The Important Question

The Sivan raised a crooked finger. "You are leaving because of loyalty, yes?"

Zoysana nodded. "I want to be loyal to my friends, to the king, to the realm. And now those loyalties are all pulling me in different directions, and I can't..."

"Loyalty is not an end in itself. It is the means to an end. What do you really want?"

"I told you. I want to show my allegiance. But I'm not sure where."

"In my experience, there is no deep, emotional drive in the human soul to be loyal. You are trying to be loyal in order to fulfill a need. What is it that you need?"

"Need?" She frowned, staring into the sharp eyes that saw so much. "I don't know..."

ZOYSANA'S CHOICE

Gordon A. Long

AIRBORN PRESS
Delta, B. C.

Zoysana's Choice

Gordon A. Long

Published by
AIRBORN PRESS
4958 10A Ave, Delta, B. C.
V4M 1X8
Canada

ISBN: 978-0-9952687-0-8
Printed by CreateSpace

Cover Design by Mihaela Voicu

More from Gordon A. Long

Other Titles Available at Smashwords, Amazon and
other outlets

"Out of Mischief" World of Change Book 1
"Into Trouble" World of Change Book 2
"Mountains of Mischief" World of Change Book 3
"The Trouble with Tents" World of Change Book 4

"A Sword Called...Kitten?" Romantic Comedy with an Edge
"The Cat with Many Claws" Sword Called Kitten Book 2

"Why Are People So Stupid?" Social Humour with a Point

Look for Gordon's books, selected reviews, poetry and short
stories at <airbornpress.ca>

Gordon's opinions on humanity are at the
"Are People Really That Stupid?" blog

Find his weekly reviews and his ideas on writing at
"Renaissance Writer"

CONTENTS

Thanks to all my beta readers for their tough love.

PROLOGUE
A NEW TENANT

"Mother, Mother! Uncle Barent's coming home."

"Wonderful. Have you seen him?"

"No, Mother, but the Sivan says he's coming. Any moment now."

She smiled. "If the Sivan says he's coming, then he'll be here soon. You go up on the wall and watch."

"All right."

"Gerth?"

"Yes, Mother?"

"That's an assignment. If anyone asks you why you're lollygagging around on the castle wall in the spring sunshine, you tell them you're on duty for me."

"Thank you, my Lady." He executed an acceptable bow and tore out the door.

She smiled and shook her head. Having Gerth home again was wonderful. Perhaps he should be fostered out again as a squire, as most other boys of noble blood were. However, as long as he was the only heir to the Arlyn dynasty in the next generation, his Majesty wanted to keep him close. *For once Father plays it safe. Can't complain.*

She leaned back against the stone of the wall, warmed by the sunlight that poured through the window. *It will be good to have Barent back. Things are always more interesting when he's around.* She grimaced. Part of the interest came from his frequent arguments with Alarid.

She occupied her thoughts with ways in which she could ease the tension between her brothers. Sometimes she just wanted to take the two of them by the scruff of the neck and shake them, as she used to when they were all young together.

Footsteps pattered on stone. "I have completed my assignment, my Lady. Lord Barent has arrived. And..."

"Yes?"

"He's got someone with him."

"Someone?"

"Yes, Mother. I think...I think it's a...girl!"

She sat up and looked at her son. "A girl?"

"Yes, Mother. There's somebody riding behind him. She's small and dark-skinned and she's a girl."

"How big?"

"Way smaller than me, Mother. Where did he get a girl?"

"Perhaps I should go down and find out. You have permission to join me."

"Thank you, Mother...my Lady. I will escort you."

She lifted her hand, and he responded properly, his arm there to help her rise and lead her down the hall.

They arrived in the bailey as Barent's Guardsmen were leading their horses away from the pile of luggage unloaded from the supplies wagon, leaving him alone in the middle of the courtyard.

Alone, except for the small figure that stood nearby, her eyes fixed firmly on him.

Barent's features lit up with that dazzling smile. "Kenna! Good to see you!" He strode across to her and seized her in a crushing embrace. The only possible response was a similar hug, and they held that way for a pleasant moment. Then he released her and turned immediately to Gerth.

"So, lad. Escorting your mother, are you?"

"Yes, my Lord. I have the honour."

"Good for you. It just wouldn't do to have a lady of her station wandering around unescorted, would it?"

Then his eye followed the boy's wandering attention. "Ah, yes...um, speaking of escorting..." He turned to the small figure standing forlorn in the middle of the bailey. "My Lady, will you join us?"

Relief filled the round, dark face. The girl walked sedately to Barent's side, her movements graceful and relaxed, yet perfectly controlled like those of a dancer. She was clad in worn forester's garb but seemed clean enough. She looked up at Kenna with polite interest.

Barent gave his sister a wink, and she wondered what was coming.

"Lady Kenna, I have the honour of presenting Lady Zoysana Rochenan of Borbonen."

The little girl stepped forward, bowed in a precise manner and launched into a full, formal introduction of herself and her lineage.

Kenna shot her brother one astonished glance, then concentrated on what the girl was saying. Following the ritual, she presented herself in return. Then she indicated her son. "And may I present Gerth, First Prince Ascending in the New Generation?"

Put on the spot, Gerth stumbled into his introduction, settling down as he warmed up, finishing with a flourish.

Kenna took advantage of the break to shoot her brother another enquiring glance. He rolled his eyes, made a motion of mopping sweat from his brow.

Once the children had fulfilled their duties Barent slipped his arm across Kenna's shoulders. "Now, Gerth, your mother and I have all sorts of things to talk about. Why don't you take

Lady Zoysana and show her around the castle? Make sure you introduce her to the Sivan." He started away.

Then he turned back. "And then show her the training field."

That caught Gerth's attention. "The training field?"

Barent made a 'move on' gesture.

Gerth turned to his small companion with new interest. "Will you come this way, my Lady?"

"With pleasure, my Lord. What kind of training field do you have?"

The conversation continued as the two walked away. As they passed out of sight, the last thing the adults heard from Gerth was, "Do we have to keep up this formal stuff when they aren't listening?"

The girl's response was drowned out by Barent's loud, and to his sister's attentive ear, relieved, laugh.

Kenna shook her head. "Well, Barent, I was thinking that it would be good to have you back because things were a bit boring. You seem to have outdone yourself this time. Why did you send them to the training field?"

"Because young Gerth is about to get the surprise of his life."

"He is?"

"Oh, yes. That little bundle of formality is also a master of the ancient Kyabran art of the Weaponless."

"Master of the Weaponless? That's an honorific in Kyabran society, isn't it? A social rank?"

He grinned and shook his head. "Oh, no. It is the title of someone who has taken some of the most rigorous martial training that exists. That little girl is the quickest," he took Kenna's arm, spun her to face him, and she could see that he was perfectly serious, "I tell you, the quickest human I have ever seen."

Her skeptical frown was all that he needed.

"I would not joke about such a thing, Kenna. When you watch her go through her training patterns, you will see. She has incredible grace and her speed will amaze you."

She could not keep the doubt from her face.

He leaned forward. "Let's put it this way. How good a fighter is Gerth?"

She had a ready answer for this. "He's the match of any page two years his senior and a few of the smaller squires."

He nodded. "And you put him on the practice field with a dagger, and her with her bare hands, and he won't touch her."

"But she's just a little thing."

Barent grinned. "And that will be another good lesson for your son."

"So where did you find this paragon of martial skill?"

As they walked towards his quarters, he outlined how he had found the girl. "...and there she was, living alone in a cottage in the forest. Her grandfather was her only family and he died a couple of months ago. She was doing quite well, actually. But she's nobility, Kenna. I couldn't leave her there."

Kenna nodded. "I'm beginning to put things together. Kyabran? Living with her grandfather? Of course."

"You know something about her?"

"Oh, yes. It was the Kyabran thing that reminded me. They came through here five or six years ago. The grandfather was a Kyabran. Just a small man, impeccably polite. He showed up here out of nowhere with his baby granddaughter, presented himself very correctly, had letters to prove who he was and requested permission to extend his visit to our realm. The girl was half Petrellan, as I recall. From the northeast. Remember the Borbona family?"

"The ones that never came to court and ended up killing each other off?"

"That's it. I wondered if the old man was running from someone."

"So they went off to who-knows-where."

"Now we know. They went off to the Karagata Valley, where they have been living ever since. Now the grandfather has died, and we have her."

"What are you going to do with her?"

He shrugged. "I don't know, Kenna. I didn't have any choice, in the beginning. Now, after I spent some time with her... Kenna, she's somebody special."

Kenna stared at her brother for a long time. "I've never seen you take to someone like this, Barent. And a child, at that. Maybe we should be finding you a wife."

He grinned and held up his hands protectively. "I've had it now. Once you start twirling that stick, I'm a lost man."

She turned to him, her face serious. "Barent, think about it. Your father is not well. Ulric is dead. Alarid isn't married. I'm a widow. The Arlyn family has narrowed down to Gerth, who is ten years old. Considering the dangers of the life we live, that's not very comforting."

"So you have me slated as the next sacrifice on the altar of the Arlyn dynasty."

Anger flared in her. "I paid my price."

He gave that infuriating laugh and ran a hand gently over her hair. "I know, Kenna. You always were the one to do the right thing. Go ahead with your plotting and planning. I'll follow along, as I always do."

He turned away, then spun back. "Just make sure she's pretty, will you?"

She slapped his arm, motioned to a chair. "I'll consider it. Now tell me what's going on out there in the east. Any problems?"

He flopped into the chair and began his analysis.

They were dragged from a detailed discussion of the value of raw wool by a discreet tap at the door.

"Yes?

"May we enter, my Lord?"

Barent grinned at Kenna. "Please do."

The youngsters entered decorously, but their eyes were shining.

Barent's smile widened. "Sit down, you two. You can drop the formalities. We're just family here."

The two sat in formal poses, waiting for their elders to speak.

"So, Zoysana, what do you think of our castle?"

"It's a marvelous place, Lady Kenna. I have read a lot about fortifications, but reading isn't the same as being right inside one. For example, I never understood the reason for calculating the dropping angle of the stone from a trebuchet until I saw how wide your bailey is." She gestured to demonstrate. "If I could get the right angle of fire, I could hit almost half the courtyard. You should really raise the height of the outer curtain wall."

Barent manfully kept a straight face. "Yes, but we have a clear field of fire outside the castle, so no one could set up a trebuchet close enough. You understand that rocks coming from farther away are moving at a different angle."

She rose and gave him a small, formal bow, 'pupil to instructor.' "Thank you. I have learned."

Kenna decided it was time to rescue Barent.

"So, Zoysana, I always wondered where you and your grandfather ended up."

The girl froze, wonder on her face. "You knew my grandfather?"

"I only met him once, when you passed through here on your way to the Karagata Valley about six years ago."

"Eight years and five months, my Lady. It is...was my duty to keep track of the dates."

"I bow to your expertise."

"And you knew me, too?"

"Well, you were only a baby. About two years old, I think, so I didn't get a chance to meet you properly."

"That's all right. I know about me. But some day you will have to tell me all you remember about my grandfather." She stopped, took a more formal pose. "That is, if you would prefer to, Lady Kenna."

"That would be fine. We'll have tea together and we can talk about him." *This is certainly going to be interesting.* She turned to her brother. "Where had you thought to quarter her?"

Zoysana's face clouded. "Won't I be staying with Barent?"

"No, dear. You can't be living in a man's quarters. It isn't appropriate."

"Oh."

Ignoring the pain in the girl's eyes, she turned to Barent. "What did you have in mind?"

He shrugged. "I thought we'd figure something out. She needs a family..."

Kenna smiled. "You expected me to take care of it."

"Would you?"

Kenna glanced over to see how the girl was taking this. There was a stunned look on her face, and the woman remembered what this waif had gone through.

"I could use some female company. Would that suit you, Zoysana?"

"Well...will I be staying with you, then?"

"You could. There's an extra room in my suite."

"If I can't stay with Barent..."

Kenna reached out, laid a hand on the girl's shoulder. "In the castle the women stay in the women's quarters, and the men stay with the men."

"I see."

"You're much better off with me. We can do the sort of things that ladies do together."

"Oh." She thought that over. "Lady Kenna?"

"Yes, dear?"

"I don't...really know...what ladies do in a castle."

Kenna laughed. "Then I suppose you'll have to learn."

"May I still train with Gerth and Barent?"

She glanced at the two of them: silly grins on both faces. She sighed. "Whatever you can arrange."

PART I: THE OUTER MOUNTAINS

Honourable conduct doesn't win wars. But it makes the peace easier afterwards.

> – Haskell's Code of the Mercenary

Loyalty is the lazy man's excuse for not thinking for himself.

> – Sarasha the Lame

1. WAR

"Come on, Soldier, keep that sword up. You want to lose what brains you still own?"

Clang! Sword reverberated on helmet, and the small figure reeled backwards.

"Don't quit now, kid. Just because you got a tap on the head doesn't mean it's over."

Thwack! The blade impacted on padded ribs.

"You said," the instructor continued in a conversational tone, still raining blows on the wavering sword of the student, "that you couldn't learn to fight properly because all the others were bigger than you. I'm not. So let's see what you've got, loud one."

"But you're grown up!" The protest gritted out between gasps.

"Always an excuse. When are the optimum conditions going to appear, where you can fight," a hook of the heel, "as well," a twist of the wrist, "as you talk?" A flip, and the student lay on the ground, weapon out of reach, the instructor's sword threatening an exposed throat. "If Rawden's army gets past Barent in the passes, you need to do better than that."

Pulling off her helmet, the instructor shook her heavy, dark hair free. She stood surveying the practice field, barren of its usual early morning bustle. *The time for practice is over. We are at war.* She sheathed her sword, staring at the mountains to the north.

The student sat up slowly, head drooping. "I'm sorry I said that, Zoe."

"Instructor, Ma'am! We are on the training field."

"I'm sorry I said that, Instructor, Ma'am, but..."

"There are no 'buts' on the battle field, Varli. I've never been to war myself, but I do know that either you can fight or you're dead. No matter how much talking you do."

He struggled up off the ground. "But I did better, today! You didn't touch me at all the first five exchanges..."

"Varli..."

His face fell. "I know, you could hit me any time, couldn't you? You could beat me even if you had no sword. You could, couldn't you?" He chattered on as they walked to the barracks, his spirits rising. "I told Lord Barent that yesterday. I said I bet you could handle even him with no sword. And he said that he only made that mistake once. Then he laughed. What did he mean by that, Zoe?"

"Varli, I am not some battle-trained armigerent that you can promote." A thought struck her. "What are you taking bets on now?"

A look of total innocence suffused his face. "Bets? There's nothing to bet on. I don't even go near the armigerents – big, nasty beasts. You're not doing anything to bet on...are you?"

Zoe could force a straight answer to her question and he wouldn't dare lie to her, but she chose to let it ride. He needed some way of avenging himself on the louts who battered him around on the practice field, at least until he grew a bit. "Just remember, you don't make friends with those tricks."

"Oh, I know. I never let anyone lose too much. The Sivan says there are people who..." His voice wound down.

"You've been scheming with the Sivan? Why that nasty old reprobate! How dare he? You were sent to this court to learn statesmanship and honour. Not to consort with the lowlifes...lowlives... whatever he is!"

"Don't you talk about the Sivan that way!" The boy was scandalized. "He's the Head of the Guides!"

3

"Listen, Varli, he may have created the Light Armed Reconnaissance Troop and he may be a good friend of Lord Barent, but he is also the most devious and conniving old scoundrel I know. That's why he is so good at his job. You watch your purse if you're playing betting games with him!" Secretly, she was pleased. *He's going to gamble anyway; he might as well learn from the master.* And the Sivan didn't pay attention to the squires unless they showed promise, along with a bit of brains.

They were approaching her quarters. "Want to drop in for a drink?"

"Is there any of that cold juice?" Despite living in standard Guides' rooms, Zoe had contrived a storage bin where she kept a jug of crushed fruit drink in cool water, away from the heat of the summer.

But today the cooler was empty. Standing beside it was a pair of large riding boots. As she shucked her own soft footgear, she grinned at how ludicrous the two sets looked side by side. Tossing her sword harness on a peg, she strode through the inner door and assumed a stern pose.

"Get your feet off my favourite chair, O scion of peasants. I hope you at least had the manners to leave a bit for us."

The large youth on the bed stumbled to his feet, offering her an apologetic grin. "I'm sorry, Zoe. I did take my boots off. And I didn't drink much." He looked in the jar. "At least not very much."

"Oh, sit down, Gerth. I was only joking. I'll find more cups." After pouring, she turned to see Varli hanging about the doorway, his shoes still on.

"I guess I better be going."

"What do you mean?"

"Well..." he flapped his hand helplessly towards Gerth.

"Varli, I invited you for a drink, and you deserve it. It's a hot day, and you've been working hard. Besides which," she glowered towards Gerth, "he wasn't invited. You stay."

Gerth grinned. "Sure, Varli, come on in, grab a chair."

Varli entered, still fussing, and Zoe grinned to herself. *Hero worship.*

Sure enough, the boy regained his voice and launched into a much-embellished version of some deed she had performed, with, as usual, her besting someone twice her size. As he finished, her face was hot with embarrassment.

Gerth laughed, ignoring her confusion. "You know, Varli, in two-on-two drill sometimes, if we want to shake up our opponents, she slips inside my guard and attacks the low line on my adversary, right after a high line from me. It gets them every time, even the ones who know about it."

"Say, do you think I could try that?" Varli was hopping with enthusiasm.

"From what I'm seeing on the practice field, I don't think I'm ready to let you inside my guard with anything sharp for a few years yet." Seeing the look on the boy's face, he relented. "You work on your control for a while and we'll see."

"Oh, that'll be great. Thanks." A thought struck him. "But what if you get called to go with Lord Barent to fight?"

"That won't happen. I still need my Acceptance ceremony before I can go to the field." His mouth twisted. "Until then, I'm stuck with castle defence. No battles for me."

Varli shrugged that off. "You're having a formal ceremony, aren't you?"

"Is there something wrong with a formal ceremony?"

Varli's sneer dropped. "Oh, no, nothing at all. But wouldn't it be wonderful to be Accepted on the battlefield, for bravery? To receive your cut with your king's battle-scarred blade, so that ever after your jagged scar will proclaim your honour?" His eyes gleamed.

"Varli, I would love to be Accepted on a battlefield, but I will not abandon my post here just so I can have an uglier scar on my neck. In fact, the odds are that any 'battle-scarred blade' that gets near your neck in the field won't leave you with a polite nick. It will go right on through."

"But don't you still wish you were out there right now?"

Gerth sighed. "Yes, it really irks me to sit around here while the true Warlanders are out fighting. But remember, that's the real thing out there, Varli. Rawden's army has already overrun two farmsteads. They have murdered innocent people, and more will die before the quarter-month is over. It might even be today. We are just waiting to hear. War is a serious business, and you, my lad, should be training more seriously for it."

"I see."

"I hope you do." Zoe tousled his hair. "Now will you do me a favour? Go to the Guides' Room and ask the Sivan if he has any news for us. He'll know what I mean."

"Sure, Zoe, right away. Has he got news of the war? Is there going to be a big battle? Is that why we started drill so early today?"

"Standing asking questions is not the same thing as 'right away,' young man."

"Yes, Ma'am, right away, Ma'am!" He saluted, 'soldier to commanding officer,' and was gone.

Gerth chuckled. "That one has possibilities."

"If we can keep him straightened out."

"You're doing your share. You pushed him today."

"Were you watching?"

"Yes, I've been keeping an eye on him."

"So that's why you've been hanging around. I doubted that you were picking up any fine points in swordplay."

"Never from him. Sometimes from you."

"Oh, right."

"But he has potential. And once I become Accepted, I'll need a squire. Not an ordinary squire, either."

"Varli has had plenty of experience in his father's court."

"He does. When he wants to, he can be very smooth. Out on the practice field where the others out-muscle him he may not look so marvellous, but with the nobles at court..."

"There are political implications as well."

"All of them good. We need contacts with the Inner Duchies, and every small tie like this counts. His father is big enough to influence their policies, but small enough that squiring his son to the king's nephew is a decent honour."

"Besides which, Varli will be thrilled. At least for the first day and a half, until he finds out how hard you work."

"Speaking of Varli, do I hear the whispering feet of Aislin, the gods' messenger? You know, that boy never..."

He was interrupted by the aforesaid messenger, who clattered into the room and collapsed in a chair, gasping for breath in a distinctly ungodlike fashion.

"I gather you have news?"

Varli gulped air. "Lord Barent has taken the field against Rawden. He's holding Escalon Pass. I don't know how any army would ever get through him, but in council they were arguing like mad."

"I already knew about Escalon." Zoe frowned. "Did the Sivan have any more for me?"

"He must have. He wants you in council. You know that look he gets when you've done something really stupid? Well, he was looking at the king like that. Gerth, his Majesty wants you, too. Right away. You're both to come to the War Room." He rose to his feet.

A thrill of fear went through Zoe, along with a deep satisfaction that here, at last, was action. Slipping into their harness with practised ease, the two mismatched young fighters followed the boy into the sunlight. It occurred to Zoe to wonder at what a pair they looked. She actually matched Gerth's strides perfectly – two for one. Well, if anyone found it amusing, it was no one with enough nerve to say anything out loud.

It was the last time she was to worry about such a mundane matter for some time to come.

2. A ROYAL ARGUMENT

As they entered the War Room, Zoe could feel the crackle of conflict in the air. While Gerth strode to his position at his uncle's side, she slipped into a chair just behind and to the left of the Sivan, who was at that moment giving vent to his anger, his bent body leaning forward as tense as a drawn bow.

"Your Majesty, ordering a retreat at this point could be disastrous. I say again – let Barent make his own military decisions there, in the field, where they should be made."

"But Sivan," King Alarid was using his patient voice. "We have, thanks to you, information of which he is not aware. We are in a much better position to know…"

As the king spoke on, restating old arguments and making minor points of logic, Zoe couldn't help but compare him, unfavourably, to his brothers. Especially Barent, whose strength was direct action. Alarid was a compromiser and always wanted everyone to be happy before he acted. Not a desirable trait in a king, especially a king at war. *And now, when he is definitely wrong, he wants to make a decision that is not his to make!* She listened to the king, waiting for him to say something useful. *What do they need me for?*

She did not have long to wait. Alarid looked for another target. "Zoysana, perhaps you can help us out here. You attend Lord Barent in his planning sessions. Can you tell us how you think he will act?"

That shouldn't be too hard. She stood. "I can try, Sire. Keeping in mind his reputation for improvising as the battle progresses, this is as good a guess as any." She moved to the map of local mountain passes. "He could hold Rawden in Escalon Pass with only a third of his present force. But he won't do that. A stalemate will give the invader time to consolidate his position. Barent will move forward and challenge Rawden just west of the mountains, leaving Orrick and his foot soldiers to hold the pass itself, with Light Horse as harriers. How he will handle the main attack will depend on the terrain and other considerations. He says many a battle has been lost through following a plan that became unworkable." She couldn't resist getting a dig in, but it had no effect on the king's sour expression.

"He has been training the Warlanders to work in small troops that stay together and act as a unit. This works well in broken or forested terrain, where otherwise the men tend to get scattered into individual battles.

"But if he sees an advantage, he might order a full charge with the heavy cavalry, hoping to overwhelm the enemy in one wave. Our Warlanders are superior to the knights of the Inner Duchies in the size and ferocity of our war-horses. Plus he and the other Warlanders still feel a certain satisfaction in a full-scale, headlong charge, a straightforward, man-to-man battle. More honourable." She glanced at the Sivan, who nodded once.

The king, too, nodded. "That is what we expected. Now, what do you think he will do when Lord Saxer brings his troops in from the west to cut him off and attack the city behind him?"

Zoe could not help looking to the Sivan for confirmation. The nod was there, but grimmer. *This will be harder.*

"We knew that Saxer might turn on us, but we did not figure that eventuality into the main battle plan. There are two possibilities. He can keep the two enemy forces from joining by plugging the pass at Escalon with a small number of soldiers. One choice would be to leave Rawden alone on the far side of the pass, come back and deal with Saxer, then worry about Rawden later.

"If he is already committed, perhaps he will handle Rawden first, allowing Saxer to get through. Then, when Rawden is off his back, he can attack Saxer from the rear, crushing him against the walls of the castle." When she saw the heads shaking around the council table, she hastily backtracked. "Of course, the second would be a far less desirable plan of action. I only mention it as a possibility."

"So you cannot assure us that Lord Barent has a plan which will cope with this new situation."

Zoe was speechless. *What does the man want? An omen?*

To her immense relief, the Sivan rose beside her to speak with asperity.

"What your Majesty is asking is a guarantee that we will win this battle no matter what. May I suggest that such prognostications are beyond mere mortals?"

Alarid sounded plaintive, his slim fingers twisting around each other. "But Sivan, he is now faced with two armies, each almost the size of his own!"

"Be comforted, your Majesty. I have yet to see a situation where Lord Barent has not thought of an alternate plan. The two opponents cannot join against him at the moment, and with any luck they will not join at all. Barent has come out on top under worse odds. Trust him and the strength of our Warlanders."

The king shook his head, mirrored by glum faces down the table. "Your argument depends, then, on a non-existent battle plan and a good sprinkling of luck? And what if it fails? We will be facing two armies on our doorstep, with only the Castle Guard to protect us."

Zoe was about to speak up, but a curt signal from the Sivan silenced her. Anything she could say had been chewed over several times already.

"No," the king drummed his fingers on the table. "I can only conclude that there is too great a risk. If we had our Warlanders here we could protect the whole city, not just the castle." There was general agreement among the councilors.

"So I must send to my brother and tell him to bring the army home." He sounded so satisfied that Zoe wanted to kick him. "I cannot trust this message to a mere Light Reconnaissance rider. I have decided to appoint my nephew, Gerth, as my herald. I think a fully armed messenger has a better chance to get through, and Gerth's station will assure him access to Lord Barent and add credence to the orders."

Zoe was seething. Now he was sending Gerth to take the brunt of Barent's anger. Only Alarid used the official term, 'Light Armed Reconnaissance.' The scouts were simple men, and preferred the simpler term, 'Guides.' Any of them had access to Barent at any time on the battlefield. A Guide on a light, fast horse was much quicker than a fully armed Warlander.

"Sivan, can you tell us where Lord Barent is likely to be found?"

"Near Escalon Pass is the only sure place to catch him, your Majesty. He will be moving around as he always does, but he must traverse the pass, whatever plan he decides on."

"Thank you." Alarid was so full of self-congratulatory bustle now that it was pitiful to watch. "Gerth, your instructions are to go to Escalon Pass and inform Lord Barent that he is to return with the army at once to defend the city against this double threat. And go at speed. You must find him before he engages Lord Rawden." The king raised a hand to block the protest forming on Gerth's lips. "I know there might be a temptation to hold back, thereby allowing Lord Barent to take his own decision. I adjure you, on your honour, make haste."

Gerth drew himself up to his full height and glared down at the king. His lips were a tight, frozen line, white at the ends. "I will obey, your Royal Highness." He stood there.

Alarid waited, then raised his eyebrows.

"Have I your leave to go, your Royal Highness?"

As Alarid indicated graciously that Gerth should leave, Zoe found herself on her feet, with the Sivan steering her by the elbow as he spoke. "I will follow along with the lad. I can hasten him on his way and advise him about the route as we go."

The king frowned at this but he could hardly object, so he waved them out as well.

Zoe could barely wait until the doors closed behind them before she exploded.

"The whole lot of them are afraid! They are bringing the army back to protect themselves! I told Barent he was crazy to help those merchants get places on the council. They are just worried about their warehouses down by the river."

"And their three battalions of mercenaries which they can afford to pay to protect them. Which allows us to pull more men out of the castle and thus field a larger army." The Sivan shook his head. "Those men are important, Zoe, and will become more important to the kingdom as time goes by. They must have their say."

"But if those armies besiege the city, it will give them free access to the whole surrounding area. And all the lords whose outlying estates will be overrun are out there with the army, not here on the council to defend themselves. And then to suggest that Gerth wouldn't carry out his mission with honour!"

"Yes, that was a foul blow."

Gerth, who had so far contained himself, finally burst out. "What am I to do? I have a direct order from my king that I know is wrong! What can I do?"

The Sivan looked almost cheerful. "Well, if you were the muscle-bound and not-too-creative-but-very-loyal clod that your uncle seems to think you are, what would you do?"

Gerth thought. "I would do what I was ordered."

"You would do exactly what you were ordered. You would go straight to Escalon Pass by the main road and look for Barent. You would go quickly, but in full battle armour as ordered. You would go prudently, knowing that you must arrive with your horse in good condition, because you might need to fight your way to Barent when you get there. And then your honour would be safe. So go!"

Gerth looked down into the Sivan's eyes, nodded, then spun on his heel and strode towards his quarters.

"And," the Sivan's voice dropped to a murmur, "leave the solution to those of us with a better definition of loyalty and a better brand of honour. Varli!"

The boy jumped as if struck.

Zoe grinned to herself. *He probably thought he was being unobtrusive, slipping in beside me as I left the War Room.*

"Yes, Sir?"

"Do you understand the situation here?"

"Yes, Sir. Better if Gerth didn't get to Lord Barent."

"Oh, no, he must get there. That is important. In fact, perhaps he could use some help. He has no squire to prepare his equipment, you know, and it takes a lot of...*time* to get ready to go to war. Perhaps you could go and," he paused meaningfully, "*help* him get ready in the proper...time."

Varli looked incredulous. "You want me to..."

Zoe interrupted him. "Maybe go and prepare his armour and horse while he is dressing. That takes a long *time*, doesn't it?"

A wicked grin spread across Varli's face. "Yes, I could be a lot of...*help*... couldn't I? What are you going to do?"

"We will find our own method of helping. Now be off." The Sivan turned to Zoe and hurried her along the corridor as Varli hared away. "Now we get to the real heart of the matter. Quick as you can – Guide's gear – it's all ready in your stable. Out the Guide's Postern. Over the mountain. Use that trail I showed you last month when this whole thing started.

14

"Barent must act quickly. He needs to be back through the pass and out of sight in the trees to the south before Gerth comes looking for him. That is, if Barent hasn't thought of something completely different. Gerth will take the road, about three times the distance you must travel, so he will take twice as long as you, more if Varli is successful. Good luck."

By this time she was swinging up onto her favourite mount, a lean, fast pony, smaller than the rest of the Guides' horses, but the same mottled brown in colour and more sure-footed than most. Strapped to her saddle was the usual Guide's pack: knife, water bottle, travel rations, reversible cloak, tinderbox.

Then she turned back. "What did you mean about honour and loyalty?"

"Sarasha the Lame said that honour and loyalty are often excuses for not thinking." He slapped the pony's rump. "Away you go, now."

"I'll think about that." She kneed Jobe out the door.

The postern exited the castle straight from the Guide's quarters, manned by two Guides who nodded her through and slipped the ironbound door shut behind her. The way led straight into the rock wall against which the castle was built, and she doubted if anyone could have seen her leave. Taking a deep breath, she kneed her horse into the narrow gap.

3. BATTLE

Up the rock the pony squirmed, through cracks no regular-sized horse could pass. Where it was too steep she got off and the two of them scrambled up together, helping each other. Much as her soul rebelled, she could not ease off and save Jobe, and she drove him hard. It was a hot day; they were both sweating heavily when they reached the crest. Pausing to catch her breath in the cooling breeze that swept around the shoulder of the mountain, Zoe looked out over the terrain below. Sure enough, glints of metal in the trees just northeast of the pass revealed that Barent was forming up where the Sivan had predicted. Far down the valley to the north she could see the van of Rawden's army, advancing in massed formation. Off to the south and west the forests and fields were peaceful. Saxer had not yet appeared.

Mounting Jobe, she plunged downward in a dangerous scramble of sliding scree, soon reaching the forest that cloaked the northeast side of Escalon Pass. As she entered the hot, spicy shade of the forest her view was again restricted. The trees were so close and low that she dismounted again and jogged along, leading the horse. Then the ground leveled off, and she was galloping through the thinning tree cover towards Barent's standard.

The Honour Guard parted before her, and she swung from Jobe's back almost at Barent's feet. He grabbed her arm to keep her from falling.

"You seem in a hurry to get to the war. Afraid we would start without you?" He smiled. "I'd have saved a few for you for later, if you had only let me know."

She glanced up at him and got a brief impression of a huge metallic bear. His armour accented his stocky appearance. His hair and beard bristled out around his face, held in place only by the damp band across his brow where a helmet strap had caused the sweat to gather. How comfortable and calm he looked, there at the centre of all this bustle. When the meaning of his joking words sank in she realized that this aura was partly a facade that he presented for the morale of his men, but mostly the simple fact that he was enjoying himself.

"Must talk...private..." she got out between gasps. "The Sivan..."

Motioning someone to take her equally winded horse, Barent walked her away from the others. "So, what did the Sivan send me?"

As her breath evened she outlined the situation, including Gerth's most likely route. At one point he barked out a laugh.

"Good! I never trusted that Saxer. Much too full of himself and his prowess at arms. I hope I meet him today. His people would be better off with his younger brother – what's his name? – Torey. A good lad from what I hear. Continue."

When she had finished, he called his officers together. "We have been robbed of our chance to stand up to old Rawden and see what he is made of. Saxer has finally shown his true colours and is sneaking up behind us. So we will slip back through the pass and show him the error of his ways first. Then we can come back and teach Rawden a lesson as well.

"Orrick, you now have the two companies of heavy infantry. Get them down in the pass and help with the pits and breastworks as soon as we are through. We should also double the archers up on the sides." He grinned at the grizzled infantry Captain, receiving a wolf-like snarl, which the old soldier probably considered a smile, in return. "Looks like your part in this affair just became more important. Keep them off our backs for a while, then we will come and finish off whoever you don't chew up.

"The rest of you get into the flying troops we worked on the last few months. We can't give Saxer a pitched battle. We will hit him on one flank, then retreat, pull him apart and harry him in groups. Cawbur, you take the Light Horse with a Guide up over the mountain to the west of the pass and come at them from the rear after they go by. Remember, all of you; a single Warlander is useless to me, no matter how brave he is. Stick with your troop. Strike where they are weakest, then move on before they can bring strength against you. The woods will help break them up, and our Guides will keep us in contact. Mount up, let's go!"

He turned to Zoe, and enfolded her in a quick, mercifully gentle hug. "Thanks for the warning. But I don't want to worry about you today."

"Sorry, my Lord, I forgot my helmet, and I don't think Jobe has the energy left to keep up to you in battle." She pushed a piece of his armour away from her rib. "I'll just find myself a nice, high, safe spot to watch from. You go out and do what you're so good at."

"Fine," he laughed. "You can applaud and throw flowers if I do well." He sobered, "and get back to the Sivan first with the news if I don't. He will know what to do." His squire slipped the bright red helmet into place, and he swung ponderously up onto his huge war-horse, saluted her and rode away to follow his Warlanders, who were streaming back through the pass.

Her position here would soon be exposed to the oncoming enemy. Scanning the mountain she had just descended, she picked an outcropping of rock high enough to be inaccessible and to provide a good view, and headed towards it, walking beside her pony to conserve his remaining strength.

When her route became too steep for the horse she picketed him in a small, well-hidden hollow in the mountainside with patches of grass to snack on and scrambled the rest of the way up the rock. As she approached the skyline she laid her Guide's cloak over herself grey-side-out and slid to the top. Settling into a crevice, shaded by the cloak, she looked out over the battle as it formed.

Off to her right, Rawden's army was just approaching the pass. Orrick's infantry was out of her sight because of the bulge of the mountain below her, but she could see the bowmen in the rocks on the other side.

To her left, Barent's Warlanders were spreading out in small, compact groups, threading their way through the light forestland west of the pass. There was no sign of anyone higher on the mountain across from her, and she assumed that the Light Horse, having fresher mounts than hers, had already climbed out of her sight.

It was strange, sitting up here in the silence of rock and airy space, watching the horror of a battle unfolding below her at half speed like a weapons practice.

Rawden was the first to attack. His mounted knights charged, so slowly it seemed, across the open ground and out of sight toward the pass. She could see the archers start to shoot, and then came the most horrifying sound, a combination of crashing, thundering and screaming, which rang in her ears even as high as she sat. Fortunately, it did not continue long. Rawden's knights realized that the shield wall was no easy target and came stumbling back out into the open to regroup.

However, while the first skirmish was taking place, Saxer's army had come into view, and she could see Barent's troops pounding out through the trees, converging on a point near one end of that mass of metal and bright cloth. Then those armies met, and the awful sounds of battle rolled out again, less harsh for the distance, but gut-wrenching all the same.

And Barent's plan seemed to be working. A troop would attack the main part of Saxer's army then retreat, drawing a small segment away. If the pursuers were few enough, the troop would then turn and destroy them. If a large number came after them, the riders would fade into the forest, to show up later, attacking at another spot. Soon Saxer had no centralized army; the battle had broken into a series of

19

skirmishes. Saxer's foot soldiers could find no one to fight with except the odd troop of Warlanders who would smash through their ranks sowing havoc and disappear into the trees again. Zoe could keep track of her troops by the colour of their pennants, and every so often she would glimpse a Guide, slipping from group to group to pass information.

She was startled out of her reverie by a scrabbling sound below her. She peered over the edge to see one of the Guides climbing up towards her vantage point.

"How did you know I was here?"

"Hello, Zoe." He paused to catch his breath, surveying the scene. "I didn't. This is one of the assigned watch points for the battle. Weren't you at the briefing? Of course you weren't." His curiosity was stifled by his duty. "I'm looking for Lord Siebert, and I can't get news of him. Have you been watching?"

Zoe pointed. "He's with the Blue, isn't he? They just headed west, beyond that meadow...there, with the broken fence...yes, there they are."

"I see them now. Thanks. Anything else?"

"Tell them to watch for the knights in the next clearing to the west. There is a large group rallying around that white horse. Blues are moving that way."

"Right. See you later." And he was gone.

As the battle progressed, several Guides appeared to get information from her. Twice she slipped out onto the field herself to pass urgent messages or warnings, but she didn't go far, as Jobe was still unsteady.

It was the third trip out that she ran into trouble. She had rushed down to tell the Greens that they were about to be caught between two large jaws of the enemy, and had to run her pony to escape the trap herself. He was having a blow before they continued to safety when she heard a crashing in the brush nearby. They crowded under a tree with long, overhanging branches and froze, but to no avail. A huge knight on a white war-stallion broke through the shrubbery and stopped about ten horse-lengths away.

"You – boy!" the rider snarled at her through the bars of his helm.

She said nothing.

"Boy – where is that coward Barent? I've seen a few like you around. You must know what's going on." He rattled his sword. "Tell me, boy, or I will split you in half!"

Zoe knew he could. There was no chance to run on her winded horse, and her knife was no defence against his sword. She looked around. There must be something she could use.

"Many times the enemy brings your weapon to you," her grandfather had taught her. "If nothing else, he brings his anger."

This one is certainly angry enough. Maybe I can help him along. Staring at him, she drew her dagger and flipped it to her left hand. It was an alley-fighting move, showing disdain for the opponent. She hoped he understood. To make certain, she spat on the ground between them. He stared at her. Then, with a growl of rage he flung up his weapon and drove his bloody spurs into the stallion's sides. It leapt forward, towering over her and her small pony.

But just as her assailant entered under the tree she reached up and pulled down on a low-hanging limb. He smashed into it, the forked branch catching under the chin of his helmet, forcing his neck to an impossible position. His horse slewed sideways as the rider was jerked out of the high saddle. The stallion barely missed crushing her up against the tree trunk, but its master crashed to the ground. In a breath Zoe was out of the saddle and had her dagger at his throat.

She could not push it in.

The thought of the blood gushing over her hand turned her stomach, and not even the danger that he would jump up and kill her could make her move. She stayed frozen forever it seemed, unable to strike, unable to run. Then her awareness returned, and she looked at her enemy.

The man did not move. His head, in spite of the restricting helmet, lay at an awkward angle. He was dead. She knelt there, stunned by the sudden shock of the fight. Then she realized that she was afoot in the middle of a battle. This brought her back to her full senses, and she picked up the knight's sword and slung it back on his saddle. Then she mounted Jobe and led the charger away, glancing over her shoulder as she rode.

She reached her picket spot with difficulty – the White was no mountain horse – but soon she had them both staked out munching happily on the tough grass. She sat, shivering with reaction, in her crevice.

The memory of the fear as the huge stallion rushed down upon her warred with the horrible sight of the rider's neck stretching as if clinging desperately to life, until finally the irresistible force snapped it. Her own inability to perform the final coup tore at her as well. She huddled under her cloak until the shivering passed.

4. The White Horse

Gradually the sense of the battle returned to her. Barent was still playing havoc with Saxer's fragmented army, but Rawden's forces were charging the barricaded infantry with increasing determination. A troop of Saxer's men had found their way to the pass as well and were attacking from the west. She hoped that Orrick could hold on, down there in the swirling dust and noise. The cool, clear air of the mountain seemed doubly precious to her, and she breathed deeply, relaxing. At least she could stay out of it for a while now and regain her nerve.

Then, in the middle of it all, she saw a familiar figure. Down among the trees, close below her on the east side of the pass, was Gerth. Walking slowly, leading his horse. Assessing the situation, she scrambled down, untied her pony once more, and rode to him.

"Ho, Gerth, nice day for a walk."

He spun around. "Zoe! What are you doing here?"

"I'm on assignment, too, I guess. Pelex doesn't look so spry. What happened?"

Gerth pulled off his helm and regarded his charger. There was dried blood all down the outside of its leg. "He isn't. By the time I got to the pass, Barent had already left. Rawden attacked while I was there, so I stayed to help out until we repelled the attack. Then somebody came at us from the west, and I was trapped. They're in trouble down there. Every sortie they lose a few more men. There's barely room between the two shield walls for the wounded. It's only a matter of time, I'm afraid."

"How long did you stay?"

"I must get to Barent, so I left before the next charge. I had to fight my way through, and Pelex took a spear in his shoulder. Not serious, but he can't fight, and now I can't find Barent. I guess I failed my task." His head slumped. "I shouldn't have stayed to fight, but they were really hard-pressed. They gave such a whoop when I rode in, you know?" He gazed at her earnestly.

For the first time in a while Zoe started to enjoy herself. "Cheer up. Barent knows about the situation in the pass. One of the Guides will tell him. And you can borrow my horse."

His head came up, but then he looked at her pony. "Don't be ridiculous. My feet would drag. Come to think of it, he doesn't look much spryer than Pelex."

"Not Jobe. I have an extra. Come on." She led the two towards her private pasture.

"Leave Pelex here. He can't get up this in his condition." She showed Gerth the way to where the white stallion was tied.

"What a horse! Where did you get him?"

"I found him. Climb on, and we'll go find Barent. I'm sure he will be glad to see you."

"He will?"

"Of course. Your message is going to come just at the right time. You can leave that sword here, or take it along as a spare."

"Zoe, you don't just 'find' a man's horse and sword together. What have you been doing? And how did you get here anyway? I thought you were safe back at the castle."

"If I had stayed back at the castle, nowhere would be safe. Now let's go, and I can fill you in as we ride."

She tried to downplay her actions in the story, but it was hard, since that was the only part of the battle she knew. When she had finished, he stopped the charger and shook his head.

"And you killed the knight who owned this horse?"

She felt shy, somehow. "I had some help from a tree."

24

He grinned. "I'm sure the tree won't want a share of his price. He'll bring a good bit, and he's yours by right of conquest. Unless you want to keep him for a souvenir."

"I don't want him." She wheeled her pony faster than his tired legs could handle and rode on.

Barent was easier to find than Zoe had expected. As they approached his standard, at the edge of what had once been a prosperous farm, the armies were gathering again in normal formation. The two broke in on him as he was instructing his Warlanders.

"You again. What news have you brought me this time?"

Gerth stepped forward. "Lord Barent, I bring a message from his Majesty."

"Ah, yes, the message from my dear brother."

"The first half you already know. Saxer is here. The second half, Sir..." he forged on. "The king has required me to come to you, Sir, and with his authority order you to retreat to the city and see about her defences." He stood rigidly, awaiting the outburst.

Zoe and several of the others laughed. He stared at them, his mouth open. Barent laughed loudest of all. "Retreat, is it?" He turned to the Honour Guard Captain, standing beside him in his battered armour. "What was our tactic all day, Lukin?"

"Retreating, Sir," growled the Captain. "Bloody retreating, all day. Does this mean we can't take one real bash at them, Lord Barent? Only the one?" Zoe felt a hysterical giggle forming behind her teeth as she watched this proud man coming as close to begging as he ever would, just for a chance to fight. She squashed the impulse with difficulty.

Barent was also having trouble containing his glee. He slammed a mailed hand on the Captain's steel shoulder. "Well, Lukin, perhaps we can keep everyone happy, here. As you see, Gerth, the situation has changed since you were sent. I suggest we attack Lord Saxer, drive him back far enough to give us breathing space to evacuate our troops from Escalon Pass. Then we will retreat. I don't think his Majesty will mind that small deviation from his orders.

"Besides which," a nasty smile slid across his mouth, "Saxer doesn't know that he has several squads of light cavalry lined up behind him at this moment, waiting for my signal. Could make a great deal of difference. So let's get organized. Gerth," Barent looked over his nephew's scarred armour, "I gather you saw some of this already."

"I was in the pass for a while, sir."

"Fine. There are a few holes in our front line. Could you fill in between Lukin and me?"

"Certainly. I have spent time with him in training."

Zoe was pleased and alarmed for Gerth. Barent's favourite formation was the spear point. With himself at the tip.

The lad donned his helmet, covering his huge smile.

Barent nodded. "That is settled then." As he turned to mount, he patted Gerth's white charger absently. "Nice horse."

While they had been talking, their opponents had formed up on the other side of the field. Now the two lines of mounted men faced each other.

"I don't see Saxer." Barent sounded disappointed. "Too bad. I would have liked to meet with him...what's this?"

A single knight rode out between the two armies. At the halfway point he stopped. Since the battle wasn't starting, Zoe stayed to watch this development.

"Go see what he wants, Lukin."

The Captain trotted out for a quick conversation and returned. "It's Torey, my Lord. He wants to talk. With you and Lord Gerth."

"Gerth?"

26

"He said, 'the one on the white horse,' my Lord."

"Fine. I can't see any possibility for trickery – one of him, two of us." He placed his helmet in front of him on his saddle. "Let's go, Gerth."

With a sinking feeling, Zoe trailed out behind them, stopping Jobe within hearing distance. *I know where this conversation will lead. I might as well be there when I'm needed.*

As the three reached the centre of the field, Torey pushed his steed up to Gerth. "Where did you get that horse?"

Barent bowed formally in his saddle. "Greetings, Lord Torey. I am sorry to see you involved. What can we do for you?"

"The white horse. Is it his?"

"It was a gift to my nephew from a friend."

"Today?"

"As it happens, it was today."

"Could I speak with the friend?"

"I suppose it could be arranged. Forgive my unseemly curiosity, but is this something important enough to stop a battle for? My men are eager."

"The fate of the original owner of that horse is very important to all of us, and the battle as well. Is he dead?"

"I think so. Do you need to know for sure?"

"If you could oblige me, Lord Barent."

Barent turned, and his eye fell on her, down behind him on her little horse. "Oh...there you are, Zoe. Tell this Lord about the owner of the white horse."

"He is..." The words caught in her throat. "...dead. His neck broke."

Torey burst out. "You killed him? You vanquished him and took his charger?"

"And his sword." Gerth slapped the pommel that swung near his hand.

Barent broke in. "Is this Lord Saxer we are talking about?"

"Yes. And he has been killed, you say. And by a boy?"

"I am NOT a boy!" Zoe tore off her leather helmet. "Don't make the same mistake HE did!" She flung her hand towards the White, who tossed his head in response.

"My apologies, I am sure, my Lady. There have been several mistakes of that sort made today. Mostly by my late brother." Torey turned formally to Barent.

"My Lord, I suggest we cease hostilities and I ask permission to withdraw my troops from your kingdom. I assume that you will require reparation for the damage done, and I will leave high-ranking hostages to prove my intentions."

"I don't suppose the light cavalry coming up behind you helped you make this decision?" Barent grinned. "Oh, you hadn't discovered them yet?"

"Fresh cavalry? Another mistake. Look, Barent, this war was my brother's idea. He cobbled together this army of brigands by bluff and promises. I told him it was wrong to antagonize you, with the Inari just waiting to pour across the Barrier, that we might need your help soon, but he wouldn't listen.

"When word gets out that he was killed, and by a girl...excuse me, by a lady...they'll just fade away. In fact, I must get home with my loyal troops before that rabble gets there. I must maintain order and protect my own holdings."

"And Rawden?"

"I never liked the man. This was all his idea."

"Good. Forget the hostages. If the barbarians are getting stronger we'll have to trust each other in the next few months, so let's start now. Just give me a moment and I will call off my Warlanders. Oh, and would you let a messenger through your ranks to take a message to my Light Horse?"

"You mean there really are...?"

"Why should I lie to someone who had just surrendered?"

"Please, no insult intended, my Lord. It's just that..." he seemed at a loss for words. "And you can find all your Warlanders, and give them orders, just like that?"

Barent merely smiled.

The young noble clashed his metal glove against his thigh. Wheeling his horse, he returned slowly to his waiting troops. As he rode away, Zoe heard him mutter, "I told him, I told him..."

Barent was immediately in action. A few brief words with the Guides, and their long-legged horses were racing in different directions, one following Torey back through his lines.

"Now there is the small matter of Lord Rawden." Barent's smile became grim. "Let's deal with that."

5. BROKEN WALL

Followed by the majority of his force, Barent moved in good order towards the pass. As they approached the mountain they came upon about thirty of Saxer's knights. This troop was considering another charge against the western shield wall, which plugged the narrow opening, still bristling with long spears, although not so many as before.

Barent rode up to them, his hands folded in front of him on his saddle. "Your war is over. Go home."

Seeing the size of his company, they shrugged at each other and complied.

Barent's forces entered the mouth of the pass, welcomed by grins and cheers of relief from the defending infantry. As the wounded were evacuated Barent held another lightning strategy meeting.

"Orrick, how long do you think your shields would have stayed up?"

"We've quite a few men out, my Lord. Might have gone down on the next charge if they really pushed it home. I think they're getting ready for a big one."

"Will Rawden believe that?"

"If I believe it, who shouldn't, then he definitely will, who needs to!"

"I gather that means yes?"

"Yes, Sir, it does, Sir."

"Good. Then let's have it break on the next charge. Oh, I know," he grinned at the Captain's scandalized expression. "The most dangerous trick your men will work today. A shield wall is a pretty comfortable place to be. A broken wall is another matter. On the next attack, let us have the wall break. Not right away, but soon. Prepare your men with protected spots to gather in. Just open the wall and let Rawden and his men through. Then comes the important part.

"When a bit less than half of them are through, I will bring in my Guard, here, at the western exit, and help you close the pass again. Then we will deal with Lord Rawden at our leisure."

It was a grim but satisfied-looking group of Warlanders and soldiers who deployed towards their appointed positions. As they had come to expect, Lord Barent had provided a battle plan containing the two ingredients they liked best: a good fight and a better-than-average chance to win.

While they waited for the next developments, Orrick stood with Barent, Gerth, and Zoe near their horses.

"Glad to see the young fella made it, my Lord. He was fair use to us here, with that big sword of his. Plugged up the one breach we had all day. Four or five of their biggest chargers got through – looked rough, and us with nothing heavy enough to match them. Then Lord Gerth blasts into all of them like a whirlwind. Knocked two horses off their feet, killed the third knight out of hand, and had the others running for their lives.

"We're sorry we all laughed, Lord Gerth, but it looked real funny, you charging at those last ones like a maniac, and them whipping their horses as madly to get away. Broke the force of the charge completely, it did." He looked at the bloody ground. "About the best laugh we had all day, I guess.

"Then they came at us from the other direction. Had us penned, they did, but he says he can't stay. 'Got to get to Lord Barent,' he says. 'Important message from the king.' So I suggest that he goes up over the mountain, like the Light Horse did, but no, he has to go out through the middle of them. So we open the wall, and out he charges, straight into half a dozen this time. Went straight through like a knife through cheese. I tell you we were worried when someone said his horse took a spear. He kept going, though. Why didn't you come back?"

"Better still," Barent pointed east, "why not go over the mountain?"

"His Majesty's orders were specific, sir. I was to reach you or my honour would suffer. And I couldn't go over the mountain. What if Rawden's men saw me and followed?"

"So you went straight through the whole of Saxer's army."

Gerth straightened his back. "My Lord, I'm not quite that foolhardy. I angled over to the left, there, near those boulders. You can see the advantage of the rocks and small trees to a lone fighter. Also there were only four or five of them there."

"Six, Orrick says."

"Well, maybe six." Gerth gave an exaggerated sigh. "I suppose if it were you, Uncle, you would have found a better way."

"Of course he would," Zoe chimed in. "Maybe he would have been the first Warlander ever to fly, complete with warhorse and armour. That would have been a better way."

A great gust of laughter burst from everyone within hearing. She hadn't thought it was that funny, but she had done a perfect job of breaking the tension of the wait.

Serious again, Barent raised his sword and held its battered, bloody blade high. "Your mother will kill me for this, lad, but raise your chin."

As the youth stood with his head high, meeting his uncle's gaze, Barent drew his sword across the left side of Gerth's neck, just above the collar of his armour. A thin, jagged line appeared, and as a small drop of blood trickled down his neck, Gerth intoned the oath that made him an Accepted Warlander.

Zoe watched the brief ceremony, her heart glowing with pride. When the oath was administered, Barent turned Gerth and presented him to the company.

"Behold the new Warlander. May his friends remember his face." The men all cheered. Barent raised the helmet and placed it on Gerth's head. "Behold his helm. May his enemies fear its visage." The cheer again.

At that moment Zoe was struck by a strange feeling. The rest of the ceremony faded into the background as she puzzled. She ran the preceding events through her mind and studied them. Then she had it. The picture of Gerth, standing proud and tall, and Barent stretching to lift the helm above his head. It was the first time she had ever seen Barent look awkward, or physically dominated by any other person. It had never occurred to her that Barent wasn't much over average height.

The final cheer for the new Warlander was fading when the cry of "They come!" echoed down from the bowmen up the canyon. The cheer swelled on a more sinister note as the men turned to their positions. Several of the Warlanders slammed Gerth on the breastplate with their gauntlets as he passed.

As Zoe approached him, she wished there were some way she could reach him, away inside all that steel. Instead, she had to settle for squeezing his gauntleted hand as she passed him a lance. "Fight well, Warlander."

Gerth leaned down from his horse and laid a heavy hand on her shoulder. "Watch him for me, will you?" and he was gone.

As Zoe scrambled up to another watch-point near the archers she pondered Gerth's strange comment. Anyone trained by the Sivan couldn't help but take a wider, more cynical view of people's motives.

Gerth's Acceptance on the battlefield was a deserved honour, and far from unusual. But this simple act had other effects. While it might seem ludicrous for the youthful Gerth to feel protective towards a Warlander as powerful as Barent, there was no denying that a life-long bond, already strong, had just been welded more firmly. Not so bad for Barent, now the First Prince Ascending, to hold his immediate successor so tightly to him. *I'm going to enjoy discussing the political implications of this with the Sivan.*

And then all thought was drowned out in the thunder of battle, so horribly near to her now.

And of course the action went exactly as planned. Even as it passed through her mind, she knew the thought was a dangerous one. She was falling for the kind of morale-boosting tricks she and the Sivan were always planning. Everyone was to think that Barent was invincible. But it was so easy to believe as she watched Rawden's jubilant horsemen pouring through the gap, not noticing that the shield wall had broken in an orderly fashion instead of fragmenting as it normally would. It took a stiff fight to close the pass again, but Barent had chosen his attack point well, at a gap between the aggressive leading knights and the more cautious followers.

The predicted result was that Rawden found himself and a portion of his men surrounded by a far superior force. The rest of his army milled, frustrated and leaderless, on the other side of the pass, held at bay by a renewed shield wall, this time reinforced by mounted Warlanders.

Ambitious but no fool, Rawden had no choice but to surrender. He could afford the ransom if he squeezed his serfs this harvest.

Zoe arrived on level ground just as Rawden was submitting his sword to the triumphant Barent. He grimaced when he saw Gerth ride up on the big White.

"Saxer's horse. That explains a lot. You take him down yourself, lad?"

While Gerth was trying to form a reply to this patronizing attitude, Barent took charge. "Saxer was undone by his own weaknesses. Don't let the same happen to you." The threat set the tone for the discussion. This time, Barent wasn't shy in taking hostages and setting steep reparation payments before allowing a single enemy lord to go free.

Then the army gathered itself together and patched itself up for the triumphant return to the city.

6. Triumph for Some

For Zoe, the triumphal entry was a letdown.

Gerth, the newly Accepted Warlander, rode proudly behind Barent, the triumphant general, each receiving the adulation he deserved. The hostlers had bandaged Pelex well enough for the occasion, and Gerth rode the brown destrier at an easy walk, looking confused when the crowds cheered them wildly.

The huge white stallion was in the baggage train with the other prizes of the conflict. It was a small enough group of wagons, since Barent had allowed Torey to take his supplies home with him. Rawden's equipment train, warned of how battle was going, had turned back to the protection of his own borders. So the White was prominent in its lowly place in the procession. Gerth had refused to ride it because that would be going under false pretenses. Zoe was glad it was out of her hands. Every time she looked at it she shuddered, half in horror of what she had done, half in fear of what she had escaped.

Of more importance to the crowd was the group of prisoners, stripped of their armour and led by Rawden himself, riding borrowed horses, protected by the mercenary infantry. The citizens were quick to voice their displeasure, and at times the mercenaries were hard pressed to keep order.

Barent received the lion's share of the applause, as was his due. By now everyone knew how his military genius had saved the city, and every section of the crowd burst into hysterical cheering when he passed.

As the sun set, the procession wound through the streets and formed up on the parade ground before the castle, the lengthening shadows of the Warlanders stretching out towards the city below.

There, with his Warlanders row upon row behind him, his foot soldiers and mercenaries in front and the townspeople crowding into every vantage point, he cantered his warhorse to the centre of all eyes.

"People of Petrella," his voice, hoarse from the battle, carried over the stillness. "People of Petrella, today we won more than a battle. Today our enemies who could learn from their mistakes have become our friends. Those who could not learn are dead or in chains.

"We have paid a price for our victory. For those who did not return, I mourn with their families. For those in pain, I feel hurt as well. But for all of us, I feel joy. We have shown everyone that Petrella is not a kingdom to be trifled with.

"So, go to your homes, your barracks, your taverns," a chuckle ran through the common soldiers, "and enjoy your rest – or whatever suits you." Another appreciative murmur from the ranks. "You deserve it. We...are...victorious!"

He jabbed his sword to the sky and posed, his burly figure outlined against the setting sun. From the foot soldiers a deep chant of "Barent, Barent, Barent," began, to be taken up by the crowd and then the Warlanders. He held the pose longer while the sound swelled around him. Then he bowed to the city and with a flourish, pivoted his stallion around on its hind legs and galloped towards the castle. The Warlanders parted like water before him, then flowed after through the huge gates.

Zoe followed with the supplies and the wounded, wondering. She admired the way Barent worked the crowd, but how wise was it? The king or one of his watchers saw it for certain. It wasn't smart for the First Prince to be seen trying to be popular. She mentally shook herself. *Maybe I'm being too cynical, but that's how I feel.*

Or maybe I'm just being grouchy. In contrast to Gerth and Barent, she had ridden with the rest of the off-duty Guides in the rear. As far as the Sivan was concerned, the place for an information gathering organization was out of the public eye. So for the Armed Light Reconnaissance, there would be no awards, no shouts from the crowd. Even less recognition for her, since her presence must not be advertised at all. So no glory. Oh, there was the respect of those she respected, the true reward of the professional. But sometimes she could wish for just a bit more.

With thoughts like these churning in her weary mind, she left Barent and Gerth to whatever reception awaited them in the castle and turned aside to the Guides' stables. There, in accord with regulations, she took care of her pony.

"You and me, Jobe," she rested her cheek against his smooth flank. "The only reward we get is a warm place to sleep and a good meal. Well, why should we complain? Though, come to think of it, I doubt if there's anyone waiting to give me a rub-down."

These maudlin thoughts were broken by the sound of running feet on the flagstones. A smile spread across her face as she raised her head. *I might have known.*

Varli pelted around the corner of the stall and threw his arms around her, knocking her back against Jobe, who moved uneasily, disturbed but too tired to take serious offence.

"You made it! I knew you would!" As she untangled him and set him upright, he babbled on, "I was in the Sivan's quarters when the advance Guides reported. You were right in the battle! And you killed the enemy leader! A knight in full armour? In face-to-face combat!"

"Varli, it wasn't like that at all."

"Don't try to brush it off this time; I heard the report. But the Sivan said not to talk about it. Why not?"

Zoe handed him a curry comb and turned back to her work. "Varli, this may cause you to strangle on your own busy tongue, but if the Sivan says don't talk..."

"...I won't even mention it in my sleep. Anyway, the Sivan is expecting you to report, but the Lady Kenna sent for me, too.

She wants to see you right away. I told her about your orders, and she said for once she would pull rank. She gets you first! You aren't even supposed to clean up – I'm to finish for you here, and you go. Now. That's what she said. How did she know you'd be here?"

"Varli, you may admire the Sivan's knowledge and Barent's fighting skill, but believe me, when it comes to power and politics, Lady Kenna can match either one. Maybe both!"

"You're not going to the Sivan?"

Zoe sighed. "Whatever Lady Kenna wants. If she says go to her first, that's where I go." She checked the last hoof, patted her pony. "We're finished here. You report back to the Sivan. He'll understand."

They parted near the main hall. As she stumbled up the stairs to Kenna's quarters, she wondered what the king's sister wanted that could be so important. She hoped it wasn't going to take too long. *All I want to do is crawl into bed, pull the covers over my head and sleep for a week.* However, when she entered Kenna's private sitting room, she was greeted with warmth.

She had always enjoyed the other woman's choice of residence. Instead of the larger, more formal chambers of the rest of the king's family, Kenna had chosen a smaller suite of rooms close to the busiest corridors. She spent much of her time in a cosy den: always a sense of warmth and comfort, the walls and floors covered with tapestry and deep furs, the lights softly glowing. Kenna resided at the centre of this, and also in a deep spot at the centre of Zoe's affections. When she was younger Kenna's soft arms had been her only place of refuge in the harsh, martial world of the castle. Now, once again, her friend greeted her with a warm hug.

"Be careful, Kenna, you've got one of your nicest gowns on, and I'm covered with dust!"

"Nonsense!" An arm around her shoulders, the older woman guided her to a comfortable couch and sat opposite. "Now you tell me all about it."

"I'm sure you heard about the battle. Barent..."

"No, dear, not that. Your own little adventure."

"Please Kenna, I don't want to talk about that. Couldn't you ask Gerth later? I told him."

"Zoe, I know it is difficult for you, but you need to talk about it."

Zoe's voice rose "I just killed a man! In case you don't remember, I haven't done that before. I botched it up, it wasn't much fun and I don't want to discuss it!"

Kenna's voice stayed calm and low. "What do you mean, you botched it up? Barent seems to think you did rather well."

"He wasn't there. I failed at just about everything! First, I got caught where I shouldn't have been, on my poor, exhausted horse, by a huge, clumsy oaf who never should have known I was there. I was lucky with the branch, but when he was on the ground, I took my knife," she drew out her Guide's dagger, "but I couldn't finish him. I was frozen. If he hadn't been already dead, he could have got up and killed me! Oh, Kenna, I'm such a coward! When I close my eyes, I can still see that huge sword coming at me. And the sound when he hit the branch! I'll be hearing that the rest of my life. Why did they bother with all that training?" She held up the dagger. "I'm not made for it. I'm not a killer – I don't want to kill people!" She flung it wildly away from her and burst into heavy sobbing.

Kenna was beside her, holding her tight. "I know, I know. It's very hard. But it is important not to keep it inside you." She straightened the smaller woman up and wiped her cheeks with a dainty handkerchief. "Now let's get this straight. Why were you out in the battle?"

"Well, Purvan's Green troop was about to ride into a trap. None of the other Guides knew, so I had to go and warn them."

"And did it help?"

"Yes, they avoided the enemy and attacked them on the flank."

"So you saved quite a few men. Score one for you. Why was the horse so tired?"

"It was the climb over the mountain. I had to get to Barent before Saxer did," she looked sideways at Kenna, "and before Gerth did."

Kenna laughed. "A race he was pleased to lose, I gather. Score two. Now about the branch. Was that only luck?"

"It was the best I could do at the time. The only alternative meant my pony being run down."

"So that worked out well. Now, about killing the downed man. Surely all your training tells you not to kill a vanquished enemy?"

"Yes, but this was war. He would have killed me. What kind of honourable Warlander attacks a defenceless opponent?"

"Still, you know how difficult it is to break lifelong training. But the man was dead, so you were fine. What kind of man was he?"

"He was awful! He had no honour at all. He had an agreement with Alarid and he broke it. He's the one that caused the whole battle. When he was dead, his army went home."

"Another score for you – a big one. It sounds to me as if you handled yourself very well. Now, about the killing. That's harder. You must get used to the idea. It will probably bother you for some time. It does you credit that you feel this way."

Kenna put her hands on Zoe's shoulders and looked her straight in the eyes. "And you were lucky. This was a straightforward attack, with no choice on your part and a good

40

result from your act. I hope you are never required to kill in cold blood, or where you are not sure you are in the right. Because," she gestured across the room, "you were right about one thing."

"What?" Zoe spoke before she turned to look.

"Your training." There, imbedded chest-high in the centre of a bedpost, was Zoe's dagger.

"You have been trained more intensively than any Warlander your age. You, my sweet young friend, are a very potent weapon. It is your responsibility to be sure you are used for a good purpose, not for evil. It is an important stage of your development to learn this, and we could not deal with it until you reached this point. So don't dwell on the fear and the horror. That is not productive worrying. Think instead about right and wrong. How do you decide? How *will* you decide? That is enough to worry about, and it is valuable worrying."

Zoe laid a grateful hand on her friend's arm. "Thank you for your help. You know, you are really good at that."

"Hmm. Practice."

"Practice?"

Kenna nodded. "Long ago, Barent. Last year – Gerth."

Zoe was astounded. "Gerth!"

"Think about it. Yes, he loves fighting, but how do you think he feels about killing? Don't mention to him...on second thought, he wouldn't mind if you knew."

Zoe smiled for the first time. "I held his head after his first drinking bout. I've held his hand after several of his puppy loves fell apart. This new revelation won't change anything. And it does help me to know."

A thought struck her. "Are you angry at Barent?"

"Because of Gerth? How could I be?"

"Didn't you want a big ceremony for his Acceptance?"

Kenna's face sobered. "Being there for his Acceptance was an event I anticipated with great pleasure. But being Accepted on the battlefield by my brother, whom he admires greatly, was the highest point in his life so far. Even if it was given to me, what choice could I make? And the choice was not given. How could I begrudge him?"

"Kenna, no wonder he loves you so much!"

A wry smile. "Does he? You might remind him that he hasn't mentioned it lately. However, duty calls us. I had your gown brought over from your quarters. My page tells me it is your only one. We shall mend that state of affairs at our leisure. You can bathe here, and we'll go straight to the banquet. You will go with me? I feel in need of an extra retainer tonight. Just because we must sit on the side and watch others receive their glory doesn't mean we can't enjoy ourselves."

She held up a restraining hand. "The Sivan will wait until tomorrow. You will come with me," she tapped Zoe on the chest. "You will enjoy!"

7. A NEW SLANT

Her interview early the next day with the Sivan was equally surprising. Not as comfortable, but surprising. *How can anyone be comfortable at this time of the morning?* He had stayed at the banquet the night before as long as she had. She glanced at him as she groped for a chair. There he sat, the same as always: no better, no worse, scarred hands folded on the scarred old table. Arranged behind him in a system no one else would ever figure out were rows and rows of pigeonholes, each full of papers. The man had a copious memory, yet he used more paper in a year than five average scribes. His intense, pale eyes bored back at her. He did not speak.

"I didn't do anything stupid last night, did I?"

"No, you handled your liquor rather well, considering your state of mind."

"I'm still in a bit of a state, if you don't mind."

This wan attempt at humour fell flat, as usual. "Please concentrate your scattered wits on our discussion. I understand the necessity of postponing your report yesterday, but I still need the information. From the moment you left the castle. Give."

As she related the events of the battle, she was quite sure that a glow of what might almost be pleasure stole over the wooden countenance facing her. A few times he backtracked her for specifics, but generally he let her talk, making a few notes as she spoke. When she had finished, including her conversation with Kenna, all he did was nod.

"Very satisfactory. I always maintain that the goddess of luck needs a nudge now and then. We were able to take advantage of her help yesterday. Too bad Barent slipped up, but I suppose he had other things on his mind."

"Barent! Slipped up?"

"Yes. He brought you out in the open. I understand his reasoning. He wanted to impress upon Torey the nature of his defeat. But he has done us a disservice in the process."

Zoe frowned. "Why is that a problem?"

A soft sigh, like a breeze through leaves. "Has all my training been completely wasted?"

Lesson time again. They fell so easily into the pattern. "Right. The Guides are supposed to show a low profile. But I'm not a full member of the Guides. They won't mind. So why the problem?"

"In demonstrating your ability, Barent was giving in to his justifiable pride in you. However, in doing so he has devalued your usefulness. Consider the attributes of the concealed weapon."

"Why must you speak of me as a weapon? Can't I be a person?"

"That is an unjust accusation. You have no idea the difficulty it causes me, having to cope with my own feelings when considering your assignments. It is an unusual situation for me and I am attempting to learn from it. Now...consider the attributes of the concealed weapon."

Zoe stared at the spymaster. That was as close to an admission of personal attachment as she had ever heard from him. Pleased, she threw her mind whole-heartedly against the problem. "The main strength of the concealed weapon is not its power but its element of surprise. Evidence of its concealment draws attention to it and devalues its power." That was the easy answer, so she went on. "This is why the weapon concealed in plain sight is the most effective. There is no evidence of concealment, therefore less chance of drawing attention to its power. My grandfather taught me that."

"Oh, yes, your famous grandfather. A truly fine mind. I have learned much from him."

"You never said you knew my grandfather."

His head shook slowly. "I didn't say that. But you quote him at me with great regularity. Continue your analysis. It grows interesting."

She thought some more. "So you consider my effectiveness is due to my visibility, combined with the concealment of my abilities."

I can carry this further. "Perhaps Barent did us a favour, then. By bringing me into the public eye, he has assured that no one will ever realize I am a concealed weapon."

"But a double-blind is only effective for an enemy sophisticated enough to see through the first bluff, but not intelligent enough to perceive the falsehood in the second. A technique of limited usefulness, but we will keep it in mind. Tell me again about Torey's reaction when Barent called off our troops."

Zoe was used to these sudden changes of topic; there was always a connection, somewhere. "He was impressed by Barent's ability to contact his Warlanders and the fact that they obeyed orders coming from a distance in the heat of battle." Then she caught it. "He knows about us! Has the value of our Guides been diminished as well?"

"Only against Torey, and I don't mind that. He's not going to attack us. In fact, if the barbarians over the Barrier get any more troublesome, we may be allies in the near future, so he would have found out anyway. However, if we are to maintain our superiority we must enter a new phase. Any ideas?"

She pondered. "I suppose there must be ways of improving the effectiveness of the Guides in battle. But that's just touching up what we already do. Do you mean to expand our activities into different areas?"

"Yes and no." A typical response from him.

"Am I supposed to guess what that means?"

"This is not an idle game I play. If I tell you a plan complete, I restrict your ability to give any imaginative contribution. If you think it through on your own you will come up with ideas I hadn't considered."

She had heard this before, many times. "We decided that trying to improve the Guides in their present role is not enough. So you must mean yes to expansion, but not the Guides. Nothing very imaginative there. Sorry."

"As usual, save your wit for the subject at hand. Where do we expand?"

"At the risk of seeming facetious, may I assume we are restricting ourselves to information gathering and communications, or do we move into campaign planning as well?"

He started with a withering look. "You may assume..." There was a pause and his expression changed. "Why assume any such thing? I had intended to discuss the creation of a new information system, but why restrict ourselves? There are other areas. Information has more to it than collecting and sending."

"Yes," Zoe jumped in. "Creating!"

"What do you mean?"

"Oh, no. You tell me."

One of his rare grins split the Sivan's weathered face. "You learn your lessons well. If I were creating new information, I suppose it would be false stories to mislead the enemy."

"How typical of your devious mind. No, I was thinking of finding out new things. For example, what if our ironsmiths could make a lighter, stronger steel? Wouldn't that be a great advantage to our Warlanders?"

"I see what you mean. Although in the case you mention, the knowledge already exists. In your grandfather's native land they know how to forge very strong and supple swords. A laborious process, I believe, and a closely guarded secret, but effective. We could send someone to find out more, and we might work on it here, too."

"And while he was visiting, I'm sure they have more battle lore than what I was able to learn from my grandfather."

"Let us consider that line of thought in future," he scribbled a note. "What other areas do we need to look into where we could improve our armies?"

"Food, transport, weapons..." and on they went.

Much later, the twinges in Zoe's stomach brought her back to the real world. From her position hunched forward over the papers now covering the table, she straightened up and looked out the small window. The sun was almost at noon.

"I can't believe it. I come in here with no food, little sleep and a hangover to boot. I end up spending the whole morning and I don't even notice it!"

Her companion also stretched, more slowly. "Ah, the heady young vintage of new ideas. Be careful – it can become addictive. You don't eat, you don't sleep. You sacrifice all for the sake of learning. A terrible fate, yet so enticing."

Zoe was bemused. "This has been a new experience for me."

"No wonder. This is not a time of new ideas. For that reason, I came to Petrella. At least the Arlyn family has a reputation for listening. Especially Barent. This is why he is so successful, yet has so much trouble getting anything done. There is great resistance to change, mostly among the landed families. So I applaud the admission to the council of the merchants, craven though they may be in war. Merchants are travellers; they see new places, hear new ideas. They make profits on new things. They will be useful to us."

"Not if we starve to death in the process. Let's go to the kitchen and see what's lying around."

47

"Perhaps that would not be kind. I know my reputation. If I show up in the kitchens, the head cook will harass his staff for a week trying to find out what I was looking for."

"That means you are working against your own precepts." Zoe held the door open and waited until he joined her. "If you wish to be unobtrusive, it would be better if you habitually wandered the castle more. It would also help you keep in touch with what is happening at a more direct level. You spend too much time tied to that table. How can you function if all your information is second hand at best?"

He paused in his stride and looked at her, forcing her to stop as well. "Again the teacher learns from his student," he executed a full formal bow. "I shall remember. I thank you."

She laughed, caught his arm and propelled him towards the kitchens; he followed willingly enough.

It was only later, looking back on it, that she realized he had been serious.

8. DILEMMA

Even the meal was a revelation. She often ate at unscheduled times, a habit she had developed as a child. The warm, noisy camaraderie of the kitchen, so opposed to the austere quiet of her grandfather's life, had appealed to her. Today, the presence of an outside observer gave her a new perspective on her old habits.

He sat, taking everything in, as she expressed concern to one of the workers over the illness of a child. He would be filing it away in his mental pigeonholes to be considered at a future time. As she gave the head cook her opinion about the spicing of Barent's supper, it occurred to her that she was one of the few people in the castle who conversed so freely with so many levels of the hierarchy. Her familiarity did not end with the kitchen staff; it extended from the stables and armoury through the personal quarters staff and up to the king's own family. Seeking a reason, she thought of her lack of specific status in this structured society.

Looking at her situation through the Sivan's eyes, she saw how valuable she could be in gathering information. *But I don't want to start using my friends as sources of information.* She hoped the Sivan wasn't going to consider her as part of his extended spy system. *With his reluctance to waste resources, the prospect looks dim.*

She was lost in thought as she crossed the main courtyard. She hadn't been good company at lunch, but the Sivan seemed satisfied. She had left him to return to his plotting and was wandering wherever her feet took her. Her abstraction was so deep that she jumped when a hand descended on her shoulder and Barent's voice growled in her ear.

"You look about the way I feel right now. What's wrong?"

Recovering her balance, she grinned up at him. "Wrong? Nothing. Just thinking. A great deal has happened in my life in the past day. Takes rearranging. What about you?" She regarded his bristling demeanour. "You're looking rather grim. What could be of such great importance to bother the hero of the Battle of Escalon Pass? Besides the dregs of last night's wine."

He tried to match her mood, but the attempt fell flat. He only looked angrier. "It seems I impressed everyone except the man who counts."

"If you've had another of your famous 'disagreements' with your dear brother, we should move to a more appropriate spot before you sound off. Some of the things you say about the king don't bear repeating in public." As she took his arm to lead him away, she could feel the tension in his body and changed her mind.

"Come on. You need the full treatment. A nice workout to warm you up and a cup of tea after to relax you. It's probably the change in the weather that's bothering you." As she said the words she realized that they could be true. She had been too preoccupied to notice, but clouds had covered the sky and a light rain was falling, settling the dust and cooling the air. Pleasant as this might be, darker billows rolled on the horizon, promising more than a spatter soon.

She dragged him over to the training bars. "Hurry up or you'll get more cooling than you want." She insisted that he follow her through a full set of exercises before she would allow him to quit, in spite of the increasing rainfall. They finished just in time, and they scurried through the beginning of the downpour to her quarters, laughing. Once there, he sat on a low stool while she kneaded the tension out of his neck and shoulders. She refused to heed his protests.

"Listen. If you come to me for help, you get it, but it will be my kind of help. That means I'm in charge. You know when your muscles are solid like this your mind is too. Now hold still."

He suffered her ministrations, wincing when she dug in harder. "You are bossier than usual today. Have you been talking with Kenna again?"

She squeezed again. "That's an uncomplimentary thing to say about your favourite sister."

"Ouch!" He squirmed. "Say, would you mind if I went out and found a battle to calm me down instead? Just a small one? It might hurt less. My favourite sister. My only one, thanks to the gods. I gather that means you have been talking to her?"

"Yes and no." She chuckled when she realized whom that sounded like. "I mean, yes, I was talking to her last night, but no, she isn't the cause of what I would prefer to call a change of attitude." She didn't mind discussing her problems with him. It had been that way since he first helped her over her grandfather's death. His back relaxed under her fingers as he listened.

"I did a little forced growing up recently. Until yesterday, all my training was just sport, and all my battle strategy lessons were merely pins on a map. It has been pointed out to me that I must accept my share of the responsibility for what I do, instead of only following along. If I am to be involved in these less delicate parts of life, I want to make some of my own choices. Having experienced the destruction of yesterday's battle, today I am choosing to be constructive. You were the handiest victim." She winced, sharing with him the irony of the term, then continued. "So come over and sit somewhere comfortable, and I will pour tea."

As she expected, the comforting predictability of the ritual calmed him more. The wild look left his face, and his tense motions tamed down as well. She also cheated; the blend she chose, while not exactly a soporific, had relaxing properties. Through habit, she allowed all her own weighty thoughts to be pushed aside, and she rounded off the ceremony in a mood of pleasant serenity.

"Now you may tell me about his Majesty, your dear brother."

"I don't know why I was so upset. There's nothing new to tell. As you might expect, he was less than enthusiastic at my interpretation of his commands. I gently pointed out that if I had done as he wished, we would be sitting here like a bear surrounded by hounds, with two armies outside our gates, giving him a chance to perform his much-vaunted negotiation technique to save our necks. He observed that if my 'schemes' hadn't worked, he would be negotiating with no army to back him, which I must agree is hardly beneficial. But I won yesterday, in spite of his interference! He couldn't argue with that.

"I tried to tell him how much better it would be if he stayed with his duty of being king, and how I would be happy to stick to my duty, which was running the army. You know what he answered?"

"I could come up with several good guesses, since we've been through this all before, but go ahead – surprise me."

"How about, 'That's what I thought we were doing'? At that point I felt it would be healthier for both of us if I left."

Zoe mulled it over. "Were those the exact words you used, 'I would be happy to stick to my duty'?"

"Near enough. Why?"

"An unfortunate choice of expression. Did he see your little show on the parade ground yesterday?"

"Show?"

She raised her eyebrows and waited.

"He mentioned it in passing. Was that a problem?"

"If you aren't happy with your duties, whose is the occupation you are likely to try for?"

She watched the light dawn. "I see."

"You can understand why Alarid might find your activities disquieting."

"But Zoe, I don't want to be king! I wouldn't like it, and I don't think I'm suited for it. I'm too apt to charge ahead and force every issue – too much the soldier. You need to be a politician like Alarid. We could be such a good team! But he won't let me do my part. He's always looking over my shoulder as he used to when I was a kid playing Markers, showing me a better move. You do a lot of studying. You're a thinker. Tell me. If he orders me to do the wrong thing, what should I do?"

"The Codes make it simple. Be loyal. Obey."

"The Codes are always simple. That doesn't help."

"Maybe it does. You want him to let you do your job, not look over your shoulder; trust you and wait for results. So you give him the same opportunity. Maybe in the long run he's right."

"Like he was yesterday?"

"We all make mistakes."

His anger was returning. His shoulders hunched, and he seemed to bristle. "And I should sit by and let my country be overrun by that swindler, Rawden? So Alarid can practice at being a general? No. A king can't afford to make mistakes like that. If he can't do a proper job, then maybe someone else should do it."

Zoe drew herself up and stared coldly at him. "I suggest, my Lord, that you take care what you say."

"Oh Zoe, don't go all formal on me."

She relented. "Barent, what you just said could be considered treason."

"I suppose. So who can hear it?"

"You forget where we are. This is the barracks of the Light Armed Reconnaissance – our information service. Even if you

53

and the Sivan did hire them all, perhaps one of them is more loyal to the king than to you."

"I suppose that possibility exists."

"And what about me?"

"You?"

"Yes. You ask me to help you decide. Where should my loyalty lie?"

"I remember when your loyalty was to me. Then, you let me worry about loyalty to the king."

"That was yesterday – about a hundred years ago. You know, for the first eight years of my life my loyalty was to my grandfather and the Codes. Then you came along and told me the Codes could not cover everything, that sometimes we have to improvise. For the past ten years I have been loyal to you. That, too, was easy. There was no conflict. But now I am learning that in the end I am responsible for what I do. Kenna showed me that last night. And now you want me to make a choice between you and what the Codes say is right. Please, Barent, don't make me choose."

He laughed. "You have grown up, I see. I'm sorry I said anything. I wouldn't dream of putting you in that situation. Let's have more tea." And their talk turned to other things. But she was not reassured. While they chatted, Barent didn't seem to be completely there. He was thinking deeper thoughts, and she didn't want to know what they were. Soon he departed, leaving her with her own pondering.

She had seen the possibility of a split between Barent and Alarid coming for years, but had not dwelt on the consequences of such a division, especially to her, personally. She cursed this 'growing up' she was doing. Oh, there were benefits. By taking part in a battle she had passed a kind of test in the eyes of the castle people. The Sivan had certainly changed towards her. But if she had decisions to make, she had to think about them. She marvelled at how simple life had been a few days ago. Problems that had seemed mountainous were now trifling.

Her life seemed to go in steps. Just when she thought she had everything pretty well under control, circumstances came along and showed her a whole new vista of problems to be solved in their turn. Following this idea, it would seem that her present difficulties would soon be solved, which was comforting. That they might be replaced by another set, the complexity of which she hadn't even thought of yet, was disquieting.

She skipped supper, sitting in her quarters sipping tea, watching aimless rivulets run across the courtyard outside her door. She went through her evening chores in a daze. Even a visit from Gerth and Varli didn't rouse her, although their account of Varli's 'help' in getting Gerth's horse and armour ready the previous day was hilarious. They didn't stay long but went off in search of more responsive company. Late into the night she sat, not bothering with a light, her mind going round in the same circles. The lulling rhythm of the rain failed to help her. Finally, when the objects around her were starting to reappear with the first dawn light, she crawled into bed and an exhausted sleep, with nothing resolved.

9. NEW DUTIES

As a result of her thought-filled night, she was less than receptive when Varli, at his cheerful noisiest, roused her at a ghastly hour the next morning. He announced his arrival by pounding thunderously on her door, then stomping through in response to her mumbled query and proceeding to throw open her shutters, allowing the sunlight to strike her unprotected eyes.

"Though I appreciate the service, isn't this the sort of torture you are supposed to inflict on Gerth? What are you doing, practising on a more defenceless victim?"

"Not a bit. I will not be officially assigned to Gerth until the proper ceremonies are completed, so I am available to help in any capacity. I am here on the instructions of the king himself."

That got through. "Alarid? What does he want in the middle of the night?" The king was known for the long hours he spent on state business, starting at an hour when many of his nobles were stumbling off to bed.

"My Lady! You are summoned to a private audience with His Majesty!" He poured a chilling stream of water into a bowl and stood stiffly holding a towel on his arm. "It hardly becomes a lady to enquire as to his purposes. What kind of example are you setting for an impressionable young Squire, just beginning to learn his duties?"

"Varli, one thing you must begin to learn is that sometimes it is not smart to be completely insufferable. Perhaps this will help make an impression on you." Finished washing, she flung a handful of water into his face, lifting the towel off his arm before he could react. While he was still spluttering she steered him outside. "Now get out of here and let me dress."

A moment later, she opened the door and popped her head out. "What am I supposed to wear for this?"

He was standing there, perhaps a little chastised. "How fast can you get dressed?"

"Do I get breakfast?"

"If you don't stop to dress."

"Then whip over to the kitchen and pick me up something while I get semi-decent at least." Varli scrambled off, pleased to be indulging two of his favourite pastimes: being useful and moving quickly.

She stood outside the king's daily reception room brushing the crumbs of a hasty snack off a light formal robe, wondering again what was going on. As she entered with Varli trailing, the smiling faces of Kenna, Gerth, Barent and the Sivan greeted her. So this was a family event. When Alarid motioned her to a chair opposite him, she relaxed more, regarding the king in the light of the present conflict. He carried the stamp of the Arlyn line, with the same bristling hair – smoothed more than Barent would ever bother – and the same piercing eyes. He was slimmer than his siblings, though, and with lines beside his mouth and a touch of grey at his temples, he looked a great deal older. Which he wasn't. *He has only been king for five years. Could it age him that much?*

"You may be at your ease, Zoysana. This is a pleasant occasion. I have heard the reports of our recent battle, and it seems that you have done us good service. Why the Sivan would use you as Battle Reconnaissance escapes me, but you acquitted yourself well."

She told herself to keep looking straight at the king. She could imagine the report the Sivan and Barent had concocted, and the king had fallen for it. "I am pleased to be of service, your Majesty."

"And your superior has, for his own obscure reasons, requested that you should not be recognized publicly for your service. Although I do not understand this, I do recognize the

Sivan's style, and I must not interfere if he is to do his duties properly."

She kept her expression schooled. That sounded like a dig at Barent.

"There is also the difficulty of which I have become more aware with your increasing age: a young woman residing here with no official position. While everyone seems to accept you at face value, this is not a normal situation and could lead to misunderstanding. I believe in solving problems before they arise, whenever possible. So I have found a solution that should satisfy all.

"There is an obscure position in the castle, unfilled for many years, which is not onerous in its duties, yet carries with it a small yearly stipend. No princely sum, but enough to allow its holder to live independently." He stood, and she rose as well. He picked up a scroll and a chain with a key on it from the table by his chair. With a brief flourish, he held it out to her.

"We hereby bestow upon you the official title of Keeper of the Royal Archives. It is our hope and expectation that you will fulfill your responsibilities with the diligence you have shown in your past service to us."

She knelt to receive the scroll and chain. "I am deeply honoured, my liege, and I swear to uphold these responsibilities as a willing part of my duty to the throne." It was an interesting choice of ceremony. Trust Alarid to pick one stressing responsibility and diligence.

She rose, and he smiled benignly at her, then lifted his gaze to include everyone in the room. They were all looking at her with different degrees of satisfaction. They gathered around her with smiles and words of congratulation, moving her towards the door. The audience was over.

As they entered the corridor, Barent chuckled wryly. "All these years I foster your independence, and what do you end up with? A castle sinecure."

"Don't be so sure, Barent." The Sivan's usually grim expression now resembled that of a cat with a small feather at the corner of its mouth. As he departed, he turned to Varli. "Next time you can't find Zoe, lad, you'll know where to look."

She had been to the Archives before, halfway up a smaller turret above the central keep. She doubted if Varli even knew of its existence.

Kenna chuckled. "Brother, you must allow the Sivan to practice his little plots. It would not do to interfere; how could he get his duties done properly?"

So Kenna had caught it too. Zoe watched her turn her innocent smile to her son. "Since this is a private honour, it cannot be officially celebrated. That is no reason to ignore it. Why don't you take Zoe down into the city for a small celebration? I hear the Jolly Watchman spreads a good meal." She paused to let it sink in. "Although some might feel that before noon is a bit early for strong ale." She took Barent's arm, "Come, my Lord, walk me to my quarters. There are matters to discuss."

As they turned away, Barent grinned over his shoulder at the three of them, standing flat-footed in a row with their mouths open. Recently, Gerth had spent a full day and night in the Watchman, quenching his sorrow at the unfaithfulness of a certain young lady. In the end, Zoe had taken two of the castle Guard down to carry him home, and Varli had helped put him to bed, very quietly. So much for keeping anything from Kenna.

Recovering their composure, they looked at each other. Gerth broke the silence. "Well, we have our orders. How could we disobey? But I agree – not so early. You two need time for your usual workout. Just because Varli is going to be my Squire doesn't mean he should stop his weapons training. In fact, Zoe, I'd like you to give him more help, because our schedule won't allow him to make all the regular practice sessions." He realized she was staring at him. "Oh... I didn't mean it to sound that way. Is that all right with you, Zoe? Um…if your new duties…"

She laughed. "I would enjoy that. And maybe you can join us sometimes – pick up a few pointers."

He ignored the jibe. "Thank you so much. So let's go into the city about mid-afternoon. That means you two can work out after lunch. The rest of the morning," he glared at the squire, "I am going to teach him a quicker way to saddle a horse!" With a burst of laughter, they turned away, leaving Zoe moving up the stairs.

When she reached the Archives it was somewhat as she had remembered, except dirtier. At one time, someone who cared very much about books had spent considerable effort on the room. Though it was small, it was an ideal place for paper – warm and dry. It took up half the tower, so there were enough windows, though they were merely glazed arrow slits, to provide both illumination and ventilation.

However, the position of Keeper had not been filled recently. Increasing layers of dust showed which areas were used least often. The floor was filthy. What had once been an orderly system had broken down and now books, scrolls, papers, and individual parchments were strewn helter-skelter.

She descended to the kitchen to scare up help and equipment. She commandeered one of the kitchen maids, an older girl who had often helped her in the past. As they lugged hot water up the stairs, Zoe noted that her new aerie had its disadvantages. They entered, and she surveyed the room, wondering where to start. She turned to her assistant to find her stopped, openmouthed, in the doorway.

"What's wrong, Loreline?"

"Books," was the awed response. "Look at all the books!"

"Aye, those are books. And those are…"

"Scrolls – parchments – paper." The young woman entered the room with growing enthusiasm. "I never knew there were so many books in the whole world!"

Zoe was amused and intrigued. "You have experience with books."

"Oh, no, not much. Well..."

Zoe glanced at the girl. "Do you know how to read?"

"Well...yes."

"How does a kitchen maid know how to read?"

Loreline gave a crooked grin. "Might be better to ask how someone who can read ended up a kitchen maid."

"Right. So, how did she? If you don't mind my asking."

"My father was a scholar. He taught me. Then he died. And here I am."

"Well, it's the kitchen's loss and my gain. You can help me here, if you like."

"Does that mean I can read the books?"

"If you finish the work I give you. And the work right now involves cleaning up this mess."

"Yes. It's hard to know what's trash and what's good."

"I think it safe to assume that nothing's trash."

The older girl picked up a loose sheet. "Fair enough. Look at this. It isn't even written in Petrellan. I wonder how old it is."

Zoe glanced at it. "That's Kyabran. I can read most of it."

Loreline laid it down carefully. "Well, we'll make a pile of that sort of thing, and you can go through it, all right?"

"We'll do that. Let's start over here." She was pleased to discover that her assistant's reverential attitude towards books meant that she could be relied on to treat all the materials with utmost care.

They chatted as they scoured and brushed their way through years of dust and grime, and she began to think that Loreline was very bright. She had a decent grasp of what was going on in the kingdom and a command of castle politics that was amazing.

When Zoe expressed surprise, she grinned. "Oh, you know how people talk when there's only servants listening."

"But you remember it all."

She shrugged. "It keeps my mind alive. Scrubbing a mountain of potatoes is rather boring. I can tell you the names of everyone in the castle, their husbands, wives, children, and most of their lovers."

"Now you're showing off."

"I certainly am, my Lady. This is my first opportunity to better myself in many years. I'm not going to let it slip."

By the time the morning was over Zoe had not only a better idea of what her library contained, but also an able assistant eager to help with its reorganization. Loreline offered to come up in what little leisure time she had, but Zoe refused.

"If you are assisting the Keeper of the Archives, you are doing a service commanded by the king himself. So you will be officially assigned to me for the time you spend. I'll clear it with the head cook. He'll understand."

Zoe came to her own decision. "In fact, we're finished now, but come back this afternoon and clean up this floor. I'm sure you could read for a while once you're done. You keep the key. I know where to find you if I need to get in here before I have another one made."

Locking the door behind them, she handed over the key. Loreline pulled a thong from around her neck under her blouse and tied the key to it. Zoe had a glimpse of a small circular medallion attached to the thong before the girl tucked it back out of sight. Each well satisfied with her new position, they parted company at the bottom of the stairs.

After the noon meal Zoe found Varli, and they headed for the field. She insisted that they run through a full set of exercises on her training bars first. Varli's attitude had improved because of the battle and his coming promotion, but he put up a token protest.

"But we'll be tired before we even start training."

"Let me tell you one important thing I learned about battles. You begin all fiery, and it doesn't seem you could ever wear out. But you can't keep that up. Soon you find yourself dead tired, but the battle isn't over yet."

"So you spend most of the battle tired, but still fighting?"

"Right. You get to rest sometimes, but it's never long enough. At least, that's how it affected me, and my poor horse too. And I didn't even lift a sword."

"You did pretty well without one. Can you teach me more of that stuff?"

"Let's stick to the lesson at hand. There is another advantage of training when you are tired. When your muscles are strong you can carry out any movement easily, and you don't realize how inefficient you are – how much extra force you are using. When you are exhausted, you find the easiest and smoothest path, using the smallest number of muscles and the least energy. That will be the most efficient way to perform that move. Besides which," she grunted as she swung into the first pattern, "we will get into shape so we don't tire out. Let's get to it."

"Since you put it that way..."

They had a good workout, first physically, then with swords. At the end she tried him on a few simple weaponless combat moves, which he found fascinating.

"It's a whole new way of looking at fighting. The idea of using the weight of the opponent's body against himself!"

"If you think that is a new concept, you haven't been listening to the Weaponsmaster. You should be using the power of your opponent's blow to throw him off balance in swordplay as well. If you try to meet him strength against strength, the stronger one will always win. Which is not a good plan for a twig like you."

He ducked the cuff she aimed at his head. "I'll think about it. Can we stop now? My brain works better when it's not upside down."

"Sure – get cleaned up and change your clothes, nothing too fancy, then go tell Gerth we'll meet at my quarters."

"You mean I can come too?"

"I think so. After my big celebration, Gerth will need you to hold doors open when he carries me home."

"Hah! I've never heard of you getting drunk."

"I hope you never do. It might spoil your glamorous image of me. On second thought, maybe...anyway, scat! I must prepare myself for our great night in the city."

10. An Evening Out

When the three entered the Jolly Watchman it was too early for a meal, so they ordered small beer and looked around. Varli, given the responsibility, chose a table in a secluded corner.

"Low profile, eh? Has the Sivan been talking to you?"

"Both of us." Gerth shook his head. "You're allowed to do anything you want, be as loud as you wish, but the moment you start talking about the battle, home you go. Oh, and no fights. Weirdest set of instructions I ever heard; he was positively effusive about instructing us to make sure you had a great time; nothing was too good for you. Then he started on the 'but-ifs.' What's going on?"

Zoe shrugged morosely. "I guess he has plans for me, and they might be spoiled if I sully my hands with any public attention. You know something? I wish I could enjoy some of that glory the balladeers sing about. Can't the Sivan see that? Why does he always treat me like a weapon in his arsenal instead of like a live person?"

Gerth chuckled and stretched his long legs out beside the table. "Strange to hear that coming from you. In all the years I've known him, which is most of my life, you are the only one he treats like a person. The rest of us, yes, you are right. He moves us around like playing pieces in a huge, complicated game of Markers."

"Except Lady Kenna." With his coming assignment to Gerth, Varli had become more formal in talking about his family.

The prince nodded. "He doesn't treat her like a playing piece. More like an opponent."

"Not even that," Zoe entered the game. "I think he treats your mother more like an elemental force – a river or a mountain. The kind of thing you must consider in all your planning, because it's always there and you couldn't consider budging it."

"That's good for him. Everyone needs someone around to tell him when he steps out of line."

Varli considered this point. "I wonder what it would be like to be king with no one above you to tell you what to do."

Gerth snorted. "Next time you attend a Council meeting, try listening. When you're king, everybody tells you your duty. And no matter what you do, you can't make the whole world happy."

Zoe leaned forward and dropped her voice. "That's where Alarid has trouble. He always tries to make everyone happy, and in the end no one is." She relaxed back and grinned. "The moral of the story, as my grandfather used to say, is not to slander any man's task. You may be performing it one day."

Gerth slapped her on the shoulder. "And don't be too envious of those of us with all the glory. I've had my share and more the last few days. Do you see me complaining about this quiet spot? We could have gone to a number of nicer inns. But in the first place, it would look strange for my squire to be eating with me," He clapped his other hand on Varli's shoulder, "and more important - no peace. All night there would be people coming over to make sure they were seen talking to me. Varli, I know you find this hard to believe, but after a short while you get to wishing for simple things, like finishing a conversation with a friend without being interrupted five times."

Varli looked unconvinced, but Zoe considered Gerth's words. He would never rush forward to be king. *I could wish that Barent had a bit of his nephew's humility. After all, who is there who can keep Barent in line? Certainly not Alarid. Maybe Kenna.*

Gerth's voice interrupted her train of thought. "But this is too much serious talk for a night of celebration. I think if we want the choicest food, we should order now."

The room had been filling as they talked: local craftsmen, dropping in for a drink between work and supper, who ignored the trio in the corner; a few of the Castle Guard, who greeted them but respected their privacy; and four Guides, who slipped in and took no overt notice of them, although soon a pitcher of the inn's best ale appeared in front of Zoe. When they questioned the server, he simply shrugged, his eyes sliding towards the Guides. Zoe caught the eye of one and signalled her thanks. He smiled in return, then resumed his conversation with his companions.

Varli was trying to take this all in. "Was that from those Guides? Aren't you going to thank them?"

"She did," Gerth interpreted. "She said, 'Thank you very much. This is marvellous ale, but a bit strong for a squire,' and he said, 'You're welcome, enjoy yourselves.' Right, Zoe?"

Varli looked astonished. "They said all that?"

Zoe poured the dark, rich ale into Gerth's mug, then hers. "More or less. He made up the part about the squire, but I agree. This is heady stuff. You'd best stick to the light beer. Gerth doesn't want to carry both of us home."

"Maybe if I had some food."

"Maybe if the squire fulfilled his duties, he could find food and order himself another small beer while he was at it."

"Yes, my Lord, right away." Varli self-importantly called the server over and took care of the ordering. It wasn't difficult, as the inn only offered one main dish. Soon they were digging into a rich stew, full of vegetables and large bites of meat, with big chunks of rough bread on the side for sopping up the juice.

While they ate, a balladeer wandered in and set up his instrument and stool in a prominent spot. As they finished he strolled over to their table and bowed. He was a tall, slim man of about fifty, who had maintained the graceful movements of a minstrel's acrobatic apprenticeship.

"Is it permitted for a mere songsmith to sit with the local heroes, my Lord? The time has not come for me to play."

"Pull up a stool and wet your throat before you start. I believe you know Zoysana. Perhaps you have not met my squire, Varli? Varli, this is Solonstan, most loved and feared coiner of slanderous wit in twenty kingdoms."

The singer bowed again. "My Lord is too kind, as usual. Varlinden. Ah, yes, I passed through the Inner Duchies about three years ago. In the late fall, I believe."

"Did you? I don't recall you playing at my father's court."

"No?...ah, no. Your father had a steward – big man, heavy, not much of a way with horses?"

Varli's mouth fell open. "Yes, he did."

"Ah, him I remember. Very unfortunate. You see, when I met the man, he was going up a steep hill. He is a large man, and had a small horse pulling his cart. Ah, yes, unfortunately, I tried the song out at the inn before I asked admittance to your grandfather's hall. I suppose word must have gone round before me. No sense of humour, your father's steward, I must say. Quite unfortunate."

"You wrote 'Fat Man on a Hill'?"

"Ah, yes. My small reputation does precede me. How fortunate."

"Yes it does. Zoe, watch your tongue around this man. One small slip could be," he grinned at Solonstan, "unfortunate?"

Zoe waited. "Well...? Give."

Varli was pleased to be the centre of attention. "My father's steward was a hard man. Hard with horses, hard with people. He was a good steward for all that – a worker, and honest –

but'not well liked. Then the song came out. There was no doubt it was about him. He couldn't escape it. Everywhere he went, everyone sang it. In the end, he had to leave. You can't give orders to people who are laughing at you. Believe me, a lot of folk would thank you if they knew."

"Perhaps one small horse, as well?"

"No, it was his own horse, and he took it with him. I always felt sorry for that horse."

"Ah, yes, a small success, a small failure. How unfortunate, how near to life. Now I must thank you for the libation and go to my avocation." He made a flourish, "I have tried to be kind. Please to be kind." The balladeer made his graceful way to the stool and began tuning his instrument.

Varli was impressed. "What a memory! He knew who I was, who my father was, even my father's steward."

"It is his job to know," Zoe reminded him, "and to remember."

"But what did he mean about trying to be kind?"

"Well, 'Please to be kind,' is the traditional minstrels' introduction. You hear it all the time. For the rest, I'm not so sure. I suggest all will be made clear when we hear his songs. As you are now aware, he has no reputation for being kind."

In truth, Solonstan had a wicked tongue. He was merciless with the effete foibles of the upper classes, an attitude the tavern audience appreciated. He also showed no quarter to the cruel, the bully, the sneak. After each song, the inn erupted in violent appreciation, although several times Zoe noticed those in the crowd whose laughter seemed forced. One well-dressed group even got up and left after an acerbic treatment of usurious moneylenders.

When he sang "Fat Man on a Hill," she listened with more appreciation than she had given the song before. It was nasty, it was hilarious and it had a ring of truth. Instead of taking the moralist's stance, Solonstan had chosen the horse's point of view. Each verse ended with the man berating the horse for its lack of observational skill.

"You stupid horse, why can't you hear?
The road is dry, the way is clear.
I said go faster, stupid nag."

To which the horse always replied with an uncomplimentary comparison to a different part of the man's anatomy. *Well, it's a tavern song, and not for the ladies' chambers.* At the end the man falls off and rolls down the muddy hill, and the horse decides that the man was right, after all, because the carriage really is light, and he willingly runs home, apologizing for his mistake. The audience responded with thunderous applause and a shower of coins. The singer rose and bowed with his usual flourish.

"And now to present times of glory and honour. For those who risked their lives and bodies in defence of our city. Perhaps some are here tonight."

Gerth rolled his eyes at his companions and eased his bulk back into the shadows. Fortunately the room's attention was taken by a group of mercenaries in another corner, cheering several of their number. It took a while for a merchant nearby to insist on buying drinks for the whole table of them.

Then Solonstan touched the first few chords. "I claim the honour of presenting to you a new song." Another murmur of appreciation greeted this. "I give you, 'The Battle of Escalon Pass.' Please to be kind."

As he sang, Zoe had several reactions. The first was pleasure, to hear her battle immortalized as so many she had dreamed about. The second was amazement at the accuracy of his knowledge. Except for a few minor errors, he knew the battle as if he had sat with her in her perch that day. Next came amusement, at the heroic colouring that tinted every event. It was fascinating how the noise, dirt, exhaustion, and horror of the battle could, in a matter of days, turn into a glorious conflict of splendour, daring, and skill.

Her last reaction was embarrassment. When it came to the death of Saxer, it was obvious the poet knew more than he was telling. Twice came the line asking "Who rode the White Horse?' and the question was unanswered at the end.

Again the audience was appreciative, and another merchant offered drinks for "anyone who fought on that glorious day." To the landlord's enquiring look, Gerth shook his head. Then the balladeer, pleading fatigue, left his position, bringing his equipment over to their table and perching there on his tall stool.

"Well written, well played, well sung," was Gerth's greeting. The other two chimed in with similar sentiments.

Zoe regarded him frankly, "Not your usual fare for the tavern crowd."

"True, but, fortunately, I had more than the usual crowd, and when I am honored by such an audience, I must perform accordingly."

Gerth signalled Varli to fill the singer's mug. "We are honoured that you are honoured, sir, but there is one small way in which you could credit us further."

"Anything within my power, my Lord."

Gerth seemed to find the right words escaping him. "While, perhaps, I am not used to discussing the merits of poetry with one as experienced as yourself, I couldn't help but notice that a few lines, for example those about the white horse, are possibly not in keeping with the style of the piece. Also, they ask a question, the answer to which might remain comfortably obscure. Could those lines be removed without harming the integrity of the work or its composer?"

The musician stared at Gerth for a moment. "The person making this request could admit to some self-interest in mind, having been involved in the action? Would you prefer the song to indicate that you were the one..."

Gerth cut him off in immediate distress. "No, no, not that. I would never ask that I...."

In his turn, Solonstan interrupted. "Unless, of course, the request is on behalf of someone else? Who would prefer not to advertise his or her presence?"

As Gerth smiled and nodded in relief, Zoe studied their guest. "You are perceptive. While we are dealing with possibilities, might there be items to discuss at another time?"

"Straight and to the point. Ah, my Lady, in some ways you are so like your grandfather."

"Grandfather?"

"Ah, yes. Our paths crossed frequently at one time. Both your grandfathers, I suppose. The Lord Borbonen's court was one of my regular visits in those days. I was well received there, and the talks I had with your maternal grandfather were fascinating. I learned much from him. Much of our land, much of the world."

"Then you must come and see me, and tell me more about him! I was so young when he died."

"Ah, yes, so unfortunate. So sad for you, and a loss to us all. Not even a song to be made for him. Whatever he did was always hidden. Like your Sivan in that respect."

"The Sivan. Yes, I suppose. Come at noon and eat with me. There may be others who would like to speak to you, too."

"You think there may be? How fortunate. Till noon tomorrow, then. I must rest now." He drained his mug and stood. Receiving once more their compliments on his performance, he made his way to the stairs that led to the sleeping rooms.

Varli rounded on Zoe as soon as the singer was gone. "There's something going on here."

72

Gerth had a puzzled frown as well. "Very quick, lad, very quick. Zoe, what just happened under our noses?"

"I guess I wasn't that subtle, was I? I'm not sure, but I think he wants an excuse to meet the Sivan."

Varli couldn't see it. "Why doesn't he just come up to the castle and ask for him?"

Gerth answered. "I don't think he wants to make a big deal about it. He'll probably enjoy a nice public visit with Zoe, then just run into the Sivan on the way out. It sounds as if they know each other already.

"It also occurs to me that if Solonstan wants a last verse to his song, it will be convenient to be at the castle tomorrow morning when Alarid announces the final form of the treaty he and Rawden are discussing."

Varli's eyebrows rose. "But Rawden's ransom money hasn't even showed up yet."

"That may be part of the deal. Who knows? All we know for sure is that he is making the agreement public tomorrow."

"And that Barent won't like it." Zoe's shoulders sagged. "You can count on that."

"Probably," Gerth grinned, "but my uncles' differences are not what we are here to talk about. We came to celebrate, remember? It hasn't been a bad evening so far – the ale bought for us, and our song's first performance."

From there, the talk turned to lighter things.

11. A Rough Night

After a time, a companionable silence fell over the table as they turned their attention to the rest of the room. No entertainment being provided at the moment, the patrons were amusing themselves in their own fashions: joking, talking, story-telling, gambling and showing off standard tavern tricks – feats of strength and skill.

As they watched they heard voices coming from the next table, separated from theirs by the small partition that gave them their privacy. As the evening and the drinking progressed, these voices had been getting louder. Now individual words and phrases could be heard. What had arrested their attention was the unmistakable use of Barent's name. Then, in one of those lulls that happen every so often in a crowd, came loud and clear, "...Barent and those damned foreigners of his."

Before either Zoe or Varli could react, Gerth reached out and laid a hand, gently but firmly, on the shoulder of each. "Now don't get in a hurry. Low profile, remember."

"But that's me they're talking about – and the Sivan!"

"And even me!" Varli was indignant. "I'm not exactly from the next village."

Gerth shook his head. "Don't let it get to you. I hear that sort of thing all the time." He grinned. "Part of the price of fame."

"But we can't just let them get away with it!"

Zoe could see the wheels turn. Varli and his sense of justice. "Low profile, Varli."

"Oh, sure." That look was on his face. He picked up the now-empty pitcher from the table, and started for the bar. Just past the partition he stopped and called back, "Oh, Lord Gerth, did you want some as well?"

Gerth caught on. "No, lad, I've had enough to get me in fighting trim. Maybe it's time we went and found ourselves more active entertainment."

Varli returned, still talking just a bit louder than necessary. "Right away, my Lord. Here, let me get your sword for you." He sat down, and they all waited, listening. There was a pause, mumbling, then hasty movement at the next table. Three figures pushed their way to the door with an exaggerated lack of concern and hurried out into the night.

Varli was in stitches, and Zoe felt better. "As the man said earlier, Gerth, it seems your reputation has preceded you. However, at the risk of disappointing Varli, I think I am ready to go home on my own feet."

Satisfying as the ending of the incident had been, it had cast a pall over the evening. They kept their eyes open on the way back to the castle, especially in the unlighted sections of their way, but nothing untoward happened. Zoe didn't know whether she was relieved or not. She felt the need to strike out at anyone who dared to question how Barent conducted himself. "Ungrateful louts! Why, if it hadn't been for Barent and his 'foreigners' the city would show a whole different aspect today. Did you recognize any of them, Varli?"

"I think so, one of them. And I could describe the others."

"Write it down and give it to the Sivan tomorrow. He might be interested."

"Certainly!"

Varli would be doubly pleased. He was proud of his handwriting ability, which far exceeded what his peers could scratch out. That, and to be reporting officially to the Sivan!

I wish my life was that simple.

They parted near the barracks, and Zoe went to her rooms and another restless night. It had been a long and active day, and nothing that happened had relieved her anxiety. The king's generous act, bringing her a bit of the recognition she had bemoaned the lack of, had bound her further to him. The final incident in the tavern had revealed that all was not well in the kingdom's political life. And to top it all off, she was getting deeper in the Sivan's plans; Loreline was an ideal subject for recruiting, and Zoe had facilitated tomorrow's meeting with the balladeer. Not that any of it had been hard. Solonstan had set it up beautifully. Experience told her that there would be a more difficult duty following, late or soon.

It occurred to her that she had no idea where the Sivan's loyalties lay. If it came to a division between the two brothers, which way would he go? It was not inconceivable that he was playing some devious game of his own, although she didn't want to believe that.

The news that Alarid was making the treaty public in the morning added to her unease. Word about the castle had it that the king was treating Rawden more as an ally than as a conquered enemy, and a treacherous one, at that. She could imagine how Barent regarded this turn of events.

She tried to think of the pleasant things that had happened recently. She had enjoyed the session with the Sivan so much. It felt like the strategy sessions years ago with her grandfather. Except that this time she knew that her ideas really counted. Which brought her back to her loyalties. What if the Sivan and Barent took opposite sides?

She tried to think of pleasant things. Her new position was going to be interesting. Think of all that information, hidden away there for years. Loreline was such a joy to work with. What a knowledge of castle life from a different perspective! *I must put her in touch with the Sivan. There goes another friend.*

She looked for other happy thoughts. What about in the Inn, when those idiots had upset them so? *Not Gerth. Idiots like that don't bother him.* It was strange. Growing up, she had always treated him as a younger boy, although they were about the same age. Of course, she had been so serious and old when she was little, at least that's what everyone teased her about now. And here was Gerth, when the gauntlet was down, doing the calm, mature thing, while she reacted exactly like Varli. She probably needed to reassess Gerth as well, and she wasn't sure she wanted to. They had a very comfortable relationship right now. But it couldn't last. Sooner or later Gerth would be making a political marriage, and that would be the end of any friendship with her. She had never faced that possibility squarely before, and the thought hurt.

Her body twisted on the bed as the thoughts churned through her mind. She considered getting up and making herself a pot of tea. Who was going to come around and perform a soothing rite for her when she needed it? She pictured herself marching up to Barent's quarters at this time of night and demanding a tea ritual. *The guard would probably be scandalized, but Barent would comply, I must admit.*

She thought fondly of Barent, ten years ago, riding out on a patrol of the farther reaches of the kingdom, returning with a midget nine-year-old in tow. The whole castle was amused. In those days, Barent was always coming up with something new, and not always something that was appreciated. It had taken years of monumental patience, combined with a certain amount of browbeating and a few brilliant successes, for him to get to the point where his Warlanders, and sometimes even the council, would follow his lead. Well, he had proved himself again.

And through it all, he had found time to help her out as much as his conscience would allow. There had been no handouts, but he seemed to enjoy helping her make a living. They'd joked about 'Barent the Merchant' as they decided on appropriate prices for the special blends of tea she sold. They had chuckled together when he charmed court ladies until they simply *had* to have Zoe 'do tea' for them. He had also seen to her training, some of it personally, and to her schooling, and spent a lot of his precious free time with her.

The fact was, since her grandfather, he was the only family she had. The fact was, she loved him, and she owed him a great deal. What if he went against everyone? What would she do?

The fact was, she was no farther ahead than she had been when she went to bed.

She tried to think of pleasant things...

12. BETRAYED

The king's choice of ceremony for the morning was, again, revealing. While normally the attainment of an agreement between two rulers was a matter for small ceremony – a handshake over a parchment, the branding of seals, perhaps a signature if both could write – Alarid had decided to make this a state occasion. All members of the council and the royal family were to be present in the Main Hall. When Zoe and the Sivan entered by a side door, Rawden was already in place, lounging in an ornate chair near to the king's own, his sallow face a study in smug contentment, his short beard neatly trimmed, his clothing immaculate.

In the Sivan's opinion, there was no harm in treating Rawden to a bit of inexpensive panoply. "His kind thrive on flattery. If this little display makes him more amenable to keeping his part of the bargain, so much the better."

Zoe wasn't so sure. "As long as he doesn't take all Alarid's 'diplomacy' as weakness. A little coddling is good for a vain man, I suppose, if it makes it easier for him to swallow a bitter draught later. I think Alarid has picked the wrong patient for this treatment. Rawden is the type to take it as his due, then ask for more. Besides, he knows what's in the agreement. Does he look like someone about to experience a bad taste?"

The Sivan looked grimmer than usual. He must know what was in the scroll that lay between Alarid's bejewelled fingers. "No, the one who is about to receive the unpleasant medicine is on the other side." She followed his gaze to Barent.

The king's brother and general was placed, symbolically, opposite Rawden. He refused to sit, but stood unbending. He had worn his long sword slung on his back in battle harness, rather than his ceremonial belted weapon. She knew the message the choice was intended to convey. Observing Barent's restrained anger surging against Rawden's

79

complacency, she wondered whether the king's placement between the two was practical as well as symbolic.

"I wonder," she lowered her voice. "How much of this has nothing to do with Rawden?"

The Sivan merely raised his pale eyebrows.

"Alarid got his report of Barent's return from the battle. The king now has taken his chance to publicize his own expertise."

The Sivan nodded gloomily. "It is a poor situation when rivals compete for the attention of the crowd. It is not good for the king, the kingdom, or the people."

"Not good? Hah!"

At that moment the king raised his voice to begin the ceremony. During the ritual words of the opening Zoe looked around the room: Barent, grim and angry. Kenna, not happy, either; she also knew what was in the agreement. Gerth, worried but keeping it to himself. The rest seemed normal – bored or interested as their inclination took them, although she saw a few of the Warlander lords looking with puzzled faces towards Rawden's position. The merchant representatives acted fittingly solemn with the dignity of the occasion. New to the council and used to their own brand of bargaining, they could be swayed by a show of diplomatic skill on Alarid's part, especially if they could derive a profit from it. Zoe herself still hoped. If the king had somehow managed to keep Rawden both happy and under control...

But the king started to read from the parchment and her heart fell. As he continued, she became incredulous. Rawden's only concession seemed to be in the area of trade. In return for agreeing to open his borders to Petrellan merchants, he seemed to be getting off free. His personal ransom was being waived as a 'gesture of confidence'."

As the concessions grew there were quiet murmurs among the assembled nobles. At one point, a sharp hiss of indrawn breath nearby turned her head. An older Warlander nearby was listening, his face a mask of anger. He had lost his eldest son in the battle. She noticed a restrained ripple of movement surge through the crowd. Only the merchants looked happy.

And Alarid. "So to this document we affix our seal on this, the seventh day of the sixth month of the sixth year of our reign," he finished triumphantly, lowering the scroll and looking around. There was dead silence. Then, instead of the applause he expected, his brother's voice cut harshly.

"My liege."

Alarid turned in mild surprise.

Barent took a long stride forward. "Your Majesty, I must speak."

Alarid frowned. "I do not feel that this is the time or place for one to speak who carries such anger in his tone. I suggest..."

A chopping gesture of Barent's hand cut him off. "Before you affix my father's seal, with fire and iron, on that despicable travesty of cowardice, I will speak!" he thundered out. A quiet murmur of agreement rumbled from the nobles behind him. "That dishonoured snake lounging there has underhandedly attacked this kingdom in spite of existing agreements similar to this one!" A sweeping motion of his hand, and the contents of the table scattered through the air like frightened chickens. With a lightning grab, he somehow snatched the agreement before it hit the floor.

"And this," he shook the crumpled sheet, "is a formula to strengthen Rawden just so he can attack us again, maybe dredge up enough scum like Saxer that he can win the next time."

He turned slowly and fixed his brother with an icy stare, and spoke in a quiet, controlled voice. "You cannot keep making these blunders forever, you know. I may not always be around to pull you out of the deep water."

81

The king half rose, his hands corded on the edges of the table, his face deathly white. Then he sank back to his throne and stared at his brother. "You presume too much upon our relationship. You also overestimate your importance to this kingdom. Soon there will come a day when your primitive way of solving conflicts will be unnecessary, and," his voice quavered dangerously, "you will not be allowed to bring your insolence into this court! Guards!"

Four of the Castle Guard hesitated forward.

"Remove this man from our presence!"

The Guards stood rooted to the floor in stunned dismay.

"Remove him!" Alarid snapped out. The soldiers, taking comfort in each other's support, moved forward again. Barent spun in a slow circle and crouched, his hand part way to his greatsword. The Guards stopped. After a frozen moment, Barent relaxed. Slowly, he walked to the table and gently spread the parchment in front of the king.

"I'm sorry I spoiled your fun, Alarid. Here's your toy back." He straightened and started towards the main exit. The guard in front of him scrambled aside, then followed him at a respectful distance. Anticipating him, the huge doors at the end of the hall parted. He stopped between them, wheeled back to face the room and hesitated. Then he slowly shook his head, turned his back and strode away.

"A beautiful exit," whispered the Sivan's voice beside her. "The man should be on the stage."

"I'm afraid this is a bit more important than a play." She was still staring at Barent's retreating figure. "What is he going to do now?" She turned to the Sivan. "What are you going to do?"

The Sivan raised his eyebrows at the question. "Me?" He considered. "I think your grandfather would suggest it was time for the Terrapin Approach."

"Pull in your head and await developments."

He nodded towards Alarid, who was rearranging the papers that two Squires were hastily gathering. "There will be some very unhappy people around here for a while. What about you?"

"I'm afraid my shell isn't thick enough for all of this."

"There are other options."

"Believe me, they look equally unpleasant." She twisted her face to a semblance of a smile. "In fact, some of them could be quite fatal."

Before her companion could respond, Alarid's herald called their attention to the continuation of the ceremony, which trickled away into a quagmire of self-congratulation on both sides, sounding hollow in light of the preceding events.

As she drifted out of the hall with the muttering crowd of notables, she pondered her course of action. Her feet had carried her almost to the top of the stairs before she knew that she was headed for the Archives room and realized that she had no key.

However, the door was open and Loreline was there, completely involved in a book. She started with guilt, then relaxed at Zoe's wan smile. Zoe flopped on the bench opposite.

"Found something interesting?"

"It's a list. There seems to be a lot of food and equipment, but it doesn't say what for."

Zoe spun the book towards herself. "Yes, it's a record of the supplies required for an expeditionary force. Doesn't say where they're going, just the number of men – see here – and wagons – here –" As she showed the girl the words she did a bit of calculation. After a while she summed it up.

"It was a raiding party, say to the Inner Duchies, probably Poligny or Falticeni. Summer, I'd say, about fifty years ago."

"Where did you find that?"

"Facts like these are useless if you can't interpret them. Look – wagons – they aren't going into the mountains. Supplies – light, nourishing, for both man and beast – long distance, speed. More wagons than they need…"

"They expect to bring something back!" Loreline's voice rose. "And summer because of the clothing, and…and…no vegetables! They were going to forage. But how did you figure out the number of wagons so fast?"

Zoe laughed. It felt good to laugh. "Training. By the time I was eight I could rough out the supplies, including transportation, for an army of any size, for almost any distance of march. My grandfather and I had this game we used to play…" Her voice faded out. Loreline waited in silence. Finally Zoe came around. "Oh… I'm sorry. Just thinking. Do you know the Sivan?"

Loreline was taken aback by this sudden shift. "Pardon?"

Zoe gestured impatiently. "The Sivan…"

"Of course, I know who he is. But I don't really know him. Why?"

"He'll want to talk to you. Keep on with your job here. Great improvement. Use whatever books you like to practise. Talk to the Sivan. Can you remember that?"

"Of course I can. But why are you giving me all these instructions? Are you going away?"

Zoe looked at her new friend, thinking. "I guess I must be. I hadn't made up my mind until now. Don't mention it around." She selected a few volumes from a pile she had made earlier, those she intended to read.

"Keep the key. I won't need it till I get back. The Sivan – remember!" She patted Loreline on the shoulder in farewell and was off down the stairs, books under her arm.

13. A STRATEGIC DEPARTURE

The Sivan was unfazed. "Discretionary withdrawal in the face of mutually destructive engagement patterns. Good choice. Going to your grandfather's hideout?"

"Is it that obvious?"

"Only to those of us who know about it. I'll take care of your friend Loreline. Thank you for the suggestion. Do you want me to say goodbyes for you?"

"Still protecting your secret weapon?"

"Among other things."

"Thanks, in any case. I'll talk to Barent myself. For the others, though, Kenna and Gerth, it would help. Yes, and Varli."

"Ah, yes, the irrepressible Varli. He might not find life so pleasant here as the alliances shift. His father is no friend to Rawden. Going alone, are you?"

"I thought so."

"Perhaps..." His face cleared, as if he had made a decision. "Yes, that will do. Well, stay in touch."

"I...thought not. I want to work this out with no distractions."

"If I need you, I have a vague idea where to look."

"Let's leave it at that, then."

He raised a crooked finger. "A thought."

"Yes?"

"You are leaving because of loyalty, yes?"

"That's right. I want to be loyal to my friends, to the king, to the realm. And now those loyalties are all pulling me in different directions, and I can't..."

"It might help you to realize that loyalty is not an end in itself. It is the means to an end. What do you really want?"

85

"I told you. I want to show my allegiance. But I'm not sure where."

"You know what Sarasha the Lame called loyalty."

"I think she said it was weak substitute for independent thought. Why?"

"Is it enough just to be loyal? In my experience, there is no deep, emotional drive in the human soul to be loyal. You are trying to be loyal in order to fulfill a need. What is it that you need?""

"Need?" She frowned, staring down into the sharp eyes that saw so much. "I don't know..."

"You might think on that need. A profitable use of your time."

"Ah."

He gave a wintery smile. "And now I have given you your assignment. Thus I fulfill my need to be useful. You are free to accomplish that task as you see fit."

"Thank you." There was an awkward pause. "I know I'm not just a secret weapon."

"No."

She leaned across and squeezed his roughened fingers where they lay on the table in front of him. As she turned away, her last impression was of his other hand covering the spot she had touched. Then she was out the door and on her way to Barent's quarters.

When she got there, it was as she expected. Two of his Personal Guard were standing uncertainly outside his door, while inside she could hear him pacing, punctuating his movement with an occasional crash of furniture.

She shouldered the door aside. "I hope you enjoyed that."

"Oh, I hope so. There's going to be the gods' due to pay for it."

"Yes, and both you and the kingdom are likely to be doing the paying."

"What else could I do?"

"I don't know, Barent. You're the one with the reputation for finding a way. The question is – what are you going to think up?"

"Well, what am I doing right now?"

"Thinking about it. I can tell by the cries of abused furniture. You aren't getting anywhere, though. Sit down, let me work the kinks out, then we'll do tea and talk it over."

He sat, his rigid back towards her. "Sounds like a productive idea. Go to it. You don't need to be gentle." He winced as her weapon-strengthened fingers dug in. "I didn't say use a knife!"

She laughed a bit. "Remember when I used to walk on your back to make this work?"

"Don't try it today. You'd forget to take your boots off first."

"And would you deserve it?"

"Oh, I'm sure. Gods, Zoe, what am I going to do?"

"Might I suggest low profile for the next twenty years?"

"I know I overdid it. But Gods! He's my brother, and I love him dearly, but sometimes he is so pigheaded stubborn, I could just strangle him."

"I wouldn't suggest that as one of our options."

All the muscles under her hands snapped taut, then slowly loosened. He turned to face her.

"Why not?" He looked speculative, but deadly serious.

"Barent, he's your brother! He's the king!"

"He is also selling the kingdom out from under us. To Rawden! He has given him everything! Trade concessions, power; you name it."

"I don't know that having to trade with our merchants but receiving no tariff is a benefit. Also, it doesn't do any good to drive potential trading partners into poverty. This whole connection with the merchants is your idea, you know. Maybe Alarid has simply taken your plans one step further. Besides, Velikii has been punished enough by the number of their people lost in battle."

Barent shook his head. "This is the same old pattern of negotiation, settlement, peace, then treachery and war. Then it starts all over again. It never stopped thugs like Rawden before, and it will not stop him this time. I want to bypass Rawden and make deals directly with the Velikan merchants. If we are tied to them financially, and they get powerful enough, Rawden won't be able to attack us. They won't let him."

"Sounds good. Maybe your brother is doing just that. The question is whether the king is a superior statesman, as he believes, or weak or stupid, as you believe. You are ahead of your time in warfare. Is he ahead on diplomacy? Is he too far ahead? Is this part of the world ready for him? You act according to your own personal answer to that. But you don't kill anyone. Once you start that, it catches on too fast."

"But if it could stop at the one death…"

"Barent. There may be a time to break the rules, but there is also a time to obey them. You told me before; those rules are what hold the kingdom together."

"But he is breaking the kingdom apart!" came the anguished cry. "My duty is to the realm, not the king!"

"That's a revolutionary thought, coming from the First Prince Ascending." But she wondered if he even heard her. She made the ceremony and served the tea, and their talk turned to other matters. After a while she left him relaxing in a comfortable chair. He sounded thankful, but hardly seemed to notice her exit. She shrugged with a rueful shake of her head at the two Guards, who smiled gratefully at her. She envied them the lack of complexity in their lives.

She strode down the corridor deciding that she was miffed. This was the second time this quarter-month Barent had needed her to calm him down. *How much does he really appreciate my effort? He could get the same effect from a mug of comfrey tea.* She noted the similarity of the two occasions. He was always open to her and considered her ideas at the beginning when he needed her, but after he got calmed down he seemed to shut her out of his thoughts.

Why doesn't he just find himself a wife? They're supposed to be good for that sort of thing. She wondered idly why neither Barent nor Alarid was married yet. Poor Alarid. With a mother like his and a sister like Kenna, he was probably too scared. She doubted if that was a problem with Barent. He seemed quite happy with his life as it was. After all, he had someone to look after him, calm him down, nag him about his clothes, see that he ate right. For the first time she could be angry at her grandfather for bringing her up to be such a little housewife. As far as sex was concerned, she knew full well that a man of Barent's physical and social stature had no difficulties. Many a morning she had stood a polite distance down the corridor while a sweep of silk rustled away from his door. *So why should he want a change? Why would he want a wife?*

Well, sooner or later, he would have to change. *I have needs of my own, after all. Who knows, I might even find a man I want to marry some day.* Then what would Barent do? Better he should start practicing sooner.

Especially if he wasn't going to listen to her. In fact, she wondered what she had accomplished. By bringing Barent's problems out in the open, she had made them accessible to his fertile mind, and soon he would be solving them. And she didn't want to be around when he succeeded. Then she realized that she hadn't even told him she was leaving.

She muttered a few choice curses under her breath as she added a book of philosophy to the small pile on her bed. Besides the books she had brought from the Archives and her own volumes of the Code and Haskell's, all she packed was standard traveller's gear, Guides' issue survival kit, weapons, and bedroll. At least she had enough money to last her a considerable time. Not that there would be much to buy in the tiny village near the cottage.

Swinging past the kitchen on her way to the stables, she picked up a few staples and some luxuries that would not be available in the forest, such as salt and sugar.

But as she entered the stable she found her horse waiting, already saddled, and there was a familiar form seated on a pile of straw nearby.

"Why Varli, thank you so much. Did the Sivan send you?" As he rose, she noticed his clothing. "But I don't need anyone to see me off, not even a little ways. I want to make this quick and subtle."

"Uh...Zoe?" He turned and opened the next stall. There was another horse, caparisoned for travel.

"Oh."

"Please, Zoe. I talked to the Sivan. I can explain it all to you as we ride along. Let's go, all right?"

She slung her pack up behind her saddle. "No need. Rawden's next move is to turn his ambitions towards the Inner Duchies, and you might be in a touchy situation here, with his supposed ally."

"And this whole thing has messed up my Squire position, too."

"How could this affect your relationship with Gerth?"

"My father hates Rawden. With this new treaty, Father won't want me too closely connected to Petrella. He might even bring me home."

"So if he calls and you're not available...?"

He brightened. "Out of sight, out of mind. It's not as if I'm running away. That would look bad, too. I'm just on a training mission!" He looked positively enthused.

"A training mission, is it?" She swung onto her horse with a grim smile. "We can arrange that, too. We wouldn't want to disappoint anyone, would we?"

Varli looked puzzled at this comment, but he knew enough to stay silent when he was winning. He mounted and followed her out.

It was mid-afternoon when they emerged from the shadow of the castle wall at the Guides' Postern. Taking a roundabout route, Zoe led them to a spot away from the castle where they could blend in with the travellers on the main road east.

At the top of a rise she stopped her horse and turned to look back. Observed from this angle in the westering sun, the castle had a dark and foreboding aspect even in the bright day, and she shivered.

Turning to the path she had chosen, she realized that the sun was warm on her back and the birds were chirping in the hedges beside the road. She felt her spirit lift as they jogged along, the jingle of their harness blending blithely with the sounds of nature. She grinned at Varli, riding beside her.

He glanced over. "How did your meeting with the balladeer go?"

She felt a momentary qualm, then smiled again. "You know, in all that excitement, I forgot about him completely. I didn't even eat lunch. Well, he's a big boy. He can look after himself. Besides, it wasn't me he wanted to see – he'll find the Sivan, don't worry."

She pulled her pony over near the hedge and leaning down, plucked a buttery yellow blossom. "Isn't it a beautiful afternoon?"

14. INTO THE PAST

Over the next few days they ambled through the golden countryside. They were in no hurry and took their time getting hardened to the road, going a bit farther and waking up a bit less stiff each day. It was beautiful weather for the harvest, and in many fields they passed the workers were putting the hay up in coils or binding sheaves of grain and standing them in stooks. Harvesting was a dirty, sweaty job, especially in hot weather, but there seemed to be little complaining from the occasional farmer they spoke with. Zoe and Varli took a private satisfaction in knowing that they had contributed in their small way to the contentment of the country people. They could guess what the situation here might be, had Rawden succeeded in his plans.

To give purpose to their idle time, Zoe considered her threat to continue Varli's education. They continued their weapons training in the evening after the day's travel, but she was beginning to form a more ambitious plan.

She questioned him about his upbringing, then plumbed his knowledge of the working of the two courts with which he was familiar: his father's and that of Petrella. After a couple of days of this, she began to bring out the books they carried. When they were settled down after supper she would point out a passage for him to look over. The next day as they travelled she would question him on what he thought of the material. Since there was little else for his youthful mind to dwell on he was happy to go along with this, although sometimes he found her methods frustrating.

"You've read this a hundred times," he burst out once. "Why don't you just tell me what it means?"

She shrugged. "What good is my opinion to you? Wouldn't you rather form your own? I've been proven wrong, the odd occasion."

"Some chance." But after that he paid more careful attention to his reading.

They camped out every night for a variety of reasons, the first being that the weather was beautiful. However, one morning Zoe had trouble rousting her companion from his sleeping robes.

"It's too cold!" was his verdict, and he snuggled in deeper. His nose crept out again. "Can we get a room tonight?"

"A room! It will get a lot colder than this, come midwinter. Besides, I'd rather not stop at an inn. It might be cool in the mornings, especially as we go higher in the foothills, but we don't want to draw too much attention to ourselves. Inns are notorious centres of gossip. Travellers with nothing else to think about, I suppose. We aren't after information at the moment, and we don't want to become the subject of someone else's stories. Now get up. There is ground to cover today."

As they travelled, Zoe felt a new sense of purpose, which Varli noted as she hurried him through his lunch.

"Why are you in such a rush all of a sudden? Did I miss something?"

"The weather. I've just realized that there is lot to do between now and the first snowfall. If we want to survive the winter, that is."

"Snowfall? That's months from now!"

"And busy months they must be, my little squirrel. Where we're going, there is no huge storehouse full of food waiting and no inn to pop over to if you don't like what's served for supper in the hall. What you eat for the next eight months will be what you harvest yourself, and now is the best gathering time."

"But couldn't we just buy what we need?"

"In the first place, there is no telling how much surplus is available. Harvests haven't been too plentiful the past few years, and we don't know how hard our area has been hit. Second, gold is an uncommon commodity here, and we don't want to advertise that we are rich. Which we aren't. We don't have a great deal of protection, you know. Our best course of action is to be small, quiet and well camouflaged. And quick. Mount up." She swung into the saddle and rode away, not looking back. A few moments later he caught up, stuffing the last of his meal into his mouth as he rode.

"So are we getting close?"

"I think so."

"You think?"

"I only travelled this path once when I was old enough to remember. I know the general area, and when we get closer I should start to recognize landmarks. We have already passed through the right number of lower hill ranges and we have gained a lot of elevation. If I figured it right, we leave this road some time tomorrow. I don't want to show up at the village like lords on horseback. We'll go straight to the cottage. Later when we need to, we can go to town on foot."

"So there is a village nearby?"

"Not too near. But there are people who will remember me. Some were very kind to us, and it will be good to see them again."

The following day Zoe was up early. Stomping around in the pre-dawn chill, she started a fire and had breakfast on as the treetops above their heads were catching the first rays of the sun. This time Varli didn't linger either, and they were soon on their way.

At mid day they took their lunch sitting on a mossy boulder at the top of a low pass through yet another range of wooded hills. Before them stretched a long, wide valley angling down to the southeast, with snowcapped mountains rising into the haze behind it.

Varli glanced at her, seemed about to speak, then went back to his food. Finally he spoke quietly. "So this is it."

After a moment Zoe registered. "Hmm...? Oh, yes."

Varli leaned back and watched the clouds moving overhead. Then he tried again. "It's beautiful, isn't it?"

"Yes, I guess it is."

He regarded her curiously. "Are you finding this difficult?"

She considered, then smiled at him. "No, not really. Thank you for the thought, though. I wouldn't say it was difficult. I don't know what to call it. Sour and sweet at the same time, I suppose. You see, until I was nine, this valley was my life. This valley and my grandfather. And now I'm back. And he won't be.

"I only ever looked out over the valley from here once before. On my way out with Barent. We stopped here, turned our horses around and looked back. I was pretty mixed up then, too, I remember. My grandfather's death was still fresh in my mind, yet here I was, going off with a bunch of soldiers to live in a castle!

"They were a noisy lot, that light cavalry troop Barent used to travel with – equipment jingling, a verse of a song, a joke, a shout of laughter somewhere along the line. But right then they were very, very quiet and we all looked out over there." She gestured with her hand. "That was nice of them, wasn't it?

"Then we turned and were off – into the big world of adventure and glory," her smile faded. "And now it's all backwards. Here I am, running away from the big world because it's too adventurous for me and the glory wasn't so great after all. It occurs to me that all this may be a waste of time. Barent says you can't go back, you know. The past won't help; you must keep forging ahead. So," she jumped up, brushing crumbs from her tunic, "shall we forge on?"

As she rode, the Sivan's words drummed in her head. *If I can't go back, what did I come here for? What do I really need?*

15. HOME

Throwing off her funk, she turned to Varli, all business. "What is the first thing a Guide does when entering new terrain?"

"Identify landmarks."

"Right. Now, one or two you know from the maps back at the castle, so I'll show you those first. Then there are some that I know the local people's names for, especially those near the village, over there." She pointed northwest, where a haze of smoke drifted from the trees. Farther on, small fields scattered across the rolling valley floor. Here and there a glimmer of water showed the winding path of the river. Further up the sides, stone walls enclosed the white dots of sheep.

Then Zoe turned and looked to their left, at the mountains opposite them. "Over there on our side of the valley we pretty much made up our own names for things. For example, see that lower peak which sticks out of the mountainside alone? That's the Sleeper. Our cottage is in a fold of the mountains close under the peak." She grinned. "So close that Grandfather used to say that he hoped the Sleeper wouldn't roll over in bed one night."

"Why did you call it the Sleeper? It looks like a normal crag to me. Steep, though."

"There's a tight canyon around the north side. When there's a west wind the gusts come in a regular pattern and it sounds like someone snoring. Very slowly. I'll take you up there, if you like. For now, that's where we're headed, in case you get lost." She moved her horse towards the road again and they began the gradual descent into the valley.

Whenever a gap in the trees afforded a view she would indicate points of interest to Varli, often with an anecdote of her life here to assist his memory. He knew that according to standard Guides' practice he would be expected to demonstrate perfect recall some time on the following day.

Suddenly Zoe stopped and swung off her horse. "Raspberries! I thought they'd be finished."

Varli remained mounted. "Shouldn't we be getting on? We want to reach the cottage in good time, don't we?"

Zoe looked up at him, then down at the berries in her hand. "When I was sitting up there in the pass I realized something. Up to now, we were travelling. Now we have arrived and we are no longer under pressure to make distance. Now we are surviving. The pressure is to find food. That's what life here is all about. If you're in such a hurry, jump down and pick your hat full and we can eat as we ride. We'll scout for more near home. We must figure out a way to preserve some."

Soon they were riding on, savouring the sweet, tangy berries. A mile or two later, they passed a narrow trail leading off to the west.

"Where does that go?"

"Where we're going."

Varli looked back at the trail. "Then why aren't we going on it?"

"Soft ground."

The lack of a more succinct reply would cue Varli to the fact that he was supposed to be learning something. Farther down the road where the surface was gravelly, Zoe turned her horse, making sure his feet stayed on the road. Varli did the same, and they rode back, this time angling onto the trail when they reached it.

"Was that necessary?"

"Just a precaution. If someone was trailing us that wouldn't fool them for a moment, but for the casual passer-by, there's no need to make everything obvious."

97

"But for the not-so-casual passer-by, doesn't that draw attention to the fact that we're trying to hide something? Isn't that a double-blind?"

She looked at him in astonishment. "That's very good, Varli! Where did you hear that?"

He regarded her smugly. "The Sivan told me."

"Well, you remembered it, and you're right. If just the wrong person were to come along that trick might pique his curiosity enough that he would want to find out what we want to hide. And that would be the person with the skills to find us. Fortunately, it's not an unusual technique – some people use it all the time, whether they have anything to hide or not – and someone with a lot of skill and not too much curiosity might decide it wasn't worth investigating. A double-double-blind, you might say."

"Could get complicated. Where does this trail lead?"

"It's a route the fur traders use when they go up into the mountains in the spring to trade with the Inari."

"You mean this leads directly to the steppes on the other side of the Barrier? Isn't that dangerous?"

"Not really. It's a narrow and difficult trail over the pass. You wouldn't want to try bringing an army through. A raiding party, perhaps, but there isn't much on this side that the barbarians want. Besides, there's a truce on the fur routes. The tribes that hunt furs won't let any of the others spoil their chance to get at the riches they can trade for. Because of the trading those tribes are the more powerful ones, so it works out quite well. This village hasn't been raided at all in a hundred years or more that I know of.

"It's the same to the north, except more so. Right over the mountains, as the crow flies, it's not far at all to the Inner Duchies. But the trail is only passable for two months in the summer, and you can't get a horse over at any time of year. So,

98

while a few spies probably risk it once in a while, it's useless otherwise. Makes it a peaceful place, this valley. The Arlyns send a troop out here once a month or so when the weather permits, and that's about all. That is what Barent was doing when he found me. He had come out with his own patrol to learn more about his country, he said. Personally, I think it was an excuse to get away from the castle for a while."

"Why would he want to do that?"

"I don't suppose you ever met the old king and queen?"

"No, but I've heard a bit. They were the ones who expanded the kingdom, weren't they?"

"True, and that shows what good monarchs they were. But think. Lady Kenna gets her strength of character from her mother. King Alarid gets his habit of making unilateral decisions from his father. I gather that the 'old folks' were a formidable pair when they worked together for the good of the kingdom. But living together on a daily basis?" She shook her head.

"Oops, time to water the horses."

"Water the horses." Varli looked around. The trail followed the west bank of the river at this point. It was hardly a river, more like a large creek, and in many places a man could wade across without getting wet above the knees. The spot Zoe had chosen had, from the evidence of old tracks, been used to water animals before, but Varli was puzzled at this departure from their usual travel routine. Nevertheless, he complied.

"Don't let him drink too much. It's quite cold, even in the summer."

"Sure, but why water him at all? He doesn't really need it."

"Just keep him in the river." *He has to figure this one out for himself.* She rode her horse out onto the trail, then slowly backed him down again into the water.

"I get it! Two tracks going down to the water, two pointing back up."

"Exactly. Again, that won't fool a real tracker. It took a lot of training to get Jobe to take long steps backing up, and the track doesn't really look the same as going forward, but for the average observer, it's enough. One rain shower to blur our tracks on the main trail and it's perfect. Now we head upstream."

For the next hour, Zoe used all her woodcraft to make it look as if two riderless horses had wandered through the area. She knew she was overdoing it because once they had the horses installed in a secure mountain meadow, she didn't plan to use them much. However, she felt it was good for Varli, not only as a training session, but also to impress upon him from the start the approach they would take to their life here.

"You will notice as you learn the area around the cottage that all the trails in this part of the woods run past our clearing. None of them lead directly to us. People and animals do not walk a straight line through the forest. They follow natural open ways, or paths made by others. Immediately around the cottage, these paths of least resistance through the brush all lead away to either side. It would be virtually impossible for a stranger to stumble on us. As long as we always use different ways to approach and don't wear a path, we are safe."

Varli was taking all this in. "What about in the winter? Isn't there snow here?"

"There is, and then the risk will be greater, but very few people wander in the woods at that time, so it all evens out. No one found us while we lived here, and I will not be surprised if no one has found the cottage in all the years I've been gone. I really hope not. This is going to be difficult enough, even if everything here is fine."

"This? Do you mean your homecoming, or our winter?"

100

"A bit of both, I guess." She gestured him to take the lead. "We're getting close, now. Look around. See what you can find."

Leading his horse, Varli stepped ahead of her and moved forward. After a few steps he turned to see Zoe following, her finger pointing off to the left.

"We were headed that way."

"No, I've been going in a straight line."

"Then the forest is moving. That way. Try again."

A moment later her finger was off to the right.

"Over there?"

"Aye."

"Fine. I know what's going on, and I still can't find it. I believe you. So will you show me?"

"You did quite well. You made it within a spear-cast. Look around."

He complied, then shrugged. "Just looks like forest to me."

She pointed. "Up there. What do you see?"

He stared. "Flowers. Wait a minute. Why are there flowers up there?" He bashed his way through a screen of brush. "The roof! It has flowers growing on the roof!"

Taking a deep breath, Zoe pushed through after him.

The clearing was overgrown with brambles and small bushes. The training posts were weathered and loose in the ground, but still strong enough for tethering the horses. Zoe had expected the house to seem smaller, but she was shocked at how shabby it looked, in spite of the profusion of flowers growing on the roof. Ten years of summer sun and winter frost had performed their usual role. She showed Varli the special twist required to release the primitive-looking latch and eased the door open.

The emotional impact hit her with almost physical force. Except for a thick coat of dust filtered down from the sod roof above, the room was exactly as she had left it all those years ago.

She had insisted, before she and Barent departed, on leaving everything exactly as her grandfather had taught her, as they had always left it: kindling on the hearth, chairs set in to the table, utensils placed on the shelves and hangers. She had stood at this exact point in the doorway, looking around for the last time to be sure that it was perfect. And now she stood there again, tears pouring down her face at the memory of the little girl who had done everything she could in the vain hope that her grandfather would somehow approve and return to her, if only she performed the task well enough.

She snuffled and looked sheepishly at Varli, who was standing just outside, his head bowed.

"Well, I guess I got that over with. Would you like to come in?" She stood aside but, instead of walking past her, he reached one arm around her shoulders and gave her a hug and an understanding smile. Then he entered and gazed around.

"Hey, this is cute."

"Cute?"

"Yeah," he knocked the dust off a chair and sat down. "Everything's my size! I like it." He rose again and circled the small room. "Wow, it really is! This place is like an arsenal! Look at those table legs; one tug and – Boom!" He made a clubbing motion. "And there they are. A set of Nadhi throwing sticks. I knew it!" He reached up, pulled them from the wall and, with a twist, disengaged them.

She collapsed in a chair, stirring up a cloud of dust. "How do you know...?"

"I'm the little guy who's always asking dumb questions, remember? The armourer back at the castle has a set of these.

Quite his pride and joy, but he let me look at them. Wouldn't teach me how to throw them though. Will you?"

Zoe was just regaining her composure. "But how did you know...?"

"Oh, I heard all about this place." He waved a hand at the curtained doorway. "Two bedrooms and cold storage back there, along with the spring. Do you think any of your stored food lasted? I guess not, after this length of time."

Finally he took pity on her, sitting there with her mouth open. "Oh, Zoe! Gerth described it to me when he heard we were leaving. Barent told him years ago. This place is a bit of a legend among those few of us who were let in on the secret. I couldn't wait to see it. I wasn't going to say much at first, but then... well, I wanted to take your mind off..." He lifted a shoulder.

"Hah! It did take my mind off. But that gave me a chance to think of other things. Like how dirty this place is. Since you're so informed, you'll know that back beside the spring there is a wooden bucket. It needs to be put in the water to soak and swell up so it doesn't leak. Then you can start up the fire, first checking to see that the chimney is clear, and heat a ton of water in the big pot from the cupboard over there. I will meanwhile go unpack the horses and look for our precious soap. I was hoping to save it for ourselves, but the house needs it more, I'm afraid. We'll just have to start making our own sooner. Now, let's snap to it!"

A few hours later, after giving the whole house a scrubbing, she got up the nerve to step around the corner of the cottage to her grandfather's Resting. But it wasn't as bad as she had imagined. It, too, was sort of cute. She cleared away the weeds and bushes that had grown over the small mound. A corner stone had fallen down. She used only one hand to right it, remembering how difficult it had been for her to move it when she had first placed it there. The marker had also fallen, and she held it for a while before she replaced it, running her fingers over the carving, now weathered to illegibility. She grinned and rubbed the scar on her left index finger. The letters hadn't been too clear in the first place.

Gently, she tamped the earth back around it. That was the only thing she intended to change. She had brought a good chisel with her, and would go up on the Sleeper soon to look for a suitable piece of stone.

She looked up to see Varli peering around the corner at her.

"Oh, stop looking like a mother hen. I'm fine. Let's get supper going!"

His smile was both relieved and proud. "It's going already. I was just coming to call you. You've been out here quite a while, you know."

16. Fall Harvest

Between Varli's training and preparing for winter, the remaining days of summer passed quickly.

The cottage needed even more repair than she had first thought. It wasn't the first time she had wondered at the necessity of a sod roof, camouflage or no. Now she heard herself on the opposite side of the argument.

As they hauled, sweaty and dirty, on the replacement for a rotted beam, it was difficult to explain the glories of the art of blending in with the environment. For Varli, with his charge-ahead-to-glory attitude towards conflict, it was a completely foreign concept.

"Why do we care if anyone knows where we live? You said no big raiding parties come through here. We're not helpless, you know."

"Speaking of helpful, if you give one more really hard shove, this joist will go into place." He snorted, but complied willingly enough. As the beam settled into its notch, they could hear a patter of dirt on the floor.

"So, now we go inside and clean up!"

"Again," they groaned in unison.

As they worked, she returned to their former topic of conversation. "What do you think would happen if a couple or three bandits wandered through here and saw this place? No – let me guess. You thought about it, didn't you? They come pounding on the door. You meet them with flashing steel. They force their way in. Back-to-back, we fend them off. Your sword is struck from your hand. With a bound, you wrench off a table leg and, catching him by surprise, you crush the biggest thug's skull. Dodging a slash, you whip the throwing sticks from the wall and expertly skewer both the others. If you're feeling magnanimous, you let me wound one or two first. Does that sound like it?"

He had the grace to look sheepish.

"Come here." She led him outside and into the forest across the clearing, then turned him around. "Consider this as a training exercise. Here's your problem. You're lost in enemy territory. No food, no money. Then you see, through the trees ahead, a small cottage. What do you do? Go up and knock on the door?"

"Of course not. Let me think." He stood looking at the cottage.

"You're doing fine so far."

"I am?" He looked for evidence of sarcasm.

"First thing you do is stop, look, think. Why rush? Now, what do you need to know?"

"Who is here, how many, how well armed."

"Right. And...?"

"Um...What they are doing, how long they are staying, umm...Are there others who might be coming up behind me."

"Good start. How long will this take?"

"Quite a while, maybe."

"True. So you decide it is a small force and you might best them in a fight." She waited. "What are your considerations now?"

"To find a way to beat them for sure."

"But..." She made a rolling motion with her hand.

"But...?"

"Is beating them good enough?"

"Oh, yes, I must make sure no one gets away to tell the enemy. So I have two choices, I suppose. If I attack with all of them inside no one will get away, but then we probably wouldn't get in. So I guess I would wait till one left, then take him alone. Yes, and then if we wait long enough," his voice quickened, "one of the others will come looking for the first, and we can get him alone, too."

"But..."

"But...but he'll be more careful, so we need a really good way to get him. And by that time, the last ones inside will be suspicious, so we'll take them by force. How am I doing?"

"Fine. Now what are you going to do when someone pulls that same plan on us? Since we are only two people."

"Oh."

"Yes. 'Oh.' You see how easy it is once someone knows we're here?"

"I get the picture. It really works best if no one finds us."

"I believe I mentioned that before. Ninety-five percent of our defence is in not being found."

"Ninety-five what?"

And that was the way it went. She was a good teacher. She had beaten the rudiments of battle into enough offspring of the local nobility to know this. But being responsible for the total training of the student was a new experience for her. No sooner had she filled one gap in his knowledge than another fell open.

He was a great planner. He loved battle stories and caught on quickly to basic tactics. From there it was a simple step to troop movement and supply. Once he discovered the importance of arithmetic in figuring weapons, food and transport, his enthusiasm for mathematics lessons increased dramatically.

One evening as he was labouring over Haskell's, he looked up at Zoe. "Does Barent do all this every time he makes a new deployment?"

"I haven't seen him pick up the "Mercenary" for years. He has most of it memorized. Remember also that these are simple theoretical problems. In real life, nothing ever goes that smoothly. Barent figures in weather, road surface, morale of troops, attitude of the local populace and several other things that could go wrong but no one else even considered. He has a plan figured out ahead of time to solve every problem he can predict.

"You know, he has this great reputation for improvising in the field, but I don't think it's accurate. A lot of his creativity comes from following an alternate plan he already thought up.

"It comes to him naturally. In case you hadn't heard, the old king was a perfect demon for protocol, tactics, and memorizing large quantities of useless information. Barent has put to good use the techniques he learned." She gave Varli's head a playful push. "So get back to it. Finish that battle plan before the light fails and be glad it's only me cramming things into your receptive little mind."

If Varli was good at planning, his execution suffered by comparison. Sending him out to forage was useless. He would return with a few berries in the bottom of his basket and colourful stains around his mouth, offering 'her share' with a proud grin.

Finally, she blew up at him.

"Varli, this is not just an extended picnic we are on. How can I get it through your head that we are going to be very hungry this winter if we don't store enough food?"

He was contrite. Sort of. "But I thought we were doing fine! We got all that hay put up yesterday, and we've got lots of dried meat now. You said yourself it's still months till the first snowfall."

She gave up on that tactic. "Here. You're a wonderful provisioner. Plan five months supply of food for two smaller-type people, let's say two-thirds soldiers rations, garrison

108

assignment, with capability to forage twenty-five percent of supplies."

"This sounds familiar."

"That's right; it's us. Figure it out. Then we'll look at what we have. Using that, we can compare how much we are collecting on the average day and see whether, at this rate, we will end up with enough to last. Use the fractions I taught you last week."

When he was finished, Varli was not impressed. "Can we continue gathering right up to the first snow? Also, surely we can find more than a quarter of our needs in the winter."

"Why should we?"

He grimaced. "Because continuing at this rate right up to winter, we will have exactly half enough food to last. Unless," he looked hopeful, "I made a mistake somewhere?"

She laughed. "I don't think I've ever heard you anxious to admit to an error before, and I'm sorry to disappoint you, but I agree with your assessment. Especially when you realize that most of the gatherables are gone before the first snowfall. We aren't the only ones storing up, you know. All the other squirrels are way ahead of us. We started late, and we're not working hard enough."

"You mean I'm not working hard enough."

"I didn't say that."

"You didn't need to."

"So..."

"So let's go berry-picking. I found a huge patch of the ones we use to grind up with the dried meat."

"I know."

"How...? Oh, you saw the basket."

"No, they're all over your face."

After that, their progress began to improve, and soon they were far enough ahead that Zoe decreed a visit to the village. Varli was not as pleased as he might have been when he discovered they were walking.

"But that will take almost half the day! We could ride there in far less time, even if we had to go round-about so as not to leave tracks."

"It's not that. We don't want to attract more attention than necessary. No horses, no good clothes, not much money. This is an information-gathering trip only, to see what they have, what they need. No sense taking a load of stuff only to find out they either have lots or can't afford any. Waste of energy. I think I'll just take a few packets of herbs. Give them as presents, smooth our way."

She made a careful selection from her stores and they set out. It was a pleasant walk. The early autumn frosts had wilted the undergrowth, and movement through the forest was getting easier. When they reached the river they removed their footgear and waded across, then swung down the trail to the wagon road. By the time they neared the village, their clothes were dry again.

17. OLD FRIENDS

Instead of heading straight for the centre of town, Zoe swung up the hill to the right and took a path through the trees.

"There's someone I'd like to visit. She was good to me when I was small. I hope she's still here. She was awfully old, and people live a rough life here. I hope..." Coming to a large clearing, she stopped in confusion. The cottage was the same as she remembered, but there was a general air of neatness and prosperity that seemed different.

"This doesn't quite look the same. She was a widow, and she was finding it hard to get by alone."

"Maybe she got married again."

"Perhaps. Not likely, at her age. Maybe she died, and someone else lives here."

The cottage door opened and a woman stepped out, nodding politely. Then a frown creased her brow, and she stepped forward. "Zoe?"

"Erla!"

The woman Zoe threw her arms around was not exactly the aging crone she had expected. In fact, Erla was a sturdy matron of middle age.

"Erla, you look so good! I always thought you were so...well...old!"

"Ah, I might o' known it. First thing she does, she insults me."

"Oh, Erla, I'm sorry. You know how kids are about the age of adults. I thought you must be at least as old as my grandfather. It's good to see you again. You've done so well!"

"Yes, it was hard goin', back then. I guess I was lookin' tired a lot. But I just dug in, and it went. Oh, it went all right. Then I got a cow and I started sellin' the milk. That brings in a bita coin." She glanced at Varli. "And who's your little friend here?"

"Erla, this is Varli, who is travelling with me. Varli, I'm so pleased you can meet Erla, who was kind to me when I needed it."

This time Varli was quick to present his hand in the proper manner, but it was no use. After the clasp, instead of releasing his hand she turned it over and glanced at the calluses.

"Sword, is it? And you so young, and too pretty to be a bandit. Maybe it's a curtsey I should be makin'?"

Varli reddened. "No, no, please, I'm...I'm just a friend of Zoe's. I'm...um very...anyone who was good to her, I am glad to know."

She laughed and slapped his hand lightly as she dropped it. "Whatever ye be, you'll go farther yet, lad. Trust me. So what are you doin', Zoe, back after all these years?"

"A bit of a holiday, a bit of a training session, a bit of a sabbatical."

"So I suppose you're staying at the cottage between the rocks?"

Zoe stared at her. "How did you know about the rocks?"

"It did take a bit of findin' all right. In fact, the way I got there finally was by goin' every place it looked like I wasn't supposed to."

Varli loved this. "Double-blind again. How can you fight that, Zoe?"

"Remember what I said. Our methods only protect us from most of the population. Fortunately, only our friends know us well enough to try that trick. So you found the cottage. But it didn't look as if anyone had been there."

"Oh, I didn't go inside. I only looked for it out of curiosity, and for the challenge of finding it. It was years after you'd left when I found leisure to go that far. I wouldn't touch any of your things. Besides," she grinned sheepishly, "I couldn't get the door latch open."

"Erla, that latch was only made to keep out honest people. I'm impressed. Nobody else found the cottage. Say," she dug in her pack, "I brought something for you."

"Not in the yard, please. What are we, naked barbarians from the south? Come in the house for tea. Have ye had lunch? Of course not. You go in and stoke up the fire and I'll bring us a bit o' the oldest cheese from the spring house."

Erla bustled about, bringing them into the cottage and settling them down. It was no manor house, but it was scrupulously clean and sparkled with polished wood and stone. The cooking, eating and workspace took up the lower floor, a hand loom leaning to one side. In the middle of the back wall a ladder led to a sleeping space in the loft. A new door in the west wall showed the lean-to extension built for the cow. The pervading presence of farm odour confirmed this, although with the door and shutters open, it was not obtrusive.

As they ate fresh bread and cheese and drank of the special blend that Zoe had brought, they caught up on each other's gossip.

But when lunch was over, she decided not to stay. "We're keeping you from your work, and I want to check on business prospects in the rest of the village before we go home, so..."

They rose and went outside. Erla embraced Zoe heartily. "So glad to see ye back, and lookin' so well." She clasped Varli's hand. "You're a lucky young man, friend of Zoe's. She was a smart one when I knew her long since, and out here with her, you'll be learnin' more about what real life's like than back at any castle."

"Why Erla, what do you know about castle life?" Zoe had never inquired into Erla's past.

113

"Nothin' but what I've heard and what I've surmised, but I can tell you, I've not been impressed. All that schemin' an' plottin' don't sound like a healthy way to live. Out here in the valley you know where you stand with everyone, and it's the weather and the earth you must worry about."

"Right, and that's what we are worrying about now. We started late, getting our winter supplies in, and I hope we can find a way to earn some extra here – bring in game or furs or something."

"I suppose it'll be hard, providin' for the horses, too." Erla gave a knowing smile as Varli's jaw dropped open. She nodded towards their stirrup-polished riding boots. "Now would ye like to borrow a big scythe? My hay's all up long since, so I won't be wantin' it for months."

"Oh, thank you, Erla. That would help a lot. We'll pick it up on our way out."

"I'm so glad you're back, Zoe. Will you be visiting again soon?"

She looked around the tidy farm, mostly harvested. "I imagine, at this time of year, we will be even busier than you are. Why don't you come out and see us? Seems a shame to miss the inside of the cottage, when you went to all that bother to find it."

Erla positively glowed at this. "Of course. I'll come next time I've a day free."

"That will be great." Zoe realized that she was finding it difficult to leave, so she took direct action. "We'll be going now, or we'll stand all day talking, and nothing done. We'll stop back in a while for the scythe."

Varli made his polite goodbyes, and they continued on their way into the village.

Later, as they strode home after a successful visit, Varli broached a subject with hesitation.

"I don't understand, Zoe. I didn't realize you had such good friends. I thought from the stories that you were some sort of wild child, living on your own out here, and Barent rescued you. Why didn't you just go and stay with Erla? She seems to be really nice."

Zoe mulled it over for a few strides. "I hadn't thought about it until today, simple as it may seem in retrospect. I suppose if Barent hadn't come, I would have ended up with her.

"At the time though, going to them never even occurred to me. I guess I was so caught up in my grandfather's attitudes I thought his was the only way to live. And those were pretty lean times for Erla, trying to make a go of it by herself after her husband died. I always thought she was terribly poor. She didn't eat as well as we did. Grandfather used to take some treat or other when we went to visit, which, as I said before, was only a few times a year.

"There wasn't much in the village that we needed. In fact I wonder why Grandfather went at all, except for conversation. After all, even a smart nine-year-old is a poor substitute for stimulating intellectual debate. Erla's pretty sharp, you know."

He grinned. "She had me labelled from the moment she set eyes on me. Do you think the rest of the people we met in the village figured out that much?"

"Maybe some of them. Being illiterate isn't the same as being stupid. People are pretty much the same, all over. These folks have equal abilities to everyone you know back home, just turned to different uses. They read the world around them: the weather, the woods, the tracks on the ground, the same as you would pick up the allusions of a poem or the nuances of a diplomatic missive."

"I suppose so."

"And I'll tell you something else. Grandfather once told me that Erla was one of the most honorable people he knew."

"In spite of not knowing the Codes?"

"That's right. He said she lived by a code of her own."

"I suppose that's possible, if you thought it out clearly and stuck to it."

"There. You learned something today. That makes it a successful trip all round. Now let's finish it off by having you find our route home. Make it a new one, but not too long. We don't want to be stumbling around in the dark."

18. Decision on The Sleeper

The next day they used the scythe and cut a larger quantity of hay than they had managed in three days without it. When supper was over, Zoe got out a length of thin, strong rope she had brought with her from the castle. Varli watched her as she went over it from one end to the other, examining it with hand and eye.

"Is there something wrong with that?"

"I hope not. I want it to be in perfect condition. We'll need it in a couple of days."

"What are we doing, swinging from tree to tree, or chasing wild mountain sheep?"

"Good guess, but no trees where we're going."

"A mountain." He jumped up. "We're going to climb a mountain. The Sleeper? Do you think the wind will be right to hear him snore?"

"Yes, we'll try the Sleeper, but there's no predicting the wind. We'll have to wait and see about that. Erla told me she could use the top of a certain small plant, the Shepherd's Hat, that only grows at high altitudes. She makes dye with it for the wool she spins. The area above the village has been over-picked recently, and I could sell a lot of it to the other cottagers. So, when we're ready, we go out harvesting. There used to be a big bed of Hat on the Sleeper, so we'll go there first."

"Let's go!"

"It's already too late in the day. We'll be starting at sunup."

"Sunup!"

"For another, you need training. Come over here." Throwing the coil over her shoulder, she strolled around the boulder on the north side of the cottage. "Let's see you climb up there."

He looked dubiously at the rock. "It's pretty smooth."

117

"There are ample handholds. I will always remember the first time I made it to the top. I was about six, and I'd been trying on the lower half for years. One day it seemed to come together, and I got all the way up. We were both so proud! It was the first time I had ever done anything my grandfather couldn't. He was too stiff to make some of the stretches. He would walk up the other side and throw the rope down to me."

"So are you going to throw it down to me?"

"Varli, I was only six years old and half your size. You don't need a rope for this height of rock. But we will practice with it later. You have climbed before?"

"Of course. Remember that day we went up behind the castle with Gerth? That was fun."

"Oh, yes, the day you kicked all those rocks down on our heads. I was hoping you would remember that and not repeat it." He looked suitably chastened, and she continued. "That was just rock scrambling, not real climbing, but it gives you some idea. Now take another look at the rock and up you go."

Varli stepped up to the boulder, and finding positions for both hands, started to climb. He reached about his own height above the ground and stopped.

"What's the problem?"

"I don't see any more places to grab."

"You're right. There are no more holds there. Come back down."

"Come down?"

"Unless you plan to stay there all night. Just use the same holds you went up on."

He tried to look below his feet. "I can't see any."

"Probably not. Your stomach is in the way. Don't cling to the rock like a baby to its mother. Push away."

"I can't lean any farther. I'll fall!"

"Don't lean. Keep your weight centred, just like in swordplay."

"I don't have a spare hand for my sword right now," he gritted out, "and I can't hold onto this rock much longer."

"Then come back down."

He gave her a disgusted look over his shoulder. "I'm trying."

"Here, look at this." Choosing a route near him, she quickly reached his height, balanced on finger and toe-tips, body held well away from the rock.

"Isn't that what I'm doing?"

"Not quite. You look like this," she imitated his stance, hips pushed in and shoulders leaning back, "like you're about to fall over backwards."

"Oh." He corrected somewhat. "Like this?...hey! I can see it. I remember now!" He clambered down. Soon they were both at ground level. He grinned proudly. "That was better."

"You somewhat resemble an arthritic spider, but yes, that was better. Now try again, but this time, check your route farther up the wall before you start. The one you chose dead-ended."

"I noticed."

"Also, make a conscious effort to remember where the holds are. You could have found that last one without seeing it."

"Right. So where should I try now?"

"Anywhere you like."

"You are too generous." His sarcasm turned to a frown of concentration, and he stood back, gazing upward. "I think perhaps..." He walked to the wall and started up again.

He tried several more routes, but did not make much progress. The sun had set, the light was getting dim and his arms were shaking. When she called a halt, he had reached a point just above her head. He let go and jumped down beside her, landing in a cloud of dust.

"Another lesson you had better learn is that most accidents happen late in the day when you are tired. People do silly things like taking a jump when it's too dim to see the landing and they break an ankle."

Varli was rubbing his roughened hands together, undismayed. "But I did pretty well, didn't I? I got a long way up."

"Yes, you did. When you can get all the way up, we go to the Sleeper."

* * *

What with the foraging and a bit of rainy weather, it was eight days before Varli finally made it to the top of the boulder unaided, and even at that it was a bit of a scramble. He had made it up several different ways, but each time he had needed support from the rope at a critical moment. Zoe was patient, because the rope practice was essential as well. She had also given him practice in belaying while she climbed.

Finally he made it. He was trying a different route and, fingers shaking from fatigue, he made the final pitch to where she was lying, chin on hands, waiting for him.

"I did it!"

"You did."

"I suppose you could have done better."

"Faster, perhaps, but that's the only route I ever found. Once you discover you have to go over and down in the middle section, it's quite obvious."

He grinned. "Sort of like life." He dusted his hands together. "When do we try the Sleeper? Tomorrow?"

"We might. Depends on the weather."

He lost his humor in an instant. "Do you think it's going to rain? Can't we go if it does?"

"You tried to climb wet rock yesterday."

"Aye."

"The weather's unsettled." She started down. "We'll get up early and see."

He stood, looking up at the mountain towering over them in the gloom. "Get up early? I guess I can handle that."

"Not often I hear that sentiment from you." She tossed the comment into the dimness above her as she descended. "Now come down before it gets so dark you have to stay there all night."

* * *

Compared to the rock face, the Sleeper was an easy climb. After all, she had done it when she was six years old, although she had to admit her strength-to-weight ratio was formidable at that age. Still, she felt worried as she climbed, watching Varli's progress carefully. It just wouldn't do to bring him out here and let him fall off a mountain. Not good diplomacy. Varli, ebullient as usual, scoffed at her concern and climbed blithely.

There was a small area on one shoulder of the peak, just before the final stretch to the top, where the rock formed a shallow dish. It was around on the north side and this orientation, combined with its form, created a damp pocket. Shepherd's Hat thrived in this environment. They deposited their packs and Zoe gave a short lesson in harvesting.

"We want an equal number of leaves and seed pods. Don't take more than a third of either from any plant. They regenerate slowly. Don't even step on any." This last was hardly necessary, as the plants grew about a pace apart, but Varli was too polite to complain. "On the other hand, don't miss any. Just from looking around, I'd say the crop is not plentiful this year. Probably why the villagers are short."

They picked side by side, sweeping across the small meadow. Soon they reached the limit of spread of the plants and started back. In a very short time they were finished. They tried a broader sweep but found little more. Zoe looked at their harvest.

"I suppose the only consolation is that, with the stuff so scarce, the price will be higher."

"Couldn't we pick more?"

"We had better not. One over-picking combined with a bad winter and we could wipe out the whole patch. There used to be more on the very top, but that's a harder climb."

"You mean we aren't going to the top?"

"Varli, stop whining. No, we are not going to the top. I still don't like the look of the weather, and it's too hard."

Varli looked at her, his head to one side. "Zoe, is something wrong? You're getting all moody on me. My sister does that." Zoe didn't know his sister, but this sounded like the ultimate insult.

"I'm sorry, Varli, it's just that I'm disappointed in how small the crop is."

"I don't know anything about dyes. Can you explain how much difference it will make?"

"Well, take a look at this." She held two handfuls of the herb. "That amount is enough to dye your shirt a medium red. In the village, we could trade that for enough mutton to take the place of all the rabbits we could trap in a week, maybe more. And rabbit meat is too lean in the winter. It's not sustaining enough."

"You mean, if we pick that much more Shepherd's Hat, we can rest for a full week? Let's find more!"

She laughed. His enthusiasm was catching. "Well, since we found the climb easier than I thought, we should get down quicker than I thought, so I guess we had better hit the top."

"That's better. If you're going to be in a mood, it might as well be a good one." He started off towards the final peak.

At the base they roped together again, and she led off. Again the climb went well, and soon they were at the last pitch. Zoe stopped to belay on a narrow ledge and soon Varli was beside her.

"That's the last bit, just there," she pointed. "It's not too hard, but it's a long way down if you fall." They looked between their toes, then both hastily looked up again. Varli swallowed.

"Can I lead for this bit?"

"Not by any means!"

"Zoe, you're being an old woman again. You said yourself this wasn't that hard. It looks easier than the parts I led on below. Is there something about the rock that makes it dangerous?"

Zoe couldn't figure it out. There was no real reason to refuse him. Maybe it was the weather, or maybe her past association with the mountain, but she felt out of control in a strange way. Still, how could she answer him?

"No, not really. You must be as careful of loose bits as anywhere else on the mountain, but nothing unusual. I suppose you have to try it, don't you?"

He gave a tight grin and nodded. They moved back to a wider part of the ledge to change places and he started out. She could see that he was moving well. He had progressed so much from the limpet he had been a few days before. He was working slowly but making careful progress.

As he moved away, she became more anxious. In a moment, as he rounded a small bulge of rock, he would be out of her sight. What if he got into trouble? How could she help without going out there as well, leaving no one to belay the rope? As she watched him she slid her right foot forward on the ledge, clutching the rock near her with her right hand, leaning out to see.

He glanced back, grinned briefly, then concentrated on the rock again. He tested a handhold; it broke away, and he tossed it behind him in disgust. It fell out and down, down, down...Varli ignored it and tried again, putting his hand in the hole the rock had come from. It held. As he shifted his left foot and groped ahead for another toehold, it occurred to her that the pocket around a loose rock is often cracked as well. She leaned forward to call a warning. Then she felt the sickening give of the rock under her right foot.

19. QUICK DESCENT

As her foot slid, a million thoughts flashed through her mind. The first was that she had lost her belay, and when she hit the end of the rope, Varli would surely be jerked off the mountain with her. She had no time to cut or untie the rope. Strangely, she also had time for an overriding awareness of how stupid it was for her to be thinking of having time to untie herself, and she should be using the last moment of her life thinking of something more useful. She could think of nothing useful.

As the edge of the ledge gave way, her foot dropped back and out, spinning her until her back was to the rock and most of her weight hung by the fingers of her left hand, twisted as they were into a small crack. The rope, freed of the belay, hung down, useless. Her left foot was still firmly on the ledge, but she had no purchase to lift her weight back over it. At least she hadn't fallen yet.

She tried to pull herself up by exerting sideways pressure on her leg. The higher she pulled with her leg, the more weight came on her fingers, and she felt them start to slip. She scrabbled for a solid spot with her right foot, dangling over nothingness, but the ledge crumbled when she touched it, the small pieces spinning away silently into space.

She froze, then took one slow breath and calmed herself. Her only chance was her other hand. Afraid to turn her head, she watched out of the corner of her eye as her right hand groped across the uneven rock, trying for even a finger-hold. There were several nubs there, but she couldn't risk them. Then the tip of her middle finger found a crack. She lifted again with her left leg, just enough to worm her first knuckles over the edge. She tested. It held. More confident now, she leaned her head out to see. It looked firm. She took more weight on it. She had a perfect, firm grip. Easing the pressure off her aching

125

left hand, she swung around to face the mountain. Both feet again on the ledge, she clutched the wall with both hands until her breathing slowed. Then she remembered the belay. She flipped the rope into a new position and looked over to Varli.

Facing away from her, he was blithely swinging the last step up onto the rim of the cliff. Looping the line over an outcropping, he settled into the stance she had taught him and looked back.

"All clear here. Come ahead." He grinned, confident and proud.

She hesitated. The last thing in the world she wanted to do was go further along that ledge. She was about to call him back when she realized that she would be asking him to cross an area she considered unsafe for herself. She looked again. Little had changed, except the ledge was one rock narrower. Had she really stepped that close to the edge? What a fool! She had allowed her fear to influence her good climbing practice. She considered the rest of the pitch. It wasn't that hard. *I crossed it when I was six years old.* She nerved herself. *I can sit here shaking, or I can go on. Not much of a choice.* Avoiding the broken end of the ledge, she started out.

Hand by hand, foot by foot, she eased across and up. Varli was taking up the slack in the rope perfectly. It really was an easy passage. In a moment, she was beside him. She moved away from the edge.

"That was great. I made it clean, didn't I? Are you ready to go on?"

Going on was not her first priority. Now that she was off the face she could feel the shakes starting. She looked up at him, about to refuse. She opened her mouth, then realized that she must either tell him what had happened or suggest that they start back down. She couldn't face either prospect, so she simply nodded. He started out, and she stumbled to her feet and followed.

The top of the peak was only a few minutes away: an easy scramble. By the time they got there, Zoe was back in control of herself and was able to dredge up a weak response to Varli's enthusiasm.

"We made it! Say, look out there!" He pointed out their cottage, the river ford, the village. Between the two of them they figured out which was Erla's field, and they shared a thrill that here they were, so far removed, yet they could see the thread of smoke rising from the chimney of Erla's cottage.

Then Varli turned his attention closer. "Look! Shepherd's Hat!"

There was only a small area of the herb, again on the north side of the peak, but this time the leaves were packed together, carpeting the rock and the stony soil.

"This is as thick as I've ever seen it grow. We should take a lot from this patch. Look. Don't you think the plants and the seedpods are smaller here than below? This soil isn't deep at all, and I think they are choking each other out. It will do the patch good to be thinned."

Varli's voice took on the deeper tones of the balladeer. "How fortunate!" He set to work, laughing. She followed more slowly, still bemused by her reactions to what was happening. They picked steadily, filling the bags they had brought. Soon, as usual, Varli's enthusiasm waned and he took a break, looking out over the valley again.

"Why can't I see any sheep out in the fields? There were lots when we came over the pass on our way in."

Zoe did not consider her answer seriously. "I guess the shepherds have brought them down for the winter."

"I thought you said they didn't do that until the first snowfall?"

"Can you see them in the pens? They might bring them in for some other reason. Look lower down, in sheltered spots with trees around."

"Oh, yes, I found a flock. Why would they pen them now, in the middle of the afternoon?"

"I don't know, maybe..." Her head jerked up, and she stared at the mountain peaks to the southwest. Or at where they should be. They were disappearing in a mass of dark, roiling clouds. She jumped to her feet. "Picking time is over, my friend. Pack your gear. We have a very short amount of time to get off this mountain or we will spend a very uncomfortable night."

They swung into action like a well-rehearsed team and started down, Zoe leading. "Remember, the most dangerous part is descending."

"I know that part from my first lesson!"

"Good. Don't forget it. There should be time to get to the bottom without rushing. If we must, we can hole up in the rock pile at the foot of the wall. So just keep moving methodically and we'll be fine."

There was no idle chatter, and the rock flowed by under them. Zoe felt good. The uncertainties of the morning were brushed aside by the need for action, and for the first time that day, she felt sharp. She climbed quickly but carefully, finding it no problem at all to keep an eye on her own path and guide Varli on his, although he needed little help. In truth, she could see how much easier this was than she had remembered. She found spots, now that she was looking, where the stretches would have been very difficult for a child. Now, they were comfortable.

As they entered the last crevice, there was a roll of thunder in the distance. The clouds had filled the valley as they climbed and were reaching over them.

"Let's get a move on. It could get dicey in the crevice if the water starts pouring through," and down they went again. As they reached the bottom, the first big drops of rain splattered and disappeared on the sun-heated stone. They moved carefully out over the jumbled rock pile and Zoe kept an eye out for a sheltered spot. Just as the rock was starting to get slippery, she saw one. It was a huge flat plate, supported at an angle by another boulder. Smaller stones had piled around the uphill side of the opening, leaving a snug cave underneath. They dropped their packs inside and scouted for firewood. There were broken pieces of avalanche-killed trees all over, and soon they had a small, cheery blaze going, reflecting heat off the rock wall into their backs and faces. In this weather, it was too much, and they moved back.

"We may not find this soft, but if we need to spend the night here, we'll at least be warm and dry."

Varli looked around. "Spend the night?"

"It's possible, although I doubt it. These fall thunderstorms may be dillies, but they roll through quickly. With any luck, it will get over with and we can still make it down before dark. Now sit back and watch the show." She indicated the view down the valley in front of them.

The rain had stopped, and the air was still warm and heavy. Looking over, they could see the lightning striking the hills on the other side. So far, the storm seemed to be missing them and charging straight up the middle of the valley. They could hear the thunder roaring, but still at a distance, not threatening. Then the storm overwhelmed the scenery, veiling the western range in sheets of rain. The leading edge of the storm was well past them, and they watched it crash up against the mountains at the head of the valley, the clouds massing, confused in the enclosed space, smashing at everything with lightning bolts, the thunder growling in frustration. Then a sweep of water washed over them, obscuring everything.

In the cooler air, they moved closer to the fire, and both sat for a long while, staring into it.

"Varli, what would you do if I was hurt or killed, and you were left alone here?"

"You mean like if you had fallen off the mountain when the ledge crumbled back there? I guess I'd go and stay with Erla until the next Patrol showed up, unless I heard something about the political situation to make me decide to head over the pass to the Inner Duchies. Although if I believe your stories, I'm probably not enough of a climber to do that. But don't worry, you wouldn't have fallen. That's what the rope is for, remember?" He continued to chatter on, seeming oblivious to her astonishment. "When I heard the rock go, I flipped a loop over a projection. For a moment, I didn't know whether it was you or me that was going, so I did what I could. When I turned to look, you were just swinging back onto the ledge, so I went on."

Zoe nodded in agreement, since there didn't seem to be much she could say, and continued to stare into the fire while the rain pattered down through the mist around them. She wondered if she would ever get to the point where the twists of fate ceased to astound her. She thought she knew Varli, yet here was evidence that he learned her lessons far better than she expected, and also that he had a much cooler head in an emergency than she could have hoped for. Before, she had been weighed down by the responsibility of his training, but now she realized that he was capable of making his own way.

She shook her head. *This is always happening. I think I'm doing fine, but I'm missing something that seems obvious when I find out about it. I think my problem is loyalty, but the Sivan says it's something else. What do I need? How can I know?*

She took up her time with thoughts that swirled and eddied like the mist outside until she came to full awareness. The rain had stopped. She got up, went outside and looked around.

"Want to try heading down? We're almost at the bottom of the rocks, so it's not too dangerous. We may slip around a bit and we'll get soaked as soon as we hit the undergrowth, but a warm, dry home waits at the end."

"Sounds like a good idea if we can find our way in this fog."

"No problem there. Just keep going down. When it gets level, start looking for landmarks. I suspect we'll come out below the mist before we hit the bottom. It's really a low cloud, you know."

Kicking their fire apart, they scrambled out into the wet greyness and started home.

20. DISCOVERED

When trouble came, there was more of it than she had expected, but it was stupider than she had hoped, so that evened things out.

The weather had returned to its wonted cold in the weeks after their climb, and when the first snow fell it stayed on the frozen ground. They had been out once or twice and no new snow had fallen to hide their tracks, so the danger of discovery was in the back of her mind. Still, the noise of the hammer she was using to repair the windowsill covered their approach until it was too late. She spun round to see four ragged men approaching across the clearing. She glanced to both sides. Her staff was to her left, leaning against the corner of the cottage; the doorway was an equal distance to her right. Zoe surprised herself. She went for the weapon.

She started to edge back along the wall, but one of them made it to the door first and cut her off. He tried the handle, but it wouldn't open. She got as far as the window, whispered, "Varli! The bow!" then turned to face her visitors.

"So the little girl has a stick, has she?" The leader was a loudmouth and a bully, she could tell already by his stance and his malicious sneer. He was larger than the others and carried a staff of his own. A short sword hung at his belt. The others were less well armed, with staves and various metal-studded leather protectors hung about their arms and bodies.

"What do you say, boys? This looks like a neat hole to sit out the winter. Got our own little slavey girl, too. Who's inside, girlie? Any bigger than you?" He took a pace forward. "Put down the stick, sweetie. Little girls don't have sticks. They have other things that are much more fun. Only boys know what sticks are all about." He laughed uproariously at his own crude joke, then suddenly aimed a vicious swipe at her head with his staff.

She parried, making it look like a startled reaction, his wood skimming over her head. He stopped, looked at her, laughed again. "Oho! She wants to play boys' games! Try this one."

He poked the end of his staff straight at her. She dodged aside as if she had forgotten her own weapon.

"Look at her dance, boys! We'll get our entertainment out of this one before she wears out."

"Just make sure we all get our share of the fun!" The one who spoke had stepped back and was leaning on his staff in a bored fashion. The others followed suit, allowing the leader room to show off. The quickness of the attack and the lack of serious conversation made this a deadly game. The only alternative outcome was death for Varli and worse for her unless she could outwit and outfight them. She had heard nothing from inside and she took this as a good sign. If Varli would only stay far enough back in the shadows that they didn't see the bow, she could even the odds out here.

"What do you want?" It was not hard to put a quaver in her voice. If they all rushed her at once, she was done for.

"If you don't know, girlie, I'm the man can show you. Drop the stick and come on over here." She knew from the way he said it that he didn't want her to drop it at all. A bully for sure.

"No!" She held her staff inexpertly before her.

"Time for fun!" He prowled around her. When he got too close, she swung, forcing him back. He stalked in again, enjoying himself. This time when she attacked, he met her staff with his, stopping it easily. She allowed one of her hands to slip off the wood, then recovered quickly but ineptly.

He reached out towards her, and again she skipped away. He came at her more seriously now, and she put up a clumsy defence, keeping him just out of reach, and at the same time testing his skill. He was none too smooth and had an awkward move of his own, caused by what seemed to be a weakness in

133

his left arm. As he pressed harder, she whaled away more and more desperately, allowing him to get closer and closer. Then, when he was well within reach, she made a frantic, wild swing, complete with frightened scream, and clipped him a solid blow below the left ear. Before he fell, as she was jumping away from him along the wall, she brought the other end of her staff around and slashed him viciously across the throat, hoping the others wouldn't notice the second blow. He hit the ground like a sack of meal and lay perfectly still.

For a frozen moment they all looked at the fallen man. Now was the crucial point. Did they still buy it? She screamed again and cowered against the cottage wall.

The bandit who had spoken before laughed. "Well, well, well. Ol' Jorge finally met his match. Dropped by a brown-skinned slut who barely knows one end of a stick from the other. Let's quit this playing around and get down to the serious fun."

There was no sense of humour, no bullying, in this man. More dangerous, there seemed to be a streak of meanness. There would be no testing or playing here. He moved forward smoothly, intent on his victim. Again, she set herself up awkwardly, but he didn't give her any room for acting. He was a decent fighter, and she had to reveal some of her ability to protect herself.

"Well, well, well," he mused between blows. "So she conned old Jorge. That's a real smart girl. Too bad you won't con me. You did me a favour, though, gettin' him out of the way. I'll remember that, maybe go a little easy on you sometimes."

She stayed on the defensive, waiting for an opening that didn't come. She knew now that she couldn't make this look like an accident, with a single blow. It would take several good ones, and her cover would be blown for sure.

But it was already too late. This man had little pride, and if the fight became too difficult, he had no problem with calling for help. "This is getting boring, boys. Give me a hand here, and we'll finish her off."

Bandits and bullies they might have been, but their lives depended on quick action, and the other two sprang towards her. With a loud cry of "Now, Varli," she attacked the new leader as hard as she could. The bandit from the doorway, stepping past the window with his staff raised, faltered with the feathers of an arrow growing from under his arm. Then he fell, and she concentrated on her present assailant.

She had the advantage of surprise, because the man had no idea she was superior to him. It only took her a few strokes to break his guard and bring another smashing blow spear-wise to the centre of his face. He fell, leaving her to face the last enemy.

He was a younger lad, ill-favoured, standing there with a look of stupid amazement on his face. Then he dropped his staff and took to his heels.

Zoe dropped to the ground, shouting, "Shoot, Varli, shoot! Now!" Nothing happened. She turned. Varli stood in the open doorway, bow half pulled, looking at the running youth. She was at his side in a bound, grabbing the bow, but the bandit had disappeared among the trees that screened the clearing.

She shook the bow in Varli's face. "Why didn't you shoot?"

He stuttered, at a loss for words. "He...he was running away. I couldn't shoot him in the back!"

She threw the bow down in disgust and turned away. Then she calmed herself until she could speak to him.

"Don't you understand? We must get him. He's a bandit, probably a murderer and at least a thief. He might even have friends nearby. You could have made it easy, but now I have to go and find him and bring him back or kill him myself." She picked up her staff, reached inside and grabbed her short cloak from its peg and set off. "Get inside, bar the door, and watch them," she tossed over her shoulder. "If I'm not home by tomorrow morning, find a roundabout way and go to the village." Then she settled into the chase.

It didn't take long. A short distance from the cottage she could tell by the tracks in the snow that her quarry was faltering. As his footprints got closer together, she moved more cautiously. Soon she heard laboured breathing, almost sobbing. Moving forward with all her skill, she stopped, muttering a soft curse to herself.

The young bandit was leaning against a tree gasping for breath, his bony body showing through gaps in his clothing. He was unarmed.

She crept up behind him, then swung her staff under his chin, grasping it again in her other hand, and pulling his head back against the tree. The pressure on his throat cut his gasps short. She eased off.

"Where are your friends?" she hissed in his ear.

"B...b...back there." His hand wavered in the direction of the cottage.

"All of them?"

"Yes."

He sounded so frightened and pathetic that she had to believe him. Now what was she to do? She couldn't kill such a poor specimen in cold blood, and she didn't want to take him back to the cottage again. After a moment's thought, she came to a decision.

She twisted him around until he was facing the tree. "Grab the tree with your arms."

He did so, and she pulled her staff away. She walked around in front of him. "Stick out your foot."

He did so. As she grabbed it, she couldn't help but notice that his feet were unshod, only wrapped in rags.

136

"Now support your weight with your arms and stick out your other foot."

"What are you doing?"

"Nothing painful. I just want to be sure you don't go away. The alternative is to hit you on the head. Give me your other foot."

Grabbing both his feet, she bent his legs until, as he slid down, he seemed to be sitting tailor-fashion, with his legs around the tree. However, they were folded in such a position that the only way to get them straight was to lift his body up, and the tree was too smooth and large for him to get purchase enough for that.

"I won't be long." She turned away. Then she turned back with a snort of disgust, threw her cloak around his shoulders and departed.

Back at the cottage she found everything as she had left it, with Varli inside and the three prone figures in the clearing. When he saw her returning he came out, and they examined their attackers.

The one with the arrow was dead. The leader was also dead; whether from the head blow or the shattered throat, it didn't matter. Her second antagonist wasn't quite finished. A faint pulse beat in his neck as Zoe turned him over, but his face was a smashed ruin, the bridge of his nose driven deep into his forehead. Zoe pulled out her dagger.

"You're not going to…?"

She looked up at Varli. "What else? Look at him. The bone splinters driven into his brain will probably kill him anyway. If he were to survive, chances are his mind wouldn't be right. If it was, he is the one member of the group I would fear the most – a cold, mean killer. Besides, we would only take him into the village, and the soldiers would hang him when they came. So this is the only choice. You don't need to watch."

137

He shook his head dumbly and stood his ground.

"Well, let's at least drag him out of the yard." Together, they hauled the bandit out of sight of the cottage.

"I suppose we should say a prayer or something, but this situation certainly isn't covered in the Codes, and I can't quite bring myself to be charitable. Do you realize what they had in mind for us?"

He nodded.

"Try to concentrate on that. I think being angry might help. I don't know. Last time I tried this, I couldn't do it."

She drew her dagger again and, with a steady, sure cut, opened the bandit's throat. Wiping the blade on the snow, she sheathed it, took Varli's shoulder, and steered him back to the clearing. It had been easier than she thought, but she got them busy right away, so as not to think any more.

"No time to bury the dead ones. I left the last one tied to a tree and we need to take him to the village today. We'll drag the bodies along the hillside and pile rocks on them to keep the scavengers off until we can do a better job when everything thaws."

They did as she suggested, not having the strength of arm or will to recover the arrow. Zoe did keep the leader's sword, as a useful tool not to be wasted. The bandits had been a poor lot, having nothing but the clothes they wore and a few items in pouches, which she left alone. The men's clothing, though over-worn, spoke of a time when they had been better equipped to fight, and Zoe wondered if the remnants of Saxer's foot soldiers had made it this far. They left the one she had just killed until last, trying not to look at the red trail that dragged out behind him in the snow.

When that grim task was finished, they packed together their winter travelling gear along with a piece of rope, and set off to retrieve their prisoner and take him to the village.

21. EXECUTION

They found the young bandit in a dejected slump against his tree. Zoe hauled him up and had Varli untangle his legs. Then she tied his hands behind him and, taking the long end of the rope, started him off.

"Take the lead, Varli. We want a straight path to the village. I'll keep an eye on our friend here."

As they walked, she talked with the miscreant to keep his mind off the route they were taking and to gain as much information as possible. The group had been a part of Saxer's army, recruited in the slums of several large towns with promises of easy loot. When the mounted nobility had returned with Torey, there had been nowhere for the rabble of foot soldiers to go, and they had split up. This bunch, led by Jorge, had tried to make their way by banditry, but had been pushed farther and farther in the wrong direction by the soldiers and bailiffs of Petrella. In the end, they had decided to hole up for the cold weather and try to get out in the spring.

Zoe could hardly feel too sorry for the boy, young as he was. He certainly was no angel, travelling with that rough crowd, and she wondered what deeds had given him enough status to be allowed to stay. Not his fighting skill or courage. More than likely petty thievery and backstabbing. She resolved to keep a close watch for the remainder of the trip. When she was satisfied that, to his knowledge, there were no more of his kind wandering in this part of the kingdom, she left him to his own thoughts as they walked along.

It was only when they got onto the main road and turned towards the village that he showed any spirit at all.

He stopped, turned and faced her. "Where are we going?"

"To the village. Where else?"

"I ain't goin' there!"

"Why not?"

"I ain't goin'."

She poked him ungently with the end of her staff. "You lost your chance to make that choice a while ago. Move."

She wondered at this reluctance as she prodded him along. He seemed to get more and more afraid the closer they got. The reason for this fear worried her. What had the bandits been up to?

She was hardly shocked to be challenged, just outside the town. Three angry-looking farmers barred the road, staves at the ready.

"What do we have here?"

"I don't know if you remember me, but I'm Zoe, a friend of Erla's. This," she jerked her chin at her prisoner, "is one of a party of bandits that attacked us. We'd like the king's soldiers to deal with him."

The spokesman, a tall fellow with a long, hollow face, grabbed the boy roughly. "So this is one of them, is it? I doubt we'll need the soldiers to handle him." He looked at Zoe and Varli. "You're Zoe, hey? Heard you were back. Sorry about Erla." He focused on the prisoner again. "So you got the little one. Where's the rest gone?"

"They won't be going anywhere. They're dead." Zoe took no satisfaction in the pronouncement. In fact, she was reluctant to say anything, although the villagers needed the information.

The farmer looked at Zoe more closely. "Dead, you say? All three of 'em?" He turned to his fellows. "This story the rest'll want to hear. One of us best stay here just in case and the other two can go with these." His head indicated Zoe's party. She didn't like being lumped in with the criminal, but she could understand the farmer's distrust. The bandits had been here.

"What did you mean about Erla?"

"They got her." He gave the boy in front of him a blow between the shoulder blades that almost sent him to the ground. "Cut her down with a sword, they did. And we couldn't get there in time to save her."

Zoe strode along beside her lanky companion in stunned silence. Erla dead, and killed by this same group of criminals. She paid no attention to the fearful moaning of the prisoner in front of her as the meaning sank in.

Erla, dead. The steadfast, hardworking, loving woman, struck down for no reason by evil men. Pain burned in her: anger with no outlet. She took a greater satisfaction in her deed now. It was her only solace. *Some day I must find a way to stop this sort of tragedy.*

She regarded her prisoner, holding back the urge to attack, to beat, to kill. *Dishonourable behavior is no solution. There must be a better way.*

As they entered the main square of the village, word spread quickly and a crowd gathered. It was not a pleasant crowd, and Zoe could understand how they felt. Their little haven had been violated. For a hundred years they had tolerated the visits of the soldiers, not realizing the worth of the king's protection. Now they were vulnerable. It was not an agreeable feeling.

Village justice was merciless, but mercifully swift. The young bandit was standing, his hands still tied with Zoe's rope. Two of the stronger farmers led him over to a tree, threw a noose over a branch, put it around his neck and hauled him off the ground. It all happened so quickly that the victim hardly registered what was going on. When he had stopped kicking they waited a while, then lowered the body down. A thriftier and less squeamish villager untied the ropes and brought Zoe hers. She steeled herself to accept it graciously, then tossed the coil over her shoulder.

Once this last criminal was disposed of, the people relaxed. They gathered around, casting glances at Zoe and Varli, hoping for an explanation. Zoe began to feel exposed and uncomfortable and she could see Varli getting edgy as well. She made a quick round of the group, talking with people she remembered, and then they took their leave.

On the way home, Zoe stopped at the town resting ground and had a private cry over the fresh grave, a nondescript pile of dirt among all the others. That was something she could take care of. Her chisel was still in good shape. If you couldn't keep your loved ones alive, at least you could make sure they were buried well.

Varli knelt beside her, looking down in sombre silence. Then he turned to her. "Being honourable isn't much protection."

She rose, looking down at the grave. "It isn't, and that's why we must protect each other. So that honourable deeds can overcome the evil of the dishonourable."

She wiped her face, squared her shoulders, and set off home.

22. Fatal Slip

It was a poor time then, back at the cottage. The weather settled in, cold and grey. There was no more gathering to do, except checking the snares every few days. In spite of the clouds, no new snow fell to freshen the ground, and soon the pristine white began to take on dirty tinges.

And Zoe worried. Like the villagers, she felt her perfect refuge had been sullied. The large number of tracks in the snow caused by the fight seemed to scream and point to the cottage, yet when she tried to brush them away the crust was too hard from freezing and thawing to cooperate.

Nor did Varli cooperate. He was suffering from the after-effects of the killing as well, and Zoe either hadn't the skill, or wasn't in the mood herself, to help him as Kenna had helped her. So he alternated between obnoxious bragging and sullen silence, either one enough to make her want to throw him out on his own for a quarter-month or so.

It was a hopeless situation, and Zoe wondered how much worse it would get as winter went on. The only time things went well was in their training sessions, where, by unspoken agreement, they worked harder than ever.

But as the days went by Zoe came around enough to realize her responsibilities and started to look for something to raise their morale. She found it in the bag she had brought from the Archives.

She caught Varli in a relatively normal mood, just after a good swordplay session, and slapped a small book in front of him. "I've been pushing war plans at you all fall. War isn't everything. What do you know about running a country in peace-time?"

He held the book up. "Not a lot. I never thought about where kings and dukes get their knowledge, except as pages and squires. I guess I thought it was sort of train-as-you-work."

143

"Sounds like a disastrous way to begin such a crucial task."

"Now that you mention it, I agree. So what's this? The Monarch's Rules of Kingsmanship?"

"It's a record of the important decisions handed down in the king's council in the past hundred years."

"Interesting reading for future kings. Is it any good for the rest of us?"

"I think so. Most of our laws aren't made up by anybody in particular. Each decision is made on its own merit, taking into account the needs of the realm and the rules of the Codes, but also based on similar decisions of earlier times. The more familiar you are with what happened in other courts, the more likely you are to win your argument. Better still, you can plan your actions so you aren't so likely to wind up before the king in the first place."

This idea should appeal to Varli, whose main objective in life so far was to get away with all the trouble he caused. He thumbed through the book, reading passages that caught his eye.

"Hey, look at this!" he chuckled. "These two farmers get in an argument over who owns a valuable ram. The king suggests they chop it in half and each get his share. Do you think they really cut it up?"

Zoe, in her turn, was interested. "You mean that's true? I always thought that was a joke, or something Sarasha the Lame cooked up to prove a point. I don't imagine they cut up a valuable stud animal. More likely the king was telling them that he didn't want to be bothered with their petty quarrel and if they didn't solve it themselves, they were both going to lose. I bet they figured it out pretty quickly after that."

Varli's nose was back in the book, and all that evening he kept breaking out to read her chosen bits, sometimes for her opinion, sometimes for laughter. It did them both good.

The next few days they went about all their tasks with increased speed and purpose so they could work on their new project. Zoe looked through the rest of her small library for more information, and several times they hauled out the Codes to see how they applied in a given case.

One evening Varli threw down the book he was reading. "These laws don't seem to be talking about our realm at all."

"What do you mean?"

"All this about serfs being tied to the land, and owing chickens to the Lord. Nobody does that old stuff."

"So some of our laws are not valid any more."

"Everyone says things are changing, but I thought that was just the way people talk. I'm not so sure, now."

"A leader like Barent couldn't function unless people were willing to change. Something must be different."

"Does that mean that laws should always be changing to meet the needs of the kingdom?"

"My, we are thinking deep thoughts tonight, aren't we?"

"Be serious, Zoe. Isn't it true? We are living by laws that don't work any more. By holding on to them, are we holding ourselves back?"

"Perhaps. Can you think of any examples?"

"Give me an hour or so."

It took him several days. He refused to show her what he was doing, but spent every spare moment with his face hidden by their small stack of books, which looked like ragged-plumed birds because of all the bookmarks he put in. The only sign she had of his progress was the length of the list he was making; she wondered if she had brought enough blank paper along.

Finally, one evening after supper he raised his head and proclaimed, "They aren't going to work."

"Sorry to hear that, Varli. What went wrong?"

"No, no, my work is going fine. Too fine. It's our system of laws that's out of whack. It's not going to work."

"Is everything really that bad?"

"Not yet." He tossed his pen on the table. "But it soon will be."

"Why soon? What's going to change?"

"It's those traders and merchants. Do you agree that they are going to be trading more and more in this area?"

"That's the only policy Barent and Alarid agree on. It's the one they fight about the most, too."

"Exactly. And the reason they're fighting is that they're trying to use a system that won't work."

"Tell me why."

"No, you tell me. You're a trader. You want to do some selling and buying in Petrella. I'm the king. What do you want? What problems do you foresee?"

"Varli, are you using the Sivan's techniques on me?"

He grinned. "You know me, I pick up a few things, here and there."

Again my pupil listens a lot more than it seems.

"I'm a trader. I guess I want to get money straightened out first. And security. Then I want a set of constant rules that I can work by and incidentally try to get around. How am I doing so far?"

"Not bad. Do you think you will find what you need in Petrella?"

She smiled. "With Barent around, security is no problem. The money is more difficult, but we do know the value of our coins relative to those put out by all the other kingdoms in the area."

"Now what about the laws?"

"I can tell by the look on your face that there's a problem. Why? Our laws work pretty well. They're fairly consistent; they're backed by a powerful system. They should work."

Varli slapped the book of council decisions in front of her. "Find one. Find one that applies to a trader."

She frowned. "Not one?"

"Not one that counts. All the decisions are based on the idea that everyone has a place in the society and looks to someone else for responsibility. There are no laws for a free individual. Nope. It's not going to work."

"Aha! But I'm the merchant. I have a lot to offer you. You're the king. You figure something out. Any ideas?"

Varli looked pained. "You've turned it around on me again."

"That's why I'm the teacher, and you're the student. Well?"

"I'm not that far, yet."

Zoe relented. "I think this could take two of us. Let's start with the kind of laws we'd need...."

They burned the candles short that night and for several nights to come.

Then one day, on their monthly trip into the village for sugar and flour, everything changed.

As the shopkeeper was wrapping up their bundle, Zoe asked him if anything new had happened in town. She made the request out of good manners, not expecting much. However, the man tilted his head and looked at her.

"Now, that's somethin' I never thought of. You'd wanta know."

"What's that?"

"There's big news from the outside world. The king's dead."

A shock went through her. "Dead? How did he die?"

The man shrugged. "Went ridin' on the wrong horse, I guess. Big white one, they said. Spoil of battle or somethin'. Slipped on the ice, threw him off, bashed his head in. Now Lord Barent's king."

Zoe was trying to take this all in and seem calm. "How did you find out?"

"Soldiers was here. Like the reg'lar patrol, but they never come in winter. That's what I was talkin' about. They was askin' questions, subtle-like. Maybe it was you they wanted."

"Did anyone tell them?"

He grinned. "They was too subtle, I guess. Nobody made the connection."

Alarid dead, with his head bashed in. The unwelcome thought wormed into her mind. *I wonder where Barent was when it happened.*

She refused to even think about the white horse. *That wasn't my responsibility, and it would be stupid to worry about it. But now Barent is king. And I wasn't there. I should have been there. If I'd been there, maybe Barent wouldn't have... but maybe he didn't. Why would I think that he'd do something like that? How disloyal can I be?*

And I can't even tell Varli. After all, it may be nothing. People fall off horses. Horses slip on the ice. It's a dangerous world we live in.

And politics is the most dangerous part of that world.

23. FUGITIVE

To stop the errant thoughts, Zoe threw herself into their research even harder, but on the fourth night after their return from the village Zoe realized it was hopeless and put a stop to it. "Look, Varli, this is ridiculous." She dropped her book and stretched her aching muscles. "We've been slaving away at this for days and wasting our energy and candles. There's no need to rush it. We have all winter."

"I guess. We didn't exactly overdo our arms practice today, either."

"That we didn't. I think we need to settle down to a schedule so we only work on this a little while every day. Otherwise, we may burn out on it and lose enthusiasm from trying too hard."

"I suppose..." Varli's head came up, and he stared at the door. He glanced at Zoe.

"I heard it too, don't worry." Varli had been quite bothersome in the early stages of their trip, with the noises he kept hearing in the night, but this one was real.

"What was that, a fox?"

"No fox makes a yap like that. Sort of half a whine." She went to the window and looked out. It was too dark for her eyes, used to the lit interior, to see much. There seemed to be an unfamiliar mass near the door, but nothing moved, and she couldn't tell...

Motioning Varli to pick up his sword, she took her own and padded to the door. Cautiously she opened it, allowing the candlelight to fall unrestricted on whatever it was out there.

Varli leaned over her shoulder. "It's a dog!"

"Not quite." The beast stood there, head and tail low. He was the size of a large coursing hound, but his gangly feet and huge, widely spaced eyes showed that he had not reached his full growth yet.

"Why, he's just a puppy!"

The head did not move, the dark eyes looking up at her, but the tip of the tail twitched – once, twice – that was all.

"And a polite one, at that!" She stood aside and made a sweeping motion. "Would you like to come in?"

The animal stumbled into the warm room, then moved as if drawn by a magnet toward the fire. As he entered the full light, Zoe could see that he was in bad shape. His coat was roughened and torn, and he staggered as he moved. The prints he left were too dark to be snow water. He hesitated as he approached the fire and turned the stumble into an ungainly flop to the floor. He lay on his side, his eyes lifted to Zoe apologetically. Then, with a sigh, the huge head came to rest on the planks.

Varli looked on, eyes wide. "That's an armigerent, isn't it?"

Zoe was kneeling by their visitor, gently examining him. "He will be if he survives. He's only about eight months old, and he's been through a lot. His feet are torn to ribbons. He hasn't eaten properly for days, either – look at his stomach."

"Where did he come from?"

"Not too many options." Zoe rose and bustled around, preparing a broth. "There aren't any armigerents any closer than Arlyn Castle on this side of the mountains. And where else did he get his feet cut up like that?"

"You think he came over the pass from the Inner Duchies? I thought it was closed during the winter."

"I don't suppose anyone thought to tell him that before he ran away."

"Ran away?"

"In the first place, he's a tame beast, used to people. Second, there are no wild armigerents. If there were, they would be hunted down at once. Too dangerous. I believe they were bred up from big sheep dogs, so they still have herding instincts.

150

Even so, a wild one could kill a lot of stock. Which is why we need to make a decision about this one. If we revive him, we keep him. No other choice. We can't let him go, and no one else will want him, that's for sure. Most of the villagers won't be happy that he's anywhere in the district. They all own sheep. So what do you think?"

"Keep him. What else?"

"He's going to be a real complication in our lives. He'll eat as much as one of us. Our supplies aren't up to that."

"Will he be able to help us hunt?"

"Later on, when the wild sheep move down lower because of the deep snow, we should be able to get a few if he will hunt with us. He'll also require a lot of training."

"We're living a simple life here. We just decided we couldn't spend all our time on law books. Besides, what else are we going to do? Stand here and let him die or kill him quickly?"

Zoe shuddered. "Since you put it that way, give me a hand, here."

She sat down on the floor and lifted the big head into her lap. Varli handed her the leftover soup from supper, and she allowed a small spoonful of broth to slip between the half-closed fangs. After a moment the throat constricted. She took that as a good sign and poured another spoonful. A definite swallow this time. She grinned up at Varli and continued. When the bowl was empty, she sat there.

"That's all, fellow. Supper's over. When you gain enough strength to lift your head, you can eat again." The left eye opened a slit and the rough, pink tongue touched her hand. There was no other reaction. She slipped out from under the weight of the head. "Get a blanket, Varli, and we'll cover him where he lies."

Varli, glad to be of assistance, rushed out to his room and came back with a spare blanket, which he flipped open. A deep, barely audible rumble came from the chest of the armigerent. Varli jumped back.

"You're moving too quickly. He knows he's in trouble and he doesn't want to fight, but he's warning you. Slow down and treat him gently."

"But he's too weak to raise his head. How could he fight?"

"It's called spirit, Varli. He's barely conscious, weak from hunger, cold and exhaustion, but if he had to he could still take your arm off. It might kill him, but he seems to think he could do it. He just told you, didn't he?"

"Why do you know so much about these things?"

"My grandfather told me stories. In his country there are a lot of them, or used to be. When I was a kid I dreamed of owning one. No puppy dogs for me. I wanted a war beast." She laughed and ran her hand slowly over the domed forehead. "According to the stories they're supposed to be very intelligent. They become attached to one master as sheep dogs do, and are very loyal. I think that's why they don't use them much any more. If a master gets killed in the battle they've been known to run amok. But generally they're easygoing. They're tough as sword-metal. Cold and pain don't bother them, so it takes a lot to anger them. Of course, this fellow's weak and sick. We'll be more careful with him."

"And you say he's just a puppy?"

"Look at his huge feet – all out of proportion, same with his head and ears. He might grow to be twice this large."

"But the ones in the kennels at the castle are no bigger than he is now."

"I never thought they were very good specimens. Nothing like the stories, anyway. Oh, I played with them sometimes, but it wasn't like I expected."

"You played with the armigerents?"

152

"They seemed to like me, but the trainers didn't want me around. Anyway, they didn't have much spirit, so they weren't much fun."

"The armigerents or the trainers?"

"Both, I guess. If that's a sample of your sense of humour, then it's time for bed. We'll just leave him here. I'll check on him a few times in the night, and we'll see how he is in the morning." She looked her patient over. Satisfied that he was warm enough and sleeping normally, she put out the candle and left him lying there in the glow of the dying coals.

Twice she rose and checked him, replenishing the fire. Neither time did he move or in any way acknowledge her presence, though his breathing was regular, so there seemed nothing to worry about. Either he was very near the end of his resources or he felt very comfortable with her, she couldn't tell: maybe a little of both.

With the late night and the disturbed sleep, she was slow to rise the next morning. When she arrived in the main room, Varli was before her.

"He certainly has improved," was his exasperated comment. "He won't let me anywhere near him." To demonstrate, he stepped closer to the fire. The deep rumble sounded again, stronger than last night. "How are we going to do any cooking?"

"I don't think he'll be much trouble." Zoe knelt in front of the armigerent, and laid her hand on his head. "Now don't you be mean to Varli. If you don't let him fix the fire, then I have to do all the cooking. We don't want that, do we?" The intelligent brown eyes looked deeply into hers, and the rough tongue touched her wrist. "There, I told you. Go ahead, get the fire going and I'll start breakfast. Regular fare for us, more broth for our guest here."

Varli began his morning chores, keeping an eye on the beast, which seemed to accept his presence now. "How did you do that?"

"I didn't do anything. He did it. He's decided that I'm in charge and he has to answer to me. If I accept you, so does he. He wasn't sure when you came out this morning alone because he probably has very muddled memories of last night. Now we have everything straight. Here, you feed him."

"Will he let me?"

"If he's hungry enough, he will."

Varli gingerly inserted his leg under the animal's head and began spooning the broth. The job went faster this morning, and when the bowl was empty, it was obvious that more was required. "Will you get some more, please, Zoe? I don't want to disturb him."

Zoe refilled the bowl. "He's probably much stronger than you think. He's just seeing what he can get away with. He likes being pampered."

"Really?"

"Find out. Put the bowl down by his paw."

Varli did so, slipping out of his position at the same time. The armigerent lifted his head and stared at Varli reproachfully. They waited. He waited. Finally, with an exasperated sigh, the animal heaved his head and shoulders erect, his forepaws spread wide. Varli shoved the bowl under the shaggy muzzle.

"See what I mean? Just playing games. He's very intelligent. He has figured me for the pack leader and now he's trying to place you. You must be firm with him for a while or he will decide you are lower than him in the pack hierarchy. If that happens you won't be able to work with him at all."

"Be firm with an animal that can rip my arm off. Sure. No trouble at all."

"Oh, come on, Varli, you've handled horses all your life. This fellow is just a bit more intelligent, that's all."

"I suppose."

By this time they had all finished eating. Zoe passed Varli the bowl to be cleaned and went into her bedroom, returning with a brush. "Let's see what we can read on our friend's hide and clean him up at the same time."

The armigerent had lowered his head to the floor again, too weak to keep it up for long, and he lay quiescent as Zoe examined him, brushing his pelt of wiry hair as she did so. "His teeth are in very good shape. He's been fed well, except for recently. No large scars at all on his head or ears."

"No fighting, then?"

"Definitely well reared. He probably has a pedigree as long as yours. From the hair on his neck, I'd say he's worn a wide collar all his life, but the bruises make it look like he broke it through main force. Nothing serious, though. Oh, what have we here?"

She parted the hair over the left shoulder, revealing a long, purple bruise. Moving further down his back, she found several others. She looked up, scowling. "He's been beaten – with a heavy stick. I hope nothing's broken. Watch his mouth. If he starts to snarl, tell me immediately." She probed carefully but more firmly along the weals, feeling the muscles quiver as she touched the sore places, but her patient did not move. There was only one place, lower on his rib cage, where he was very tender. There the flesh was torn as well as bruised.

"He must have had a fall coming over the mountains. Might be a cracked rib, but nothing serious. The beating did no permanent injury, I hope." She checked his pelvis and legs, but all seemed sound. She ruffled his ears as she stood up. "Nothing wrong with you that a few weeks' rest and good meals won't cure. You'll be pussy-footing around a while, if you'll pardon a mention of cats, but it won't be long until you're raring to go.

155

That'll be just fine. Gives us enough time to get you trained, so once you're healthy we can keep you under control." She bent and looked directly into the animal's eyes. "And that's what you're going to be for the next few months. Under control!"

The huge head held for a moment, then the eyes dropped, and the tail thumped the floor a few times.

"He understands every word you said!"

"Not the words. It's a combination of the body movements and the tone of voice. I just re-asserted my position as leader, and he agreed. Now, the invalid needs his rest and we need to do our chores so we can get down to our little project. He's going to take up more of our time, so we better be moving!"

24. A New Set of Rules

And so the winter passed. They talked and read and wrote and trained. And they hunted. It was here that the armigerent earned his name, which Zoe got from ancient Kyabran mythology: Patu the Hunter.

True to Zoe's prediction, the growing beast was a serious drain on their resources, especially since he ate a limited diet. Their meat supply dwindled, and it wasn't long before they decided to try hunting. The snow wasn't deep enough in the mountains nor the cold harsh enough to drive the wild sheep down, so they had to climb to quite an altitude before they found any quarry. Fortunately, it all turned out simpler than they had any right to expect.

It became believable that Patu had made it over the pass. His over-sized feet glued to the rock, and in spite of his awkward appearance his balance was impeccable. He flowed over the mountain like a cat, and his greyish-brown hide blended in with his surroundings. Hunting was a matter of the two humans finding hiding spots with a good field of fire and sending the armigerent to herd the chosen game to them.

The first expedition they couldn't believe it was that easy. They killed three sheep to ensure they had a decent supply, then had a terrible time getting the meat off the mountain. She and Varli could, with difficulty, each carry a dressed animal, and Zoe refused to leave the third behind to waste.

Fortunately, she had rigged Patu with a harness, thinking she might need to help him up the harder climbs with a rope. She mentioned this to Varli as she tied the last carcass across the armigerent's shoulders.

"I'm glad I didn't tell him that was what it was for. He might have been so insulted he would refuse to put it on."

"If he was smart enough to understand that, he's smart enough to realize that it's his supper he's packing."

Patu had no problem with his new role, and Zoe wondered if he had been trained to it. Instead of roaming around as he had done all day, he now settled into line and the three of them started downhill, each staggering under the weight.

What with the icy rock and the frequent rest stops, it was dusk before they got below the timber line, and they only made it home by following Patu through the deepening winter night.

"Thanks again to our war beast turned coursing hound, turned pack horse, turned Guide." They were finishing a fashionably late supper of fresh roast mutton. "It would have been a cold night if we hadn't made it home."

"In any case, it wouldn't have been a hungry one. What are we going to do to keep all this meat?" Varli tossed another bone to Patu, who, sated already, nibbled at it, more out of good manners than hunger.

"We need to make a cache nearby. If the meat is outside it will freeze and stay that way as long as the weather continues this cold. We can keep a few days' supply in the cold room."

"That was sure easy – the hunting part, I mean – do you think he can do it again?"

"I'm beginning to think so. Next time we'll be much more careful and only shoot one good animal. That old ram you knocked over – well, let's just say it's a good thing Patu will eat him, because I don't think my teeth are up to the job."

"It will be a much easier trip home afterwards."

And so the pattern was set. They hunted often and took only as much meat as they needed for a short period, spreading their forays over a wide area so as not to deplete supplies near home. As a result they climbed, hiked, waded through snowdrifts and generally had a marvellous time. In the process Varli and Zoe became tough and wind-burned, and Patu's heavy pelt grew even thicker. He was also growing rapidly and putting on muscle. Now, when he reared up and put his paws on Zoe's shoulders his head towered above her, and it was only because of her new strength that she could hold him up at all.

One day, as they stood in the clearing, she swung up and sat on his back sideways. He stood firm as a rock.

Varli's eyes opened wide. "Can I try? Do you think he would let me? I'm lighter than you."

She slipped off, and he tried it. Patu stood still, then looked around at Varli and deliberately dropped one shoulder, dumping the boy to the frozen ground. Then, as Varli got up, the armigerent nudged him with his nose and he fell again.

"Don't let him get away with that, Varli," Zoe got out between gasps of laughter. "Have at him!"

Varli, rising from the ground, launched himself, tackling Patu around the neck, hitting him squarely in the shoulder with all his weight. The surprised armigerent stumbled sideways a few steps, then regained his balance and twisted away.

Both regained their feet, and Patu attacked this time, rearing up and putting his paws on Varli's chest, trying to knock him over. The boy squirmed aside, and they broke apart, spinning again to face each other.

Zoe had recovered from her laughing fit and was watching with interest. "We haven't tried to handle Patu barehanded."

Varli backed away, signalling Patu to stop. "Not too likely. What chance would we have?"

"Let me try."

She stepped forward, inviting Patu to attack. For a while they circled warily, feinting. Then he rushed, and she ducked to the left. He rushed, and she ducked again in the same direction. The third time he was ready for her, and as she moved, he angled to her left. This was what she had hoped for, and she shifted the other way, catching him with her weight against his shoulder sideways as Varli had. However, instead of grabbing around his neck, she reached under and fastened both hands around his far foreleg, pulling towards her and levering up at the same time. It happened so quickly that the armigerent was still driving in the same direction as her push, so he helped to throw himself on his side on the ground. Zoe pinned him, her legs locked around his neck, his forelegs crossed in her hands. All he could do was scrabble at the air with his hind legs. When he gave up on that, she let him up, and patted him, rubbing his ears in the gesture he loved.

"Not too bad, fellow. Want to try again?"

This time she stood her ground as he charged, and he reared up to knock her over. He tried this from several different angles, and each time she was able to duck away. Finally she got the timing right, and as he rose up she twisted, reaching in with one foot, sweeping both hind feet from under him. Again he went to his side with a thud, but as he rose she jumped behind him and got a firm grip near the base of that long, expressive tail he was so proud of. After a few fruitless attempts to reach her with his jaws, he stood still, looking reproachfully over his shoulder at her.

Just as she started to relax, he lunged forward, almost jerking her off her feet. Losing her purchase on the frozen snow, she could not hold him back, and he took off at full speed around the clearing. For the first few steps she kept up, but then she tripped and he dragged her, still hanging on, the rest of the way around. When he got back to Varli, who was taking his turn to be incapacitated with laughter, he stopped and Zoe let go. He then came back and lay down beside her in the snow. She reached over with both hands and grabbed him by the hair on either side of the jaw, shaking him with mock ferocity.

"If you develop a sense of humour like Varli's, this will be a very long winter!"

They both laughed at her.

* * *

When the cold snaps and blizzards kept them inside they concentrated on their legal system. They were working backwards from the book of council decisions, selecting the verdicts that seemed to be based on rational principles and trying to decide what those principles were. Considering the intricacies and inconsistencies of the decisions, it wasn't easy, and they often wondered whether they were doing more inventing than discovering.

"Well, I guess that's not so bad an idea." She paused in the middle of one long session. "After all, we are going into a new situation. There's no point in getting distracted by what happened years ago. We know that a set of basic principles is necessary, but who is to say that the principles they had then are the same as we want now?"

"You mean principles can change, just like that?"

"Not 'just like that', but over years and centuries, yes. Take for example the one principle the Codes hold firmly, that everyone in society is born to be responsible to someone.

"Now we have all these merchants and shopkeepers, and these people are getting powerful. We must develop new basic rules, and they had better be based on ideas that merchants also believe in, or we will have real problems making them work."

Varli smiled. "Now there's a new concept – creating a law and taking into consideration the people affected, so they will agree to abide by it. I doubt if any king would like that."

"It doesn't sound like an idea that any king would agree with, but it's one of the principles we have to make our laws by. What would your father say if he heard you talking like this?"

"Probably throw me in the cellar for a few months to straighten my thinking out."

"You realize that we can't go home and start preaching this on the streets."

"The thought never entered my mind. I've been around the Sivan long enough to figure out better ways."

"There must be better ways, but what are they? I think we're going at this with a handicap, like a man who has never fought with anything but a sword; that's how he thinks."

"I get what you mean. A bow is even worse. It's a weapon of offence only, no defence at all. That's why bowmen get laughed at. They do a lot of running away."

"You know, I used to think that carrying no weapon at all, as my grandfather taught me, was the only way. But I have since realized how restricting that is to one's thoughts. You notice now that I always carry my dagger with me, and whenever I ride I sling a sword on the saddle. Yes, it's definitely a time of compromise."

"But can we get anyone else to believe in our compromises?"

"I don't know, Varli, but if we can break out of our old ways of thinking, we can try. Say, speaking of compromises, you remember what I always told you about my grandfather's teaching?"

"All that weaponless technique? How could I forget?"

"As I think about it, he wasn't that rigid about weapons. For one, he kept the cottage well stocked. For another, he did train me on sword and staff."

"So he wasn't against weapons at all, just against relying too heavily on the standard ones."

"I think you put your finger on it. I want to show you something." She went into her room, and brought back a small, plain wooden case with a tight-fitting lid. "I was checking out my clothes the other day and I decided they were wearing out too fast. So I looked in this box to see if my grandfather had left anything I could wear. Look what I found."

She pulled out a short robe made of a strange, mottled material that shone and wavered in the candlelight. A few simple designs ran down one sleeve, and that was all.

"It looks like silk. What is it?"

"I don't remember exactly. My grandfather used to wear it for special occasions. I think it may be an insignia of rank."

"Put it on."

"Do you think I should?"

"Look at it this way. If it's any sort of insignia, and it was his, who has inherited that rank?"

"Me, I guess."

"Right. Besides, who is here to know, that would mind?"

"I follow your idea if not your syntax. I'll try it."

But they had forgotten the other member of the group. When Zoe put the robe on and belted it with its thick sash, Patu went wild. He set up a howling that threatened to blow the walls out, and tore around the small room, sending things helter-skelter. Then he bounded up to Zoe and knocked her over, his tail wagging furiously as he smothered her with his wet tongue, intermittently sniffing deeply at the robe.

Varli stood, his mouth wide with alarm. "What's wrong with him?"

Zoe struggled upright and managed to get the animal to settle down. "I think he's happy. There must be some relationship with his past life, and not the one where he was beaten."

"I wasn't sure for a moment there."

"Neither was I. He seems all right now, though."

"Full of surprises, isn't he?"

Zoe mopped her face and rubbed a bruised elbow. "As he gets bigger, I hope those surprises come smaller and fewer."

"Anyway, go on about the robe."

"For one thing, it fits! Do you see? I must be the same size my grandfather was!" She had mixed emotions about that.

"I guess you are. What else? You were talking about weapons."

"I already knew it, but I forgot. I washed this plenty of times, and he showed me as well. There are quite a few places inside it where you can keep various weapons and tools. Look."

She demonstrated how she could put her dagger in one place, a garrote in another, and several small sharp instruments in various places, including the sash, where they couldn't be seen. "Look at me now. I'm a walking arsenal, and you'd never know it."

"Wow, you sure wouldn't! Any other secrets?"

"Not that I've figured out, yet."

"Well, wear it around, and something may show up. It sure looks great on you."

"Why thank you, Sir!"

"You're welcome, my Lady."

She smoothed a sleeve, watching the lay of the cloth in the candlelight. "Still, I don't think I'll wear it much. I'll save it for the next time we have company. Come to think of it, my grandfather used to practice patterns in it, too. Maybe I should try that."

They cleared away the furniture Patu had knocked over, and she started one of the weaponless patterns she knew: The Open Fist. It seemed to go very well, as if the robe enhanced the movements. How, she wasn't sure.

Varli was more impressed than she was. "It looks strange. I know that pattern and I can't see the moves."

"What do you mean?"

"The robe seems to hide what you are doing. I can't be more specific, but your movements look all blurred, and I can't follow them."

A thought struck her. "Here, I'll try another. Watch this." She launched into a new pattern, more complicated than the first. Again, it seemed to be better than ever. When she had finished, she felt exhilarated. "How was that?"

"Fantastic! You just seemed to flow! I haven't seen you practice that one before...or have I? What's it called?"

"No, you haven't seen it. It's one I never could get to feel right somehow, so I always practice it alone. It went this time, didn't it? Know what it's called? The Cloak!"

"It would be. It looks like that robe was designed for it."

"Perhaps not. I suspect the pattern was designed for the robe."

"Maybe. Try another one."

While the storm blew itself out they experimented with the robe. They found that many of the moves of weaponless combat flowed better when wearing it, and, to Varli's dismay, were much harder to counter. He had just reached the point in his lessons where he was starting to give her a fight, and now he couldn't put a hand on her.

Later, when they could work outside again, she found that it required only a slight accommodation in her sword work to produce the same effect. Time and again, Varli found himself aiming at a part of her body that turned out not to be where he thought it was. Once she got used to the swirling material, it felt light and effortless to move in.

One thing that puzzled her was the wear. It was in remarkable shape, considering the age of the garment, but there was one spot on the inside of the left sleeve, just where the loose cuff dropped from her wrist, that was worn and tattered.

One day during a workout it all came together. She had been concentrating on the feel of the robe as she and Varli sparred with their swords and had not been paying much attention to him. As she was getting into the flow of the fight, it seemed that he was, too, and they were working faster than usual. Finally he made a good clean lunge at her. Instead of parrying with her sword, she could feel herself falling into a familiar movement. In a moment of stillness, Varli's point seemed to come at her slowly, and she reached out gently with her left hand, flipping the sleeve of her robe in an arc as she did so. The cloth wrapped itself around the blade and, as she pulled her arm back, the hilt was wrenched from Varli's startled grasp.

"How did you do that?"

She was bemused. "I'm not sure. It's a move out of The Cloak that I hadn't understood before. It just sort of came to me out of nowhere that it would work, so I tried it. It was so easy."

"Next time warn me when you're going to try something like that. I almost died when I saw you reach out with your bare hand towards my blade."

"I didn't plan it. I guess my feet were moving in the pattern and the rest of me just followed. I've been practicing that one a lot lately. Gives me an advantage, wouldn't you say?"

The other advantage was that Patu, having recovered from his ecstasy, obeyed her even faster when she wore the robe. More evidence to mull over concerning the mystery of his past life.

25. Minds Turn Outward

As the winter tapered off, Zoe's thoughts turned often to home, and to speculation of events there. While she had run from the complications of castle politics, she had no intention of avoiding them forever. She had reached the stage where she could consider with equanimity the idea of returning to her everyday work and the tensions involved. She knew that as she stayed away longer her attitude would turn to eagerness. Then it would be time to go back.

So they continued with their rustic life: hunting, training, studying. Now when they left the cottage they formed a compact and trusting unit, each sure of the capabilities of the other two, each fulfilling his or her share of the task unprompted.

In a strange way, Zoe felt much safer than she had ever been before. Oh, she had never felt threatened during her life at the castle, but this was different. Before, she had always been the one dependent upon others for her security. Now, she was an integral part of an efficient unit. Now, they also depended on her as well. It was a powerful feeling, and very satisfying. *I wonder if this is what the Sivan meant. I needed this, whatever it is.*

As the cold weather broke and the snow receded up the mountainsides they ranged farther afield, following the fur packers' trail up into the mountains to the south and exploring Patu's backtrail up to the pass into the Inner Duchies.

The day they were turned back by snowfall and avalanche, Zoe probed Varli's feelings. "Just think; in a straight line, you're not more than a few days' journey from home right now. Doesn't it make you homesick?"

"Homesick isn't the right word. I got over that the first six months I was in Petrella. I would like to go back for a while, though. It's been a couple of years. It would be nice to see how my mother and sisters are getting along. Most of all I want to talk to my father. I think we'd find a lot to say to each other.

"You know, my mother never was too keen on me being fostered out to 'those barbarians.' My father thought it would be good for me to hone my fighting skills. I imagine he'll be surprised to discover my new interest in statesmanship."

"I imagine he'll be other than amused at some of the ideas you come home with. What we're working on is pretty revolutionary, you know. What kind of man is your father? Will he embrace new ideas?"

"When I show him how they will benefit us? He hasn't kept us a power in the Duchies through the strength of our army, you know. He'll pay attention, don't worry."

She wished she could be so sure anyone in Arlyn Castle would listen to her.

Contrary to the popular ideal, spring is one of the dreariest times in the forest. Everything is grey and dead. Small, dirty piles of snow lie in shady spots, maintaining the damp chill of the air. The ground is wet and slippery underfoot, and many paths are inundated with overflowing streams. There is no new growth yet. The storage advantages of freezing weather are gone, and the winter's supply of food is stale. Still, the days are getting longer, and the spirit lifts with the expectation of warmth.

The ground of the clearing, being bare and solid, kept none of the meltwater and was soon dry. The three began to spend more time outdoors, and their training increased. Varli was especially interested in the unarmed combat techniques they had been practicing all winter in the confines of the cottage. He felt he had made good progress, but until they had a chance to spar with solid footing and space to move it was not possible to tell how much. He therefore monitored the condition of their outside training ground daily. One warm spring day, he decreed that it was dry enough.

"Let's do unarmed drill outside today, Zoe. The ground's dry, the sun's warm, and I think I'll toss you around."

She laughed. "You do, do you? Think you've picked up something over the winter to go with the extra height you've put on? Well, look at me. Am I trembling in my shoes? Are my hands shaking? Does that tell you something?"

"Yes. That you're over-confident. Come on, oh great and mighty teacher, and find out how well your student has learned!"

As he reached the door, she jerked him aside and tried to get through ahead of him, but he put one hand against the doorjamb, resisting. She pulled at him again; he tried to push her back, and the two of them tumbled into the clearing laughing, with Patu gamboling around them in high expectation.

They did a thorough, strenuous warm up, instructed Patu to stay out of it, and squared off. It was a no-holds-barred but friendly fight, with punching, kicking and wrestling as the basic ingredients. Biting, scratching, pulling of hair and hidden weapons were only mimed. An informal scoring of points accrued from an advantage gained over the opponent, whether by a hit, a throw, or a pin.

They sparred easily at first, getting used to the expanded space and the opponent's reactions to it. Varli did not realize it, but Zoe was testing him thoroughly, both offence and defence, to see how well he had progressed. She was satisfied with his responses to clean and simple attacks so she started to mix it up, grabbing at his clothing, trying to catch his fingers and bend them and generally acting like a street brawler would. In the middle of one of these scuffles she made her mistake.

He had just attacked, and she had grabbed his sleeve and thrown him off balance so she could slip behind him. In reaching over his shoulder to pretend a claw at his eyes, she allowed her hand to come too far into his line of vision. Before

169

she could pull back, he had grabbed her wrist and hunched his back, and she was flying over his head, to land on her back in front of him. He dove to pin her, throwing his chest against hers, clasping her arms tight against her, and jamming his knee hard into her crotch.

For one moment he held her, immobile, face to face. Then his cheeks reddened and he let her go, stumbling to his feet, mumbling an apology.

She scrambled up. "Good throw, Varli. I deserved that. I should never have let my hand get so far in front of you. Come on, let's try again."

He tried, but he couldn't get back into the mood. He fought too carefully, trying to keep too much distance between them, and as a result he was always on the defensive. Zoe finally stopped.

"All right, let's give up. We're not going to make any more progress today."

He agreed, standing back to allow her to enter the cottage first. In fact, that was how he treated her all the rest of the day – with the kind of good manners he used when dealing with the ladies in court. For Zoe, this was dismaying. She knew what the problem was; she just had no idea how to approach a solution. One thing she knew for sure. It was time to leave.

The next day the atmosphere was more relaxed, but Varli was still overly formal. In the end, she decided to have it out. He was sitting in front of the cottage, braiding a new strap for Patu's carry harness. She went out and sat beside him, not too close.

"What kind of shape is that harness in?"

"Not too bad, really. I'm only replacing that strap with one that looks better. What do you think?" He held it out to her.

"I wonder what your family would think, you being able to do work like that?"

"I hope they'd be proud. It looks good to me."

"I agree, and we're going to need it soon."

He glanced up, then away. "Are we leaving?"

"Are you pleased?"

"Is it because of what I did yesterday? I told you, Zoe; I didn't mean it, and I'm sorry!"

The anguished look on his face made her cringe. "No, Varli, don't be sorry. It was just one of those things that happen. I don't see why it bothers you so much."

"I hate that sort of thing. It's exactly what Crel and his moron friends would make a huge joke of. I always thought I was better than that. I..." he was having trouble finding the right words, but he plunged on. "I have a lot of respect for you, Zoe, and that wasn't respectful. It was incredibly rude. I'm not supposed to think of you like that!"

The light was beginning dawn. "So it wasn't what you did, it was what you thought?"

"I guess so."

"Because a true Warlander would never think about a friend and an older lady like that."

"Exactly. But I did."

"Just because you aren't supposed to, doesn't mean you won't."

"What do you mean?"

"Varli, if everybody didn't experience that kind of problem, why would they make up rules about it?"

"I...guess they wouldn't."

"Believe me, everybody has problems like that. It's a part of growing up. The point is not your thoughts, it's what you do about them – how you control yourself. So far you're fine, except you've overdone it. For example, it would be nice to sit down beside you without you moving away. It would be nice to try a round of combat training without feeling that you're taking it easy because I'm a female. In fact, I would consider that insulting, I think."

"I can see how you would."

"This will take time for you to come to terms with. After a while it will become part of your natural good manners and only bother you occasionally, with someone special. But, now that you understand things better, I will say that this problem is one of the reasons we're leaving. You have matured a lot this winter. This is a part of growing up that I don't feel I'm the best person to help you with. So, because of that, and the fact that I'm ready to go back anyway, I think we should start preparing for our trip. All right?"

"Sounds fine with me. I'm ready to go home too. When?"

"In the next half-month, I suppose. I want to leave this place closed up a little better than I did last time. I like it here. I know I'll come back."

"Can I come back too?"

"Consider this a standing invitation."

"Great!" He jumped up. "What do we do to get ready?"

"First, you could sit down and finish off Patu's harness. He'll carry his own gear. Then we can see what else needs to be done. We'll go to the village and sell off our surplus supplies, such as they are. This time of year, there are bound to be shortages there."

Varli bent over his work with renewed vigour. A moment later he looked up. "What are you doing, sitting there? Get packing!"

172

26. Foreigners

It was a good thing they were prepared, because the decision as to their departure date was taken out of their hands. A few days after their trip to the village Zoe was in the cottage repairing a bridle when Varli called her to the door in a worried tone.

"Look at Patu."

One look at the armigerent put Zoe on the alert. "Weapons, Varli. I don't understand this, but we'd best be ready."

Zoe had thought she knew her huge friend well enough to read all his emotions, but this was something new. He was pacing the western edge of the clearing, but he couldn't seem to make up his mind if he was threatened or excited by what he sensed. His hackles would rise, and he would half-growl, then his ears would go up, and he would whine. Then he would pace farther, sniff and go through the whole procedure again.

Varli stepped out the door, an arrow strung on his bow. "There's something out there."

"Yes, but he doesn't know if it's friendly or not. Why don't you hold secure here and we'll go out and investigate?"

"Right. I'll leave the door open in case you come back in a hurry."

Giving Patu the 'hunt' signal to calm him, Zoe took the time to put her mind into the proper frame as well. Then the two of them ranged silently through the bare forest, all senses alert. It wasn't long before Zoe picked up the sounds. Riders moving through the woods. Even before she saw them, she knew they were small in number, and by the racket, at least some of them were armed. They were not trying to be subtle.

Bringing Patu close, she sought a hidden point where the invaders would pass nearby, but she could escape unseen if need be. She found one under the spreading boughs of a stand of young evergreens. As she lay in wait the tension built in her. Who could be coming through the forest? And in armour? She put her ear to the ground. There was one large horse along with a few smaller ones. That could only mean that there was a Warlander in the group. And what might a Warlander be doing, moving slowly through this remote area as if he were searching for something? The only reason she could think of was not reassuring. *He is looking for us.*

The noisy progress came closer and she could see movement through the trees some distance away. She dug her fingers deep into the ruff on Patu's neck, not as a signal – she was confident in his hunting skills – but more for her own reassurance.

She saw them more clearly as they crossed through a patch of young poplars whose leaves had not yet sprouted. There were four of them and one packhorse in single file, the leader a Warlander on a brown charger. He looked very large, or else his companions were quite small. She stared. They came closer. Then a leap of joy ran through her. Only one person sat a horse like that. Was it Gerth? She forgot herself and leaned forward, nearly out of her cover.

Yes, it was Gerth on Pelex, followed by three strangers, dressed in unusual clothing. Because of them, she restrained herself from rushing forward. If they were with Gerth, they must be all right, but she was still reluctant to reveal her hideout to anyone else.

She needed a plan, but the first thing to do was inform Varli. Sliding backwards through the trees, she retreated, the armigerent gliding beside her.

By the time she reached the cottage she had it figured out. "Varli, it's Gerth! He's come looking for us!"

"Where is he? Didn't you talk to him?"

"No, he brought three others with him – dark men in strange clothes. I don't want to bring them straight in. I'll go meet them, lead them roundabout."

"So Gerth thought he could just trot out here and find us, did he?" Varli's smile held the old mischievous flavour.

"Some chance. The route they are on, they would have missed us by a long way. If Patu hadn't smelled them they could have blundered around these woods for days, or until we heard the racket they made or spotted their tracks."

"Bring them in, but don't make it easy."

Zoe returned his malicious grin. "Don't worry, I won't."

She still had the grin on her face when she caught up with Gerth's party a while later. They were already past the cottage, headed on up the valley. *Good. That's the first step in mixing them up.* Hurrying around and placing herself to one side and in front of them, she gave the whistle signal, "Who goes?"

The answered was, "Friend."

She waited a while, then moved to the other side of their route, and gave the call for "home" with the "question" trill at the end.

The answer was affirmative, but there was a following call that she couldn't interpret. It had the "home" and "question" in it, but it also said something else, much more complex. Since she had taught Gerth the only signals he knew, she couldn't place this. That response was too confident to be an error.

Until she knew more, she couldn't do much about it, so she started them moving directly towards the cottage, gave them 'keep going straight,' and dashed back herself. By the time she reached home Varli had cleaned up everything. From the outside, door and shutters closed, the cottage looked deserted. Varli was spruced up in his best tunic, and she darted in and put on her grandfather's ceremonial robe. Secreting themselves in the woods outside, they waited.

175

Soon the crashing and stumbling noises drew near. Twice they faded, and Zoe gave the signal equivalent to "over here, stupid" to get them back on track.

She had brought her visitors in on a side of the house where the brush was tight evergreens, so they entered the clearing leading their horses. Gerth was first, and he stopped at the edge, signalling his companions forward. As she had noted, they were short and dark. The two who spread on either side in defensive positions were well armed, but the older one who stood by Gerth seemed to carry no weapons. More interesting, his robe looked similar to the one she was wearing! Filing this away for future thought, she continued with her plan.

Their attention was riveted on the cottage, and she took that time to pull her appearing trick. She and Patu glided forward so slowly and smoothly that they didn't seem to move at all. They were fully in view when a flick of Patu's ear brought the eyes of the visitors snapping towards them.

After giving the party their moment of stunned silence, she draped an arm casually over Patu's shoulders and ruffled him behind the ears. "Well, Gerth, you took long enough getting here. Did you have a good journey?"

Gerth dropped his reins and stepped forward, smiling joyfully. "Zoe!"

His pleasure to see her removed all thought of continuing the act. She broke her pose and ran across the clearing, jumping and throwing her arms around his neck, while he caught her in a bear hug.

Then he put her on the ground and set her at arms length, intending to get a look at her. However, he was forced back by a furry shoulder that placed itself between them. Patu stood there, looking up at Gerth with a guardedly neutral expression. He was making his position clear. *"If Zoe thinks you're all right, then that's fine for the moment. I reserve judgement."*

Zoe laughed and folded her arms, leaning them over Patu's back.

"I guess Patu isn't quite sure you're a friend yet."

"From the look of him, I guess I better persuade Patu I'm a friend!"

"I'll take care of that right now." She reached out and took Gerth's hand. "Patu, this is a very good friend. You talk to him." She held the hand near Patu's nose to be investigated, then guided it to the tender spot behind the armigerent's ears.

Zoe had been so intent on Gerth that she had not been paying any attention to his companions. She now turned to see them in a certain amount of disorder. The older man was frowning in a bemused manner. One of the fighters was retrieving his sword from where it seemed to have fallen, and the other was just getting up off the ground. If Gerth noted their disarray he chose to ignore it.

"Zoe, I have the honour of presenting Lord Janitra Omanisa, merchant of Kyabra, who has come a long way out of his normal path to meet with you."

Zoe could tell by the phrasing that this was no ordinary merchant. "I am Zoysana, my Lord. My humble home is yours."

As she spoke, the merchant bowed in a certain way, and before she could stop herself, she added a phrase that came from somewhere deep in her past. His response was familiar to her, and she gave the same bow in her turn. There was a buzz of whispering, instantly stifled, from the two men behind him. Then he said something else, and she was lost. She looked at him quizzically. "I'm sorry, my Lord, but I don't quite understand."

He smiled. "But you knew the first part, my Lady?" He spoke in Petrellan, but with an accent that thrilled her.

"Yes. It came to me, as from a long distance. Was that Kyabran?"

"It is the formal greeting of lords in our country, those who wear the robes we two wear."

She looked down in confusion. "Oh, but this is my grandfather's robe. I just..."

"But I understand your grandfather is dead."

"Yes..."

"And his only daughter, your mother, as well."

"Yes, long ago."

"Then perhaps it is your robe." He repeated the Kyabran phrase, and sketched the bow again, as if to confirm the ceremony. "Now may I present my nephew and guard-of-life Maksa Silabu," here the larger of the guards approached and stood stiffly before her, "and my other guard-of-life, as yet unsponsored, Tadeo Priya." The second young man stepped forward, not so far, and spoke a phrase she did not catch.

Janitra Omanisa laughed. "Well put. I could not express the experience better myself." He turned to Zoe. "In my young friend's words, Very few are allowed to feel so close to the Goddess. It may sound exaggerated in your language, but believe me, in Kyabran it is very poetic, and I assure you he means every word."

Looking at the fighter, who had not moved a muscle since he spoke, she could see that he did. Smiling at him, she answered with a word her grandfather had used to commend her when she had performed a practice move exceptionally well. The fighter's impassive face lit up with a pleased smile, and he relaxed and bowed. Both guards stepped back. Relieved, she turned to introduce Varli, but Gerth was already beside him.

"You might have a special interest in the boy, but he is my future squire. May I present him?"

Zoe was quite happy to be removed from the ceremony. Everything she had done so far had seemed like walking a submerged log across a dark pond; the only way you knew you

178

had made the right step was when you looked around and you were still above the surface.

When that round of formalities was over and Zoe invited them inside to sit down, Varli asked what to do about the horses. Both Zoe and Gerth started to answer him at the same time. They laughed together.

"I can see a small division of loyalties for the poor lad. Who is he supposed to obey?"

"Well, he is on the way to being your squire. Take him and welcome."

"Do I detect relief in your voice?"

"Can you imagine being shut up with that sense of humour all winter?"

"You still seem sane."

"It's all a facade. Just keep an eye on me if I start twitching!"

The others had been waiting through this exchange, the Kyabrans with amused politeness, Varli with exaggerated disgust.

"By the time they finish insulting me and each other," Varli confided to Tadeo Priya, who was standing nearby, "I could have all the horses stripped, rubbed down and fed."

The young Kyabran nodded hesitantly. "Insult – smile together. Good friends?"

"Oh, very good friends. And when they get together and start giving orders, watch out!" He could see his companion was not getting it all, so he simply pointed at the two of them, then at himself, "Lots of work for me."

Tadeo Priya clapped him on the shoulder. "We fix horses."

"Right! Come on you two, what about it?"

Zoe turned to Gerth. "What's the plan? Are you staying a while?"

"How long we stay depends on you, but we are carrying all our gear, so I suppose we could set up camp in your front yard, here?"

"Then you're setting up for tonight, but not much longer. I was just packing myself. You heard that, Varli. Snap to it!"

Varli smiled, but did not move.

"What's wrong?"

"The squire awaits his lord's instructions. Am I to listen to this woman?"

They both took a threatening step towards him and he fled, his laughter ringing behind him.

Gerth looked at Zoe, half serious this time. "How did you ever put up with him?"

She laughed again in pleasure to have Gerth here to join in their fun. "He's good company when you have him by himself. He may even turn out to be a real person soon!"

She turned to Janitra Omanisa. "Please treat this as your home and relax. I will prepare tea to welcome you, but it will require some time, as many things are packed away. She opened the door. "Do come in and sit down."

27. Old and New

Leaving Varli and the younger guard to see to the horses, the others entered the cottage. When they were seated, she excused herself and went to her room and changed into her regular clothes. She had no idea what was bothering the Kyabrans, but perhaps it was the robe. When she appeared with the tea service she saw the two older men exchange glances, but that was all.

When Varli and Tadeo Priya came in she served a formal tea to welcome the visitors. She was nervous, as she was using her grandfather's ritual, one that she did not normally perform. She was gratified when the merchant's response was similar to Barent's, so long ago.

"It is not often that a maiden performs the Fighter's Welcome, even at home in Kyabra. I congratulate you on your grace."

"Thank you. I hope it was…appropriate?"

"Oh, yes, it was a pleasant ceremony." He cleared his throat. "I hope you will pardon us. Lord Gerth had prepared us somewhat for meeting you, but we Kyabrans are a careful people. It was impossible to be completely prepared."

In other words, there is a problem. And this man wouldn't be travelling with Gerth unless he was important in some way. I must be very careful, here. "I understand, my Lord."

The Kyabran's eyes moved to Patu, lying at ease in his usual place by the hearth. "That is an unusually large beast." He frowned, as if choosing his words carefully. "How is…what is his temperament?"

She snapped her fingers and the armigerent rolled to attention, lying with his front paws spread, his ears perked. "Oh, he's a real sweetheart."

181

Omanisa frowned. "Sweetheart? I have not heard that term applied to an animal..."

"Oh, I'm sorry. I mean that he is very well behaved."

"At all times?"

She tried for a grin. "Better than Varli, I'd say." This brought a hint of a smile. "Are you familiar with armigerents? I thought they came originally from Kyabra."

"Yes, we have many of them. But we are more careful with them than you seem to be."

"Our trainers think the same, I'm afraid. It just didn't seem like that sort of thing would work with Patu. I assure you he will be no trouble."

"I sincerely hope you are correct."

Back to the stiff formality. I'd better watch that Patu is on his best behaviour. It occurred to her that she had never seen him with other people, or with a larger group. *I'll have to watch him closely. As well as myself.*

And so it went all evening. Zoe still felt she was fumbling in the dark. Only Tadeo Priya, the younger Guard of Life, seemed open and friendly. The larger man, Maksa Silabu, hardly spoke, sitting and...well, not really glowering. Just sitting.

Janitra Omanisa carried the conversation, and it was difficult to tell what was going on in his mind. Just when she thought she saw a chink in his armour, the Kyabran would retreat into formality. Always perfectly correct, never openly disapproving, but showing that she had stepped over some line she couldn't see. She was feeling increasingly frustrated. *I'm tired of this game. These people come into my home and make me feel like I'm doing something wrong. Well, if I am, I want to know about it.*

She steeled herself and spoke directly to Lord Omanisa. "It is not hard for me to understand, from the accent you use and your wearing of a similar robe, that your country is where my grandfather came from. Please tell me, did I commit an error in wearing his robe? It seems to have special meaning."

Janitra Omanisa leaned back, relaxing for the first time. "I thought at first that there had been an error, but not a serious one. The privilege of wearing the robe comes in two ways. It is your birthright to wear it, if only because you are the heir to it through your grandfather. However, except on ceremonial occasions, no one in Kyabra, especially a young woman, would wear the robe unless she had also undertaken the training. It would not be a social error to wear it, but it would be looked upon as boastful. The robe is a symbol of the highest level of fighter our land possesses. Oh, one need not be of the best, but one must have the appropriate lineage and the proper basic schooling in the arts of war. I can see you have had some Kyabran training. From your grandfather?"

"Yes, until I was nine years old."

"That is proper, then, but how much had you learned?"

Gerth could contribute here. "From what I can gather, a whole lot. When Barent first brought her in, she was a terror on the practice field. None of the squires could touch her in staff work, and her unarmed skills were unbelievable."

The Kyabran smiled. "Intending no offence, Lord Gerth, but that was perhaps by your local standards? We emphasize the weaponless work more in our land. Be that as it may, it could be enough. Had you, Zoysana, reached the level of the practice Patterns?"

"Oh, yes, he taught me many of those. I have worked them alone ever since, though, so it is difficult to know if I remember them correctly. Would you like to see one?"

"My Lady, I had no intention of forcing you to any kind of test!"

"No, I would love to try. I have been practising for ten years on my own, and now I have a chance to perform for a Master. May I show you? In the morning, when the light is good?"

He smiled. "It would be my pleasure."

Which guaranteed that she would sleep poorly. It was pleasant when the visitors retired to their tents, and she and Varli had their home back. They sat for a moment before the fire, looking at each other.

Varli grinned. "Well, I wasn't expecting that."

"Nor I. What do you think of them?"

"Tadeo's great. I like him. His Petrellan is better that it seems. He's too shy to speak out. The other one, Maksa? He's threatening, isn't he? Never says anything. Gerth told me he's a formidable fighter. Any weapon, weaponless, you name it."

"What about Lord Omanisa?"

"Can't read him. He's too polite."

"He's hiding behind it. There's something going on, and I don't know what it is. But he's important to Gerth, so we have to figure it out and keep him happy."

"And he's Kyabran, so that makes it twice as difficult for you."

"You pinned it exactly."

He rose, yawning, and slapped her on the shoulder. "Don't worry. You'll figure it out. You always do."

She stood as well and headed for her bedroom. "I wish I had your confidence."

* * *

184

The next morning when Zoe was clearing away the breakfast plates the Kyabran lord looked up at her. "Are you still willing to show us your Patterns?"

"I am. It would be best to get this out of the way."

"I agree. And I'm sure you have duties to attend to before we leave."

"Shall we go outside, then?"

They all went out into the clearing. Gerth and Varli stood to one side, but the Kyabrans knelt in a line. Calming herself, she took her position facing them. She bowed, and they responded. After three calming breaths, she started.

For Pattern One, a simple training exercise, she ran through the steps confidently, as she had been performing them ever since she could remember. When she was finished she was well warmed up. She did not look to her audience, but went on to a more complicated one, Pattern Four. Again, she felt that she had performed it creditably; she was even starting to enjoy herself. With the added incentive of appreciative onlookers, she found her intensity higher than usual. However, these had been simple exercises, showing only the basic skills. Now she moved on to the Patterns with individual names. For the next one, *Gammal sar Damis*, she had to concentrate.

She was less pleased with her performance of the harder Pattern, because there was one section of it where she did not understand the flow, and she felt that her intensity dropped at that point. Still, it was a good Pattern. She had practised it many times this winter as it involved defence against a variety of weapons, suiting her changing philosophy of fighting. When she finished, she stopped and knelt again, bowing. The three Kyabrans bowed in return, more deeply than before. The youngest, Tadeo, held his bow much longer. She took this as a good sign.

"What do you think, my Lord?"

185

"If you will give me leave, my Lady, this is an educational occasion not to be passed over. My guards have never had the opportunity to watch a fighter whose training has been so different from their own. May I allow them to comment first?"

Zoe had no reason to refuse. "By all means."

"Tadeo, would you start?"

The chosen fighter squirmed. Then he spoke haltingly, "I will...would not presume...to critic...criticize?"

"Nothing, Tadeo?"

The youth held his ground. "I not...am not worthy." He bowed to Zoe again.

Smiling, his master responded in Kyabran, then turned to the others. "He is perhaps hard on himself. His quality is very high for his age. Now, my nephew, what do you say?"

Until now, Zoe had hardly heard this larger fighter's voice. His speech was accented but fluent. "I, too, have little to say, my Lord. Perhaps the lower defence in the last quarter of, what is it called in this language, Knives and Forks?"

Janitra Omanisa nodded. "Yes, I saw that as well. An interesting interpretation. Do you have any comment, Zoysana?"

She made a helpless gesture. "What can I say? I could not remember my grandfather's explanation of that move, and I have never been able to figure it out to my satisfaction. I have assumed that it is a defence against a weapon I am unfamiliar with. The extended block to the side seems to indicate something with an angle to it, otherwise why reach so far from centre?"

"Do you understand the meaning of the name, *Gammal sar Damis*?"

"Half of it. *gammal* is 'dagger,' isn't it?"

"And you don't know what a *damis* is?"

186

"No idea, my Lord."

"It will not be a revelation to you that a damis is a weapon made by the peasants of our land, formed by bending the tines of a hay fork at a right angle to the handle, to give a grasping action to pull the opponent towards you. It is very hard for the inexperienced fighter to block it, as the tines extend so far in from the line of the weapon. There is a tendency to block too close, and the tines are sharp. I am impressed that you had figured that out. Some day I must show you the real instrument. The form of the Pattern will come clear, I am sure."

"Thank you, my Lord. I will be honoured to learn."

"And now, my Lady Zoysana, have you any more to show us? We are already very impressed."

In spite of the warmth in Omanisa's voice, Zoe felt shy. "I would like to try one more, if I may. I have not understood it at all until recently, but I have worked hard on it." She rose, picked up her robe, and put it on. Taking a few breaths to calm herself, she commenced The Cloak.

She started slowly, setting her timing to the movement of the robe. As it swirled around her, she picked up the pace and a strange feeling came over her. Everything began to flow. She had never been so light on her feet. Time became extended, and she knew and understood her movements more clearly than ever before. She had leisure to notice every muscle, every minute gesture, as she floated from one move to the next. Her leaps extended forever, and her landings were feather-light. Then she reached the section of rapid movements, and her hands and feet rapped a staccato that blended into a single stretch of sound.

Up, down and away she moved, up and down again. The shadows of the trees stretching across the clearing were solid, and she wove unerringly around and between them. She felt she could hide in them, disappear, then burst forth, high into the sunlight and float gently to the ground. The robe supported her, hid her, strengthened her. She spun and struck and dodged and spun again and spun again, slower and slower...

And then it was over. The robe settled, and she stood perfectly still, dazed by her return to reality. There was dead silence in the clearing. A bit of seed-fluff drifted down in front of her, illuminated by the sunlight shining through it, and she watched its progress. She remained motionless, unable to break the spell. Then she was aware of movement. The three Kyabrans were circling her, pressing against each others' hands, palm to palm at shoulder level, forming an unbroken shield around her. Slowly, they moved their arms inwards, closing until their hands encircled her shoulders. As complete awareness returned to her, she realized that they were making a deep, soothing, humming down in their chests. When they could see that she was recovered, their hands dropped, and the sound died away.

"Wh...what...?"

Lord Janitra placed his hand on her brow. "It is not altogether unusual, my Lady. I, myself have experienced the Trance but twice: once on my sponsoring day, once in battle. It is brought on by the ecstasy of the movement and is usually preceded by some great fear or joy, which seems to set it off." He smiled and shook his head slowly. "There can no longer be any doubt of your right to wear the robe, and with pride. To feel the Trance is the stigma of the Master. You cannot be otherwise. We all feel humbled and grateful. It is a rare boon to see any Pattern, especially The Cloak, performed during Entrancement. Truly a beautiful experience for us, as well. Now I think you must speak to your friends." The three bowed even lower before her and faded back.

Gerth and Varli were standing there, unsure of what to do or say. When she moved towards them, they rushed forward, only to stop in some confusion.

"Zoe, what happened? I've never seen you move like that!"

"It was the robe, wasn't it? You were even better than before!"

"Varli, I don't think 'better than before' quite covers it. I have never had such an experience in my life." She still felt a glow within her. She had felt so strong, so light. Her warmth seemed to spread from her and encompass her friends in an aura of love. She laid a hand on the chest of each, looked into Varli's face, then Gerth's.

"It was marvellous. I am so glad you were here to see. It has made me more than I was. It has shown me the potential I have, what I can strive to perfect."

As the three stood together, a small sound turned them.

"I believe there is one more member of your circle you must attend to, Zoysana," came the soft voice of Lord Janitra.

Patu was crouched close to the ground as if in fear. He looked up at Zoe as she approached, but he did not move. When she signalled him to her, he crawled on his belly and laid his head on her foot. Disturbed, she raised his head up. He stood, but with his tail between his legs, his head turned aside. She looked around in wonder. "What's wrong with him?"

"The armigerent is sensitive to his master's feelings, as no doubt you have noticed. The Trance is the most powerful of moods, and you have completely overwhelmed him. He is a young animal, though almost full grown. He has no way to handle this raw emotion. The only thing he can do is reaffirm his allegiance to you as his pack leader. See how he offers his throat. It is a very important moment in his life as well."

As Zoe bowed to Lord Janitra in gratitude, Gerth fingered the small scar on his throat.

She bent over and threw her arms around the armigerent's neck, hugging him hard. Then she ruffled the special spot behind his ears and gave the signal for him to run. He dashed off across the clearing, gambolling joyfully around and over the

189

luggage in his way. With sudden confidence, Zoe stepped forward to command his attention. Then, with a sweep of her hand, she sent him bounding towards Pelex, who was tethered nearby, away from the other horses. In a single leap, so quick that the stallion had no time to react, the armigerent soared over the horse's back without touching, landed gracefully, then trotted over to Zoe and stood, panting joyfully, looking up at her. Again she hugged him, and he squirmed all over. There was still a lot of puppy in that huge body.

Zoe turned to the others proudly. Varli's face contained the smug complacency of the already initiated. Gerth was astounded. The Kyabrans looked much less surprised, but very impressed.

There was a pause, and Zoe began to feel the tiniest bit uncomfortable. Finally she had to break the silence. "Well, I guess that's enough circus. Shall we get ourselves organized for the trail?"

28. RETURN JOURNEY

So their departure was speeded considerably. What with entertaining guests, packing, and preparing the cottage for another extended vacancy, Zoe had little spare time in the next two days. Again she took great care that everything was in order, but for different reasons and with a better idea of what she was doing. Now when she turned at the doorway for a last look, the room did not seem as if its occupants could return at any moment. All loose items were taken down and packed away properly, hung out of the reach of any rodents or flooding that might threaten. Not as dramatic as last time, she thought as she turned away, but much more practical.

Her farewell at her grandfather's Resting was also more subdued. Fondly rubbing the smoothly chiselled stone, she murmured her thanks, with more appreciation of exactly what she had to thank him for. Again she was leaving on a new adventure, but now her awareness of how well prepared she was filled her with keen anticipation.

She was sure that her troubles at the castle had not been solved. Barent being king, especially if her suspicions of his method of achieving that rank were true, would only compound the tension and intrigue. However, she felt rested and ready for whatever came. Besides, a whole new life had opened up for her.

As she grew up she had maintained an unusual position, or lack of position, in Petrella's tightly ranked society. Cushioned by Barent's patronage, she had only explored the positive aspects of the situation, and ignored her need for a sense of belonging. Discovering that she held a rank of her own, even in so far a country as Kyabra, made her aware of an emptiness she had not noticed until it was filled. So she took to the road on a fine spring day, full of optimism and surrounded by friends. Time enough for the problems when they came. For now, she would enjoy herself.

Except for the roundabout route she used to lead her party away from the cottage, everything was changed. Now there was no need, nor even any chance, of subtlety. She totaled up their strength: a Warlander and his Squire, two Kyabran Masters of Weaponless Combat, one with a fully trained armigerent, (strange to think of herself in those terms) and the other with two competent Guards-of-life. All they needed now was a troop of soldiers to make a full foraging party.

* * *

At the village the rest of Gerth's party, the ten Private Guard who came with his new position of First Prince Ascending, were ready to move. They lined out along the street in fine formation, making a great display for the villagers, but dissolving into a more relaxed pattern as soon as they were on the road. Zoe and Varli found it easy to create some of the privacy they craved by riding side by side.

"Are you feeling like I'm feeling?"

She glanced over at him. "Busy lot, aren't they?"

"Yes. Sometimes I just want some time to myself. Or time to talk over things with you, like usual."

"Did you have something you wanted to talk over? Something private?"

He nudged his horse closer and lowered his voice. "Did you figure out what happened when Lord Janitra and his men first met us?"

"There was some kind of misunderstanding, but I didn't want to make a fuss out of it. Since then things are friendly but formal, and I didn't want to embarrass anyone, so I let it go.

Besides, I've been too busy to indulge my curiosity. I didn't really see much, anyway."

"You better let me tell you about it, then." Varli gave his usual impish grin.

"I suppose if I wish to hear this tale, I must put up with the teller."

Varli sobered. "It was more than weird, Zoe. When those three saw you and Patu, they went absolutely stiff. Then the two fighters drew their swords and laid them on the ground in front of them, like in a ritual, with the hilts in your direction. Then the bigger one, Maksa, knelt, and Tadeo got right down on both knees, his forehead on the ground and his arms spread to the sides. Lord Janitra didn't go so far, but he looked as if he had decided to kneel, too, then changed his mind, at least twice. Then when you ran and Gerth hugged you, he gave a signal and they sort of got themselves back together. If they hadn't been so serious about it, it would have been hilarious!"

Zoe was even more puzzled. It sounded as if a mistake had been made, but she was still not sure if it would be a good idea to broach the subject with her new friends. They had their own system of honour, and she did not want to make any false steps, since she wanted to learn more about it. Finally she decided that any slip on her part might be forgiven. *After all, they are strangers in my country, not the other way around. When I find my chance, I will ask.*

But before anything else, she had one more ritual to complete.

Once more, with a Royal Warlander and his Personal Guard, she mounted the low pass through the hills above the valley. Once more she turned to look back over the home of her childhood. At least this time she knew more of what the outside world contained. *Although come to think of it, I have as little idea of what it holds for me.* She looked up at Gerth, high above her on Pelex, and shrugged her shoulders. "At least this time I know I can come back." She wheeled her pony and led the way down the hill towards Arlyn Castle and her old life.

They camped beside a small stream the first night, as the weather was good and there were no towns nearby. When dinner was over Lord Janitra strolled out, looking at the stars. Zoe also wandered away from camp and was sitting on a mossy boulder along the bank when he returned.

"May I join you for a while?"

"I was hoping you would. There was a question I wanted to ask you."

"Any way in which I can assist you..." He sat beside her.

"I'm not sure you will want to. I am not asking this out of idle curiosity and I do not wish to offend in any way, but I...I feel that when we first met there were a lot of things going on that I did not understand. Part of it, I now see. Because of my robe, my appearance and my partial knowledge of your customs, you must have assumed that I knew much that I did not. However, there seemed to be more to it than that. Am I reading more into the situation than actually existed?"

He smiled at the recollection. "Oh, no. It was truly something out of an ancient tale, Zoysana. I gather you have no knowledge of our heritage of stories and legends?"

"My grandfather told me some."

"Did he tell you any about armigerents, and their place with the gods?"

"About armigerents, yes. The gods, no. I don't think he wanted me to hear about his old gods. He only told me about the Petrellan ones."

"A strange choice, but understandable, in the circumstances."

Zoe wondered what circumstances he meant, but decided to save that for later. "What do armigerents have to do with your gods?"

194

"Not our gods exactly. With our Goddess. She is the First of our pantheon, the one original Spirit. In your language, she would be called The Lady, although Mother or even Woman would be more accurate. She has two aspects: the Nurturer and the Defender. In her duty of Nurture, she is seen in the fields with a lamb, colt, or other young one. As the Defender, she is found most often in the forest…"

"…with an armigerent!"

He smiled wryly. "With a huge armigerent, and in most stories dressed as a Master of the Weaponless. You can see our amazement when you appeared in exactly that form. Your Kyabran heritage is strong, and your armigerent is a credit to his breeders. I don't think Tadeo has recovered from the shock yet. His time on the Wheel has been short, and he sees what he wishes to see. When you affected such an old skeptic as me, how could we expect otherwise?" He smiled in the young guard's direction. "Tadeo came with me to find something. There is a place in his soul that yearns for that which it might never attain. It is often so with the young, is it not?"

Zoe smiled inside at the thought of her opinion being asked on such a question.

The trader lord continued. "It is a source of sadness to those of us who witness it time and again. The ones for whom the flame burns brightest are affected the strongest. For most, the desire will fade with the realities of life, and they will become resigned to their place. Others find a quest to follow, good or bad, and from that group come the great successes and glorious failures of the Ballads."

Zoe could follow this. "Then there are some who never find a quest, never get their chance."

"And those are the bitterest, both to themselves and to those who love them. I pray that Tadeo does not follow that path. It is the most sorrowful to see, and most often trodden by those with the highest and most noble aspirations."

"Tadeo...?"

"Yes. Be it for good or ill, Tadeo aspires greatly. Not for wealth or glory. Only to follow a marvellous dream. He is too much outward turning, my young guard-of-life. He would do better to seek strength within himself. It is there, in full quantity, but he is too modest to accept it. I fear he will never be a great leader."

"There are other roles than leading ones, many with great honour. It must be so, since there are so few places where one may lead."

Janitra laughed. "Astute, my young friend, and it would be better if most of our aspiring leaders were more aware of this!"

She laughed as well. "But if they knew, they would not aspire any more and what would they do then?"

Lord Janitra looked at her. "Your time on the Wheel of Life has been short but the track has worn deep. What do you seek?"

This serious question brought Zoe's humour up short. "I am too skeptical to seek greatness and glory. I have seen the downward side of that path. It is something I have spent much time on but have come to no simple conclusion."

"But you understand enough to realize that conclusions are not that simple."

She sighed and got up from the rock. "One reason I took this time away was to find answers, and I did find some. But I wonder if I asked myself all the proper questions."

He rose as well. "Not to seem trite, but is that not the nature of the best kind of question? The answer only serves to lead one onward."

She started back towards the glow of the fire. "It seems the wisdom of Sarasha the Lame has filtered all the way to the Inner Sea. But it would be nice, don't you think, to find a simple, straightforward solution, just once in a while?"

He chuckled lightly. "If I may give you the benefit of my many years of experience, those are the solutions that are to be trusted the least."

A chill ran through her. "I think I knew that already."

29. TESTING IDEAS

Zoe was glad they had camped away from any town the first night. Accustomed as they were to solitude, both she and Varli found the noise and chatter of even this small number of companions irritating. As they rode on the next day, Zoe drifted back so that she was following the group at a distance. Just as she was beginning to enjoy her solitude, Tadeo pulled his horse aside to wait. As she reached him she stopped, and he bowed gracefully in his saddle.

"I do not wish to burden you with my presence, my Lady, but it is...good that I follow after, if you wish to ride here, from the group. Please ride on, and I will follow after."

"Oh, no, please, Tadeo Priya. There is no need for you to follow me."

He was adamant. "Please, my Lady. It is...my duty...my occupation."

"But aren't you supposed to be guarding your Master?"

"Yes, but not, if he sends me on another...place."

"And he...?"

He smiled. "You...we have no choice. If...you must argue with my Master."

She found him much easier to talk to when he smiled. "Would you be fulfilling your duty if you were to ride beside me? No ponderous thoughts to occupy my mind; it's just that all that noise was too much for me. I have lived in the quiet so long."

"Yes, I understand. Large groups have no serenity, and your soldiers," he shook his head sadly, "not subtle."

"Not to offend, my Lady," he added, glancing over at her anxiously.

She laughed. "Don't be too hard on them. This is a pleasant outing for men who live a hard life. A patrol through the farthest, safest section of the kingdom, in fine weather and no rush is looked upon as a holiday. Gerth has his pick of men for his own Guard. Any of these could qualify as Guides. Have you seen our Guides at work?"

"Oh, yes, I had...was honoured of accompanying your Sivan's men. They are good. For soldiers." Again, he glanced at her, to see if she was upset by the faint praise.

She was not. "I quite agree. On foot, they definitely leave something to be desired, something that only a childhood of practice can cure. On horseback, you must admit, they move very well. By the way, why do you call him 'my Sivan'? Or do you mean 'our Sivan'? His name, as we call him, is 'the Sivan'."

"Sorry. I do not speak well."

"No, you are doing fine. His name is not usual here, either."

"Oh, thank you. I call him 'your Sivan' because he talks of you. When we are coming to see you, I think him very happy."

"Was he?" It was good to think that someone was concerned about her and would be glad to see her back.

They rode in companionable silence for a while, then he looked over at her several times, hesitating. "Lady Zoysana?"

"Yes?"

"Your names, in Petrella. What is 'shortened name'?"

"Oh, we don't call each other by our full names most of the time. Especially mine; it's much too long. My full name is Zoysana Rochenan, but most people call me Zoe. Much easier."

"Ah, I see. For us, the same. We only use one name, too. I am Tadeo. Will you say that?"

"Tadeo? You mean call you that?"

"Yes, I think. Call me 'Tadeo.' Other name is family, many Priyas. One Tadeo." He smiled and his back straightened.

"Fine. Then you can call me 'Zoe', too."

"Oh, no. That is not right."

"Not right? In this kingdom, many people use the short name."

"No. I am Tadeo. You call me that. You are the Lady. I cannot use short name."

Zoe looked over at him, then down at Patu, trotting along with his head at her knee level. "Tadeo, I am not the Lady. I am Zoe. I don't even know your Lady."

He seemed embarrassed. "No, no, not The Lady." He made a sign with his left hand, touching the centre of his chest. "Not The Lady, not...truly. But you are Master, you are Lady. It cannot be other."

She gave up. There was no use arguing against another's culture; who knew what rules she might be asking him to break? "Will you at least call me 'Lady Zoe?' The rest is just too formal."

"Lady Zoe." He glanced sideways at her. "This is right?"

"Yes, Tadeo. I guess so." She smiled at him.

"Lady Zoe. Good."

She wondered how traders ever managed it, if this was an example of how difficult it was to communicate, even with someone who knew her language fairly well. She could hardly imagine going into a new kingdom every month or so. The different laws would be bad enough, but if it took this long each time just to figure out what people should call each other!

That evening she had the experience of immersing herself in a foreign culture, except that the culture was her own, made strange by her absence from it. They stopped in at the manor of the local lord, a man named Turnhout, and were invited for the night. This was one of Gerth's official functions during this trip: visit the lords and receive their hospitality, their fealty and their complaints. Again, Zoe's weakened resistance to noise and confusion caused her to be less than her usual outgoing self. This was fine, as she was hardly important here, so she let Gerth and Janitra bear the brunt of the social whirl.

She and Varli contrived to sit as far away from the centre of the Hall as possible, with a willing Tadeo to serve as a buffer. Whenever anyone came to talk to them, he seized the opportunity to practice his Petrellan speech and thus kept them insulated. It also helped that Patu wasn't comfortable with the bustle, either. He never quite settled down from his 'on guard' attitude. He stared and raised his lip at any sudden movement nearby, clearing an empty space around them. Zoe appreciated his help and allowed him to continue.

A much more pleasurable aspect of the journey was the training they did each day after the travelling was done. Skilled as she was, Zoe knew that she had much to learn, both in conventional warfare from Gerth and his soldiers and in her grandfather's ways from the Kyabrans. Varli was proud to show off his improving skills to Gerth, although there was a new deference in him, and he acted almost as if he knew he was the poorest fighter in the company.

They spent hour after hour in the lengthening spring evenings, working with every weapon they carried, in every combination they could think of. When they camped out, they practised in any glade or field nearby. When they visited a local manor, they borrowed the practice field and worked with anyone who wished to join. Few took the opportunity, preferring instead to stand around and stare, with varying degrees of suspicion or amazement, at the outlandish techniques.

The soldiers of Gerth's Guard were hesitant at first to attempt the strange gyrations of the Kyabrans, but when they saw Zoe working them so smoothly and Gerth laughing as he tumbled through, they soon joined in both the exercises and the laughter. Here Varli, with his winter's training, was far ahead of them. Zoe could see how pleased he was, showing a toughened fighter twice his age the intricacies of a movement he had mastered. He turned out to be a patient and careful teacher, and rose in the esteem of the rest of the party because of it.

He also gained from the companionship of this group. Laugh and horseplay as they might, these were all tested fighters, and their attitude underneath was deadly serious. He mentioned this point to Zoe one day as they stood watching a sort of melee, in which Gerth and Tadeo with swords and Maksa with a staff were standing their ground against five of the Guard.

"This is all rather fun, but a thought just occurred to me."

"A thought. How original."

"Zoe, listen. We are all having fun doing this, but to them it's serious, isn't it?"

"Mm-hm."

"I mean, look at Gerth's soldiers. They take all the standard training in Foot and Light Horse work, and they are some of our best or they wouldn't be assigned to this position. But they are learning things they have never seen before. I was thinking. One short session with Tadeo or Maksa, and one of those men might learn a simple twist of the sword or change of balance that might save his life one day."

"An interesting point. Can you apply it to yourself?"

"I suppose so. You mean that any training session might be the one where I learn the move that may save my life?"

"There's no doubt about it. Believe me, there will come times when you are using every variation you know and they won't seem to be enough."

Varli grinned. "I guess it would be too late then to wish you'd practised more. No wonder they go at it so hard."

It was Zoe's turn to grin. "Besides which, apart from drinking, betting, wenching and tavern brawling, it's the only sport they have." They walked over to where the three defenders stood, backs to a large tree, a frustrated ring of attackers standing at a respectful distance.

"That's an incredible combination, my Lord," one of the soldiers was panting. "We can't get into proper range because of his staff, and if we do, the two of you have the high and low lines well protected."

"Yes," another chimed in, "and I don't see how Lord Tadeo moves so quickly. Several times I thought he was completely engaged, then suddenly he was there in front of me."

A third grunted in disgust. "I had you for sure, my Lord, with your side exposed, when Maksa went after Tursko, there. Then he," his head jerked towards the grinning Tadeo, "kicked the sword out of my hand. I guess his foot was all he had free at the moment."

Most of the others had missed this and they clamoured for a demonstration. The soldier stepped forward with his sword, and to his dismay Tadeo dropped his weapon and moved within range, motioning the man to attack. Unsure, the soldier jabbed with his point. Tadeo was elsewhere. He made a few quick slashes, but they all went wild. Realizing that he could try harder without too much danger of hurting his opponent, the Petrellan leaned back for a longer swing.

This was what Tadeo was waiting for. He ducked, and the sword whizzed by a finger-width above his hair. Then his left foot whipped out, deftly lifting his opponent's helmet off his head. He was out of range again before the backswing could even start. The soldier looked around and raised his hands with a 'see what I mean?' expression, then sheathed his sword and went looking for his helmet while his companions roared with laughter. Then they all shucked their weapons and got down to learning how it was done. Here Tadeo's lack of fluent speech made little difference, as his demonstration was eloquence itself.

Gerth strolled over to Zoe. "Now guess what we'll have to put up with."

"They'll be kicking each other's hats off for days. And you think I had a hard time putting up with Varli!"

* * *

Because of the number of stops Gerth had to make for political reasons, it took them almost a month to reach the castle. As they neared the western end of the kingdom, Zoe got the feeling they were meeting more bands of armed men than she expected. She mentioned this to Gerth one evening as they strolled away from the camp in the deepening dusk.

He nodded. "We've had some trouble. Seems as though a bunch of Saxer's army didn't go home with the rest, but stayed here to pick up what they could. But I shouldn't need to tell you about that." He looked at her expectantly.

"How did you know?"

"There was a story came through at mid-winter about a little girl in the east who took on half a dozen of them, all by herself, with a staff. We thought it was a sign that you were thriving."

"That's ridiculous! There were only four of them. Varli took one with an arrow, and the villagers hanged one."

"So you only got two. With your staff?"

"They deserved it! They killed a friend of mine in the village, and who knows how many others!"

"All right, Zoe, I wasn't arguing. We were all very proud of you, as a matter of fact."

"Oh."

"Those are desperate men. Most of them are not real soldiers, just tavern brawlers. There is no other solution."

"So these patrols we see are looking for others? Surely there aren't that many left. This is the civilized part of the kingdom. There are few places for them to hide."

He kicked at a small stick in his path. "There has been other unrest as well. The more aggressive lords are pushing at their neighbours. We've had a few minor skirmishes between retainers and one full battle including all the forces both lords could muster. Several men killed, not a few injured and nothing proven. Stupid. Why does Barent let it happen?"

"Barent lets it happen?"

"Well, he hasn't done anything to stop it."

"He's the king. He must have something in mind." She looked anxiously up at Gerth. "He always has."

"I hope so. If he has, he didn't let me in on it. Just sent me out and told me to 'settle them down.' Some duty!"

"Gerth, you are so good at that. The lords I've seen so far sound very loyal. You're doing a fine job."

He smiled. "Thanks, Zoe. It's good when someone believes in you."

She wound her arm around his and squeezed it. "Of course I do. You make it easy!"

She couldn't tell properly in the dim light, but she could have sworn he was blushing. "Uh...really?"

She released his arm, then reached up and punched his shoulder. "Really." They walked on.

The next day they passed through another range of hills where, as usual, one of the quickly moving streams was being used to power a mill. This mill, unlike the ones they had passed before, was emitting a rhythmic thumping sound. Janitra was interested and when Gerth told him that this was a fulling mill, he requested more information.

"I'm not the miller. Maybe we should ask him."

"But Lord Gerth, a foreigner can't just walk in and bother him like that."

"Sure you can. He'll be flattered. Especially if I go too!"

The rest of the travellers watered their horses in the stream and lounged about on its banks while Gerth and Janitra went to talk. When they returned and the party took to the road again, Zoe noticed that Gerth and Janitra rode on side by side, their heads together. Intrigued, she pulled up beside them. They were deep in conversation and looked up blankly at her.

"What did you find in that mill worthy of such mental effort?"

Gerth raised his eyebrows at her interest. "It's what they need, back in your village. They have the wool and the fast water. All they need is a mill. They could double their output of cloth, maybe even triple it. Thus it would be economical for merchants to trade with them. I'm sure there are many other villages in the same situation."

"Sounds great. So what's the trouble?"

Janitra frowned. "It is not a simple matter, just to build a mill. Money is not difficult. I, myself, would be interested in a venture of this sort. But there are many factors to consider.

"First, as to the ownership of the mill. I am told a mill usually belongs to the lord in whose demesne it rests. We would need a special dispensation and the cooperation of Lord Turnhout. Also we must organize the operation: responsibilities, costs and the sharing of profits."

Zoe shook her head. "Well, you won't get much help in that respect from our legal system."

The merchant stared at her. "You know about this?"

"From my information, and I am, after all, the Royal Archivist," she tried a modest grin, "our laws are very weak in the area of business contracts, the exchange of money and especially the ownership of land and property. We simply have had no need of that sort of thing. It's something we had intended to bring up with Barent on our return."

"We?"

Zoe felt embarrassed. "Varli and I...well...we did a bit of reading over the winter, and quite a bit of thinking."

"What kind of reading did you do?"

When she explained the books she had brought with her, Lord Janitra was immediately interested.

"And these sources are with you now? We can look at them when we break for the noon meal? And what are the results of this thinking?"

Faced by the reality of a merchant prince of considerable experience, all the talk and planning that she and Varli had done over the winter seemed simple and foolish. What do we know, after all? "We...uh...we had a few general ideas, some theories, that's all."

"Aha! And now that I ask you to bring them out into the light of day, they suddenly seem pale and weak, and perhaps not so worthy as they did in the enthusiasm of the moment?"

She nodded her head glumly.

He laughed. "Of course they do. It is always so. But the ideas must come out in the day if they are to be more than dreams, must they not? You see yourselves as young and untutored, trying to think in a field with no one to guide you. Look at it another way. Who else in the kingdom is working on this serious matter? The right or wrong of your thoughts is unimportant; making a start is what counts. It puts you far ahead. It is noon. We must look at books and speak." He gave a whistling call, and Maksa, who was riding at the front of the column, turned his horse aside into a clearing. The rest followed and began to dismount.

Zoe watched all this, wondering if she would ever have enough self-confidence to wave her hand and expect twenty people to defer to her. He had chosen a scenic area, though; a small stream ran between mossy banks, with water-rounded boulders sticking up through the grass nearby. Janitra appropriated a group that was bunched together and gestured to Zoe to place her books on the largest.

Gerth wandered over, slapping the dust from his gloves. "A pleasant spot, my Lord, but you seem to be spreading your table for other than lunch."

Janitra swept his open hand above the books. "There are times, my Lord, when the mind and the soul must be taken care of before the hunger of the mere stomach can be considered. We will read and talk and snack the while, if time allows."

Gerth looked more closely at the books. "Would it be appropriate for a mere soldier to listen in?"

The older man raised his eyebrows, looking up at his companion. "I doubt if a mere soldier would find any of this interesting. However, a person such as the First Prince Ascending..."

"I take your point." Gerth leaned against one of the larger rocks. "Pray speak on; the House of Arlyn listens."

"Oh, no, my Lord. The House of Omanisa listens as well. It is our young hermits who bring us wisdom from the wilderness."

At this Zoe felt even more reticent. She looked helplessly at Varli, who had brought her the books from the pack animal. He looked pleased at the opportunity. She calmed herself as if before a battle, and began.

"Well, my Lords, we started with this volume, which documents legal decisions of past years..." It got easier as she went along. Once again she could feel the rightness of their findings. No one could fault their conclusion about the lack of consistent legal precedent upon which to judge business dealings.

She never did reach the end. As she got into the more theoretical side of their studies, both listeners began to ask questions and pose ideas of their own. Varli brought in his support and soon a full-blown discussion was under way.

A short time later, or so it seemed, they were distracted by the clearing of a throat. All looked up to see Tadeo standing over them, his arms full of food and drink, and a look on his face that the young sometimes get when they have their elders at a disadvantage. He said something in Kyabran, of which Zoe only caught a bit, but which made Janitra burst out laughing.

"Tell them Tadeo. You have the words."

The young fighter looked around shyly but firmly. "It is the job of the guard-of-life to protect the Master from all harm. Also that which he does to himself. Like hunger. Now you must move the books and eat. There is time for talk on the road."

Properly chastened and reminded of their empty stomachs, they complied, although the topic of conversation did not change. As Zoe had feared, the vast experience and knowledge of the merchant allowed him to see farther than they had on many points of the discussion and to find what seemed, in retrospect, to be obvious flaws in their plans. But he was impressed with their progress and said so.

"I have wished many times that the leaders of a kingdom I was opening trade with had made half the progress you two reveal on this issue. Lord Gerth, how receptive do you think King Barent will be to these ideas?"

"My uncle is known as a progressive thinker. It was his influence, even before he was king, that gave the local merchants their status on the council. I see no reason to expect any resistance, as long as the good of Petrella is kept in mind."

...and the talk ran on.

So with optimistic plans, good company and warm spring weather, Zoe once again entered Arlyn Castle.

30. STRANGER IN HER OWN HOME

It felt like coming home, covering that last busy stretch of road through fields where farmers were sowing the first seeds of spring. *Of course. This is my home. Has been for years. Well, I learned something, didn't I?* As they made their way through the crowd of drovers, tradesmen, messengers and the ever-present soldiers funnelling towards the main gates of the city, Zoe found her eyes drawn more and more to the castle, looming above it all in the hot midday sun. She and Varli rode with Patu between their horses; he was feeling nervous in the press. They grinned at each other as they passed under the shadow of the city wall and plunged into the narrow streets, drinking in the sounds, sights and smells.

Varli was enjoying himself. He was wearing a new robe, resplendent with Gerth's arms on it, and was looking quite dashing. The crowd flowed aside for Gerth's standard-bearer, and many exchanged greetings with the prince himself. Zoe had opted for her normal riding wear, but this was a wasted attempt at subtlety. Most citizens were casting curious glances at her companions, with their strange clothing and the huge armigerent in their midst. Varli loved it.

The night before, Gerth had come to Zoe, a bit worried. He had given his Squire the new robe, but had been disappointed at Varli's reaction. "Knowing the old Varli, I thought he'd be ecstatic over it. But he wasn't, you know. Oh, he was appreciative, but it didn't mean as much to him as I expected. Has he lost interest in being a Warlander?"

Zoe had laughed. "Not at all. But he begins to realize that there is a lot more to it than parading around in fancy clothes. Besides which, there weren't any mirrors handy!"

Now Varli looked over at Zoe and grinned again. "You might as well relax and enjoy it. No one is going to notice you in all

210

this resplendent company." He looked down at himself. "Especially with someone as beautiful as me to admire!"

Zoe reached down, snagged a clod of dirt from the wheel of a slow-moving farm cart she was passing and lobbed it at him. He ducked, and it disappeared into the crowd. He gave her a knowing smile and they rode on.

Everything looked the same but seemed different. For one thing, the city was smaller and shabbier than she had remembered. She chuckled at herself, recalling her reaction to the cottage when she first saw it again last summer.

But the major difference, which caused her no laughter, was the larger number of armed men in evidence. They met several troops of soldiers, both mounted and afoot, moving out of the city at regular intervals, fresh and clean, and passed others returning, travel-stained and weary, from their patrols. Men with weapons but wearing no specific livery strolled the streets and lounged in front of the taverns.

As this all sank in she started to watch the citizenry more closely. There was bustle – a lot of business going on – but little merriment, few smiling faces. She realized what else was missing. There were almost no children around. The usual street urchins were present, slipping through the crowds, eyes open for the main chance. But any other youngsters she saw were in the presence of several adults and sticking closely, at that.

"Varli, stop posing and open your eyes. I want a full report on the condition of the city tomorrow. Analyze it as if you were a stranger here. What's going on?"

Varli looked at her, then at Gerth's back, and shrugged. "Sure, why not? He can take care of the public for a while. I was getting bored with being gracious, anyway. It doesn't become me, I find."

In spite of his flippant words, Zoe could see him settle down to watching. After a while he glanced over at her and frowned, then raised his eyebrows. She held her palms up helplessly. He shook his head and went back to his observations, a grim expression on his face.

There was more than the usual number of men drilling on the parade ground in front of the castle gates. At the appearance of Gerth's standard they stopped as one and stood stiffly at attention until the party had passed. It was an impressive display of discipline. Looking up, Zoe could see extra sentries on the battlements, and she noticed that the mess of sheds, stalls, and general detritus that usually built up along the outside of the wall in peacetime had been cleared away.

Passing by a queue of merchants, servants and soldiers waiting to be checked in at the main gate, they entered the castle. All was bustle and business here as well, but to Zoe's trained eye it was a more disciplined vigour; the arrival of the First Prince Ascending caused only a minor eddy in the flow of the day. Refusing the hostler who offered to take Jobe, she gave instructions as to the disposition of her goods on the packhorses and slipped away to the Guides' Quarters to stable her pony and think.

The city contained all the evidence of a kingdom preparing for war. *Why have I heard nothing of it? Why hasn't Gerth said anything? Surely he must know!* And who would attack? Not the Inner Duchies, or Gerth never would have brought Varli back. Surely Barent had solidified his ties with Torey? If the Inari were about to invade, there would be no secret about it. Rawden again? Probably not. Lenient though the peace terms had been, he had been given no time to build up his resources yet. There was no power she could think of that they needed to defend themselves against.

She must talk to Barent about this. No, not Barent. He was the king now. He wouldn't have that much time for her. The Sivan, then. He would know, and he would tell her. She had to report to him anyway.

So she found Patu a stall next to Jobe and instructed him not to eat Ardu, the stable boy. Then, her livestock taken care of and her riding gear put away, she lugged her equipment over to her quarters.

It was strange, walking into her old rooms. They seemed so large and bare, compared to the cottage. She resolved to put up some decorations, of both the aesthetic and the useful variety. After stowing and tidying her belongings, she cleaned herself up and went off in search of food.

By this time it was mid-afternoon, and the only way she would get anything to eat was to fall back on her old habits and go on a kitchen foray. It occurred to her that she might also find Loreline there. When she strolled in she discovered not only Loreline but the Sivan as well, sitting over a cup of tea at one of the corner tables, deep in conversation.

"Well, I didn't expect you to take my advice so much to heart. I see it has paid off, though!"

The Sivan, as usual, looked knowing, although Loreline seemed flustered. "You didn't tell me Zoe was back!"

"Who says I knew she was back?"

The two women looked at each other, then back at him. "The day you don't know what's going on in the furthest, dirtiest corner of this castle will be the day they bury you."

Loreline laughed. "Even then, he could probably make a guess."

"Yes, everyone with something to hide will be celebrating."

"If you two have finished your morbid discussion of my early demise, perhaps we could offer Zoe a cup of tea, a few scraps to eat?"

Loreline jumped up with a guilty smile. "Yes sir. I forgot; the King's Archivist has returned, and I am her lowly assistant." She hurried off to talk to one of the cooks.

Zoe sat down in her vacated spot. "Well, she has certainly come along while I was away. I gather she has been of use?"

The Sivan's knowing look flitted across his face. "Not a touch jealous, are you?"

Before allowing the abrupt denial that sprang to her lips, Zoe remembered the incisive mind she confronted. "Yes, I suppose I am, a little. But more than that, I am pleased to see her doing well. Anyone with her ambition and tenacity deserves it. That's why I put her in touch with you."

"A good move. Input from one of her class has been invaluable – a point of view I had regarded too little in the past. She also has an insubordinate air which I find refreshing after all the toadying I deal with."

Zoe thought about the Loreline she knew. "Do you find her insubordinate?"

"Not at all. She just talks that way. Thinks that way, too. Little formal training, no set patterns of thought, no dogma. Very stimulating."

"I'm glad you feel that way. Varli and I have some very un-dogmatic ideas we have been working on."

"So the Hermits found their withdrawal from society to be enlightening?"

"Not you, too!"

"Oh, yes. That's what we have all been calling you. The Hermits. Also, in moments of levity, the Wise Ones of the Wilderness."

Zoe felt a pang of hurt. "We did a lot of serious thinking, you know!"

"I never doubted it. But the other was a convenient device. Used with a certain degree of envy, I might add. Who would not wish the opportunity to abandon the flow of his life for a while? I also thought it expedient to draw attention from your other motives."

By this time, Loreline was returning with fresh tea for all and a plate heaped with a variety of rather new-looking 'scraps.'

"It's all prepared for the banquet tonight." She set it in front of Zoe and slapped the Sivan's hand when he reached for a morsel. "Eat hearty, oh Master of the Archives, while I tell you of my progress."

"Progress?"

"Wait until you see how I've organized the Archives!"

"One shock at a time." She looked Loreline up and down. "I noticed that you weren't dressed for the kitchen. I thought it was your half-day off, or something."

"Oh, no. I don't work here much any more. Between what I do in the Archives and what the Sivan needs done, I am left with little time for kitchen work. Only when there's a big banquet or someone is sick."

"I see. Second surprise. What's the big banquet for?"

"What do you mean? The First Prince Ascending has just returned, in the company of a Lord of a foreign land. Of course there's a banquet. Don't eat too much right now; save a good appetite for later."

"Right. Now the last. What have you done to the Archives?"

Loreline laughed again, a fine, carefree sound. "Don't worry, Zoe. I didn't mess things up." Her voice dropped and its intensity increased. "It's so easy to find things now."

"How did you organize them?"

"Well, first there are different sections: laws, histories, medical, religious. Then, in each section, the books and papers are in alphabetical order."

"Alphabetical order? What's that?"

215

"By where the first letter of the name comes in the alphabet. Books are always organized that way. Didn't you know? Oh. I'm..."

"No, that's great, Loreline. I never had to deal with a lot of books like that. Just shows how right you are for the duties. Do you want to show me now? I'd like to see it. I'm going to be spending more time there, now, and it would help if the books I need are easier to find. Unless you two were busy...?"

The Sivan waved a lazy hand. "No, you go ahead. You want to see your precious room again." The hand fell with a sharp smack to the table. "But tomorrow morning is my time. You owe me eight months' report, young lady."

"But Sivan, there's a banquet tonight!"

He glowered. "I remember you the day after a banquet. I suppose you think it's ladylike to be 'indisposed' at the tail end of a late night. Well, we could start at noon. But be prepared to talk!" He rose and strode away, ignoring everyone around him in the busy kitchen.

Zoe watched him go, then stood, and the two women moved towards the stairs. "Is he upset with me?"

Loreline glanced down at her, amused. "Why would you think that?"

"Well...he's usually rather brusque, but for a moment there, I thought he looked a bit...well...hurt?"

Again that clear laugh rang out. "Zoe, he's been impossible for the past week. I couldn't figure out why. Now I realize that it was because he knew you were coming back."

"He knew a week ago?" Then she grinned. "Of course he did. Especially at the speed we were travelling. But why would that upset him? There was no danger. I doubt if he missed me much, with the upheaval of Alarid's death, and all. Besides, he had you, didn't he? You two are getting along pretty well."

"Oh, Zoe, are you jealous? Don't be, please! You must realize how much he thinks of you. He talked about you all the time you were away. He thinks of you like he would a daughter, you know. With me, it's different. I'm older, he didn't know me as a child and I'm," she ran a hand from her hip, up the side of her rather snug-fitting dress, ending in an open-handed shrug, "not so innocent, you know?"

"Loreline, you haven't...!"

"No, as it happens, we haven't. But would it bother you if we did?" Her head rose and she turned to stare at Zoe. "You aren't jealous, are you?"

"No, no, of course not, but he's so, well..." Again, the words failed her.

"Old? Ugly?" There was a dangerous tone entering the taller girl's voice.

Again, Zoe found herself backing down. "No, not ugly. I mean, I've known him so long. I couldn't say. But he's old enough..."

"...to be my father. Maybe. Just. I bet he's not much past forty-five. It's the weather and the scars that make him look older. Zoe, you look on him as a father-type; I don't. I see him as a very interesting man who can offer me something I've never had before. And he's so intelligent! Of course, I don't have to tell you that.

"I'm twenty-seven, you know. I was getting to the end of my time in the kitchen. I was holding out, trying to better myself, and I wasn't making much progress. After a few more years, I would have given up and got married to one of the stable hands, maybe a lead groom if I was lucky. But this is what I was looking for. For as long as it lasts." She looked down at her companion. "And I have you to thank for it. I'll never forget that."

Zoe squirmed. "Oh, share the credit. If you hadn't been who you are, I never could have given you the chance." She stopped on the landing outside the Archives and turned.

"Loreline, is this girl-talk?"

The other shook her head, confused. "What?"

"Girl-talk. You know. I'd be going off to somewhere like the practice field, and I used to see the kitchen girls, or the lords' daughters when they visited, sitting with their heads together, giggling. I thought that was girl-talk. It always seemed pretty silly to me. I knew the older ones were talking about the men. So this must be girl-talk?"

Loreline's head canted to one side, and she regarded Zoe as if in a new light. "Yes, I guess it is. And of course it's silly, some of it. You have to be silly sometimes, you know."

"Do you? I suppose so. I guess I never got in the habit."

"No, I guess you didn't. Maybe you should work on it. Anyway," she swirled around to face the door, her hair flying out, "here we are." She fished in her bodice for the key and opened the door. Again Zoe caught the flash of a round object on the chain, quickly gone again. "Do you want the key back?"

"No, I won't get in here again before tomorrow night, now. Do you think you could find another one by then?"

"No difficulty at all. You would be amazed at what I can do, now that I'm not a kitchen wench any more. Now," she swung the door wide and motioned grandly, "will His Majesty's Keeper of the Archives deign to enter her domain?"

31. BANQUET

The two spent a pleasant and productive afternoon in the Archives. True to her word, Loreline had organized things completely. What she had not mentioned was that she had spent considerable time in making the room comfortable. Since there could never be any fire because of the danger of an accident, she had found a well-worn but still serviceable carpet to warm the floor. To the usual hard wooden benches she had added two old but well-padded chairs. Zoe looked around her domain with a sense of welcome, and threw herself into learning how it was organized.

Much later, Zoe returned to her rooms with a few more books under her arm, ones she had wished for all winter. She couldn't wait to look at them, to try her new ideas against what they held.

It turned out she wasn't to get the chance, however. Varli showed up with a message. "His Majesty assumes you will attend the banquet tonight, and Lord Janitra requests that you wear your Master's robe and sit with him at the head table."

Zoe was intrigued. "Why would he do that?"

"No idea. That's all I was told. By Janitra's request."

She shrugged and moved to her pack. "I'd better get my robe out and brush it up. At least I washed it yesterday."

"Don't be too long. The grand entrance will be just after the sunset chime, which is any time now. I'm going to get changed, too. I'm serving Gerth tonight, of course."

They grinned at each other. "So the Hermits are getting a big welcome back to society, are they?"

Zoe sobered. "I wonder what kind of society we have come back to. Have you heard anything?"

"Nothing at all. It seems like Barent is preparing for war. He hasn't told anyone who he thinks might attack us."

"That leaves one other unpleasant possibility."

"Yes, I know. But Barent wouldn't attack anyone first." Varli's brow furrowed. "Would he?"

"I don't think so. I hope not. But apply the Orchard Pruner's Solution. Get rid of all the impossible ideas, and whatever is left, no matter how unlikely, is the right answer."

On that sombre note, they parted to prepare for the banquet.

She was just finishing up and ready to leave when there was a discreet tap on her door. It was soft but firm, different enough from the thumping used by most of her friends that she went over and opened the door instead of just calling a welcome. There stood Tadeo, dressed in what must be his finest: a robe similar in design to hers but of plain silk, soft leggings of the same material and a complex set of leather harness to hold his sword and dagger. His hair was tied up in a complicated braid, all pulled to the left, leaving the other side of his head and neck clear of adornment.

"My Lord Janitra has commanded me to come and prepare you for the banquet. May I be of help?"

"I don't know. I put my robe on as he requested. What's going on?"

The young guard-of-life smiled. "No idea. But Janitra says you must be like Master of the Robe from Kyabra. So I do head, yes?"

"What? Oh, my hair." She brushed a hand through her thick, dark hair, grown long over the winter. "I meant to get it cut when I got..."

"Oh, no, no, it is just getting right." He urged her back inside, and she sat down. "Must be long enough for the Braid." He ran his fingers through the heavy tresses, pulled them to the left side, and began to twist them deftly together. In a short time she had the same smooth right side, from crown to collarbone, and an even more intricate design of braids on the left.

"This is a special ceremonial arrangement, isn't it? Does it mean anything in particular?"

"Yes, most particular. It is the mark of honour for the fighter. It is his code. If his honour is gone, he will use the *gammal* on the neck, here, see?" He touched a point on her exposed throat where the pulse throbbed near the surface. "So the hair is pulled away to tell all he is willing. Also so not to make a mess."

"Oh." She ran a hand past her ear, feeling the strange bareness of it. "And I must follow this code of honour?"

"Yes, when you have taken the Oath. But in real, you have not taken the Oath, so you do not say you will follow the code. But you are Master anyway, because of birth and training." He finished complacently, "Some day you must take the Oath."

She fingered her throat again. "I suppose I must."

"You look very good, now. Now we go, yes?" He was looking at her strangely, a combination of sorrow and affection on his face.

"Is something wrong?"

"No, nothing wrong. I thought about my sister."

"You have a sister!"

"Four. Jaddie is one of them. She is young."

"Why are you sad?"

"I look at you and think of her. She is smaller, but the same. But she is not serious. She sings, she dances, she rides, she goes to parties. That is all. She will never wear the Robe."

"How old is she?"

"Sixteen."

"Tadeo, all sixteen-year-old girls are like that. Give her a chance!"

"Were you like that at sixteen?"

"No, but everyone tells me I'm too serious. You are also probably too serious. Come on, we're going to a big party. Let's not be too serious!"

"Not serious?" He frowned. "This is formal banquet. We must be serious."

"Fine. We'll be formal, but not serious." She smiled at him, and they glided off into the gathering dusk towards the central keep. It was strange to be walking with another fighter so close to her in size, dress and movement.

When they reached the doors of the main hall, the other Kyabrans were there, as well as many of the local nobility, all dressed in their formal best. Barent's steward was fussing around trying to get everyone in the proper order for the entrance.

Janitra was resplendent in a Master's robe that shimmered and glowed in the lantern light. Zoe looked down at her shabby garment and grimaced at the comparison. He noticed this and smiled.

"Do not worry, Master. My robe is my ceremonial best, never to be worn even in practice. It is much more honour for you to wear your grandfather's robe, earned twice over. Besides, there is not enough light for anyone to notice."

"Lord Janitra, why…?"

His upraised hand silenced her. "While to the people here, you are Zoe, a friend of many years, to me you are Zoysana Rochenan, Master of the Robe, and a noble of my land in your own right. When I am here, Barent does me honour by doing you honour." He smiled. "Besides, I am in this kingdom with a very small entourage. I see an opportunity to increase our numbers, and the merchant spirit in me cannot resist. There, the steward has everyone ordered to his liking. We will go in."

"But Barent is not here yet."

"I think he plays the host tonight, so he and his close family members will be seated when we enter. Come."

It felt so strange to be entering the hall with the visitors instead of sitting and watching the procession as she usually did. Her group was first, and stood just inside the open end of the U of the banquet table while the other guests moved to stand at their places.

When all were present the steward called out, in his 'official' voice, introducing them.

"Your Majesty, may I present Lord Janitra Omanisa, Merchant Lord of the ancient land of Kyabra, and his retainers."

Janitra stepped forward and bowed a perfect 'ambassador to foreign monarch.' Again Zoe was reminded of the amount of information a merchant needed to smooth his way in a strange realm.

She was pleased to see Barent rise from his chair in response and pass through the gap at the corner of the table to approach them. "I have long respected the Merchant Lords of Kyabra. They come of an ancient race, but do not fear new things and modern ways. I suspect you will be leading us into the future, once given the opportunity. Please be welcome, and make known to us your companions."

"Thank you, your highness. May I present my nephew and warranted guard-of-life Maksa Silabu, and my kinsman and guard-of-life, but unsponsored, Tadeo Priya." The two fighters gave their stiffest and most formal bows.

"You, too, are welcome, my Lords."

"And also, my kinswoman and fellow Master of the Robe, Zoysana Rochenan, who is of course known to you." The 'kinswoman' appellation was not precisely fiction. Janitra had explained to her on the road that almost all the noble families of Kyabra had become related through centuries of intertwining alliances. He had worked out, as near as possible from memory, that he and she could be third cousins by marriage, one generation removed.

Until this moment, Zoe had not been sure what response she should choose, so she took her cue from the situation. She was with the Kyabrans, dressed like them, and introduced as a Kyabran. She stepped closer to Barent and bowed, a very deep and respectful 'noble to foreign monarch.'

He stepped forward, and put both hands on her shoulders. Too quietly for anyone else to hear, he murmured, "So you are leaving me too, Zoe."

Her gaze flew up to his face. It was paler than usual. There were lines she had not seen before, and the easy smile seemed far away.

"Bar... your Majesty, I thought you would be proud!"

The smile, when it came, was slow and a touch bitter. "I suppose I am. But it is also sad to see you go."

"But I just got back! I'm not going anywhere!"

"Aren't you? But that's not exactly what I meant."

"Oh."

He turned her around, putting an arm across her shoulders, and spoke to the Kyabrans. "Come, my Lords. This is a joyous homecoming for several of our friends," his glance took in Gerth, with Varli standing behind him at the right of Barent's chair, "and we will celebrate accordingly."

He guided them around to their places, with Janitra at his left and Zoe immediately left again. Maksa sat beside her and Tadeo took his place behind Janitra's chair. As she sat down, Zoe leaned forward far enough to exchange a wink with Kenna, who was seated next to her son. When all were settled Barent himself sat, and the banquet began.

It was a fine meal, although not completely new to Zoe, as she had sampled the dishes earlier. She was impressed by

Tadeo's smoothness and style in serving; he was able to keep his lord cared for while seeing to her needs as well. At one point she leaned back as he reached forward to fill her goblet.

"Are you supposed to be serving me, too? I usually do for myself."

"Tonight is not usually. Tonight you are Master from Kyabra. I honour you, and so honour my Master."

"Whatever keeps us all happy. I'm sure you'll forget all about this on the practice field tomorrow."

He smiled serenely, standing up in his position, staring straight ahead. She reached back and gave him a sharp jab in the leg with her elbow. His face remained the same. She grinned and returned to her meal.

It was a typical formal banquet such as she had sat through many times. She always enjoyed them, but it was quite different, she found, to be a guest of honour. Whenever she looked around, smiling faces were turned her way. Anything she wanted was there before she knew she had a need. A small nagging thought arose that she had done nothing to deserve all this, but she squashed that idea and had another sip of the fine wine they served only to the head table.

When the serious eating and the meaningless speeches were over there was a less formal time before the entertainment started, when the guests felt free to stretch their legs and mingle. Zoe wandered around in a daze, accepting compliments from those she knew and gracious conversation from those she didn't. It was quite funny. One recently appointed and rather young ambassador commented on her unaccented speech and was so embarrassed when his companions put him in the picture. She managed a few words with Kenna, who was eager to hear all about her adventures and dropped a standing invitation to come and visit at any time during the next few days.

Alone for a moment, Zoe noticed the Sivan, still sitting in his usual place farther down the tables. A familiar figure was bending over him, removing his empty plate.

"Well, we do get around, don't we?"

Loreline straightened with a grimace. "I'm not sure that the servers have much over the kitchen staff, with all these heavy platters and things to lift. However, 'any difference is better than the same old job,' as Sarasha taught us. Are you having a good time, my Lady?"

"I suppose I am. A difference for me, too, I suppose. I'll try not to get used to it." She turned to the Sivan. "I could make it by the second chime tomorrow if I went home soon."

He looked up at Loreline with a 'see what I mean' gesture, then gave an exaggerated sigh. "Zoe, go have a good time. Please?"

A load was lifted from her. "Really?" *How could I ever think he isn't serious?* "All right. I will." She turned and moved briskly through the eddying crowd, swirling her robe as she moved, conscious of how graceful it made her appear. She looked around and found Gerth in conversation with several of the younger lords. *I'm a guest of honour. They should be glad to talk to me.* She nudged Varli aside from his position at Gerth's shoulder and slid into the banter.

32. HANGOVER

She was glad she had the whole morning for her recovery, as the entertainment and dancing went on until almost daylight. However, at the third chime she was standing at the familiar table, with the familiar hung-over feeling. The Sivan was polite enough not to notice. She wondered when it would be best to ask about Barent's plans. Not just now, she decided, as he looked up at her for a long, appraising moment. She realized, standing there, that it was the first time since Gerth had appeared at the cottage that she had spent any thought on her public image. The one she was supposed to be avoiding.

"So you cannot hide. Given that fact, what is your plan now?"

I should be thankful when the Devious One comes directly to the point. But her wit collapsed under the weight of her chagrin. "I don't have one any more, I suppose. I allowed circumstance and my own pleasure to guide me. I'm sorry, I just wasn't thinking."

He shook his head wearily. "No, do not apologize. It was shortsighted of me to try to be so simple." He raised a crooked forefinger:

"Moving water will be found,

By its ripple, by its sound."

"How could I expect to hide one whose talents could not help but become so obvious? But it would still be good to formulate a line of conduct."

Zoe thought, then laughed at the irony. "Line of conduct! Right now, I suspect all I have achieved is confusion. I have been so many different things I don't have them straight myself."

"Not bad, not bad. Confusion is a good tactic. Let us be charitable and assume it was intuitive. After all, one should always take one's liabilities and turn them into strengths. Now, how to take it farther...?"

Zoe thought back to her lessons so long ago. "Taken to the extreme, the logical extension of what I should do would be the opposite of what I was doing. Therefore, instead of trying to hide what I am, I should be trying to display what I am not. How would that work?"

The Sivan's head came up. "You have already done that, but with a twist. So far, all you have shown are facets of what you really are, but they are so disparate most observers would not believe them. Truth is the most devious of evasions, as Sarasha would say."

"Full of little quotes today, aren't we?"

"I know. I taught you that to fall back on old maxims is the first step in the long downward path to stagnation. I will correct myself." He looked up at her peevishly. "They still apply though. Sit down, and we shall talk."

Midday came and went, and the two of them hammered at it. Leaning back comfortably or forward in enthusiasm, stretching when their tortured bodies complained of postures held too long, they discussed the ramifications of her observations over the past weeks. When they had finished with the outlying districts and she had given her report of the town, she found her time and asked her question. He merely looked at her.

"You already know the answer."

"I do?"

"Apply the rule. Whatever fits is the correct answer, no matter how little you like it."

She leaned forward and spoke quietly. "So Barent plans to attack Rawden as soon as the roads are dry?"

"He hasn't said so."

"Not in words."

"Shall we discuss his loudest actions?"

"Sivan, you're just ducking the point."

"There is no need for me to tell you. I trained you well, if I say it as shouldn't."

"To speak honestly, you trained me, so I will see what you see."

He gestured with an open hand. "Honest, if not charitable."

"So are you going to let him?"

"Why should I stop him?"

"But it's wrong!"

"Wrong in what manner? No. Do not answer. Take the king's position. Tell me why he should attack."

The king. Barent. How strange to think of him that way.

"Barent sees it as correcting a mistake made by his brother. Also as protecting himself from an attack that is sure to come, sooner or later. To be honest, it will take the pressure off him here at home. Many of those who oppose his moves here will be too busy fighting the common enemy to worry about local events. They may not like his policies as a king, but they all know how successful he is as a general. Most would look on this war as an easy ride with rich pickings at the end. And surely Rawden's people would be better off with Barent as their ruler. It should also warn other rulers with similar ambitions and regain any status we lost by seeming to give in to Rawden last year." She shrugged. "That's all I can think of on short notice."

"Pretty convincing, even at that, don't you think?"

"But it's wrong!"

"Still didn't persuade yourself?"

"You don't attack first if you have any honour! Starting a war is a horrible thing! Do you have any idea what it's like?"

Her companion regarded the scars on his hands. "I have seen war in many of its guises. I assure you that a battle or two is the least fearsome of them all. But that is no argument to sway the Warlanders. It sounds too close to fear. I want something that will persuade."

"How about the most potent barrier to that sort of war? It comes down to honour. When you do the wrong thing, it returns to you. When you deal with people honourably, most will treat you the same way. Then you can bargain, deal, make treaties, maintain order in your kingdom and outside it. The moment you break the Codes, you allow others the right to do so and lose the support of those who are themselves honourable. Then your kingdom falls apart with dissent from within and attack from without."

"And do you see those symptoms here?"

"Yes, and I don't understand. Barent has done nothing dishonourable..." Her voice faded away, and she stared in horror at her old friend across the table. He did not move, did not show by any sign the truth of her suspicion. But neither did he deny it. He merely looked at her.

She covered her face with her hands. "Not Barent. He wouldn't. He couldn't. Alarid was his brother. He loved him!"

"No matter how little you like the answer." That was as far as he would go.

Her head came up. "Then why would there not be war." It was not a question. "The only barrier is one that does not exist, has not existed since he took the crown. The course has been set. There will be no turning back until the end."

"No turning back. And I fear what the end will be."

"Poor Alarid. Poor Barent."

The Sivan looked at her sharply. "Poor Barent? He is still alive. He is king. He does what he has always wished to do."

"You know better than that. Can you imagine how it has affected him? I could sense something last night. I couldn't get close to him, couldn't feel him. It's like he is shut away somewhere, and can't or won't come out. Poor Barent. And poor Petrella."

"There, I agree wholeheartedly."

There didn't seem to be much more to say. They sat in mutual, silent sorrow for a while, then Zoe rose slowly. "We can speak again. There's no point, right now."

He looked up in sympathy. "It's hard, Zoe. Come back and talk to me when you need to. No one else knows. Not for certain."

"Perhaps." She was feeling cynical. "Not anyone who dares speak it aloud, anyway."

"I couldn't decide whether to tell you." It was the first time she had ever heard that uncertain note in the Sivan's voice.

She smiled gently at him. "Don't worry. I know him too well; I would have figured it out sooner or later. This way is better – now I'm prepared."

Prepared? I've known all along, really. A lot of good that did me.

She sighed. "Well, that solves my loyalty problem, doesn't it?"

He shook his grizzled head. "It does gather your targets in one field. Of course, there's always the wider view."

Zoe sighed. "And I'm supposed to guess what that is?"

He looked at the table. "This is no time for learning games." His eyes met hers. "Your other loyalty could be to the realm. Not the to king – to the people of Petrella."

She tried that on for a while. "Then where is your loyalty? You're not Petrellan."

"That's right."

"So, unlike everyone else, you are free to give your loyalty where you choose, free to go where you choose."

"Just like you."

"What if we choose wrong?"

"What if we do? We must be very careful."

"We must."

They shared a moment of understanding. Then she turned and walked slowly out into the busy castle.

PART II: THE INNER SEA

Following someone else's code never replaces thinking for yourself.

King Barent I

Unless you make a mistake.

– Sarasha the Lame would have said that

33. A New Task

The following morning brought a summons to attend his Majesty near the second chime, 'at her leisure.' An interesting form of invitation, and a between-the-lines message reassuring her of her position. In her experience, few were asked to attend the king in their own good time. In order to avoid seeming to take advantage, she showed up, dressed in Petrellan formal court robes, precisely on the appointed chime. She was admitted with a smile and a slap on the shoulder from the eldest of the Guards at the door; a man who had been in Barent's retinue since she could remember.

Barent sat in the same chair where she had last seen his brother, and she was struck as never before by their similarities. Of course, part of it was the official costume, but still, there was something about the posture, the inclination of the head, the worn look. She wondered how much of this was inherited and what portion came from the demands of the job.

Several functionaries were grouped in front of him as she entered, and she was at a loss to know what was expected of her. Barent glanced up and waved 'just a moment,' then continued his discussion. She took a seat at a polite distance and waited. Although she couldn't hear the words, she found herself interpreting the conversation from the movements and postures of the participants.

There was some kind of argument within the group. First one side – two elderly men in dark robes – presented their case. Then the leader of the other side – younger and with a larger following – disparaged his opponents' ideas. He then started his own plea with considerable eloquence and dramatics. The two elders, disgusted, heard him through. Then both raised their voices and their hands in agonized protest. Their younger adversaries joined in.

Barent sat back, observing first one side then the other with an impassive face, but Zoe could tell he was near the end of his patience. Finally, he raised his hand. Immediate silence descended. His voice carried around the room.

"You add nothing to the weight of your argument by this display of poor manners. You," he turned to the two older men, "throw no fresh light on this matter. I have heard your tale many times.

"Your ideas," he fixed the younger leader with a stern gaze, "have merit, but they are poorly thought through and the consequences will be exactly what your opponents fear. I suggest..." she could hear the italics in that word, "... that you get together and develop a plan that has a chance of succeeding. Come back one quarter-month from now in full agreement, or do not come back at all." His voice grew harsh. "Ever!"

This last pronouncement lifted them all and swept them out the door in a bobbing of heads and a hurried shuffling of feet. When they had gone, Barent rested his head back against the throne and closed his eyes. Then, unmoving, he opened them again and looked over at Zoe, lifting one eyebrow, a move she had never managed to copy.

"As the farmer said while driving his pigs to a new pasture, 'It will be better when they get there, but they sure don't act like it'."

"And where are you driving them that is so much better?"

"Into the modern world. Many fail to realize that what has worked for the past three centuries may not be the optimum method. Others want to trash everything old and improvise." He shrugged. "As the farmer also said, 'It ain't easy'."

"This is a surprise?"

"To know it is one thing. To experience it is to enter a different realm of frustration."

The irony of his complaint was getting to Zoe, and she spoke more sharply than she intended. "In this life, you get what you deserve, I suppose."

He smoothed the hair above one ear with a weary hand. "I suppose you do. How about you? Are you getting what you deserve lately?"

She thought about it, taking his question seriously. "Mostly. With extras."

"Yes, Lord Janitra filled me in. I'm very happy for you. Come over here and let's hear your version." He got up and moved to the side of the room, where a small alcove contained a table and a few chairs. Zoe made tea for them both, then began her narrative.

It was almost like old times, except for the ornate nature of the furnishings and his robe. She told her story as she had been taught, with detailed observations, and he listened keenly, commenting now and then, stopping and backing her up at times to clarify her impressions. He already knew about the bandits and was mildly approving of a fulling mill in Karagata Valley, but he was more interested in Patu, his training and his origins.

"That was a poor move on someone's part, allowing an unmanageable beast loose and not warning us."

"I doubt if anyone on the other side even thought he might come over the pass at that time of year. As to the unmanageable part, I think he was very well trained, then sold to a fool."

"Yes, that was Janitra's opinion as well. I would like to see you work the creature. Do you think an armigerent could be useful? The stories I hear about yours are hardly creditable, compared to my knowledge of the breed."

"He's not like the poor wretches we keep around here, chained, controlled, browbeaten, because everyone is afraid they'll run amok some day." Zoe's back straightened. "He's never been tied since he came to me. He's an incredible hunting partner – follows directions perfectly, but has an amazing ability to make up his own mind if he needs to. You must see him. Do you want to come now?"

He shook his head slowly. "There's nothing I would rather do, but I am not the master of my own time any more. Having you come to visit is a pleasant break in my routine. You deserved the official recognition considering your new status, but I can spare little more time at the moment."

He sat straighter. "So we have your future to think of. Have you any plans?"

She put her mind into a matching frame. "Nothing specific. I have to catch up on my work in the Archives, and Varli and I have been working on a couple of ideas that I will present to you after we polish them."

"Sounds interesting. What else?"

"Before I left last summer, the Sivan and I were discussing areas where we could make progress in learning – new techniques, new ideas. Has he told you?"

"Often, and I admit he is persuasive. Is there any specific area you are thinking of delving into?"

"No, I hadn't considered it yet. I just got back, and my other research takes up a lot of my thoughts."

"Again, Janitra has mentioned them. Ideas of law and government, I gather? A noble intent, but perhaps impractical. I had more useable information in mind."

"You already had something in mind?"

"Well, I have a suggestion..."

Remembering Barent's last 'suggestion,' Zoe grinned. "Are you going to blast me out the door with it?"

Her humour fell flat. "I hope that won't be necessary. I was considering your new status with the Kyabrans. Now, there is an old society, some would say a dying one, with much knowledge that has been forgotten or never learned in this part of the world. I thought when Janitra returns home you would like to travel with him, visit the land of your grandfather and perhaps return to us with useful ideas. How does that sound?"

She hesitated, thinking furiously. "Well, there hasn't been time to unpack. Now you want me to get out on the road again? How soon? I have a lot to do here, and..."

He made an impatient gesture. "Well, think about it and let me know. You have a while; Janitra won't be leaving for a quarter or so. But at least leave me time to get someone else if you won't do it." He rose abruptly and returned to his throne, leaving her stumbling in his wake.

"Oh, I'll go if you want, I need time to get used to the idea, that's all."

He seated himself and looked at the main door, where his steward was awaiting his signal. "Fine. We'll see you at supper, then." Like a mask had fallen over his face, he was the king again and the next supplicant approached the throne.

Zoe stood, feeling out of place, then turned and slipped out of the receiving room by the servants' door.

* * *

The following days were frenetic. Now that she was leaving again so soon, her list of projects to accomplish in her remaining time grew immense.

The main task she had planned, which she now had to turn over to Loreline, was the cataloguing of the Archives. Of all she was leaving behind, this was the one she regretted the most.

238

She had been looking forward to long hours immersed in her treasures, learning from them, sorting them, organizing them so others could learn. In spite of her rushed schedule, she allowed herself a part of every morning to this task.

It was during one of these work sessions that she found an interesting document. It was not bound in book form, but was rather a set of loose, unevenly shaped parchment pages tied up with an old leather thong. What drew her attention was the depiction of a familiar circle on the first page. When she opened it, she discovered a treatise on various religious beliefs, including the Kyabran Followers of the Lady. She slipped it into her growing pile of books to take with her.

That night before bed she took the package out and examined the pages. The first group selected for dissection was the very one she was interested in – the sect whose symbol was the mandala. She learned that it was a recent (the past two hundred years) offshoot of the Kyabran worship of the Lady. The main change seemed to be a concentration of Her in the Protector guise, with a stronger accent on its aggressive nature. For their symbol, these worshippers had taken the Wheel of Life, focusing on the reincarnative aspect of it. This philosophy made for fearless fighters, because according to the author of the tract, they all believed that the way to return to earth quickly and with higher status than the present incarnation was to die in the service of the Lady.

She could also see the pattern: a new, virile people, adapting the religion of an older society and choosing those aspects of it that most suited their own ideals.

She was disappointed in the rest of the tract, as it gave her no useful knowledge. In the end, she decided to return it to the Archives after one more glance through the important part and a closer perusal of the diagram. It was a poor representation and very old, but she could see a wheel, complete with hub and spokes. The lower half seemed darker, as if dipped in something corrosive, and the figures in that section, while less distinct, seemed to be twisted with agony. Those on the upper, lighter, half were clearer and happier. Satisfied that she had learned what she could, she blew out the lamp and went to sleep.

* * *

The next morning, Loreline came to open the Archives door as usual. Just as she was putting the key back Zoe stopped her and, reaching out, extracted the rest of the chain from her blouse. The mandala was very similar to the one on the parchment, but quite a work of art: cleanly sculpted to a fine degree of detail. She didn't say anything; she glanced at it then smiled and allowed her friend to tuck it away. They continued into the Archives and no more was said on the subject.

The cataloguing made much better progress than her legal project. For one thing, Varli was never around. With Alarid's departure, Varli's father had warmed towards Petrella, and Varli's investiture as Gerth's squire had been approved. Now he and Gerth were caught up in preparing for the reception of some dignitaries from the Inner Duchies who were taking the opportunity of the now-dry roads to pay their respects to the new king. She found the lack of progress frustrating, but at least there was one advantage. Lord Janitra had decided that he could not miss the opportunity to make contact with representatives of so many other domains, so he had delayed their departure an extra quarter. This took the pressure off Zoe and allowed her to make a thorough search in order to select the books for her trip. Travelling on tour with a dignitary and trader was going to present some advantages, at least. He had plenty of packhorses.

Even when she went back to see the Sivan, he was busy. A familiar figure was perched on her usual chair, and a lute-shaped case leaned against a stack of parchment in a corner.

Two leathery faces swung towards her as she hesitated in the doorway.

"Ah, how fortunate. The very lady we spoke of."

Zoe looked at the balladeer askance. "When Solonstan speaks of a person, that person has good reason to fear for her reputation."

"Ah, no, my Lady. Certainly not. Not in private, that is." A wicked smile flickered. "Solonstan is not the type to speak ill behind one's back."

The Sivan mirrored the expression. "Not when he does it so well in public."

"So if you weren't trading gossip about me, how did I enter your discussion?"

They looked at each other, then the Sivan shrugged. "Your forthcoming trip to Kyabra. It has been many decades since one of us has made that journey. The Kyabrans of recent years have not been overjoyed to receive 'barbarian visitors.' Your grandfather's time here was a great boon to us; it was the first access to the knowledge of the Older Races we had gained in over a century."

"Yes, it was so unfortunate that he refused to come to Court and insisted on spending his life in the backwater he chose. No offence to your maternal heritage, my Lady."

"None taken, my Lord Balladeer. So what has changed?"

The Sivan gestured towards her. "You, for one thing. There has never been one of us who would be accepted at such a high level in their court. Janitra Omanisa and his like for another. There seems to be a fresh current flowing in their stagnant river: these traders who now travel the land with goods and knowledge to sell. Oh, he is much too gracious to ask money for his information, but he is creating a store of good will, of benefit to him in the long run. And now he has offered to take you back to his country. An unprecedented opportunity, and

241

one that must be planned carefully in order to squeeze the last drop of advantage from it."

She looked at the two of them, staring innocently at her. "And when had you planned to give me my itinerary, once you had plotted it?"

Both raised their hands in protest. It was comical, yet held a touch of irony for her.

"You intended to tell me right away, of course. And now you are surprised at yourselves to realize that you forgot to include me in the planning, right? And you are ever so sorry? And now that you realize that I have grown up and have my own opinions and priorities, it will never happen again, right?"

They both nodded.

"Of course. And we can even all pretend to believe it. Your gracious apology is most graciously accepted. Now," she reached out her foot and hooked another chair over to the table, "if the flagellation ceremony is over, may we get down to work?"

34. LORDS OF THE INNER DUCHIES

The arrival of the ambassadors was diverting, at least, although Zoe considered all the panoply to be above and beyond what was required. Two days of parades, speeches, receptions, and polite socializing. She was sure that there had never been such a dusting off of copies of the Code, such concern with proprieties. The gentry of Petrella were determined to show those of the civilized Inner Duchies that there were no social amenities lacking out on the 'frontier.'

Zoe was pleased to be pressed into Janitra's entourage again. As a 'foreign dignitary,' she had a certain amount of latitude in what she attended and what she did not. She also had a great deal of fun letting people make mistakes over her. Always impeccably polite and correct, she allowed the unperceptive to label her as they chose and never disillusioned them.

But the most fun of all was watching Varli. His father had not sent his own envoy, deciding that it was about time his son earned his future position. Instead, he had sent a pack train with an ostentatious amount of giftery and several advisors to 'assist' his son in the negotiations and maneuverings that were sure to arise.

The first day's work for this new team was not the picture of polish and precision. The 'head nursemaid,' as Varli called him, had come with a rather exaggerated opinion of his own importance in the scheme. He was quite taken aback when he tried to take over Varli's itinerary and prerogatives. Instead of the callow boy he remembered he was astonished, and not especially pleased, to find an accomplished and strong-minded young noble who was not only on easy terms with the highest levels of the Court and its distinguished visitors, but who also had a propensity for slipping off to the training field with who-knows-what ruffians, soldiers, and animals of all sorts, taking part in all types of dangerous tricks and scuffles.

He only tried to remonstrate with his master once before it sank in that it truly was his master he was talking to. Zoe was there to witness it.

Varli had been enjoying his new status with his peers. It didn't do him any harm in their eyes to be seen practising with the Kyabran guards-of-life, who carried an exalted reputation with the squires because of their competence and exotic techniques. The final touch was his demonstration with the 'New Beast,' as they were calling Patu. Varli and Zoe had shown up at mid-morning, intending to finish their workout before the heat of day got serious. At first Patu had been his usual lazy self, lolling in the shade and paying little attention, as if their antics were beneath him.

However, when they brought out the quarterstaves his interest perked up. He still found the sticks frightening and was always more alert when they were being waved around. Zoe and Varli worked hard at it for a while, and Zoe was impressed at how well Varli was progressing. In fact, she was so busy planning the next stage of his training that she lost concentration and, tripping over a tussock of grass, landed on her back. At once Patu was on his feet with a questioning and not-too-friendly "Whuff!"

Zoe laughed and called him over. "Thanks for the concern, but I got just what I deserved." She ruffled his mane and looked into his eyes, so close to level with hers. "Now that you're here, do you want to play?" The answer seemed to be affirmative, so she signalled subtly to him. "Varli thinks he's so smart, why don't you go take his stick away?"

The armigerent dove at Varli, sheering away when he found the boy's staff at the ready. He backed off then rushed again, only a feint this time, stopping just outside stick range. He lowered his chest, forepaws spread in the herding position, ready to pounce in either direction. As Varli stood in front of him, his stick weaving in a complex series of feints, the half-open muzzle followed defensively, poised to snatch if the stick should come within reach.

While this stalemate went on, several others on the field broke off their own training and sauntered over to watch. Included were a few of the other squires, their numbers swelled by friends who had come to Petrella with the dignitaries. There were also more soldiers than usual, as many of the professionals who were part of the procession were catching up on the latest techniques with their counterparts from the castle.

Last to show up was Varli's 'nursemaid', who came puffing up, only to gasp in horror at what he saw. His cry of censure distracted Varli just long enough for Patu to move. Ducking past the dangerous steel tip, he lunged towards his adversary's throat. Met by a desperate push with the centre of the staff, he turned his head aside and threw the power of his huge shoulder against Varli's hip and chest. As the boy went down, the animal grabbed the staff and removed it with a simple twist, spun away and stalked over to Zoe, holding his trophy up for praise.

Varli was not finished yet. "Give that back, you monster!" He dove for one end of the staff.

Mistake.

Patu turned his head to look, and the staff swung in a short arc, catching Varli in the chest. Breath taken, he still held on as the armigerent tossed him bodily like a limp rag, his feet finding no purchase at all. Seeing that this was doing him no good, he let go of the staff and closed with the animal. Reaching under and grabbing the opposite front leg as Zoe had shown him months ago, he strained to upset his opponent.

No movement.

The crowd around began to chuckle. Grunting fiercely, Varli tried again, but only succeeded in forcing Patu to widen his stance. The watchers roared.

Giving up, Varli stood. Then he grabbed Patu by the mane and shook. "You!"

A great brown eye rolled back to look at him.

"Give that back!"

No reaction. He shook harder. "Give it back, you big bully!"

Patu glanced towards Zoe, who gave the signal. The armigerent sighed and released. It had been such fun.

"Thank you so much." Varli bowed deeply to his opponent. The armigerent lowered his head in response. Several members of the audience doubled over in laughter. Varli slapped Patu on the shoulder and turned to them. "Anyone else want to try?" There was a general good-natured refusal. He nodded slowly and smiled.

One of the visiting mercenaries stepped forward. "It looks like he's sort of a friend of yours. How do I know he'll be a friend of mine?"

Varli gave an evil grin. "Good point. You don't. But I can assure you that he's under perfect control." He canted his head in Zoe's direction.

At that the group pressed closer with questions and comments. Zoe had a moment to notice Varli walking stiffly over to his 'nursemaid', the humour gone from his face.

"If that had been a real danger there, your interference could have cost me a great deal more than a thump on the ground. I would prefer it if you would return to your quarters. Later on we will speak of your role at this gathering."

He turned back and gave Zoe a wink, dusting his hands ostentatiously, but out of the other's sight.

Then another soldier was talking, and Zoe's interest snapped to him. "We got a couple of those back in Falticeni. Not that big, but look about the same. Not trained like that, though. There used to be three, but one disappeared."

There was stillness in the crowd.

"What do you mean, disappeared?"

"I dunno. It wasn't any use - too wild. They couldn't train it good enough, and you know how dangerous they are if they're let loose too much." He paused and glanced sideways at Zoe. "Usually, anyways. Whatever, after a while that one wasn't around any more. I guess they killed it or sold it or somethin'."

Zoe was severe. "I hope so. I hope it didn't get free." She stared at the man. "I hope an unruly armigerent didn't get away and nobody was told about it."

There were murmurs of agreement in the crowd, and the soldier eased himself backward and faded away. The questions and entreaties started up again, and Zoe felt compelled to vindicate Patu's training by a further demonstration.

After they had run through their paces, Zoe reiterated Varli's offer. "I don't suggest you try the staff against him. He doesn't like sticks, and with a stranger he might not consider it a game. But he enjoys working against a sword. Only a practice sword, of course. Anyone want to try?"

The soldier who had originally spoken to Varli stepped forward. "Sure, I guess. He seems harmless enough...I mean, well, not exactly harmless..."

Zoe laughed and handed him a wooden sword. "Go ahead. Don't worry, he won't hurt you."

The man bristled. "I ain't afraida gettin' hurt!"

"Sorry. Let me try again. Don't worry. You won't hurt him."

The soldier regarded the large animal pacing in front of him. "My Lady, are you tryin' to help, here, or not?"

247

The crowd chuckled, then settled down to watch the match with interest. It didn't last long. Upon Zoe's signal to stand guard, Patu faced this new opponent in a different defensive position. The man feinted a few times. As with the staff, Patu reacted to each move with a slight movement of his head, to meet the threat with bared teeth. Finally, the soldier shrugged and pulled his arm back for a longer swing. Before the sword started forward the armigerent leapt, and the swing brought the soldier's forearm into his gaping mouth. The man froze, and the two stood there, trying to decide what to do. Then both pairs of eyes turned to Zoe.

"Okay, boys, that's enough!" She gave Patu the almost-invisible signal to release. The soldier stepped back, rubbing his arm, a shocked look on his face. "He sure has good control over his bite. I hardly felt that. For a moment, I was wonderin' if I was goin' to lose my arm!"

One of the other soldiers guffawed. "Yeah, we was all fixin' to start callin' ya 'Lefty' and then he let go!"

"I don't see you standin' out here, wantin' to try!"

"No, no, that's fine. You did real good. We don't mind just watchin', do we boys?" There was a general chorus of agreement from the others.

Zoe had made her point, but she made one more comment before she departed. "I've seen him carry a month-old lamb in his mouth, and it just stood there and looked at him when he put it down. It wasn't bothered at all. I've also seen him catch a full-sized wild mountain ram and break its neck with one snap. He's in control, all right."

The soldier grinned. "Yeah, well a friend of his is a friend of mine, my Lady. Thanks for the lesson!"

"It was a pleasure. Do the gentleman honour, Patu."

The armigerent inclined his head towards the soldier as he had to Varli, then turned to his mistress, and they walked away together, leaving their audience chortling.

Zoe was feeling pleased with herself. She and Varli were exchanging notes about the morning's events when a messenger arrived, breathless, to request her attendance on his Majesty, 'at once.' She was to bring Patu with her.

This was a different sort of summons. She looked at Varli in alarm.

"What's up now?"

He shrugged, equally mystified, and they hurried to the stables to retrieve the armigerent.

Patu was pleased to be sought out again so soon and frisked around them playfully as they crossed the bailey. For all his size, he was still such a puppy, and she felt especially protective of him. *What could have gone wrong?*

35. A MATTER OF IDENTITY

There was a considerable crowd in the main hall, and Barent was waiting for them there. She brought Patu to her side and approached. Uncertain as to her reception, she bowed formally, and signalled Patu to do likewise. A chuckle ran through the crowd. Barent was suppressing a smile, and a wave of relief rushed through her.

"Well, Lady Zoysana, I had looked forward to seeing your armigerent, but not under these circumstances. It seems the ownership of the creature is in question."

"I never hid that from anyone, Sire. I suppose the story is well known around the castle by now. I don't know who owned him."

"Well, I do!" An overdressed, medium-sized man with a dark, broad face shouldered to the front. "He's mine, your Majesty. I'm sure of it. I bought three of them from a Kyabran trader last fall. All three looked just like him. That one was a real terror. Untrainable."

"Lady Zoysana of Kyabra, may I present Lord Jaraba of Falticeni? He seems to think that this is his armigerent. I'm not sure how he thinks it got to you."

Zoe looked around. "We can't prove whose he is..."

"Oh, it's quite simple." Eyes turned to where Lord Janitra stood beside Patu, a hand on his ruff. "Your Majesty, armigerents have been bred and trained in my land for centuries. If this gentleman," he flicked a hand in the general direction of Jaraba, "truly bought him from one of my countrymen, he is marked for identification."

"And where do we find this mark?"

"Just inside the right front foreleg on the chest where the hair is thinnest. It will be a series of tiny scars in a pattern."

"Thank you, Lord Omanisa. My own handlers are here. Perhaps they can assist us."

Two leather-dressed men hesitated forward. "It's true, your Majesty. We can go and get our ropes right away."

"Ropes?"

Janitra smiled. "It is usual to rope the armigerent down securely before checking the ownership. That is one reason the marks are placed thus. It is no easy chore to meddle with them."

Barent raised an eyebrow at Zoe. "Ropes?"

She grinned weakly and shook her head. Reaching across Patu's back where he sat, she patted his side. Immediately, he lay down and rolled over to have his ribs scratched. Heads bent over to stare. He flopped to his side, staring around, his lip quivering. The crowd slid back and Zoe, with a reproving glare at them, motioned Patu to roll over on his back again. This time only Janitra bent over the animal. Placing one hand comfortingly along Patu's cheek, he used the other to search through the hair in the appropriate spot. Then he made an exclamation and searched over a wider area. Straightening up, he motioned to Barent's handlers.

"Take a look at that and tell me what you see."

The braver of the two crept forward, touched the indicated spot. Then he, too, searched through the hair all over Patu's chest.

"Well?"

"There's a scar here, your Majesty. But it's a great long one, and it covers the whole area."

"A large scar?"

Zoe, looking grim, rolled Patu onto his side and gestured. "Like this one?"

The trainer lost his fear of the animal in his curiosity. He started looking all over Patu's back and side. Finally, he looked up at Barent, his eyes angry. "There are many scars, Sire."

Zoe felt a prompt wouldn't hurt "What would you say made them?"

"Probably a heavy stick, my Lady."

"And the ones on the chest?"

The trainer looked angrier still. "Stick again, my Lady. But the animal must have been on his back when it happened. Either in the submissive position or tied down." He turned to the king. "Whichever way, your Majesty, this animal has been cruelly beaten. And it was very young at the time."

Barent did not react. "I see. And now no one can say who the animal belongs to?"

"No, Sire. The markings are obliterated. It was a heavy blow, and the flesh was opened over the rib. It has healed with a rough scar." The trainer looked to Janitra and received a confirming nod. "But if I may say so, Sire," it all came out in a rush, "whoever did this doesn't deserve to own one of these animals, especially a fine one like this. It's a miracle he isn't completely unmanageable." He looked defiantly at Lord Jaraba, then collected himself and bobbed his head in guilt to Barent. "Sorry, Sire, I didn't mean..."

Barent scowled. "Yes, you meant every word, and it does you credit. I couldn't agree more. A person who would beat any creature like that and then let such a terror loose on the countryside without warning anyone, or tracking it down, deserves much more than the loss of the animal." He regarded the assembled nobles, his glare reminding them that this was one of the fiercest fighters and most successful generals in this rugged outland. There was a subtle shrinking back: partly from Barent, but mostly from Lord Jaraba.

252

Then Barent smiled sweetly, which did nothing to reassure anyone. "However, due to that act of cruelty, there is no way of determining ownership now, so I suggest that the present owner, who has such excellent control over the animal, should continue in that role. Are there any comments?"

The smile faded slightly. There was a great deal of silence in the echoing hall. "Good. I take it we are in agreement." His smile became more genuine. "That is a good thing, because I wonder how anyone would ever manage to retrieve him, no matter what I said about it!" The tension eased in a rustle of clothing as breathing resumed.

"Lady Zoysana, Lord Omanisa, since I see you conveniently together at the moment, could I speak to you both?"

He led the way into his receiving room, leaving the growing murmur of the crowd behind. As they entered, Patu moved into his guarding stance outside. Zoe hoped no one would want to come in. When the steward had shut the door, Barent relaxed and gave a whoop of a laugh. He spun around.

"Well, we certainly gave it to him, didn't we? I've been wanting to slap that bastard down ever since he got here. Says he's part Kyabran, and has been lording it over us every chance he gets. I can't get any agreement on anything unless it's one of his ideas." He turned to Janitra. "Is it possible? Could he really be part Kyabran?"

Janitra smiled. "Why shouldn't he be? He looks it. I am flattered that anyone would think that Kyabran blood is anything special. We have our murderers, thieves, and animal-beaters, just like any other race. I suppose even an armigerent could breed with a common cur. I wouldn't worry about Lord Jaraba. You put him in his place without even mentioning his name. His credibility, especially with those who consider themselves more civilized, is gone. A very subtle piece of work."

Barent's laughter burst out. "Me! Called subtle? And by a member of an Older Race. I wish you had said that with those cultivated milksops out there listening. They think I'm only one step away from the barbarians across the Barrier, you know."

"So what is wrong with that? You are. But then, so are they."

All three laughed at that, and Barent motioned them to sit while he poured wine. When the laughter had subsided, he turned serious.

"Well, it was a good time, and we straightened out the ownership of Patu to our advantage. Now, to less entertaining topics. Lord Janitra, are you leaving soon?"

"Yes, Sire, I believe I have almost finished my business. I am disappointed with the representatives of the Inner Duchies. Closer as they are to my land, as yet they seem unaware of the realities of modern trade. I must consolidate my achievements and try again in a few years."

"You will not be shocked to find me tearless at this situation. Their loss will be to our advantage."

"Yes, I foresee a good deal of trade with your people. When the Duchies do finally join the flow of the modern world, your kingdom will be far ahead in trading technique and mechanical knowledge."

"I hope so, and that is what I wanted to speak to both of you about. Lord Janitra, I want to be sure that you treat Zoysana as my special envoy, to be given any information you would give me, to be offered any business opportunity you would offer to me. She is entrusted with the power to make any commitments of a trading nature that she deems appropriate for my kingdom. Is this clear?"

"It is a serious responsibility to place on one so young."

"Perhaps, and I place this trust also in you. It is in your best interest to ensure that she makes no mistakes. I see you as a far-thinking man, and in the long run you will benefit more by dealing fairly with her. Beside this, I see you as a strange combination, at least in this part of the world: a trader with integrity. I would deal with your kind of people. I would send my most prized possession in your safekeeping and still sleep easy."

Janitra held up a restraining hand. "I do not promise that her task will be easy." He turned to Zoe. "You saw how I reacted when I first met you. And I was only being careful. There will be many who see you as an abomination to the purity of their blood." He tossed that idea aside with a gesture. "Those people are not of my faction, and you have no obligation to deal with them. But they are there, and some who are not so bad, but unpleasant all the same. I will protect you all I can, but…"

"But if I need protecting, then I shouldn't be taking on this duty. Lord Omanisa, I heard you say of Tadeo that he should look within himself for the strength that is there. Apply that to me. I have learned recently that loyalty to an outside entity is not enough. My real strength must come from my own soul."

She glanced at Barent. "I'm sorry, your Majesty, if that makes it sound as if I am less loyal."

The king laughed. "That is one fact I know I can depend on. Your loyalty."

He faced Janitra, his body straightening as if he were making a formal proclamation. "It is an unpleasant world we live in, especially those of us who hold the reins of power. Trust is not something that comes easily at court. One thing I am sure of. Half Kyabran or no, Zoe will do what is best for me and best for Petrella. There are few of the aged, the wise, or the experienced of whom I could say that."

Zoe didn't know where to look. It was so strange to have Barent talking about her as if she wasn't present, even when what he said was complimentary.

He looked at her as she squirmed, then he smiled: the same old smile he used to have. "Ah, Zoe. Too modest as usual. And where does it send you? To the far reaches of the land. I wish you good travelling. I am sorry I did not get to see your fine beast in action, but I have no doubt he will be a good companion." He sobered. "These are not good times, my friends, and I fear there will be worse before we are much older. First, I must whip these 'civilized' lords into shape; then I will deal with those in my own kingdom who would hold me back. I wish...but no. There comes a time when the deeds are done, and to try to return to an old way is as difficult as forging onward to a new one. The flood of time is moving us forward, and I am the last one who would want to turn back."

He gave his head a quick shake. "But here I am maundering along, and you with arrangements to make. I would not rush you away, but I will not keep you one moment longer than you wish to stay. Lord Janitra, I hope to see you again soon. Take care of my Zoe. If she needs it."

He turned and caught her up off the floor and held her tightly, then set her down and looked closely at her. "You are so hard. You are not the little girl I found in the forest, are you?"

She blinked a few times, tried to smile. "That's what I found out when I went back. I'm not that little girl any more. Then he," a shrug towards Janitra, "came along and told me I was that girl, more than I thought. So I'm still not too sure. But you are right in one respect. I will do the best for you and for Petrella." It was a pledge. She knew as she said it that she would fulfill it, even to her death. Melodramatic as it sounded, that was how she felt at that moment. She tried to hold the feeling, remember it clearly. Some time in the future, she might need it.

"I will see you off officially when you leave, but for now, this is our real farewell." Barent grasped Janitra's forearm, then gathered Zoe in another hug, grimacing as she returned it firmly. Then he laughed and led the way to the door. "I wonder why the steward hasn't been in three or four times bothering me. Don't tell me he has decided to learn sensitivity...Oh."

256

He swung the door open, to reveal an interesting tableau. Patu was sitting, his back to them, the steward dancing back and forth in front while two of Barent's Guard looked on in humour.

"He wouldn't let me in, your Majesty. I didn't know what to do..."

"You did just right, Steward." Barent laughed, and heads turned towards them. Slapping Zoe on the shoulder, he steered her towards Patu. "Now if my Lady's friend will let us out, we all have work to do." Not waiting for her to move, he strode easily past Patu and out into the hall.

36. A Promise

For her final evening at court, she doffed her Kyabran guise and sat at the side table with the Sivan. They were attended by Loreline, who stood close by and, while serving only her friends, partook of their meal and their conversation. In all, the three had a great time in the fashion that suited them best: observing the actions of those on parade and discussing each one's motivation. The Sivan's capacious knowledge afforded them many interesting perspectives: a well-dressed young lord from a small Dukedom who had ridden in with a five-man entourage, caparisoned like his soldiers, as the one formal outfit was all he could afford; various older, more respectable lords whose conduct behind closed doors was anything but respectable; the Sivan knew them all, and his two young protégés enjoyed the full benefit of his acerbic analysis. Even now he couldn't help holding class. Behind this jollity was a purpose; they might find such knowledge useful in the future. With this in mind, Zoe drank less wine and watched and listened more.

When the banquet had reached the stage where everyone was free to pursue his or her own entertainment, a familiar page touched Zoe's arm.

"My Lady would speak with you, had you the time."

She looked up to the head table and saw Kenna's eyes on her. She glanced back at the Sivan, deep in conversation with Loreline, who was leaning over him, her hair brushing his neck. *They have no need for my company.* Tipping her hand to Kenna, she turned back to give the boy a formal acceptance. Then she looked up to see Kenna already paying her respects to the other main guests. By the time Zoe had made her own farewells she matched Kenna's exit, and they walked up to the royal apartments together.

"So you are off on a new adventure, Zoe. Quite the opposite direction, this time."

"As opposite as it could be, I suppose. Last time, I was running to the wilderness. Now I am sent to the centre of civilization."

"And in considerably different company."

"Oh, I don't know. My companion last time was a lord in his own land, as well."

"But this time you are not so likely to be driven mad by your comrade's sense of humour."

Zoe smiled. "Varli does get easier as he grows up."

Kenna looked down over her shoulder as she entered the door that the Guard held for her. "So do you, my dear."

Zoe stopped in the doorway, mouth open.

Kenna laughed. "Do come in. Unless you want to tell Ellic, there, all about it."

Zoe grinned an apology to the Guard and stepped through so he could close the door. Then she turned to Kenna, who had by this time arranged herself in a comfortable chair beside the small fire that kept the chill of the stone away. "What do you mean, easier? I was never difficult!"

"Were you not? I seem to remember a wild little thing who could turn on perfect manners, but only when she had a mind to. One who could dump any of the pageboys in a heap and didn't hesitate to when the occasion arose. Boys being what they are, the occasion arose frequently until they learned better. A good thing they did; you didn't. You just moved up to the squires."

Zoe sat down, staring at the fire. She had forgotten those first months at the castle.

"Up until that point, you were fine. But then you became upset, because the squires wanted nothing to do with you.

They knew better. There was no credit to be gained by bullying you – you were too small and too well connected. There was all sorts of credit to be lost if you beat them, again you being too small. Word had already travelled from the poor pages. So there you were, with no one to fight. Oh you were not easy, in those days."

"But Gerth was there."

"Yes. I am still not sure it was the best thing for him, bringing him back when his time as a page was over. But it was good for you."

"I remember. He didn't care how big I was. He would train with anyone and everyone. And when I beat him, he just dug in and worked at it until he could beat me."

"You were quite a pair. At least you got him to learn the Codes."

"I did?"

"Oh, very much so. He had no interest in anything that didn't relate to fighting. The combat etiquette sections he knew letter perfect. It wasn't until he realized that you were learning all the rest that he thought maybe there was something important in them. I remember being quite pleased with you at that point."

Zoe made a wry face. "I'm glad I was some use."

Kenna's warm hand grasped her arm. "You were a great deal of use, and we all loved you. But that doesn't mean you were an easy handful."

Zoe retained an injured expression. "But I was always polite and obedient, wasn't I? My grandfather taught me that, and I tried like anything to live up to it."

"Polite? Oh, yes. Unfailingly polite and correct. Also argumentative, overly serious, and exceptionally stubborn." Kenna stared into space a moment, then turned to her. "And now..."

Zoe waited, but Kenna seemed reluctant to continue.

"What is it? What have I done now?"

Her friend smiled. "It isn't what you've done, Zoe. It's how you are. I worry sometimes."

"Why would you worry about me?"

Kenna shrugged. "You are a very careful and controlled young woman."

"I try to be."

"But that isn't everything. You seem to be watching, analyzing...calculating."

"That is what I have been taught. I watch, I analyze, I report."

"To the Sivan."

"Or to you. Or to Barent. I am often in a position to know what none of you can find out."

"We all appreciate that, Zoe, but what about you?"

"What about me? What are you getting at, Kenna? Is something wrong?"

Her friend brushed her palm downward. "Not at all. I wonder sometimes what you're thinking...no, not your analysis. You. Your inner self. What does Zoysana need? What do you want out of life?" Kenna glanced sideways at her. "Have you ever been in love?"

"Me? Not likely. Oh, I remember having rather a crush on that handsome new Swordmaster when I was about eleven, but he moved on, and I got over it."

"Hmm. Back to being a good little agent again."

Zoe regarded her friend. "Kenna, this is a strange conversation. Of course you like to be subtle, but why don't you just, for once, come out and ask me what you want?"

Kenna laughed. "I don't want anything, Zoe. I'm just concerned about you and how you feel. We always gibe the Sivan for treating people like Markers on a board." She leaned forward. "I just don't want you to feel that is how we all see you."

Zoe laughed. "I don't feel like a Marker, Kenna. Even to the Sivan. I know how you all feel about me. I'm very comfortable with my place, if that solves your concern."

"It does..." She sat back and regarded the smaller woman. "...perhaps. I'm always concerned about your desire to be correct. Are you saying you're comfortable because you think you should be?"

"You're telling me that I'm not really happy, I just think I am."

Kenna smiled. "Put that way, it sounds rather ridiculous, doesn't it?" She shifted in her chair. "And what does the Sivan say about your new project?"

Zoe shrugged. "He thinks it was his idea. Maybe it was. But there's no need to argue the point. We agree in principle."

Kenna was silent, staring pensively into the flames. "Now, I wonder if he has anything else up his sleeve. I wouldn't be surprised. Solonstan around, then Loreline, now this other..."

"Kenna, you're losing me. What is the Sivan supposed to be doing?"

The king's sister came back from her thoughts. "I was just speculating. You know how the Sivan is – plan and counter plan, blind and double blind. He has a new system recently. Gathering information from strange places with stranger sources."

"We planned it last summer."

"You were involved?"

"Kenna, I'm having enough trouble with loyalties as it is. I don't want to get caught up between you and the Sivan,

262

worrying about what to tell whom, but it's fair to tell you that much. This trip is my part of the same plan: new sources, new knowledge. He just interpreted his part in his own way."

"His own distinctive way. That's one thing about him. When you run across one of his plans, it has his hand-marks all over it."

Zoe's smooth forehead tightened. She spoke slowly. "Kenna, when you come across one of my plans, whose hand-marks are all over it?"

"What do you mean?"

"Do my plans seem like plans of mine, or plans of his?"

"I see what you are getting at. I can't say that I have run across any of your plots lately, so I can't answer." She sat forward and stared at her smaller companion. "Do you have something on that I haven't picked up?"

Zoe just looked inscrutable, but then she couldn't stay serious. Her facade broke. "No, Kenna, you haven't missed anything. I was just wondering, that's all."

"It doesn't hurt to keep that in mind, true, but don't let it worry you. I'm sure you will develop a style all your own."

"Do you have a style?"

"You tell me. Do I?"

Zoe thought back. "Yes, a very passive one. You take in much more than you give out. You don't meddle all the time. You only give a gentle push, now and again. At least on that level. You also work on two levels. Like with Gerth."

"Gerth?"

"Yes. The first level is very obvious. Like any mother working to further her son's progress. You do all the things you are supposed to do, and a few that you aren't supposed to, but everyone does. Someone noticing that might be fooled into thinking that was all you were doing. But then there are those small nudges. I've seen it happen. You arrange a quiet chat with someone and I watch that person, and sooner or later he does something that is too smart for him to figure out himself. And Gerth profits. I'd like to listen in on one of those chats. I bet the man himself doesn't know where the idea came from." She looked up at her friend with raised eyebrows.

Kenna just smiled. "That's one way you are very like the Sivan. You are always watching, always analyzing."

"Do you ever nudge the Sivan?"

"Yes, but with one small difference. He knows he's being nudged. And then he does as he pleases. As I mentioned, we are on the same side. Usually."

"And all that's needed is one small push?"

"Always remember that any plan, no matter how complicated, at some point rests on one simple decision or one crucial fact. It is first necessary to understand the workings of the plan, but the true art is in finding that small key point of balance. Then you can influence the whole by a push, as you say, at the right spot. If you do it right, there is no need for scheming."

Kenna sat back and dusted her hands. "Enough lessons for tonight. Let's talk about your trip. There are many here and even in the Duchies who would pay dearly to be in your place."

Zoe drew herself up. "I doubt if many of them would want to give what I have given."

Kenna laughed comfortably. "Quite true. Now tell me about your plans. What route are you taking and how long do you think it will take? What kinds of knowledge are you expecting to find?"

Zoe spoke freely. This was the king's sister and a good friend. She knew that Kenna took an active part in Barent's planning; the better information she had, the better she could fulfill her role. The topics flowed and changed, and they talked about many things: the Codes, traders, Kyabra, Zoe's grandfather, Kenna's family, Gerth's father, dead in a border skirmish years ago. Even love. When they heard the middle watch called, they smiled and stretched.

"I shouldn't keep you up so late. The first day of a journey is always hard."

Zoe flexed her legs and arms. "There was no time to lose the tone I developed on our trip here, so don't feel guilty. I'm glad you asked me. I didn't want to leave without having a good long talk, but things have been moving rapidly."

"In many ways." Kenna turned to face the younger woman as they rose. "Zoe, momentous events are happening, here at home and out in the world around us. Your mission may be more important than you know. One single piece of information you find could have a profound effect on us. You are bound up in our lives, those of us who rule this kingdom. Your presence or absence might become a key balance point. If you receive a message to return, it will be for good reason. Do not hesitate."

"Kenna, what do you mean? How could I be that important?"

"I have nothing specific to tell you, but I can give you one more insight into my methods. It is not always me who does the nudging. Some day, I may need you. Then, if I must, I will call. Will you come?"

"Of course. But what kind of message will you send?"

"What seems best at the time. You will not miss it."

Zoe looked into her friend's serious eyes. "I suppose." She clasped Kenna's forearm and bowed. "And I will come."

Kenna smiled: a quiet, reminiscing smile. Zoe stood a moment longer, reluctant to release that firm, comforting arm, then turned and paced slowly back to her quarters, sober thoughts occupying her mind.

37. To the Inner Sea

Away on the road again. Zoe rediscovered how much she enjoyed travelling. The ambling pace, with plenty of time for conversation. The long, companionable silences, in the saddle or around the fire at night, with time for thoughts, deep or frivolous. The evening training sessions and tale-fests. Lessons in the speaking of different languages.

The ever-changing repetition of the roadway. Rain, sun, wind. New vistas, new people, new ideas. Inns, campsites, manors, cities, castles, mountain passes, fords, bridges, and always the clink of harness, the shuffle of shod feet, the smell of sweat. Ahead – the horizon, with only the imagination to limit the possibilities. Behind – home, a soft, warm feeling, to be brought out and enjoyed but a moment, then pushed back safely to its nest.

And always the road. Flowing beneath, bringing its changes, swirling them around, carrying some along for a while, dropping others behind, lost in the distance around the last bend, promising new meetings around the next.

It was a long journey, and with the distance and the time passing, Zoe's perspective on her problems changed, became more objective. They seemed less pressing, and she allowed them to recede from the surface of her mind, to be replaced by enthusiasm for the task ahead.

She began to question her companions about their home. As she did so, she saw that, except for ceremonial occasions, she had barely spoken to any of the Kyabrans since they had entered Arlyn Castle. It was not that she had missed the opportunity, her conscience reminded her; it was as if she had preferred not to. As soon as she realized this, she sought out Lord Janitra in his tent to apologize. His response was typically gracious and insightful.

"Do not be sorry, my young friend. It was not unexpectedd. Here I come out of nowhere and tell you that you are something other than you had always thought. Soon you would be asked to become that other to a greater degree. It is natural you should immerse yourself in your old self for as long as you could as a cushion against the change. Now you are here with us and you are prepared to begin your transformation. We are a patient people. We have been waiting. Now we can start."

"You are so understanding, Lord Janitra."

"Yes, but also the tiniest bit guilty. It is always a difficult thing to be torn from your old path, forced into another. I would not be the agent of that tearing were I not convinced that more good may come of it. But I still feel your pain and would do what I can to ease it."

She looked at him earnestly. "Please believe me, I bear you no ill will for this situation. In fact, I grow more enthused to begin plotting my new course. Tell me about Kyabran politics."

And so the journey continued: across Velikii, denying themselves the pleasure of visiting with Lord Rawden; into the Inner Duchies, where they traded the horses of the pack train for the huge wagons that rolled over well-maintained roads, finally reaching the Inner Sea.

They came out of a pass through a range of low hills, dry and barren, and wound down the lazy loops of chalky road towards a small cluster of white-washed houses that peeped out from the dark green foliage surrounding them. A warm, damp breeze freshened their faces, clearing their parched lungs. They looked out over a sheltered harbour, with natural headlands elongated by a breakwater that parted in the centre, allowing ships to glide into its protection. The wagons stopped on the dock near a low warehouse, but the riders moved on until their horses' hooves plashed in the low surf.

Zoe, having never seen a body of water larger than the long, narrow lakes that nestled among the hills of Petrella, sat silent.

267

"I had been told of the immense size of the sea, but nothing can describe the feeling."

Tadeo, who sat beside her, nodded. "I know what it is to feel this way. Before coming to your land, I never saw mountains so high that the snow always stays on them. Words cannot say what you feel."

"It's so beautiful!" Her nose wrinkled. "But the smell is strange. Not exactly nice, but rather enticing."

Janitra pulled his horse up beside them. "Perhaps it is in the blood, the call of the sea."

Zoe turned, puzzled. "What do you mean? I was never told the Kyabrans were especially a seafaring people."

"Not us. The Petrellans. Didn't you know that the nomadic barbarians who settled your area were originally fisher-folk, and probably pirates, on the Great Cold Ocean to the south?"

Zoe simply looked at him, her mouth open.

"I assure you, my Lady, this is true." Tadeo pushed his horse forward so he could speak directly to her. "Before coming on this mission, I went to our Great Archives and looked for all our material on your area. The kingdom of Petrella is only about four hundred years old. Before that, your people lived on the sea. Look at your language. It is full of words of water. If you had been a horse people, your language would be full of horses. But it is not. Your people came from the Ocean.

"But for some reason, they traded their boats for horses and moved onto the steppes south of the Barrier Range. Then, quite soon, they were driven out by the Inari, who were much fiercer and less civilized, if you could call it that. So they came north, through the passes to what is now Petrella and the other Barrier kingdoms, pushing the indigenous people out."

"But who were the people they pushed out?"

Tadeo looked discomfited and did not speak. She looked to Janitra, who smiled back at her. Her gaze went from one to the other.

"You? It was the Kyabrans?"

Janitra chuckled. "This all happened four hundred years ago, Zoysana. It is not the kind of thing we go to bed worrying about, to dream of revenge. It is the way of the world. Young races spring up to challenge the old ones. If a race is old and tired, it is pushed aside. Once, our empire covered the whole world. Now, we have our small land, our culture and our history to console us. It is sufficient for some. For me, it is not enough. I and those like me will not sit and allow our race to be obliterated. So we forge a new empire. One of goods and money. The strength of our new empire will be the power of knowledge. Kyabra has not seen its last days. Not if we and our descendants can strive in this way.

"That is why we wish to open our borders. There still are those to whom the purity of the race and the culture is everything. They wish to keep our borders closed, allowing us to decline to an immaculate death. But they are losing their power because they are stagnant. We who are moving will clear our land as this sea air clears the head, stuffed with the dust of the road." He turned his horse and spoke over his shoulder as he beckoned them to follow.

"This is why it is a good time for you to visit. You will be accepted. New blood is needed to make us strong again."

"But that means there are those who feel I am an abomination because of the impurity of my heritage."

"I will not lie to you. They exist. But there is no reason for you to contact them. As I said, they take little part in the active life, preferring to wall themselves up with their art and their memories. They will not bother you. Now come and call your beast. I think he has spotted a dead fish."

In true canine fashion, Patu had indeed found something foul, and Zoe's call came just in time to stop him from rolling in it. He came at her call, looking back over his shoulder with longing, and they rode along the waterfront to a nearby inn. Zoe took care of the stabling of her animals, requesting that Patu be placed between Jobe and the wall. As usual, the stable boys were eager to comply; impressed as they were at his apparent docility, they still had no desire to confront the huge armigerent in the course of their duties. Zoe did little to persuade them otherwise. She didn't like leaving him, and the less he was bothered, the better.

The next day, they supervised the loading of Janitra's goods onto one of the stubby, single-masted trading ships tied up at the wharf. It was his usual plan to continue by land, which was much easier for the horses.

"Besides," Tadeo confided to her later as they relaxed in front of the inn, enjoying the warm evening, "he gets seasick."

"What's seasick?"

"You do not want to find out."

She shrugged. "If you say so. Isn't it hard on a merchant, to be unable to travel by sea?"

"Oh, he can if it is necessary. He just prefers not to."

"Well, I won't complain. This is better for me. Maybe I would catch this sickness from him. Besides, I would prefer to move slowly into the Kyabran way, not be dropped suddenly on the docks of the city with no warning. How far is it now?"

"That depends on my master. It is only a few days' ride to the border of Kyabra. Then it is two days to our home. But Lord Janitra may stop to visit. He has friends to see – matters to discuss. My master is a prince of our people. It was a risk he took, going away for so long."

"What kind of risk? Is there a political problem?"

270

"Not a problem, but the shifting of power is to be considered. It will be a great help to those who wish to trade when he returns with his news and his trading goods. And you, I suppose. He will wish to tell them before he reaches our own town. He will also want to know if anything has changed. So we may stop a few days. But we will be home soon!" He smiled happily, an expression so different from his usual somber mien.

Zoe elbowed him in the ribs. "And who waits for you at home?"

He did not catch her inference and answered seriously. "My whole family – my father, mother, and sisters. They will be so pleased to see me. I was given great honour to be taken with Lord Janitra, when I am unsponsored. He has several Guards-of-life of his own following he could have taken, but he chose me. I have done my duty well, and so my honour progresses. I have learned many things, and my knowledge grows. My family will be proud!"

"You certainly have progressed in language. Your Petrellan is much better than it was a month ago."

He smiled and bowed to her. "Thank you, my Lady. If I may say, your progress with the Kyabran language is astonishing."

"Ah, but I cheated. I already spoke it well when I was a child. I only had to re-remember it."

"Re-remember? Oh, yes, I see. Remember again. Still, your accent is very good. One would not recognize you as an Outsider unless one listened carefully."

Zoe frowned. "That may be a good thing. The best I can do is to make as few waves as possible."

"Make waves? That is a fine expression. From the sea, again."

"Isn't that interesting? Can you find out that kind of thing from anyone's language?"

"I think so. If you knew that the Kyabran language has not changed at all in three hundred years, what would that say to you?"

"That nothing has changed in Kyabra for a long time."

"Right. And that is not good."

"No, I suppose not."

They sat and looked out over the water, lightly slapping the rocks at their feet as the light faded.

Tadeo's voice lilted out of the gathering darkness. "Have you ever dreamed of doing great deeds?"

"Doesn't everyone?"

"No. Many dream of great glory. They do not think of the deeds that must lead to the glory. From my reading of stories and my talking with people, I think that they dream only of the results. I dream of the struggle, the fight, the striving to win for the right cause. I do not care for the glory afterwards."

"I must agree. All that celebration is but a distraction. In my experience, a job is never that easily finished. It seems you must always keep working on it, even after the main success. If you stop to celebrate, it all just falls apart and you must start over again."

He turned earnestly towards her. "But that is not a bad thing. One must enjoy the striving. One who only enjoys the glory at the end does not last long enough to make results. Only the one who enjoys the work itself can succeed."

Zoe leaned back in her chair and stretched. "A good philosophy when one is sitting on a warm beach. More difficult when one is stranded on a mountain in a snowstorm."

"Granted, there are times when the promise of the glorious end is all that sustains the seeker. But most times..."

"I agree, and there are also times of the opposite sort, when everything is going well, and progress is being made. Times that should be enjoyed to the fullest. And this is one of them. Let's get a glass of wine before dinner. Do people always eat this late in your country?"

"Yes. It has to do with the heat, I think. For much of the year, it is too hot to eat much before sunset." He patted her arm consolingly. "It is not so bad. When one waits so long, one enjoys the food so much."

"In that case I'm going to enjoy this meal a lot!"

They strolled across the sand to the inn together as the sun set into the empty, smelly sea.

38. GUARD OF LIFE

Zoe chuckled at how naive she had been to expect any great change when they entered Kyabra. Lands around the Old Kingdom were very similar to Kyabra itself. As they rode, towns grew closer together and looked older, more worn; broken fortifications, ruined walls and in places mere humps under the turf spoke of the slow evolution of the centuries.

True, there was a delineated border, with polite but efficient guards who checked them through in a proper but thorough manner. Zoe had a moment's worry – she didn't know what about – but everything was in accordance with the rules. Janitra would have nothing less. As they pulled out, a patrol trotted in from the west along the border. Looking back later, she saw another group leave to the east. A definite border.

But nothing much changed. The same crowded, ancient towns – although the people were more often darker and rounder of face – the same ruins, the same well-kept road. She glanced at Tadeo riding beside her, a place he had claimed lately. He and the rest had changed. They rode straighter in the saddle, with their heads high and their voices louder as they called jokes to each other. Janitra's regular guards did not have Tadeo's serious innocence, and Zoe's developing command of their language allowed her to learn in graphic detail what and whom each one had waiting for him at journey's end.

Her uncertainty about her reception here was soon settled. The lords whom Janitra visited were all members of his faction and greeted her warmly, full of questions about her land. To her astonishment, a few had even known her grandfather and were happy to fill her in on his life here. In fact, it became a pleasant game to figure out how each one might be related to her. In a country where everyone's lineage was common knowledge, a rediscovered branch was quite a novelty.

The training was another story. Zoe always practised in a fashion she had understood from her grandfather to be completely correct. On the road, Janitra and his entourage worked in a very similar manner. However, she found that everyone had been quite lax, and once in their own land they reverted to the 'proper' forms.

As usual, Janitra had anticipated the situation, and he assigned Tadeo to coach her.

"And I thought the Codes were restricting."

"You think this is rigid? We are the ones who break new ground. We have relaxed many of the old strictures, but we do not wish to be seen as complete radicals. Besides, the old ways produced what we are now. It would be unwise to change too rapidly, but we make an adjustment here, a new idea there, and change comes. There are many in our land who would call us slack. They would not even appear on the same training field as one such as yourself, whose development has been so different. But do not worry. They will never be asked to train with us."

"So what are these new rules I must learn?"

"First, I suppose, you must stop training with the common guards. You, as a Master, will train with Lord Janitra, and sometimes with Maksa and myself, if you would honour us with your assistance."

"But that's ridiculous! There are many areas in which you are far beyond me."

"True. You see what a problem you would be to one of rigid thinking. It is not possible that a Master could learn from a student such as me. It would cause damage to such a one's mind, just to think about it."

She looked over at him. He glanced at her, then away, with a slight twitch to the corner of his mouth.

"Fine, fine. I get the picture. What else?"

"Your more creative style. If you wish to fit smoothly into a practice, you must restrict yourself to the standard moves."

"Completely?"

"I think not. Part of your function here, if you do not mind that we speak of it, is to demonstrate the usefulness of new ideas. However, it would be wise to use restraint. Perhaps one new movement at each practice would be correct?"

She grimaced. "If you say so. But if someone's foot is headed for my face, I'm not likely to take much time to think about which is the 'proper' response."

"Of course not. And do not worry about the rest. The minor points I will watch for and try to keep ahead of you. Then I can tell you before they happen."

"Fine. We'll just flow with it and see how it goes."

"Flow with it. A good concept. We will flow."

And flow they did. Janitra's progress swept across the ancient countryside leaving a ferment of interest and excitement tossing behind. At each castle, villa or manor house they visited, they were greeted with warmth but sent away again with enthusiasm. Though maintaining his calm demeanor, the Trader lord seemed to inspire incredible optimism, with his tales of the trading possibilities and the warm reception of his ideas in the outside world. Although Zoe herself was not party to many of the meetings, it was not difficult to surmise that great plans were underway.

She was doubly glad, now, of her intensive training in the transportation of the men and equipment of war. They were shrewd men, this new breed of Trader lords, and they asked pointed and detailed questions. It wasn't long before she had translated her guidelines for army supply trains into the terms of peaceful trading caravans and the forwarding of trade goods.

She knew that critical and proficient eyes watched her training, her animals, her comportment, even her table manners. She could be a symbol for these people, a sign that the gap could be bridged, the border crossed. All she had to do was be as like them as she could. The differences would take care of themselves.

It was not too onerous a task, as it fitted with her own intentions. First, her assignment. *I am expected to learn all that I can about this society. So I will.* Then, on a personal level. *I will honour my grandfather by learning what he would have taught me had he lived longer.* So she threw herself with a will into this challenge. It was, after all, only the newest phase of her training; there had been not a few of these in the past, and she expected the future to bring more.

So she bobbed in Janitra's wake in his procession across Kyabra, allowing herself to be put on show as required. In the process, she soaked up knowledge at every opportunity, matched question for question, and, as Tadeo would say, 'progressed.'

As his party increased in size and the meetings stretched more and more, Zoe wondered how long Janitra could continue to make time for her. It would be impolite for her to broach the subject, but she didn't see how it could work. *Well, it is his country, his procession. He will figure it out.*

On the sixth day of their 'two-day' trip from the border, Janitra jogged up beside her as she rode with Tadeo near the head of the group.

"My dear Zoysana. It seems we see so little of each other these days."

"I hardly expected otherwise, my Lord. Even so, I confess I was unprepared for your reception here. I had thought this was all a very new and tentative plan. It seems we are cresting on a wave which sweeps all before it."

Janitra signalled to Tadeo, who had fallen politely behind, to join the conversation. "I feel exactly same way. I am pleasantly surprised at the amount of progress my friends made in my absence. It seems that the very fact of my going was a catalyst; someone was doing what we had all talked about for so long. Now, my successful voyage has sparked the whole movement. We will return to my home for a greater consultation, then start our enterprises."

"Don't you need the approval of your rulers?"

"Not really. We are governed by consensus here. Whatever one lord wishes to do, if it does not hinder the others, he does. There will be those, as I told you, who disapprove, but I do not anticipate any ability on their part to mount effective opposition.

"But this does mean that I must take a much more active role in the organization, and much sooner. While this is of great importance to my plans, it also means I will not have the leisure to introduce you to our life as I had hoped."

"I quite understand, my Lord. I have no complaints. I am learning as fast as my head can fill and my hand can write. Tadeo has done a marvellous job of coaching me."

"I am very pleased to hear my conjectures confirmed in this manner. As you realize, Tadeo was bound to me only on a temporary basis for the purposes of this journey. When we return to my home in Fontenelle, he will once again be free of obligations." His raised hand anticipated the young Guard's disappointed expression. "You have always known, my young kinsman, that the life of a merchant was not for you. Under my sponsorship, you would try to become that which you cannot be. You were made for other duties."

Tadeo nodded, and Zoe grinned as he tried to look less regretful.

"So I have a request of you. When we reach Fontenelle, I will be very busy. You will not, unless you have plans I have not been made a party to?"

"Oh, no, my Lord. I had not been looking past our return. In truth, my only thoughts in that area are not reassuring. I had hoped for a place in the new enterprises, but I knew not what."

"It pleases me that you would join us, because what I wish to suggest will be of great help."

Tadeo's head came up and his back straightened. Zoe could see the dreams sparkling behind those eyes, which could be so dark and brooding.

"You see, Tadeo Priya, that Zoysana plays a larger part in this than one might expect. She is evidence to our people that our ways can be assimilated with the ways of the Outlanders. She is also more influential than perhaps she realizes in the politics of our most powerful ally at the outmost edge of our trading sphere. An ally, I must admit, for whom I feel some trepidation. So her continued progress," here he fixed the younger fighter with a meaningful stare, "and later her survival are of great importance to us. Do you see where I am leading?"

Tadeo's face brightened. "You mean, my Lord, that you need someone who has the contacts, the skills and the time to ease her through her visit here, and the ability to protect her when she returns to the Outlands?"

"Zoysana, how does this analysis strike you?"

She grinned. "You tailored the suit to fit the man you wish to wear it. I am flattered and impressed that you would assign one of your best men to assist me."

Tadeo looked pleased but uncomfortable. "I am not one of his best men, Zoe. I am only in training. He has many Sponsored who far surpass me in ability, experience, and intelligence."

"But I don't want someone who is so marvellous and intelligent that I can't keep up. I would much prefer someone nearer my own age and abilities!"

279

"Well spoken, both of you. I am not making any assignment, Zoe. I merely suggest the two of you could benefit from an association that would assist me as well. No Guard-of-Life is ever assigned. He volunteers or is invited, and both must agree upon his acceptance into Sponsorship."

Zoe smiled and reached across to poke Tadeo in the ribs, drawing forth his reluctant grin. "Well, if he can put up with me, I can put up with him." Then she sobered. "But, my Lord, this is a serious relationship we are speaking of, is it not? What are the responsibilities involved? Is this for life, or for a certain term? There seem to be areas of my upbringing that my grandfather neglected sadly."

Both Kyabrans laughed. "Nobody is asking you to marry him, Zoe. You and Tadeo will be bound together by a common aim: your mutual progress and wellbeing. The bond's only power is the honour of the two parties. If it is agreed that it should be dissolved and this can be achieved with honour to both sides, then it is done." Janitra shrugged. "It is a slight variation, having the Sponsor a female, but not unheard of. Should one of you marry, it would also depend on the new spouse whether the situation could continue. True, it is a serious relationship, but not so different from that which you enjoy now."

The two younger riders locked eyes, then both shrugged. Zoe looked over to Janitra. "You have it all figured out so well. Are you ever wrong?"

He threw back his head in a silent laugh. "Not since the noon meal, in any case. So is it settled, then?"

Both nodded.

"Good. We will hold a simple ceremony after we reach Fontenelle. You will find nothing changes much, but it is pleasant that the relationship is formalized."

39. OMANISA HOME

And Zoe did feel more comfortable after that. Especially after she witnessed the reception Janitra was subjected to when he finally returned home.

By the time they had wound their way back to the coast, they had added a considerable number of other lords to their party, each with his own retainers and advisers. Word had spread that they were coming, and most of the city of Fontenelle had turned out to greet them.

Zoe regarded the crowd with confusion as they filed along the wide thoroughfare that led to the waterfront promenade. "Fill me in, Tadeo. What is Janitra's position in your city? Why are all these people here? Is he the mayor or something?"

"Oh, no. He is only one of many lords who own land in this area. This turnout is unusual. It must be because of our journey. It has been a long time since men of our race visited the Barrier Mountains." He looked at her sidelong. "In fact, the one before us would be the last Kyabran fleeing the barbarian invaders. Our people need heroes, I think. So they will make use of us. It is pleasant, is it not?"

"Pleasant, I suppose. As long as I can keep Patu in line, we might as well enjoy it." She thought of keeping him between the horses, but then changed her mind. *These people want a show, do they?* Holding back to create a space, she sent him in front and gave the armigerent the signal to range. This cleared the throng back to the sides of the street and allowed him to feel less confined.

Most of the way he was content to walk in the centre, but once in a while he would notice something off to the side and wander that way. Each time, this caused consternation among the nearest bystanders, creating a minor stir in the normal flow of the crowd. At one point he veered close to a group of citizens and there was more movement than usual. A young child, separated from her mother, found herself confronted by the huge beast. Repeating the Kyabran equivalent of, "Doggie, doggie," she toddled over to investigate. A rough spot in the roadway proved an obstacle for the tiny feet, and the baby was dumped in the dust. She sat there, deciding whether she was injured enough to cry or interested enough to get up and keep going. Patu solved her problem by strolling to her.

Seeing the huge nose conveniently near, the little girl grabbed two good handfuls of whiskers and hauled herself to her feet then stood there, unwilling to let go of such a convenient support. Patu stood also, wondering what to do. The child's mother was in a similar quandary, but less placid about it. She had taken a step forward, but could not bring herself to approach closer. She wavered, almost in hysterics, but whether through inability or sufficient control, made no sound.

Finally the baby decided she was solid enough and let go, crowed and patted the huge, bristly nose. More "Doggie, doggie." Patu decided that this was fun. He wagged his tail and presented his nose again for more patting. There was a distinct relaxing of breath among the bystanders. Pleased by her attention, he tried to nudge his head under her arm so she would scratch his ears. The nudge was too much for her precarious balance, and she sat down again, rather hard. She looked up with the beginning of a pout. The armigerent's tail went down, and he glanced around with a guilty set to his ears. Several people laughed.

Zoe thought that this had gone on a little too long for the mother's nerves, so she whistled softly. Patu delicately reached out and caught the girl's coat near the collar and picked her up, turned her towards her mother and set her on her feet. Then he gently nudged her. The chubby legs churned in order to keep from falling and propelled their owner straight into her mother's anxious arms. From that high vantage, the toddler squirmed around, pointing and calling her "doggie" refrain proudly. When the laughter subsided enough that she could be heard, Zoe kneed her horse forward and bowed in the saddle.

"If you don't mind, madam, and your child has finished playing with my armigerent, could we go on now? We are holding up a lot of people." She gestured to the rest of the procession, filling the road behind.

The mother, flustered by the quick flurry of emotions and the laughter of her friends, gave a quick curtsey and nodded, still clinging mutely to her daughter.

Zoe bowed again and instructed Patu to do likewise. Then she sent him on ahead and they continued through the town.

Tadeo found this scene amusing. "She had little to say just now, but that young woman has a story to tell for months to come! In fact, the whole town will have a story to tell!"

Zoe glanced at him in worry. "Do you think I overdid it? There was no danger."

"Danger or no, Patu shows credit to his breeding and training. We raise many armigerents here, but none so big, ugly, and ferocious. Very few so controlled."

Zoe rode closer and spoke just over the street noise. "He's not that controlled. I think he just has good manners."

"What do you mean, not controlled? He never refuses to do anything you ask."

"True, but I don't ask him to do anything that isn't part of his training, and therefore, in his mind, the logical thing to do."

"The results are the same, are they not?"

"It might seem that way. It feels different, though."

The Kyabran looked at her with a frown. "I never thought of treating an animal like a human."

"Is that what I'm doing? I suppose so. He thinks very well for himself. He does the right thing whether I'm there or not. It's just that when I'm around, he checks with me first to make sure."

Tadeo just smiled, shook his head and rode on in silence for a while. Then he glanced over. "You must visit our kennels. The trainers of our province are well known in our country and well respected for their knowledge."

Men who train armigerents? "I would like that very much. How do I contact them?"

"When word of this afternoon spreads, they will contact you, never fear."

Leaving the town and its citizens in a joyful buzz behind them, they took a gently winding road along the coast, out to a low headland that projected into the sea. There, in a beautiful but easily defended position, was the Omanisa Home. It was defined by a long rectangular wall, low by Petrellan standards, clad with the white stucco omnipresent in this country. The buildings were all part of the facade, ranged around a huge inner courtyard with awnings lining the inner walls, creating much-needed shade. Trees and flowerbeds grew in each corner, and fountains of various sizes added their cool moisture to the air. Metal-studded wooden doors opened through the seaward-facing flank, welcoming the travellers and their entourage.

Zoe and Patu drew to one side in the bustle of the homecoming. She saw Janitra decorously greeted by a small, serious woman who moved around efficiently, directing everything.

Tadeo's welcome was quite different. Upon his horse's entering the gate he was swarmed by a mob of children, mostly girls, who clung to his legs and his equipment as he rode, with distinct danger to their bare toes. When he dismounted, they threw themselves on him, chattering and squealing. Catching Zoe's eye above this cluster, he gave an embarrassed smile and shrug. Her enquiring eyebrow brought an enthused nod, and she went to rescue him.

As she approached, the knot dissolved into two groups. The unattached ones faded back to an awed distance, and the others resolved into a line of four slim, graceful girls, of ages about twelve to eighteen. These he introduced as his sisters, with names that did not impress themselves on her memory because she was so interested in regarding their owners. When he proudly named Zoe his new Patron, they all stiffened into even more formal postures of respect. To Zoe's eye, unused to so many of this ethnic group, they looked very similar. Their slimness made them seem tall for their ages, even the youngest.

She took advantage of the momentary formal grasp of hands with each to make an assessment. "So two of you are following in your brother's footsteps, are you? We will try swordplay later." The two eldest glanced at each other, then at Tadeo, standing anxiously by. She regarded the third. "Not so the artist, I think. The strength of the sword arm is contrary to the fine movement of the painter and weaver. And, of course, the Dancer!" She turned to the youngest. "Are your ambitions toward the Veil or the Arch?"

The delicate chin rose. "Both, my Lady."

Zoe stepped back and bowed. "A laudable ambition. But for one with your poise and balance, a good choice."

"Is that why you pulled my hand?"

The older girls were shocked at this impertinence, but Zoe looked to Tadeo. "I didn't know you had a Dancer in your family."

"I suppose not."

The eldest of the group found her tongue. "You mean you didn't tell the lady about Jaddie?"

"I didn't speak about any of you. I did not think it proper conversation to boast about my family."

The four turned to Zoe with such new respect that they could not bring themselves to ask how she had done it.

Zoe smiled. "It is a matter of training. You watch, you feel, you listen. Some day you will learn." She reached out and lifted a bright-coloured thread off the gown of the third girl. They all nodded.

It had been a simple trick for one with Zoe's experience and the Sivan's tutelage. Her questioning on the journey had revealed that there were few careers open to high-born females in this society, and the differences in clothing, bearing, callouses, and several other minutiae which she did not consciously register had cued her.

The other trick, which the Dancer had registered, was a slight pull when grasping hands. It was small enough that most did not even notice it, but it allowed a quick test of balance. The fact that the untrained girl had picked it up showed her readiness to learn the complicated moves of both styles of the Dance.

"Do you Dance as well, my Lady?" The eldest girl – *Rhesia, I think* – had recovered enough to take on her role as speaker for the group.

"Not much, but certain moves, even simple ones, are valuable in both Weaponless and Sword combat. They give the fighter a distinct advantage in many situations."

The older girls looked to their youngest sister with new respect.

At this moment, Tadeo broke in. "Excuse me, my Lady, but my Lord Janitra would speak with you."

Zoe looked over to where Janitra was standing with his wife, gazing in her direction. She waved a signal, then turned briefly to Tadeo's sisters, holding out her hands impulsively. They

286

grasped hers in a non-formal jumble of fingers squeezing together. "We must speak again. I can see your dear brother has left me sadly lacking in knowledge about his family."

"Mother and Father will be so pleased to meet you. They were sorry they could not be here." The eldest had regained her formal manners, and looked to Tadeo with apology. "They knew you were coming, but Father said he wanted to bring Lord Janitra a completed package, and you know Mother." This last with a meaningful smile.

As they left the girls and made their way across the courtyard, Tadeo explained. "You will like my mother, I think. She has always refused to let anyone do anything for her. She works with my father as an equal partner, and will not back down on any task that must be done. They are a formidable pair, those two."

"Yours is a happy family."

"I think so. It is good that there are many of us. I think my mother and father spend too much time with each other, so it was necessary for my sisters and me to form a close relationship." He smiled sadly. "It is not easy to be the children of formidable parents."

Zoe grinned. "Our ancient seeress, Sarasha the Lame, said the same thing."

As they approached Janitra to be introduced to his wife, Zoe reflected that it could be more difficult to be the child of no parents, but she squelched the thought as envy, and unworthy of her.

40. Different Styles

One group that accepted Zoe with open arms was the young Guards in training who had elevated Tadeo to be their leader. These youngsters, both male and female, had no qualms about learning new ways and no prejudices against her occasional lapses of etiquette. They considered themselves to be the new generation, the ones who would put Kyabra back in the forefront of world trade and politics, and they were willing to adapt to the style of anyone who could help them. Such a group was a refreshing change from the formality of their elders, and Zoe spent what time she could with them.

One day Zoe decided to show them some moves used by village wrestlers in Petrella. They responded with enthusiasm to this test of their physical and social flexibility. She was having a wonderful time and had Tadeo down on the ground in a paralyzing hold, to the great amusement of his companions. She was concentrating, waiting for his muscles to relax in a certain way as she knew they would, so she could make the shift to an even more effective grasp, when she realized the bystanders had grown silent. Looking up, she saw that Janitra had joined the ring, a smile twitching one corner of his mouth.

Slapping her victim's shoulder in the 'truce' signal, she released him and jumped to her feet.

"Well, my Lady, may I assume this grovelling has a martial or theatrical objective?"

Zoe glanced around. The faces reminded her of a group of pages caught at the bottom of someone else's apple tree. She smiled sweetly. "Perhaps my Lord would like to discover the effectiveness of that specific technique?"

Janitra glanced down at his formal robe. "I regret that I must postpone that lesson for another time, my Lady. I go to an important meeting. It would be perhaps inappropriate to appear covered in dirt." He looked around at the other students who were taking in this repartee with amazement. "Besides, what would it do to my dignity and reputation with these gentlemen, to be seen down in the mud, with you sitting on top of me?"

She bowed graciously. "Whatever my Lord desires."

"What 'my Lord' desires at the moment is a quick word with you and Tadeo." He raised his head to include the others, who were just beginning to come out of their paralysis. "Please resume your training, ladies and gentlemen. I will return your friends to you immediately."

They walked apart from the group, leaving a hushed buzz of conversation behind. "We have a visitor coming, and I will not be here to greet him. He is Baridea Rimmon, a member of one of our oldest and most respected families. He is also one of the strongest proponents of the closing of our borders. If anyone in this area has the power and the energy to cause difficulty to our plans, this is the man. I have no idea why he is coming, but it is not inconceivable that he wants to look you over. I thought to prepare you, in case that is his purpose."

"How should I treat him?"

"I cannot help you there. He is a proud man, a leader, and you have dealt with that sort all your life. So far, you have not gone far wrong by being yourself." He smiled at her. "Why think of changing now? I doubt there is much you could do to alter his attitude toward us, one way or the other, so do not worry. I give you no specific instructions to carry out. He will come, and you will meet him. What else could he be looking for?"

Zoe was still feeling confident enough to be mildly sarcastic. "Well, thank you for all your wisdom on the matter, my Lord. I will do my best, as I always have."

"I count on that, Zoe. I would not ask for more." He grasped her upper arm, then turned away.

The two turned back to their companions, sobered by Janitra's parting words. "You haven't said anything, Tadeo. What do you know about this man?"

"While he has strong opinions on the closing of our borders, he yet commands respect from all parties, which gives him considerable power. I cannot understand how a man so talented and intelligent holds such backward views, but that is his right."

"Well, if he is at all fair and courteous, I will be able to deal with him. If he is not, I suppose there was no chance anyway. So I don't think I'll worry about it. Besides, who says he is coming to see me?"

"Lord Janitra."

Zoe grinned. "He's been wrong before. Let's go practice. Your friends are making all sorts of mistakes."

They worked on the wrestling moves for a while longer. Finally, Tadeo clambered up after being dumped by one of the others. "I think I have progressed enough in this. Can we move on to something easier on my pride?"

There was general agreement. "How about swords? I wanted Zoysana to help me with the overhand bind. I can't get it right." The speaker was a younger lad, only tolerated because he came with his older brother. He had picked up on Zoe's willingness to teach and was using the extra opportunity to good advantage.

The group separated into pairs and began sword study. Zoe watched her student as he demonstrated the move that bothered him. Forced to train too much of her life alone, she was not talented at spotting a problem. Her strength was in mimicry, and her method was to watch a move and copy it. Then she could feel the weak spot in herself and show the student how to correct it.

As they worked, she picked up a new voice that had joined the general conversation. A commanding voice that cared little who heard it. She continued training but listened with part of her mind.

"So, Tadeo Priya. It is good to find you and your friends studying the Patterns correctly. My compliments to your Masters. But where is this half-breed Outlander they say tags along with you? I hear that she is never far from your protection."

Zoe lowered her sword. The man talking to Tadeo was younger than she had pictured: about thirty and very good looking, above middle height, with a fine, upright carriage and a proud but not unfriendly eye. He glanced over the group again, then turned back to Tadeo.

Zoe sheathed her weapon and closed her anger off with equal care in a small corner, where it continued to seethe. Relaxed yet erect, she approached and bowed, very correctly. "Good day and The Lady's grace to you, my Lord. May I present myself?" And she followed with a correct self-introduction of the oldest Kyabran style, including both her mother's and her father's lineage. When she had finished, she bowed again then stood, waiting. The challenge had been offered.

Baridea glanced to Tadeo. Tadeo would normally introduce a visiting Master to another student. But Zoysana was not a student, so Tadeo provided no help. He merely stood, looking interested and polite. Baridea must either return the introduction, accepting her as equal, or show rudeness by walking away. He hesitated.

Zoe's anger began to grow, and a touch of it seeped out. "My Lord, so far in my visit to the land of my grandfather, I have been treated with the utmost in consideration and courtesy. It would be unpleasant for me to have to return to my own country and report that the Kyabrans, like the Barbarians across the Barrier, are only polite when it serves them."

291

The Kyabran lord drew into himself, and a current of anger surfaced for a flash. Then the control clamped down, but a look of what might have been surprised respect escaped. Baridea then started his own introduction. As he revealed his lineage, the angry stiffness in his bearing was replaced by the strength of pride: the pride in knowing he was, if not an equal, at least an honourable descendant of the illustrious ancestors he listed. When he finished, she sought a correct response.

"In Petrella, we have an expression," and she quoted it in her language. "It means something like, 'The quality of the forbears carries into the present generation.' I think it translates well."

He inclined his head. "I find the Outlanders not deficient in the art of flattery."

So that's how he wants it. "The Kyabrans have a saying that courtesy becomes flattery only where it is not deserved."

Baridea mulled that over, then decided that a small defeat would be the best tactic. "My Lady puts me in a position where argument would be to my own disadvantage."

Zoe could be gracious, too. "Argument is a poor way to solve difficulties. Shall we agree to cease?"

"Agreement is the end to be desired of all argument."

Zoe allowed a grin to escape. "Did you come to join us in training, my Lord, or shall we stand around all day allowing the philosophers to speak with our mouths?"

"I did not come prepared to train, my Lady. Perhaps I might stay to watch?"

"That is the exact excuse Lord Janitra used, only this morning." She turned to Tadeo. "It seems the entire older generation shuns training with us. Perhaps they are afraid?"

Tadeo rose to the occasion. "Oh, no, my Lady. They are not afraid. They wish to avoid being contaminated with any dirt or new ideas."

Zoe turned to the elder lord. "Is the younger generation not always thus? All new ideas and no respect. Of course you may watch and welcome, my Lord. But do not be surprised if my style differs from what you are used to. My training has been quite different. While I only teach the standard techniques to the students, my own repertoire varies greatly."

"Assuming that I have seen the standard moves enough, where am I likely to see your private repertoire?"

"Only in free sparring, my Lord," then she added wickedly, "with someone near to my own abilities."

"Perhaps Tadeo Priya could serve as your partner."

Tadeo had caught her hint. "Oh, no, my Lord. She is a Master of Weaponless Combat and an accomplished swordswoman. I could not pace her."

"Oblige me."

It was not a command, but it could not be politely refused. The two squared off, as Baridea and the Guards-in-training formed a loose circle.

As soon as they started, Zoe pushed hard to signal Tadeo that he was to do his best. He was a fine swordsman, her better in standard swordplay, and for a while the match was even. Then, when she had demonstrated enough Kyabran technique, Zoe began to loosen up.

And it felt so good. She had not realized how hard it was, always following the rules of another society. She felt a flicker of admiration for Janitra and the other merchants, who must do this a good part of their lives. Then all conscious thought dissolved and she allowed her instincts to flow. She overwhelmed Tadeo with a series of unexpected moves and feints. Instead of just her sword, she used her feet, her robe, her hands, even her head. Her attacks came from too many levels for his single sword to cope, and he began to give ground. He attempted an offence of his own, but the moment he got moving there was nothing in front of him to attack. Finally, during a brief respite, he grounded his sword and held his free hand up helplessly toward Lord Rimmon.

"You see, my Lord? I am stronger, so I might win eventually in standard combat. But against her combined techniques, I am helpless."

Baridea considered. "I saw that, yes." Then he made up his mind. "I did not come here to play with swords. I have another purpose, of which I will speak later. But I admit I am intrigued. There are few who can force me into a new path once my way is set. However, my Lady, I think I will oblige you. It might be instructive for both of us."

He shrugged his robe back into combat position and grasped the sword Tadeo offered him, testing its balance. It was a fine practice weapon, blunted and of soft metal but of good workmanship, and he swung it appreciatively. Then he hesitated again. "My Lady, you have not had the advantage of seeing me work. Perhaps you would like to..."

She understood his unstated worry. While it seemed that she had standard Kyabran training, there was no guarantee that such was really the case. He would not be the first man to be injured because of playing a game by conflicting rules. However, he would lose a great deal of face if he were to seem worried about such a picayune detail. "I will accept that disadvantage, my Lord. Since this is a friendly contest for demonstration on a 'touches only' basis, and with an opponent as honourable as yourself, I will have no concern."

His bow of acceptance was a hair deeper than before, as thanks to her for realizing the delicate nature of his predicament. This would, truly, be a friendly match.

Again, they started out with the standard forms, each testing the other. It was soon clear that Zoe was overmatched: no news to anyone. She was forced to throw in her personal tricks in order to keep up. Then Baridea started on his own variations, and she was in serious trouble. Janitra had never pushed her this hard. Forcing herself to stay calm, she fought grimly, attempting offensive moves when she found a chance, which was not often. She tried to come up with a move with which he would be unfamiliar, but it was impossible to think because of the pressure he placed on her.

Then she was back in the clearing facing her grandfather, who had one day decided that she was getting too pleased with her own progress and had shown her a real offence, just to put her into perspective. His words came to her. "You are trying to think it, Zoe. Don't fight with your brain. Fight with your body."

She knew what was wrong. I have been fighting poorly. *I was so much better against Tadeo a moment ago.* In the pressure to show her best to this opponent, she had been thinking the fight. She stopped forcing the thoughts. Her thinking mind moved back into a spectator's position and watched objectively as her moves loosened up, became smoother, more coordinated and quicker. Now she was in control. His attacks were more obvious, her counters surer.

But she was still in trouble. He was a Master in all senses. His swordplay was superb, and she could read the Weaponless training in his movements. The only way to survive was by defining a small defensive area around herself and maintaining it. She had lost the initiative long ago and her share of the control recently. However, she was able to keep him at bay no matter what tricks he tried. At times, she outdid herself with desperate gyrations, but still he could not invade her space.

Finally, he stepped back and lowered his weapon. He, too, was breathing heavily, and sweat stained his richly embroidered robe. This time his bow was even more respectful. "A very interesting display, my Lady. You need more control of your conscious thought processes, but after you conquered that, you were formidable."

She returned the bow, laughing. "formidable as a turtle, my Lord, without the weight to fall on anyone and squash them!"

"Yes, you do work an amazing defence. But that is a good refuge when one is bested. Often the opponent will get overconfident or frustrated and leave the opportunity for a last, desperate attack." He returned the sword to Tadeo.

"You are not as different as you might think, Lady Zoysana. There is much of the Rochenan family style in you, plus recent work with the Omanisa group, of course."

"You can see my grandfather's style?"

"Oh, yes. It had quite a distinctive curving movement in the upper arms, especially in an outside line of attack. Has, I should say. I am pleased that it has not been lost, as we feared it would be at your grandfather's departure. You have added a few individual twists, as is the right of the Master. Each one is expected to leave behind him one or two movements which enrich the Art." There was a capital letter in the way he said it.

"Of course, you have such a hodgepodge of superfluous moves, many of them would need to be trained out..." He stopped himself. "But you have no intention of doing that, do you?" He shook his head, honestly sorrowful. "Such a shame. But then, you do not have our objectives, do you?"

"I am afraid not, my Lord. While I appreciate the need to perform a move in the correct manner, I will not ignore a variation that might save my life some day." He seemed receptive, so she went on. "I fear you are too civilized here, my Lord. When fighting is performed purely at a competitive level, a certain urgency is lost. The men I train with are always looking for new techniques, new attacks, new defences, even new weapons. Their lives depend on it. When your people leave their land, this is what they will face." She stopped; she was moving into political ground, and shaky ground at that.

"And have you, yourself, been placed in such a desperate situation, and did your philosophy hold true?"

296

"Twice, my Lord, and in both cases I owe my presence here to the use of unconventional techniques."

Baridea's raised head included all the students and fighters present. "I have heard these arguments many times." Then she saw the first sign of humour he had shown since he walked on the field. "But they do carry weight, coming from one who has lived by them. I thank you, my Lady. But I am reminded that combat is not what I am here to discuss with you."

"You did say earlier you had another reason."

"Yes. There are stories of an armigerent. Do you have one?"

"What do you wish with him?"

"I understand he is of rather great size and strength?"

"In my experience, although I am not familiar with the breed as raised in Kyabra."

"Perhaps you would like to become more familiar. My home is not far from here, and I breed, if I say so myself, one of the best strains of true battle armigerents in the land. I had intended to come and see your animal and depart, but I have changed my mind. If your work with your animal is as good as what I see here, perhaps you would visit me?"

"It would be an honour. My knowledge of armigerents is restricted, mainly coming from my work with the one animal that luck sent my way. I would be pleased to learn more."

"My trainer is well thought of. I am sure you will get along famously. Would tomorrow be too soon?"

Zoe glanced at Tadeo.

"Nothing is planned, my Lady."

"Good." Baridea was all business. "Thank Lord Janitra for his courtesy. I suppose I must invite him too. Ah, well, it will be of benefit to my strength of character. Now, I must return home and change out of this robe. It seems to have picked up some dirt." He smiled again and was gone, striding across the field.

297

41. Visiting the Enemy

The following day, a small party wound its way through the fields and forests of this pleasant land towards the Rimmon estate. Janitra had decided to take advantage of the invitation, but not to make any great show. Besides Zoe and Tadeo, he had only brought Maksa.

"I must put on a proper display, even if I only bring one man." He swept his hand to cover their party. "But I do feel protected with you and your companions. After all, I am part of your following today."

Zoe glanced over at Tadeo, then down at Patu, lolloping along beside her horse, his tongue blowing back. "We are a competent group indeed, my Lord." Both of her protectors were dressed in their finest: Tadeo in full Guard-of-life costume, Patu in a set of spiked collar and flank guards which had been made over to fit him. Zoe wore her grandfather's robe. That was all she had; it was enough.

Baridea's family seat was similar in style to most others: a fortress designed to protect from men, but also from the sun. As they entered the cool shade of the walls, Zoe wondered what the heat of summer might be like if such pains were needed for protection from it.

They were greeted personally by Baridea, who came out to the central courtyard as soon as they had dismounted. His welcome was correct, although not especially warm towards Janitra. When the proprieties had been observed and the members of his family introduced, he raised his eyebrows at Zoe.

"So, where is this animal of yours? I am eager to see him."

Zoe gestured. "I left him with the horses. Should I call him?" Looking over, she could see how Baridea had missed him. Patu, seen from the bright sunlight where they stood, was hidden by the horses and the shade and could be mistaken for one of them. She whistled, and he broke free of them and bounded to her, tail wagging, to skid to a halt at her feet. She laughed at the sight of him. "He's still so much of a puppy. Sometimes he misjudges and knocks me right over."

She looked up to see the astounded face of Baridea.

The Kyabran lord stood in silent awe. Finally, he spoke. "He is magnificent! Magnificent! May I observe him closer?"

"Of course. Go and talk, Patu." She signalled the animal to approach the Kyabran. Hesitant at first, but then less cautious as his enthusiasm mounted and the animal's reactions remained placid, Baridea investigated him from nose to tail.

The lord only broke away once, to signal a nearby servant. "Bring Alphard. He must see this." Then he was back to his observations. Finally he finished, and the questions tumbled out too quickly to answer.

"He is the best example of the breed I have ever seen. Ever! Is he strong? Of course he is. Feel that muscle; I could ride on his back. Where was he bred? Are there any more like him?"

"None that I am aware of. He was possibly bred in Kyabra, though, and sold in the Inner Duchies. His two littermates, as near as we can gather, were not so exceptional."

"So he is a sport, a throwback. You realize, my Lady, that at one time all armigerents of Kyabra were almost this size. The stories tell us they were a ferocious force in battle and a useful beast of burden in peace. But they were too unstable for a placid society, so recent breeding has turned them into the weak, lazy things you see now. How did you come by him when you know so little about him? He has been severely ill-treated." He looked accusingly at her, so she told him the whole story, including the scene in the Petrellan castle.

Just as she was finishing, a small man in well-scarred leathers approached. He, too, exclaimed over Patu. Without waiting for introductions, he gave his verdict. "You fed him too much. Oh, he may look good, but he'll be weak, clumsy, and slow. They never should have sold him to you when he was so young. I'll bet he was unruly when you first got him. This one's a throwback. Should have been destroyed at birth; they're always trouble. Big, ugly, and unmanageable." He stared at Zoe's group belligerently.

Zoe could keep her anger down no longer. "He is not ugly!"

The man focused on her. "He isn't? Look at that face. Only his mother could love it. Look at his colouring, with those longer strands of lighter hair sprouting all down his back. He'll always look rough, like he just came down off a mountain."

Zoe looked with new eyes at her friend. Come to think of it, he did look out of place here, with these well-dressed people, these sleek horses. Then rebellion and pride flared in her. "That's exactly where he did come from, and I don't mind being reminded!"

"And who trained him? Who is controlling him? Why is he here in battle gear, unchained? That is a very dangerous beast, there."

Zoe advanced on the obnoxious little man, her voice held even. "I trained him, and he is under his own control. And who are you to question me?"

Lord Baridea stepped forward. "Lady Zoysana, I am sorry I was not given a chance to introduce you to my head trainer, Alphard. Alphard, this is Zoysana, the Outlander I told you was coming today. Please mind your manners!"

The little man's expression did not change. "I am sorry, my Lord, but it makes my blood boil when I see what people will do to these animals, turning them into freaks or monsters for their own amusement. Then, when the poor beast finally gets fed up and gives some back, they scream 'Dangerous animal!' and they kill him." He shot a defiant glance at Zoe.

Zoe was beginning to feel sympathy for this crusty fellow. "It's fine, my Lord Baridea. I couldn't agree with him more." She turned to the trainer. "He came to me young, wounded and starving. I couldn't do anything but bring him back to health. He ate a lot; you're right, there. But he ate nothing that he didn't chase down. We were in the mountains with no extra supplies for the winter, so we had to hunt wild sheep for his food. Believe me, if he had been weak, clumsy, or slow he would have starved or fallen off a cliff."

Grudgingly, the trainer regarded Patu again. "What was that nonsense about being under his own control?"

Zoe looked at the surrounding people, a larger group now. They all seemed interested in her answer, even her friends. "It's a matter of attitude. I discovered early on that he can't be forced to do anything. He has to feel he wants to. I can stop him from doing something because he respects me, but I can't make him do something that goes against his feelings. For example, I doubt if I could make him turn against Tadeo, because now he considers Tadeo a friend. I'm sorry about the battle gear. We wanted to dress him up for the occasion. He's not ferocious by nature. And I still don't think he's ugly!"

The little man still looked skeptical. "You mean that these throwbacks can be trained?"

Baridea seemed of a like mind. "Lady Zoysana, will you demonstrate his training?"

"Right here?"

"Do you need a special place? We have training grounds, a practice field..."

Zoe scanned the courtyard. "No, this will do fine. Patu, go get Jobe." He bounded off, slowing as he neared the horses so as not to disturb them, but the stable boys scattered anyway, leaving them unattended. Patu threaded through the milling stock and nudged Jobe with his shoulder. The little pony obediently trotted towards Zoe.

She pointed. "Now put the grey in that corner, and the white over there. Then bring Lord Janitra's horse to him." The talk was a cover; she was using her hand signals. Soon the horses stood as she had indicated and Patu stood panting before her. Tadeo's grey started to wander, but one glance in his direction by the armigerent changed his mind. Then Zoe held up a finger to ask her audience to wait, and walked behind a nearby pillar. She sent the chirping whistle ringing out, and Patu started moving again. Quickly, but without frightening them, he lined the horses up as they had been before. Zoe then whistled again, and he began to run. After their training sessions on the road the horses were used to this, so they ignored him. She repeated the stunt she had shown Janitra back at the cottage, but with four horses Patu had to touch Jobe's saddle with his forepaws in order to make the vault.

She came out to meet him as he returned, hugging and wrestling him. "The small herding dogs in Petrella can cross a flock, running on the backs of the sheep. I guess I have to find Patu a very large flock!"

Alphard regarded his master in amazement. "And we've been destroying them at birth for the last two hundred years." She had rarely seen a man so disgusted with himself, and she liked him even more. "If he was bred here, he will be marked. Can we look? I have the ropes nearby."

It was Janitra who answered. "Ropes are not needed. But you will not find what you seek."

Zoe rolled Patu on his back to display the disfiguring scar. The little trainer explored, then straightened, his face suffused with anger. He, too, had recognized the significance of the scars on the animal's undersides. "Is there no way to find the one who did this?"

"There is no official proof, but there is little doubt as to the identity of the villain. He has lost considerable face, being shamed before his peers."

Alphard was mollified. "An indication how difficult this beast was when young. I wonder how he got over it."

"When he came to me he was almost dead from exhaustion, hunger and his wounds. He had come through high mountains, considered impassable at that time of year. I gained his trust when he had no ability to argue. After that, it was all simple."

The small, dark eye glinted up at her. "Simple, was it?"

"Well, I admit there were times..."

A sardonic grin slid across the tight lips, then disappeared. "There usually are." The two exchanged a companionable look that excluded the rest of the audience. Then the trainer raised his head towards his master. "May I take the lady to see my beasts, my Lord? They are no match for hers, but I am sure she would be interested."

"I suspected she might be." He sketched a bow to them. "Please, go and enjoy yourselves. That is why I brought you together. Good may come of it. Lord Janitra and I may discover topics of mutual interest to discuss while you are gone." He did not sound hopeful of this, but at least he was willing to try. Zoe hoped it was a positive sign.

With Patu between them and Tadeo following, they started towards the kennels.

In all, it was an interesting morning. As promised, the Kyabran armigerents were no match for Patu, but they superseded Petrellan beasts in size, beauty, and personality. Alphard was at first concerned for Zoe's safety, as she showed no respect at all for the ferocious reputations of his charges. Though a stranger, she took liberties with his touchiest animals that they rarely allowed him. After a while, he realized that she was in no danger and relaxed, although he could not help but comment.

Zoe's response was a laugh. "I have never had problems with armigerents, even before Patu. The trainers in Petrella would not let me near their animals because they said I was too thoughtless. But I am also cheating. Did you see what happened when I checked her wounded leg?" She nodded towards a pregnant bitch.

"I confess I was too worried to notice much. She has an uneven temper, especially just before she whelps. She wasn't too happy about you touching her, but then she settled. How did you do that?"

"I didn't. Patu talked to her."

"He did?"

"Oh, yes. Distinctly. She raised her hackles, and he turned his head and stared at her. She knuckled under. I'm covered with his scent and he is the dominant one here. I'm part of his pack, so she would never dare to touch me. Besides, she's only an armigerent. I can read her easily. I would know before she did if she was going to snap, and I would slap her nose before it moved. She knows that, too."

The trainer was enthusiastic. "I understand. I read them, although not to the level that I would trust my hand near a wounded stranger. How did you learn?"

"I didn't. It is something I've always been able to do. Since having Patu, of course, my ability has improved."

Alphard spoke softly, as if to himself. "So he isn't the only throwback."

"What was that?"

His head snapped up. "Nothing, my Lady. I meant no offence!"

"I hear no offence, Alphard, but I am interested in what you said."

"It is not that simple, my Lady."

"There is plenty of time. Explain, please."

"It is a long lesson in our history."

She sat on the rail of a puppy fence, motioned for him to do likewise. "I am here to learn. Teach me."

He remained standing, assuming a narrator's pose.

"The story of the decline of the armigerents. Once they were much greater than they are now. Yours would be an example of the standard they rose to."

"So I gather."

"It began in the days when The Lady walked our land. Then the armigerents were great. Ferocious in war, loving in the home. But not just the animals themselves. They had a special family of Trainers. These men, and women too, had wonderful rapport with their beasts. This is why the most fearsome fighting beast could be trusted with the smallest child." He glanced at her. "Yes, I heard the story of the baby in the street, my Lady. I did not believe it until today."

He resumed his formal pose. "As the ages rolled, The Lady passed from us, but her armigerents became a power in the land. The control of these beasts became an important underpinning for anyone who wished to rule. Too important to be entrusted to an independent family. So the armigerents were taken from us, to be trained by those loyal to the rulers." He did not seem to notice the slip of the pronoun.

"There followed a terrible time. The great armigerents were not understood. They were treated as wild animals. I am sure you have heard stories of war beasts ravaging the field, killing men on both sides? This is the time of those atrocities. The rulers could no longer use the armigerents, so the strongest were destroyed and the breed became weaker."

"And what happened to the family of Trainers?"

"The legends do not say, but there remained those who had an affinity for the armigerent, who seemed to understand him better than the average man. Those who have this Talent are always normal trainers. I, myself, have some of the skill, as I mentioned to you earlier." His voice, raised in pride, became quieter. "But once in a long while, every other generation or so, one is born with the old Talent to a greater degree. Such as yourself, my Lady. The meaningful part, though, is that never, in all our recent history, has one with the Talent ever tried to train a throwback armigerent. I suppose no one thought to try; the taboos were too strong."

"Why do you say meaningful?"

"Because events of this sort are not accidental. There is an important event to come in the flow of our land's history. Perhaps you, my Lady, will be part of it." His eyes had taken on a fervid glow.

"Alphard, what do you wear around your neck, under your shirt?"

His fist jumped to his chest. "What do you mean, my Lady?"

"Do not worry. I am aware of your beliefs, and it serves to help me understand what you are talking about." She smiled and shrugged. "I don't think I'm going to do anything momentous, though."

His hand relaxed away, but he leaned forward earnestly. "My Lady, one can never predict where The Lady will move next."

"I suppose not. Have you anything else to show me?"

She had broken the moment, and they returned to their discussion of the mundane matters of the kennel. He had much information that she found fascinating, and he was keen for her opinion as well, so the time flew past. Then a boy came to bring them to the main courtyard; it was time to return if they did not wish to ride in the afternoon's heat.

They declined the offer of a meal, but finished off a cold, spiced drink in the yard before they mounted. It was a friendly leave-taking, and Zoe wondered what had happened while she was with the armigerents.

Janitra was in high spirits as they rode along. "Zoe, you have been most useful today," he crowed with an uncharacteristic enthusiasm. "It was almost worth all the trouble to go and find you, bring you here, teach you manners..."

Taking her cue from his jovial mood, she cut him off at that point with a swipe of her folded gloves at his head. "No insults, now, or I'll take my beast and go back to the wilds. What happened?"

"Please, no. Whatever you do, don't go anywhere until he's had a chance to breed his best bitch with Patu. You don't mind, do you? There would be a huge stud fee!"

Zoe laughed. "So it's bribery, is it? Don't worry. I doubt if I could stop him from breeding if he took a mind to it."

Janitra sobered. "It isn't really bribery. You forced Baridea to see our problem from another point of view. He realizes now that there are important things out there, beyond our boundaries, even Kyabran things. I think he also realizes that there are non-Kyabrans who might deserve his respect: a new thought for him. He has never met anyone like you!"

"Like Patu, you mean."

"You too. He was impressed by your sword work yesterday. Asked me all about training in Petrella. He was amazed at my descriptions of your heavy cavalry. In some of my people's eyes, our last contact was when you barbarians drove us out, centuries ago. I think he pictured Petrellans as barbaric as the Inari of the plains."

"So will that help you in your plans?"

"Immensely. He hasn't said anything specific, but he is asking questions and thinking. Baridea is a fair man, though stubborn, and once he starts to accept new information he cannot help but lean in our direction. Since he is the strongest of our opponents, that changes the power structure enough to allow us to move ahead sooner than expected." He was

307

thinking aloud, now, making plans. "That will mean more meetings, and I must make a sweep of our supporters. I won't need you for that, Zoe. You have served your purpose admirably."

His attention came back to her. "And are you getting what you came for? I have used much of your time for my purposes. How can we assure that you are repaid?"

"I am doing very well indeed, my Lord. I am taking in your culture as fast as my head can stand it. Your own library has furnished me with more ideas than I can carry home, even on the paper you toss around so freely. I learned enough today about armigerents to keep me working for a year. There may be other things I could learn of, though. Your metalworking, for example? I hear that your smiths can make blades of exceptional strength and flexibility."

Tadeo spoke up from his position at her shoulder. "You have been listening to the ballads, my Lady."

"What ballads?"

"Perhaps you haven't, then. But that is where the rumour comes from. The ballads and the legends of the Thousand-Forged Blade. I fear that is what they are: ballads and legends. I have never seen such a thing. Have you, Lord Janitra?"

"Our smiths do produce fine weapons. They command a good price wherever we take them. But the Thousand-Forged Blade? Never."

"What is this Thousand-Forged Blade? If you will pardon the expression, you whet my appetite, then give me no information. Is this part of your merchant's technique to drive the price up?"

They both laughed. "Not at all, Zoysana. You now know as much as we do. This sword is said to be extremely sharp and strong and never rusts. But I have no knowledge of how it is made, if such a thing is even possible. Do you Tadeo?"

308

"Not at all, my Lord."

"Then who does?"

"Perhaps the balladeers? But if you are serious about tracking the idea down, you must talk to the armourers. Our smith at the Omanisa Home would be a good place to start. He is a master craftsman and carries the lore of his trade in his head. Do you wish to speak with him?"

"As soon as we reach your Home!"

Janitra was still feeling informal enough to joke again. "One thing we need to cure you of, Zoe, is this barbaric habit of running around in the heat of the day. After the noon rest, please!"

42. A Thousand Folds

Suta, the Omanisa armourer, was not a smith of the type Zoe knew back in the castle or the villages of Petrella. Mainly because of his size. He was in no way remarkable. Although he was no weakling, his muscles did not stand out, and he seemed about average in size and weight. She had always assumed that a smith would show the effects of long hours at a hard job, and wondered how this man coped.

She soon understood. Janitra personally introduced them, as a sign to each of his regard for the other, then went about his own pressing business. The smith was perplexed but too polite to show his skepticism at why a lady would be interested in his work. Rather than explain the complicated politics and history involved, she suggested that he go about his tasks and allow her to observe. This suited him well enough and he turned back to his forge.

Zoe saw that he did most of his work in his head. Every piece of metal was at precisely the right temperature before he brought it to the anvil, and he returned to the forge the moment it cooled lower than the optimum working point. He did not waste one blow on hard, cooling metal. His hammer strokes were accurate, and he moved with an economy that wasted no energy. Even in the warmth of the late afternoon, he seemed unaffected by the heat of the forge.

When Zoe commented on this, he agreed. "Yes, my Lady, it was a great disappointment to my father when we realized I would grow no further. He was sure I could not follow the family trade. But I learned how to keep up. I save the light work like this," he nodded to the delicate dagger, glowing deep in the coals, "for when it's hot. Bigger stuff I handle in the morning. Interesting you should notice."

"I have done my share of sweating in the hot sun. It may not show here, but where I was raised, I was always the smallest one. I can appreciate any technique which equalizes me with my larger companions."

He glanced at her with renewed interest. "What would size or strength have to do with a lady's occupations, my Lady?"

"A sword, staff, or bow has little sympathy for the size of the person holding it."

His look rested on her longer, then he nodded, as if confirming something to himself, and turned to give the bellows several slow, even pumps. "And have you ever swung a hammer?"

"Yes, a little."

"Would you like to try on this?" He reached in with the tongs and pulled the dagger out. The blade was cherry red, blending to yellow near the narrow tip.

She seized the proffered hammer and positioned the metal on the anvil. She regarded it to see what had been done so far, then tried a few light strokes, just to get the feel of it. Encouraged, she loosened up and swung harder. The hammer head glanced, leaving a curved dent in the soft steel where the edge had dug in. She hit the same spot twice more to erase the imperfection, but it remained. She was about to strike again when she realized that repeated blows would widen the material too much and that the thin shaft was cooling and should soon be returned to the fire. She looked up at Suta, shrugged, and handed him the tongs. "I never should have tried it. I have no idea what kind of metal it is, and I'm out of touch. I need to practice on something less delicate, first."

He nodded, gave the metal two precise strokes and laid it back in the forge.

She frowned inwardly. *Who do I think I am, anyway? I have done too much showing off lately, and it has gone to my head. I hope I have not damaged an important relationship the way I marred his handiwork.*

311

He seemed to hold no grudge. "Would you like to try something else?" His hand swung in the general direction of his cluttered workbench.

"Not today, thank you. I didn't come dressed for work." She indicated her plain clothing, a castoff from Merghani, the sister who was closest to her size. Her grandfather's robe had been getting too much wear due to her lack of other 'proper' Kyabran costume. "Perhaps I can borrow something appropriate from one of Tadeo's sisters for tomorrow."

"Ah, young Lord Priya. A good lad, that. Comes around to talk. Knows his weapons, that one." He grinned at her. "Can't say as I've seen him lift a hammer, though. You'll be staying with his family, then?"

"No, I'm..." she wasn't sure of how to express it, "I'm sponsoring him."

He turned from the bellows towards her. "You are sponsoring him?"

"Yes."

Again that nod, without comment. Then, "As I said, a fine lad. Intense, though. Your work is laid out for you there. You are aware or you wouldn't have taken him."

It seemed more of a question than a statement, so she nodded. "We've been on the road together for over a month. I have a good idea of how he feels. By the way, is that dagger getting hot?"

The smith spun around and slipped the shaft out of the forge, eyeing it. The very tip held tinge of white. He held it upright, regarding her past the cooling blade. "Come here to teach me my job, have you?"

She smiled. "Not at all. In fact, I was wondering what I could learn from you."

Satisfied with its temperature, he administered his usual precise strokes, then replaced it in the heat. "You don't want to be a smith."

"No, but I will do what work I must to learn what I can. Stories say that Kyabran smiths have techniques that have been forgotten, or never learned in other lands. Lord Janitra has offered me the chance to talk to you, to see if you will give me any ideas to take to my home."

"Did you have something specific in mind?"

"Not much. Maybe you could tell me of anything you thought was especially effective. I have heard your swords are very light and strong."

He regarded her with a sigh. "You have been listening to ballads, haven't you?"

She tried to look innocent.

"It's the Thousand-Forged Blade you want, isn't it?"

Since he confronted her, she couldn't deny it.

"Legends, stories, and balladeers whose mouths are even bigger than their imaginations!"

"So there is no such thing?"

"Do you know what would happen if you folded a piece of metal a thousand times? It would become so brittle it would break if you hit it with a broomstick. Four hundred is the absolute maximum. For a sword, three hundred is ideal. But a thousand? Hah! Complete romantic twaddle!"

Zoe's hope returned. "You mean such a sword exists?"

Suta wasn't quite calmed down yet. "Were you listening?"

"Yes! You said three hundred times. What does that mean, and what is the effect? Have you ever made one?"

"Huh! Made one? I haven't the time for such a thing. Never knew anyone who had. But yes, it is possible. The method has been handed down in my family for generations. The true method, mind you, not some story singer's foolishness. Memorized word for word from my father and from his father, just like all my family's techniques. And it will work! There are those who says it won't, but if the plan is in my family lore, it works."

At her enthusiastic nod, he continued. "In simple terms, you take your piece of metal for the sword, heat it in the forge, flatten it thin and fold it over. Then flatten it again and fold it over again. Three hundred times. No more, for a sword. It makes the metal flexible, but hard as well. My father's grandfather made a razor like that once. Folded it four hundred times! Took him ages, and that was only a little razor. But it came out amazingly hard. Took an edge you wouldn't believe, kept it for months. The Old Omanisa, Lord Janitra's grandfather, gave it to the king of Trasani for a wedding present. It was well received, I hear. Something of an heirloom in their family, now. But too brittle for a sword. As I say. Three hundred." He turned back for a few delicate taps on the dagger's tip.

"Could I make one?"

For a moment he seemed not to have heard her, as he placed the finished blade on the stone that supported the forge. Then he turned. "You're serious, aren't you? You think you will come in here and work at this fire, in the hottest part of the summer, until you have folded a sword-length of steel three hundred times? Do you know arithmetic?"

It was a valid question; few needed it, so few learned more than the basic sums. "If I could do three folds a day, that would take me a hundred days. Just over three months. If I can work faster, it will take less time. If I can do less, then it will take even longer."

"And that is only the folding," he warned.

She grinned at him. "Well, by the time I get to shaping, polishing and tempering, the heat of summer will be over, won't it?"

His responding smile was grim. "By the time you reach that stage, it may be full summer again."

Zoe straightened her shoulders. "Then we shall see, won't we?"

He considered her again for a long while. *Slow to make up his mind, but sure of it afterwards. This man will instruct me well once he decides I deserve it.* There would be no showing off with her fancy skills. This would be plain hard work, and plenty of it.

"Come. We will look at steel."

He banked the coals of his forge and led her to an inner room. There they were surrounded by the usual smith's collection of metal: large bits and small, old pieces of armour and tools, new sheets, rods and roughed-out stock. The sheer amount of material present spoke volumes about the importance of the smithy in Janitra's opinion.

Suta picked up a sword blank and handed it to Zoe. She felt the heft.

"Heavy and too short."

"The metal lengthens as you flatten it, and a certain amount is always wasted with shaping and filing. By the time you are finished, it will be the right length." He indicated a rack of blades at varying degrees of completion. "What length and weight suits you?"

She regarded the selection, tried one that looked about right. "It's difficult to tell, with no pommel to balance it. But this one is the right length, though perhaps light."

"It would feel that way, with no counterweight. If you want a sword that long you want a larger piece to start with." He sorted through the pile again, discarding pieces until he found one he liked. Zoe looked at it. It was of an even colour, though it was not the smoothest.

"Do you know why I chose that over the others?"

"Well, the smoothness doesn't count; I'm sure I'll fix that in the next three hundred folds. The colour is even throughout. It also seems greyer than the others."

He nodded. "This piece came from a different merchant. His source is secret, but his general stock is better metal than most. The evenness of colour is an example; there are no impurities in the steel. There will be no weak spots in this sword that you did not put there yourself." She could see his demeanour switching from 'servant-to-lady' to 'master-to-apprentice,' and her hopes rose. *If I can win him over, my chances of success are higher.*

"So may I start with this tomorrow?"

He regarded her. "Did you not say you were out of practice? Would you spoil your handiwork with impatience?"

"I suppose not. Would you put it aside for me, then, for when I am ready?"

He smiled, the first friendly smile she had received from him. "Don't worry. You will be ready soon. I do not intend to make you serve a full apprenticeship."

She bowed, the Kyabran 'apprentice-to-master.' "I will not keep you from your work any longer. Until dawn tomorrow?"

He returned her bow, 'servant-to-lady.' "Dawn tomorrow, my Lady." He shook his head and reached for the dagger, cooling on the hearth.

Tadeo was mildly surprised when informed that they would not be having their usual morning practice session the next day. Jaddie was not quite so calm.

Her shriek of laughter attracted her other sisters from their evening occupations. "A smith? You are going to become a smith? Whatever are you thinking of? You'll have scars all over

316

you and muscles like a man's. I can just picture it!" She went off into a fit of giggling.

Rhesia frowned. "Jaddie! You will apologize! You will not speak to a guest that way." Then she turned to Zoe. "Zoysana, I cannot see what the benefit will be. As she says, you will not make yourself any prettier at that job. Can't your king afford to buy you whatever sword you want?"

"But these swords don't exist. At least not that anyone can find. There may be a few gathering dust on people's walls, but not one that I could buy."

Merghani's response was typically slower but more thoughtful. "Is this sword going to be that much better?"

"I think so. A sword can be made harder by the tempering process, but too much tempering makes it too brittle, so it breaks easily. According to the stories, and Suta agrees with this part at least, these swords are both harder and more flexible than regular steel, so they can be made lighter and still be more effective than a normal sword, with no fear they will shatter."

"But will it be worth the time and effort?"

Zoe considered. "For the one sword, no. But remember, I am not here to get a sword for myself. If that was all, I could pay enough money and someone would make me one. What I want to take away with me is the knowledge. Do you think I could just write down the instructions to take back to the armourers in Petrella? I need the experience of having done the job myself. Knowledge can be expensive, and the most important information often must be earned at the greatest cost. In answer to your question, yes, it will be worth it."

Falihea had said nothing up to this point. Now, she laid a hand on Zoe's sleeve. "Zoysana…?"

Zoe had spoken little to this quietest of the sisters and was curious what her reaction would be.

"...have you designed the hilts yet?"

"No, I hadn't even thought of it. That's months from now."

"Could I make you a design? I have an idea I could show you."

Zoe smiled. "Well, if this is to be a special sword, I suppose it needs a special hilt, and who better to design it than the family artist? Why don't you draw me a picture, and we can talk about it?"

"Could I make a model? I think better in solid forms."

"An even better idea."

There was a moment of embarrassed silence, as Zoe did not know what to say next. Falihea solved it by smiling and leaving.

With this tacit approval from her more serious siblings, Rhesia decided disapproval was a lost cause. With one admonitory glare at Jaddie, she went back to the robe she had been embroidering. The youngster gave an expressive shrug as if to absolve herself of any responsibility and left as well.

Tadeo remained, shaking his head and smiling. "You are a great trial to them, my Lady."

"How so?"

"They consider themselves to be progressive. They think that new ideas are the only ideas. But they do not realize how tied they are to their comfortable lives. Here you come, giving them a model of the new ways they think they would embrace. Then you pull a trick like this, and it throws them off balance. Except Falihea, of course. Her art is all that matters to her, and she is far from traditional in her own realm. I will be interested to see her design."

"Do you think she will accept guidance from me as to the form? I have definite ideas as to the shape of the guard, but I didn't like to interfere, so I didn't say anything."

He shrugged. "If she wants to apply her art to practical objects, she will learn to bow to the demands of function. Of course you must tell her. If it hurts her feelings, just remember that you are the one who will spend months of your life on this. You must be the one satisfied with the results, I should think."

Zoe was grateful to him for his easy ability to handle these four separate sources of trouble. Not for the first time, she wondered who should be sponsored to whom.

43. A False Start

By mid-morning the following day, she was also wondering what was wrong with her head.

Suta had given her a small piece of metal with instructions to rough out a dagger. She had pounded and sweated over it until it was what she considered an acceptable shape. Her instructor had been satisfied, putting the rough form aside and taking out her piece of grey steel, laying it on the anvil in front of her.

"Flatten it to just over twice its present width. Begin at the tip, work towards the hilt. Whatever you do, don't get in a hurry. If you burn it, the flaw cannot be repaired." Staying to see that she was in control, he had then gone about his other business.

Now he stood at her elbow, looking down at the curving, dented mass of metal she held.

"Not bad."

"Not bad? It's not even straight, and it's full of bumps!"

"Remember, it need not be straight until the last fold. You will learn." His lip twitched. "You have plenty of time. Now let us start the fold. Lay the hot spot along the edge of the anvil, thus, and tap gently, alternating to either side like this." He demonstrated on the metal, too cool now to bend, then slid it into the fire again.

"Do I try to follow the bends, or do I make the fold straight?"

"Split your path between the two possibilities. There. It seems hot enough. Try it."

Wiping the sweat from her face with a begrimed wrist, she hefted her hammer again, trying her best to follow her instructions. Balancing the steel on the edge, she soon found that every time she hit the metal it tried to twist out of her grip.

Grimly she thumped away as perspiration poured down her body.

As she struggled her way up the blade, she began to get the feel of it and the work went faster. She was concerned, a while later, to see Suta standing beside her, his leather apron removed, drying his hands on a cloth.

"Time to stop."

"Why? I want to finish the first fold. I'm not tired yet!"

"You may not be, but I am. We worked considerably past my usual time. The noon meal will be ready. I shall return this evening when it is cool."

"And I." She straightened, realizing how stiff her back was.

"No sword workout today?"

She thought this over. "I did tell the students I would help them..."

"If I might suggest, my Lady, you would be better to build into this new task gradually. Today you worked muscles you rarely use, and by this afternoon they will be telling you about it. A good dose of familiar exercise would be the best remedy. Then you will be in shape to do better work tomorrow."

She bowed to his wisdom, thanked him and departed, feeling more relieved than she thought she should. It hadn't been all that bad this morning, although the heat had bothered her more than she had expected. At least her sword-hardened hands had not blistered. She knew she would take full advantage of the midday rest period, though. The thought of moving freely in the cool evening air, sword swooping in her hand, held a marvellous appeal. Almost as wonderful as getting this grime washed off her face.

The following morning was more consistent; she felt terrible right from the start. In spite of her good condition, there were muscles she had not noticed that she was very aware of now. Looking at the twisted piece of grey metal in front of her, she wondered again what she thought she was doing. Gritting her teeth, she shoved it into the coals and pumped on the bellows.

"Gently, now. No sense in getting it too hot – just wastes the charcoal. Steady strokes, not too fast. That's the way to do it. Easier on those stiff arms, too."

She grimaced at the accuracy of his perception, picked up her hammer and stepped out into the courtyard to swing it around, stretching out the aches. When she returned, the stock was hot enough to hammer. Now, it went much better. Her arms seemed to remember yesterday's lessons, and it wasn't long before she was calling across to her teacher, "Come and look at this!"

He put down the mailed glove he was riveting and sauntered over. "Finished the first fold?"

She demonstrated. "It isn't too pretty, but I should get better."

"I hope you get faster, too. That is one day's work you are looking at."

"In a hurry to get rid of me already?"

"No, my Lady, think of the arithmetic..."

"Three hundred folds, three hundred days. Don't worry, I'll get faster. I bet I can finish another fold today."

"The second day is not a day to overdo the exercise, my Lady."

"You have the most annoying habit of getting all stiff and formal, just when you have the most disagreeable truth to lay out."

"I suppose I do. Then, as my temporary apprentice, you listen to me, young lady. You may think this is all a lark, but if I allow Lord Janitra's favourite Outlander to injure herself, guess who is in trouble? Not you: me. So listen, or go and play elsewhere!"

"I think I liked you better stiff and formal." She held up a restraining hand. "And I am listening. We quit when you say so or when I drop dead, whichever comes first, right?"

"A tempting way to solve my problems, Lady Zoysana. Let us return to our work."

She could tell he was impressed when she had almost finished the second fold by noon. He said nothing, but nodded and hung up his apron.

So on into the lengthening days and sweltering heat of the summer she toiled. Her strokes came easier and cleaner, but an endless ribbon of metal seemed to stretch before her. Still, as she improved she made two folds a day, then three and sometimes four. One rare rainy morning she announced that today was the day for five folds.

Suta was unimpressed. "Lady Zoysana, I do not advise that you hurry. The speed will come when it comes."

She grinned in confidence. "I think it has come. Just watch the hammer fly today. There are sixty folds done, and by evening it will be sixty-five." She pulled the stock out of the forge for the first blows of the day.

Sure enough, by midday she had made three complete folds. When she returned to Tadeo's family rooms for the noon meal, she was pleased with herself. The family was impressed as well, having followed her progress in this project with avid interest.

It had taken Jaddie about a week to get used to Zoe's new task, and then she had done a typical about-face, becoming her greatest encourager. "We must come down to see you working, if you are doing so well!"

Merghani was also enthused. "Yes, Zoysana. I, too, would like to see how you are doing. May we come and watch?"

"You have all watched me work, one time or another. It is scarcely an exciting pastime."

"Ah, but this is a special occasion, and we want to be there to cheer as you finish off the last stroke of the fifth fold. It will be a fine thing to celebrate, will it not, Tadeo?"

Her brother held his hands open in a gesture of agreement. "Why not? We should find something to celebrate once in a while. It is good for the morale of the family."

Rhesia threw a cushion at him. "Oh, don't be so practical. Can't we relax and do something because it's fun?"

"I thought I just said that."

It was a cheerful party that trooped down to the forges that evening as the sun slid down into the cooler angles near the horizon. Zoe started out quite enthused with this attention, but when she got out her tools to start she realized that they had all settled themselves around the shop in comfortable poses as if watching a performance.

"This isn't that exciting. I'm just going to heat this steel and hit it and then heat it up again."

Tadeo grinned from where he leaned in the doorway. "Don't worry, my Lady. Watching you work will be a treat in itself. I am surprised that there is not a larger audience." He made as if to leave. "I could probably find some."

"Tadeo, if you bring one more person here, you and I will practice Weaponless combat against the sword all day tomorrow. And guess who will get the sword?"

"My Lady speaks forcibly and to the point, as usual. Pray proceed, then."

"I will." She pumped up the bellows until the coals were blazing, then slid the steel into the middle of the bed. In a short time a dull rosy hue seeped along the blade. Soon a brighter red followed, and when she thought a goodly length was hot enough, she laid it on the anvil, and started swinging, conscious of the eyes upon her.

The first swings were awkward, but soon she got back into the rhythm, with the hammering, the bellows and the stoking of the forge, and she began to relax. Soon her self-consciousness was gone, forgotten in the pattern of the work; the ring of the hammer, the whoosh of the bellows and the roar of the fire lulled her, and she almost forgot about her audience, so that she was startled by a burst of clapping. Looking down, she realized that she had finished the fourth fold of the day and that her friends were crowding around her with congratulations.

"So far so good," she cautioned them, pushing the sword length back into the forge, "but there is still one to go."

"But you work so hard! How can you do that, hour after hour?"

She smiled at Jaddie. "How long do you practise your Dance every day?"

"Oh. But that's fun."

"Well, this isn't that much fun, but I do get a feeling of accomplishment from it."

"You get more than that." Falihea's soft voice cut through the family noise as usual.

"And?"

"You were barely here. You were somewhere else."

"That is true, now that I think about it. The rhythm of the blows and the sameness of the work are rather relaxing. It is a similar feeling to that of practice patterns. It soothes my mind, and you might even say it refreshes my soul..."

She was interrupted at this point by a deferential "My Lady," from Suta, and the alarms ringing in her head. She dove for the forge, grasping the metal in the tongs and pulling it from the flames.

Too late. The end was a glowing, lumpy white mass of metal, setting off sparks and drooping at a sad angle. She laid it on the anvil and stood back and stared. The others crowded back, and Suta stood beside her, dumb as well.

As the metal cooled, he picked up the hammer and tapped it. A few lumps fell off, to roll on the floor, smoking. He hit it harder, and a large piece at the end broke into fragments. He leaned over, then looked up at her.

"How much have I lost?"

"Only about a finger's length, my Lady."

"I will have to make the sword that much shorter?"

"Perhaps not. The stock will continue to stretch as you work it. You can lengthen it on purpose, but that will take metal from the rest of the blade. You will end up with a thinner sword of the same length."

"But if it is thinner, will it be strong enough?"

He shrugged. "That is hard to say, my Lady. We are not sure how strong this sword will be, in any case. However, we did consider this point very carefully before you started, and I do not think there is enough stock left to make a finished sword within the guidelines we discussed."

"Couldn't I weld another piece on?"

"Again, with this type of work, I cannot give you a simple answer. You can weld more metal on. There is plenty from the same source. But it would no longer be a perfect blade. The one spot would always contain a difference, perhaps a weakness, or maybe just a change of flexibility."

Zoe picked up the twisted length of metal, now cooled to an angry red, viewing it regretfully. "We did say I should work on a practice piece until I was sure I knew what I was doing."

Suta inclined his head once. "That is a whole lot of practice, my Lady."

She tossed her head. "I can be at sixty folds again in a half-month if I start now."

A stifled sob burst out. Jaddie was holding a fist to her mouth, tears on her cheeks. "It was us, wasn't it? We distracted you, and now it's ruined, isn't it?"

Suta answered. "It isn't ruined, my Lady. Even a short sword length folded sixty times is a valuable piece of stock. For example, I could make two excellent parrying daggers from that. Or you could, Lady Zoysana."

"No, Suta, you take it and make what you will." She strode to the back room, dim in the coming dusk. "I need another blank."

When she returned to place her new stock in the forge, the others were gone and Suta was busily at work on his own projects. Grimly, she set to work. Late into the night, working only by the glow of the coals, she hammered away. Long after moon-set she finally straightened up, laying the new blade aside to cool.

Suta sat in a corner of the shop, watching her.

"Five folds, my Lady?"

"At least I can fulfill one of my objectives."

He walked over to the wall where she had been keeping count and scratched a piece of charcoal just once on a new panel. "Let us count by fives, then."

She smiled, a tired smile. "Yes. After all, one fold is hardly worth walking across the room to mark down, is it?"

It was only later, after her exhausted body had the time to relax, that the full enormity of her loss pushed through the fatigue. She lay, cradling her pillow in her arms, and cried until even that was too much effort. Her sobs gradually subsided, and she slept.

44. All Over Again

The next morning she awoke slowly and late, wondering for that vulnerable instant before full consciousness why she felt so terrible. Then the memory hit her and she felt worse. She considered not getting out of bed, but then her training took over and she dragged herself to a sitting position. The moment she moved there was a light rap at her door, and Falihea's small, neat head poked around.

"Are you awake, my Lady?"

"What happened to 'Zoysana' this morning?" she grouched.

"I don't know." The other spoke with simple frankness. "My Lady just seemed better."

Zoe ran a hand through her hair, then leaned her face in her palms, elbows supported by knees. "Nothing seems much better at the moment. I slept in, I guess."

"Yes, I was waiting."

Zoysana did not lift her head. "Why?" It seemed the required response.

"I have something for you. I had not thought to show it yet, but I think today would be appropriate. Will you come?"

Zoe shrugged, with an approximation of returning grace. "Just give me time to wash and dress."

"Good. I will wait." The girl was outside with the door closed before Zoe had a chance to regain her manners. To compensate, she hurried through her morning toilet and was soon in the hallway where Falihea was waiting, a large slice of fresh bread in one hand, a chunk of cheese in the other. About to refuse, Zoe realized that the aroma of the bread was overpowering, and she was starving. Giving the girl a grateful nod over a mouthful, she waved a hand to show her willingness to be led.

Falihea's workrooms were in a limbo area of the compound, between the living spaces and the workshops. In the front room where she did her weaving, the large table where she sketched out her projects was covered with drawings of various sword hilts.

Leading the way into the back room, she stopped in front of a worktable and lifted a cloth off the object sitting there. "It is against my principles to show a half-finished work to anyone. People are so poor at visualizing the final project when there are rough edges and the colour is wrong. But I thought you might like to see it now." She made no mention of the reason, which draped over their shoulders like a dark fog.

Zoe looked at the modelled sword hilt before her, then walked around to check from another angle. It was a standard hilt, but the quillons swept back across the knuckles in several strands, to join the handle at the pommel. The strands were woven together, joining and parting, to look like a basket of willow wands.

"Go ahead. You can pick it up."

She slid her hand into the basket. The handle nestled into her palm. Holding it in fighting position, she tried several of the more awkward moves. Enclosing though it was, the basket did not hinder her wrist in any way. She held it out in front of her, regarding it critically from different angles. It protected much more of her hand than a normal hilt would.

"The form is not original," came the worried voice from her side. "I got the idea from Suta. It is a hilt designed for someone who does not wear mail gauntlets, who needs more protection. I thought you would only be wearing riding gloves most of the time, so..." She shrugged. "Is it all right?"

Zoe considered the design. "It seems to be a very good idea. I cannot think of any problems there might be with it. It's just so...so different." She turned to Falihea with a grin. "That's the problem. It's so different I don't know what to think!" She swung her arm a few times. "You can't get the feel of it, with no weight, but it seems fine."

She turned to the girl, standing anxiously to the side. "This is a switch, isn't it? You coming up with something so new that I am stymied. Has anyone else seen this?"

"Oh, no. I wanted you to see it first. The rest wouldn't like it because it's too different. They don't come in my studio. I won't let them. Some of my work is too strange. They would either laugh or get angry, so I don't show them anything unless they might comprehend it. Otherwise, I keep it back here." She gestured around.

"Could I see something?"

The younger girl ducked her head. "Not now, please. I would need to look for things that you could understand."

"Why don't you let me see about that for myself?"

Falihea favoured her with an impish smile and, walking over to the table that ran the length of one wall, selected an object, which she handed to Zoe. It was a lump of dark, heavy wood with a subtle grain. It was sculpted into a series of shapes and curves, the pattern of which Zoe was unable to see. She held it up to the window, but still could find nothing familiar in it. Puzzled, she looked to the artist.

"Faces."

"Faces?"

"Yes. That's what I call it."

Zoe looked again. "Is it...well...finished?"

Falihea looked 'I told you so' as she reached out and removed the lump from Zoe's hand, replacing the work on the table. "Can we talk about the hilt, please? Is it all right?"

"I think it will be fine. You understand that I won't be able to tell until we fix it on the actual sword and I get to work with it.

Would you like to make up a stronger model to try out on a regular blade before you make the real thing?"

"Oh, no. I won't make it. Suta will do that. I create the model he works from."

"Can Suta do work like that?"

"He makes much finer things than that – chains and bracelets and the like. He could be a goldsmith if he wanted, but he prefers armour."

Zoe brandished the hilt once more, trying to find the right words. She knew that it was too late for a polite response. She should have made an immediate exclamation, but she had missed that opportunity in her cautious curiosity. Now any protestations of enthusiasm would ring hollow. As usual, she decided on the stark truth.

"Falihea, I appreciate the work you put into this. It may turn out to be the best thing I could use. We may discover problems, or it might not work at all. I can't tell until I try it. It looks so different, it will take me some time to get used to it."

The artist nodded, satisfied.

"Right then. And you have fulfilled your other aim for the morning too, in getting me out of the funk I was in. With a marvellous new hilt to try out, I better get a sword made to put it on!" Snatching the heel of her bread up from where she had laid it, she placed the model of the hilt back on the table and strode towards the forges.

"You are not the only one upset about last night."

The smaller girl was keeping stride with Zoe. She slowed down, raising her eyebrows.

"My sisters are in a terrible state this morning. You would think someone had died. Even Tadeo looks like a puppy that chewed its master's glove. They blame themselves for what happened. Should they?"

Zoe's grandfather had long ago given her the right response for this one. "It is a poor worker who blames others for a mistake in workmanship. How can I blame them? Yes, they distracted me. But what sort of craftsman can I say I am, if I blame them? Am I only a good worker when everything is going well?

"You have learned techniques like this before, I am sure. You know how you go through stages? I was at the stage where I had learned the physical technique. I was getting good, but I had yet to learn many more things, one of which was concentration. Now I have learned that lesson. A mistake was bound to happen. I hope I do not make another one, although I will not be surprised if I do.

"You understand. You can explain it to your sisters. Tell them I am angry with them. Ask them why they didn't come and distract me when I had only done thirty folds!" Laughing, she stepped into the forge, leaving Falihea shaking her head in the doorway.

45. A Failing of a Different Sort

At times Zoe hated the new sword. It was taking her whole life, from dawn to dusk. In her determination to catch up, she was at the forge for any part of the day that was cool enough, and some parts that weren't. Her world was becoming one single, drawn-out day of hammer and pump the bellows, stoke the forge and pump, then hammer again. Ten folds, twenty, thirty, fifty. The heat was blazing, but if she concentrated on that horrible piece of steel, she could forget for a while. She focused on the sword as she swung the hammer. She let her anger flow into the sword. She could feel it. Everything was going into the sword. It was drawing the moisture from her, sucking her dry. *Soon I will be nothing but a husk, to blow away on the wind or to flare into sparks in the burning heat of the forge.*

Suta took the hammer from her hand, pulled the steel out of the forge and laid it on the stone hearth.

She looked at him, perplexed. "What are you doing?"

"It is well past the noon meal, my Lady. Have you eaten?"

"Not yet. I was going to finish the next flattening before I ate."

"It is too hot. You should not be working."

"I work when I please," she flared. The strength to make that burst of emotion used up her last reserves. The realization that she felt weak was all the excuse her body required, and she needed to sit down. The shop spun around her and she was vaguely aware of Suta's strong hand guiding her to a bench, a dipper of cool water held to her lips.

"It is too hot to work, my Lady."

With the cool drink sliding down her throat, she rallied. "But I was doing fine. Look, I'm not even sweating." She held out a dry arm.

"That is a sure sign you can no longer handle the temperature. You used up all your sweat and there is no more to cool you. If you can walk, you should come outside where the breeze will work its healing."

When she rose, a black haze crowded over her vision and she swayed. Then her sight cleared, and she stumbled out to lean on the awning post. "The wind does feel better, Suta, thank you. I'll just rest here a moment before I go back in and finish off."

Oh, no. My sword! "Is my steel out of the forge? Oh, yes, of course it is. You took it out, didn't you?"

"I did, my Lady. Sit down for a while. I will get you another drink of water, and then you can rest."

Zoe folded herself down against the wall and he brought the water. She finished half of it, then poured the rest over her head. "If I have no sweat, I'll put more on from the outside." She managed a ghost of a smile.

"That does not work as well. Your sweat has certain properties which cool you, properties that water does not have."

She wondered where he had heard such rubbish. Too much bother to argue. She sat still, feeling the coolness of her damp shirt as it flapped against her body. Then she struggled to her feet.

"Time to return to work, I suppose."

She stood waiting for Suta to stand aside and let her enter the forge. He did not move.

"Excuse me, Suta, I would like to go back inside."

He remained in the door, blocking her way.

"Suta, thank you for the drink. I'm fine now, and I want to finish the flattening."

"My Lady, you must not work any more. It is much too hot."

"Suta, get out of my way!" She stepped forward, staggering, then used the flame of her anger to push herself erect. "I am going back to work."

"Lady Zoysana, come with me. It is time for another lesson."

"Another lesson?" *I have no time for lessons.* "Where are we going?"

"Into the next building. It's cooler in there, and we can talk more comfortably."

"But my work…"

"Your stock is out of the forge. If you like, you can return to it when the lesson is done."

"All right, if you say so." *… a cool place to sit down…*

Suta guided her into the next doorway, leaving her there briefly to call out to a servant who was crossing the courtyard, something about bringing Lord Priya. *I wonder what's wrong?* Then he ushered her into the room. It seemed to be a living space. There was a simple chair, a table and a bed against the wall.

"Does someone live here?"

"I do. Come and sit down on the bed. Good. Now stay there while I get fresh water. Would you like another drink?"

"Yes, that would be nice. What's the lesson about?"

"About your work on the sword. You can lie down if you like. I'll be back soon." He was gone, and she sat there looking around the room with vague curiosity. *So this is his room. Sort of like him, I suppose. I wonder if there is a special quality hidden under the plain exterior of the room, as there is in its owner.*

The bed did look comfortable. *Perhaps I can lie down for a while. When Suta returns we can talk, then I can go back to work. Yes, that's a good idea.*

She stretched out but soon felt uncomfortable. Where she touched the sheet, it burned her. She rolled over, feeling the delicious coolness of the other side, but soon that warmed up too. She couldn't find a comfortable spot to lie. She rolled over again and again until she was tossing in a bed of flames.

Then a cool dampness bathed her forehead and spread down her arms. It felt so much better, so she lay quiet, allowing it to cover her. A long while later she heard voices, but they were far away. Then she slept.

When she awoke it was dim in the little room, and much cooler. Someone was bathing her forehead with a damp cloth. She opened her eyes; it was Tadeo. She tried to rise, but he motioned her to stay still.

"How do you feel now, Zoysana?"

She thought about it. "Weak."

"Not unusual. You used up a lot of energy today."

"It seems I did. What happened?"

"It is called the sun sickness. One gets it from being out in the sun for too long. It is a common problem here in the summer, and we all take proper precautions. I suppose you got it from the heat of the forge. It can be serious. People die from it."

She tried to argue, but her tongue seemed heavy.

"Yes, my Lady. You gave me quite a scare. I didn't realize you were still working. I should have checked on you sooner."

She peered into the growing darkness to see Suta standing at Tadeo's shoulder.

She felt irritated. "You needn't watch over me like I am a child!"

"No, my Lady, but I must see that you learn the proper lessons."

"Suta, perhaps now is not the time…"

"My Lord, she must hear it while the experience is fresh in her mind."

"What is he talking about?" Zoe was confused again. *I remember something about a lesson, but I think I fell asleep.*

"The next lesson, my Lady." Suta came and knelt beside the bed. "Can you hear and understand me?"

"I suppose," she answered with a touch of ill grace. "As long as you don't make me sit up."

"No, my Lady. You stay right there and listen. I will tell you.

"You see, Lady Zoysana, while you are not my apprentice, yet you are learning from me, so it is my responsibility to be sure that you learn all the lessons. The first lesson, the lesson of the metal, you learned quickly. You knew it already. The second, the lesson of the mind, you learned hard, when you burned the first sword."

"Don't remind me."

"You must remember that lesson so you can learn the next. The third lesson, the lesson of the body, I thought you knew, because you were so careful: not a burn, not a cut, never a dangerous move. But I was wrong. You have not learned the full lesson of the body. You are able to drive your body past its point of endurance, true, but you have not learned how to watch it and care for it when driven past that point."

"Yes I have. There are many points to be driven past, with an increasing level of watchfulness for each point. I learned that in Weaponless training." She looked over at Tadeo for confirmation, and he nodded.

Suta leaned forward. "Then, my Lady, you must learn to apply your training to more than combat. We in the forge have learned that we cannot work if our bodies are not in the proper condition. Think what would have happened to your sword if it had been in the fire when you lost consciousness."

"I wasn't going to lose consciousness!"

"You almost did twice before I got you to lie down. Then for a short while you were delirious. Then we cooled you down and you slept. But you were in a precarious state. When you stop sweating the next stage is convulsions, then unconsciousness and then death."

She thought it over. "Oh."

Tadeo moved forward as well. He seemed upset. "And what good was it? You have put yourself behind whatever schedule you are on, because you will not work this evening and you will not be strong enough to work at your usual speed for several days. You must slow down, Zoe!"

"I'll be fine tomorrow." She looked at the two stony faces confronting her. "All right. If you say I won't be fine, I won't be fine tomorrow. I'll take it easy, only do what work I feel able to, all right?" She tried to smile. "Couple of bullies. Taking advantage of me when I'm weak."

Tadeo rose. "If you feel strong enough to insult us, perhaps you are recovering."

"Oh, honoured doctor, in your opinion, might I be able to walk to my room now? I can't be putting Suta out of his bed."

Over Suta's protestations, Zoe tried to rise, but the room spun around again and she lay back. "Just a moment, I'll try that again slower." She followed her own directions the second time and made it, first to the edge of the bed, then to her feet, a solicitous helper at either elbow. She waved them off. "I'm fine. No need to mother me."

As she came outside there was an anxious whine and a dark shape rose from the ground.

"Patu! What's the matter, fellow?" She turned him around and continued walking, resting her arm across his solid shoulder.

It was Suta who answered. "What's the matter? He's been impossible all afternoon. When you were in there tossing and turning he almost tore my room apart. I had to send him outside."

"You? You sent him out when he was upset?" Tadeo sounded as if he couldn't believe his ears.

"Had to. He wouldn't let me do anything. It wasn't difficult. I told him that I couldn't help Zoe with him banging around like that, so he had to go. And he went."

"You explained it to him, and out he went?"

"Well, that's what Lady Zoysana does. She talks to him all the time and he understands. I've watched them. I wasn't sure he would understand me, but I suppose he did. He knew her name, for sure. Whined a lot out there, though. Then when she went to sleep he calmed down. How did he know you were out of danger, my Lady?"

"He can tell what I'm thinking and feeling, even when I'm not right with him. He has very good hearing, too."

"I suppose. Why do you find this funny, my Lord?"

Tadeo forced himself to stop chuckling. "Do you realize what an armigerent is, Suta? Do you know how dangerous they are?"

"Of course, my Lord. But this is different."

"It certainly is. Modern armigerents are relatively tame. This animal is a throwback to the original battle beasts. Patu must be the most dangerous animal in this land. Plus he is in a state because his mistress is delirious, and you think you can handle him by explaining it to him calmly. Most people would think you were either very brave or very stupid!"

"There is one other possibility." She had the energy now to tinge her voice with asperity.

339

"And what is that, my Lady?"

"Since he was successful, I suppose one could suspect that he was very smart."

It was Suta's turn to chuckle. "Perhaps she is recovering, my Lord."

46. A SPECIAL SWORD

At other times, she loved the sword. After the first hundred folds, she could feel the difference in the metal. It had more spring when it was cold and it took longer to heat it to a working temperature.

There were days when every blow struck true. She practised making each fold neat, so that sometimes she could see the shape of the sword growing in the metal. She could feel the power building in her arms and shoulders, and that vigour flowed into the sword, making its strength part of her own. On the rare rainy day, she would make sure she ended the evening's work with a sword-like piece. She would take it into the courtyard while it still glowed and practice her patterns, watching the fiery trail hissing and burning in the damp dimness. Already she could feel the weapon becoming a part of her.

One evening, she looked up from her practice to see Suta leaning against the forge wall, watching her.

"You are going to finish this, aren't you?"

Zoe was still flushed from the heat of the fire and the exercise. "Was there ever any reason to doubt?"

"Many times from the beginning, but not recently. I begin to know you better. I begin to believe. It is a good thing, to believe. To believe both in you and in my grandfather's method."

"You mean you allowed me to start on this, not sure...!"

He hastened to reassure her. "Oh, I believed it here," he touched his forehead. "My family's methods always prove good. But now I believe it here," his hand dropped to his chest, "and that is a different type of belief. Are you finished? Will you come with me?"

Zoe returned the sword-metal to the table and regarded her instructor. "Where to?"

"To my room. I have something for you." He led the way to the next building, to the room Zoe had never seen while she was fully aware. He stood aside to allow her to enter, then offered her a chair, the only one in the room. She was again impressed by its plainness. There seemed to be few personal touches, except for a carven, heavy-looking wooden chest in the corner, hidden by the shadows and the darkness of the material from which it was made. It was this chest that Suta opened. Reaching in, he withdrew a small leather sack. He closed the lid, turned and held the sack out to her as if in a ceremony.

She rose from her chair and received the bag in both hands. It was soft but heavy, like sand. She waited, holding it, looking at his face.

"It is a gift, my Lady. Something I want you to use. This material has been in my family for three generations, and what you hold is all that is left."

It seemed appropriate, so she opened the neck of the sack and looked in. The interior contained what seemed to be fine sand, bright silver in colour. She looked up again for an explanation.

"It doesn't look like much, but that sand is very difficult to find, almost impossible to buy. Treat it carefully, and use only a pinch at a time. As you are folding your metal, sprinkle it in the fold before you flatten it. There should be enough there for many folds. That is what makes the Thousand-Forged Blade rust-free."

"You mean that part wasn't the imagination of the songsmiths either?"

He smiled. "It wasn't. There is nothing magical about this. You still must keep the blade dry and well oiled. If you leave it

342

in a swamp for a month, I am sure it will rust. But kept dry, the blade will never decay, never become brittle.

"There is an added advantage; the steel becomes non-magnetic. It will not affect a compass."

"A compass?"

"Do you know what a compass is?"

"Of course I do. But they're too big to carry around and too fussy to use anyway."

Suta smiled. "You have not seen the Kyabran version. It is a small instrument with a fine needle inside, mounted in liquid. You can put it on a string around your neck."

"And it works?"

"Always, unless there is steel nearby. Then it will point to the steel."

"Not a tool for a Warlander in armour, then."

"Definitely not. But for a Master of the Weaponless with a magnetic-free sword, it is a fine aid for making your way across unknown territory."

"Could I get one of these compasses?"

"They are not hard to find. You must ask Lord Janitra. He carries one when he travels."

Zoe looked down at the small bag in her hand. "The compass is a good idea, but this material...are you sure you want to give it to me? It must be extremely valuable."

"I would pay much more than that to see my family's method come to reality. It has always been a dream. Not a dream to strive for, but a dream for the sake of dreaming. A dream of the old days when Kyabra was powerful and her weapons were the best in the known world. I had thought those days were over. Now, I am not so sure. When news of this sword spreads, I will be able to get more of the powder, don't worry. I must warn you, though. There is a price."

343

"Isn't there always?"

"As the powder in your sword grows you will find you need more and more heat to bring it to working temperature."

"I already do, just with the folding."

"You would, but this will make it even more so. Not for a while, but eventually. The last fifty folds will be more difficult."

Zoe smiled and shrugged her shoulders. "The way of the world. If a task is worth doing, it will be difficult. Where should we keep this?"

47. Visitor from Home

They were just leaving the forge when Jaddie came running up. "There's going to be a party, Zoysana!"

"A party! What is the occasion?"

"No real occasion, but there's an Outland minstrel here. He speaks with a strange accent. I talked to him myself! He is going to sing for us."

"A balladeer? Suta, a chance to find out about the imaginations of songsmiths. Would you like to come?"

The armourer's face lit up. "I am always at my Lady's command."

"Then I command you to appear in the main hall for the evening meal. I suggest we both go and get cleaned up."

He hurried off, and she continued towards the main buildings, Jaddie skipping beside her, chattering about songs and stories. Patu strolled along silently on the other side.

She had already guessed the identity of the balladeer. Solonstan was a renowned traveller, even among those of his own footloose occupation, and she did not think the borders of Kyabra would be a barrier to one of his wit, especially one with a certain small wheel hanging inside his shirt. He was standing talking with Janitra when she entered for the meal, and she hurried forward to greet him.

"A long way from home, minstrel!"

"Ah, Lady Zoysana. A minstrel has no home except where his music is appreciated."

"I'm sure yours will be welcomed here. Were you on the road long? When did you leave Petrella?"

"It has not taken long, as the balladeer travels. I stopped along the way to earn my living, but it has been a month or less since I left."

"You must give me all the news. How are things? How is everyone?"

The long face frowned. "Everyone is well, my Lady, but 'things,' as you so eloquently put it, are not going swimmingly. We will speak more when there is time. But all your friends were well when I left. No illness, no injuries, no one in the dungeon."

"I should hope not the dungeon!"

"Ah. An unfortunate turn of phrase, my Lady."

At that moment the meal was announced, and they went to their places. Since Solonstan had no status here other than as a minstrel, she knew he would be placed at the lower tables until his time came to entertain. She passed a word to the steward to make sure he was seated with Suta and given proper introduction. The two would find plenty to talk about.

The meal was a festive time, more formal than usual, and filled with the anticipation of entertainment to come. From conversation with Janitra, she learned that the singer had been here before and was appreciated for both his art and his knowledge.

"He was one reason I first went to Petrella. It was his information about the Arlyn kings that made me hope they might be more open to trading than the more conservative leaders in that area."

"The Arlyn kings? Who was on the throne when you first heard about us?"

"I believe it was Alarid."

"You felt that Alarid would be open to negotiations?"

"Oh, yes. From all accounts he was a progressive ruler. An unlucky blow, his death."

He turned to speak to his wife, leaving Zoe to mull over this new thought. Again she wondered what history would have

346

said of Barent's unfortunate brother, had he lived long enough to make his mark.

When the meal was over, Janitra beckoned to Solonstan. "And what do you carry from the Outlands? New songs, new poems, new gossip? Or do you bring new perspectives on old Kyabran lore as our other Outland friend has done?"

Solonstan smiled at Zoe. "I have not the advantage of Zoysana's training in your culture, but I may have a few interesting views of your society."

Zoe smiled. She wondered how far the balladeer would dare go, here in a strange land. No different from anywhere else, she surmised; he had made his reputation that way.

The performance started innocuously enough, with straight renditions of two Kyabran ballads. One of these, in reference to his dinner conversation, was one of the 'Thousand-Forged Blade' songs, and the response it received reflected the local interest in Zoe's project. When the applause continued, Janitra motioned for Zoe to rise and accept her share, which she did, bashfully.

Solonstan grinned over at her once his voice could be heard again. "It seems I have an ally in the house." He turned again to his audience. "I suppose you would be receptive to a tune about the Battle Beasts?"

Another round of applause greeted this, so he smiled and, with the usual "Please to be kind," started. Zoe didn't like that smile. She knew it was not in the nature of the man to be kind. One flattering song was more than she had any right to expect. Cringing, she composed herself for whatever might happen.

He did not disappoint her. He had rewritten one of the older Kyabran stories, that of a young lad and his armigerent who had turned the tide of an important battle through some great deed or other, she couldn't remember what. In Solonstan's rendering, the two simply couldn't get along. The handler had a poor memory and so was always asking the animal to do something it was not trained for, and the armigerent, who seemed to be less aware of things than average, was always finding new ways to misinterpret his orders. The turning point of the battle, she now remembered, had been the non-delivery of a faulty command that had been entrusted to the two heroes. In the original version, the lad had taken it upon himself, in light of information gathered en route, to correct the content of the message. In Solonstan's song, the two failed in their duty through ineptitude. Afterwards, when the battle was won and the grateful general who had sent the erroneous message showered honours on them for saving his hide, the partners accepted their accolades and bumbled off into the sunset of mythical fame, stumbling over each other as they went.

When the song was finished there was a moment of silence as these correct and polite people wondered what the proper response should be. Solonstan bowed, then, in a perfect imitation of Janitra's gesture, offered Zoe the opportunity to share in the forthcoming applause. Miming an exaggerated 'what has that to do with me?' she pointedly turned her back on him and stuck her nose in the air. With this signal, the audience loosed their laughter, all the stronger from having been suppressed. The balladeer took this as his due and switched to other topical matters.

Considering his short time in the realm, Zoe was amazed at how much local politics he had picked up, as his asides and comments between songs revealed. She could also see how such a man would be invaluable as an information source. While the entertainment was excellent, she began to chafe, wondering what bad news from home the singer had been preparing her for.

Finally, the performance was over, and Zoe asked Janitra's permission to monopolize the balladeer for a while.

"Of course, Zoysana. I had expected you two would wish to talk. I will find the opportunity later to glean what information I can from him, and then perhaps we could all speak together?

His role in your court is more than that of entertainer, I gather."

Saying nothing to confirm or deny this, Zoe bowed her thanks and went to seek her countryman, inviting him to a more private audience room off the main hall. She waited until he was comfortably seated before she spoke.

"What has Barent done?"

"Ah, straight and to the point, my Lady. What more could I expect of one trained by the Sivan? Why cloud the facts with polite evasions? The king, my Lady, is not doing well. In fact, you could say he has done very ill lately, and the kingdom suffers accordingly."

"Specifics, please." She tried to keep this as businesslike as possible.

"First, as you may not be aware, he has attacked and taken Velikii. Ah yes. The news follows me as the Petrellan armies did. Rawden at least died well defending his castle, but he was no match for Barent's tactics. You are unamazed. This is no departure from the expected course. Other than that, he has done nothing of great note. However, the kingdom is suffering. Barent maintains a large army and is using it to control supposed rebellion in his conquest and in Petrella itself. It is not only an army of Warlanders and mercenaries. It also contains several companies of foot and light horse that he uses in unlikely ways on the field, assuring him of success. But what soldiers? Not men of honour, you may guess. An unpleasant similarity to the mob Saxer gleaned last summer from the dives and taverns. Perhaps even some of the same men. So unfortunate."

Zoe took this in, trying to analyze it without emotion. "What else?"

"Gerth has gone to Arva."

"Gone? What do you mean, gone?"

"I mean gone, as in not to return. As in fled, for fear of his life, or more accurately, for fear of the strife he would cause in the kingdom by staying. He has little fear for his life, that one." A smile ghosted across the singer's thin lips.

"But why? What was the danger?"

"Word was spreading that perhaps Gerth had something to do with Alarid's death. The white horse was his, you know. Of course you do."

"The white horse was also mine! Am I implicated as well? This is ridiculous!"

"How could you be suspected? You were at the far end of the kingdom at the time. Of course, seen through the eye of the man afraid..."

"You are beginning to think like the Sivan." In an effort to keep the emotions in check, she decided that was her course of action. Cool, controlled analysis. "That would be the safest place for me, if I were involved. So where did this rumour originate?"

"Not with the Sivan's men, as you might guess, but it was being given credence at high levels of the castle, so Gerth made the safe decision. He has been well received by Torey. I believe your young friend Varlinden has joined him there."

"Is Barent likely to attack Torey? I doubt it. He sees Arva as a potential ally against the Inari. Unless something has changed there as well?"

"He seems to be making no move in that direction. In fact, he is making few moves at all at the moment. He has a lot of territory to consolidate, and little in the way of able help with which to accomplish it."

"Why has he little help?" She raised her hands, palms up. "Where are his Warlander Lords?"

"The ones who only owe their support for short periods of time have returned to their holdings, where they are needed due to the unsettled nature of the kingdom at the moment. There was also a general feeling among the less avaricious of them that many events were occurring that did not hold closely enough to the Codes. These wanted no part in such doings and have also left the Army. And then there is the Sivan."

"The Sivan? What is he doing?"

"Well, my Lady, he is doing nothing. You see, he is gone."

"He is gone, too? Where?"

"A legitimate question. Where do you think?"

"I have no idea!"

"As I suspected, my Lady, and neither does anyone else. The only one who might know is his young lady friend, and she professes complete ignorance."

"Loreline?"

"Yes. She has taken over his duties as well as she can. She is having little difficulty, though, as the Guides all seem to trust her. At least, their reports keep coming in and messages continue to be delivered. How much use she will be in the planning of new operations has yet to be seen."

"Is there any possibility that the Sivan has been..."

"Always possible, but the feeling is that his death is not likely. In fact, many are chuckling, saying that the mystery is typical of the man. Lady Kenna remarked something of the sort in my hearing. I tend to agree. The Sivan himself mentioned you in that respect. He said something like, "Zoysana's solution looks tempting at the moment." I wasn't sure what he meant, but I wonder if he wanted me to repeat that to you?"

She did not enlighten him, partly out of embarrassment. She knew exactly what the message said. When in doubt where your loyalties should lie, run away. Her cheeks burned at the thought.

"Then it means something to you, my Lady. How fortunate."

Zoe wanted to move on. "What else is happening?"

The balladeer shrugged morosely. "Is that not enough? There is nothing specific to tell, but the general feeling is not good. I travel many kingdoms in many lands, and I know a populace in fear. I know a ruler embattled, even when no army opposes him."

"And he no longer agrees with Lady Kenna."

This comment seemed to come out of nowhere, but Zoe realized it was the single most important fact of castle politics that the minstrel had picked up. For one thing, the two almost never argued about the good of the realm. Discussed, yes, sometimes heatedly, but they had a special bond, stronger than that of their other siblings. In complete agreement on the kingdom's needs, the two had developed into one formidable force. The division of that force weakened the power of the Arlyn family considerably. On a more general level, their disagreement symbolized a house divided against itself, and boded ill for the realm.

Deep in thought, Zoe escorted Solonstan to find the steward to make sure he got a comfortable bed. Then she made her way to her room, a heavy sadness on her. Undressing in the dark, she lay unmoving, almost uncaring, for half the night, until finally she slipped from her depression into troubled sleep without noticing the difference.

48. THE TEST

"So, Lady Zoysana, will you return home, now?" If Janitra found it strange that the minstrel was part of this important decision, he showed none of it.

"I am almost sure of my decision, but I would like to hear what you suggest, Solonstan."

"It is not for me to say, my Lady. I report the facts as I see them."

"And there was no message for me from anyone?"

The lanky singer looked innocent. "How, my Lady? No one knew I was on my way here."

Zoe regarded him. "No one?"

He glanced at Janitra. "Ah, well, perhaps Loreline and I did discuss the possibility of my seeing you."

"And still there was no message?"

A lean hand touched the centre of his chest as if to scratch there, then dropped. "No message as such, my Lady. We may have mentioned ways of getting you assistance if required, but nothing was decided."

"Then I thank you, Solonstan, for all your information. You wish to return to the road. I see no need for me to keep you here," she grinned, "especially if you stay to make fun of me."

"Ah, how unfortunate it is, when one sees oneself in a song. So often the singer is blamed."

Janitra laughed. "And always the singer is blameless. I, too, see no reason to hold you, and every reason to see you on your way, and happily. I would not give you an excuse to turn your talents on me!"

"Only the guilty conscience need fear the light of the truth, my Lord."

"And who has not one little corner he would prefer kept in the concealing shadows?"

The balladeer smiled and rose, bowing with courteous grace. "Then I take my leave of both, conserving the attention of my talent for more deserving subjects."

Both Zoe and Janitra accompanied Solonstan to the gate to watch him saunter away, long strides already falling into a ground-covering pace.

"Doesn't he ride?"

"In Petrella, he rides a borrowed animal if one is offered, but he refuses to own one. It would tie him down too much, having to take care of it."

Janitra looked thoughtful. "Tied down by the ownership of the means to travel. I shall consider the nature of that concept. But turning to more mundane matters, you said you had made a decision, but you failed to reveal it. Will you be leaving?"

"There is no reason. I have not completed my assignment here. I cannot go home just because of upheaval and uncertainty. Barent may have the situation under control. What then if I was to rush back, empty-handed? And besides, what good would I do there, even if conditions are poor?"

"You might underestimate your influence on those in power, but in general, I agree. You were sent for a purpose. Perhaps what you return with will help. You should finish what you started."

"On the other hand, I have no reason to delay. The sword will be finished in a month or so and I have collected all the other information I can. I shall leave before the fall rains start."

"It will be a sad thing to see you go. You are a great source of interest and pleasure to us, besides the assistance you provide. You will take Tadeo with you?"

"Should I? I would be pleased of his company. What do you think he would wish?"

354

"We will ask him, but I entertain little doubt of his answer."

She grinned. "Neither do I."

So she and Tadeo decided to leave for Petrella as soon as the sword was finished. They were into the Eighth month of the year and the hot weather would soon abate, so Zoe had hopes of being able to make better progress on the sword. If she was lucky, one more month. If not, two at the most.

* * *

The summer had passed, the days cooling and dampening into fall. The work at the forge became easier and more challenging as expected, her growing proficiency with the hammer offset by the increasing difficulty in working the hardening steel. But it was still progress toward her goal, and she suffered it gladly.

As the blade neared completion, the tension began to develop. Everyone knew that she had completed the three hundredth fold and was at work on the final shaping and polishing. Then, after a complicated tempering process, it would be finished. Falihea's design for the hilt was as complete as it could be without a tang to attach it to, painstakingly crafted by Suta to the last minute detail.

Finally, the day came when the blade was complete, the hilt attached. Zoe tapped the last rivet for the handle in place, put down her hammer, and regarded her handiwork.

The blade itself was lighter in hue than normal sword steel: an incredible shining silver. The basket of the hilt was formed of a series of twigs braided together, supporting each other, spreading out from the hilt, then twining back protectively over the hand to join at the pommel, a small orb of bronze. The grips were of a hard wood, so dense that it did not float in water. Over that was a binding made of the skin of a fish from the Inner Sea: a tough and gritty material that did not soften or stretch when wet. She stared at the weapon for a long time, marvelling. It was truly beautiful. She reached out a cautious hand.

"Time for the Testing?" Suta was before her, lifting the sword reverently on the palms of his hands. "The witnesses are ready."

"Testing?"

Suta smiled, but there was a worried wrinkle in the corner of his eye. "You only remember the parts of the ballads that suit you. You have heard of the Testing of the Blade?"

She remembered something about a testing. It hadn't been in her mind that much. "What are you going to do?"

The armourer was serious now. "My Lady and my apprentice, you have created an object that comes out of the legends of our land and the histories of my family. It would be of great disservice to them and to yourself if you were to leave any part of the ritual incomplete. And there is a practical aspect to this. Would you go into battle with an untested blade? What if there is a flaw?"

"There are no flaws!"

"Why should you risk your life when knowing is so easy?"

"What is this test?"

"A trial of the strength of the blade. We attempt to break it. If it does not break, it passes."

Zoe stared at him in anguish. "What kind of attempt? What if you break it?"

"The assessment is graded according to how strong the sword is designed to be. And what if it does break? What then?"

She looked at him while this all sank in. Then her head rose and her back straightened. "I started all over once. I can do it again!"

Suta laughed. "Lady Zoysana, I never expected you to say anything else. Come. Your friends await."

But as they left the forge, they found only Janitra and Tadeo standing outside. The rest of the courtyard was deserted except for Patu, who heaved lazily to his feet, looked at her and tightened up. His head rose, his neck hairs lifted and his nose tested the wind.

Suta nodded. "He feels your tension, my Lady. We all do. But now to the Test. There are only the few of us here. One does not make a great ceremony of the Test. It is a simple thing, easily done, and only requires the formality of witnesses."

He walked over to where two boards stood on edge, some distance apart. He laid her sword, flat as he had carried it, across the tops. They were placed so that only the hilt and the tip of the blade rested on them. The full length of the weapon was suspended between. Suta walked around so he could face the others and, kneeling down, put his palm on the middle.

"The first Test." He pressed. There was no movement. Turning the blade over, he repeated the pressure, with a similar lack of result. "The Test is passed." He placed the other hand on top of the first.

"The second Test." He leaned over, locked his elbows and pressed, the weight of half his body resting on the blade. There was a perceptible springing back as he released. Turning it over, he pressed again. "The Test is passed." He stood.

"The third Test." Placing one foot on the sword, he pushed down again. This time the metal bowed slightly. Then the other side. He stood back. "The Test is passed." He spoke directly to Zoe. "These are the trials for a normal sword of my family's making. Any fighter would take a sword tested thus into battle with confidence. For your sword to be a Truly Forged Blade, it must pass more than this."

Guessing what would come next, Zoe nodded, swallowing.

Suta stepped up to the sword, again placing his foot in the middle of the blade. Then, ever so slowly, he shifted his weight forward until more and more of it rested on the sword, which bent under the pressure. Finally, he lifted his other foot off the ground: all his weight supported by the blade. Then he got down. This time as he turned the blade over, he sighted down its length. Satisfied, he repeated the process on the other side. He sighted down it again. "The Test is passed." Zoe released her breath, hoping no one had noticed her holding it.

"The final Test I may not perform. Only the wielder of the hammer may perform it." He motioned Zoe to take his place.

She did so, looking across the sword at him. There was just one way to put more force against the blade. "Jump?"

He nodded.

"How many times? How hard?"

"That, only you can decide. How much do you trust your work? How much do you want to know about its weaknesses? How comfortable do you wish to be, wearing this sword, fighting with it in your hand?"

She looked down at the blade, shining there in front of her. She thought of all the hours, the sweat, the sparks burning her hands, the blisters, the sleepless nights because of the pain in her muscles. Would this all be for nothing? Could she start again? She looked up at her three friends, waiting patiently. She could get through this. Suta was far heavier. A few bounces would put little more stress than the tests already passed. She stepped on to the blade.

It felt rigid. She bounced, testing the spring. She bounced harder, lost her balance and stepped off, feeling foolish. She turned it over, tried again, stepped off and stood regarding the

358

blade. Then she looked up at the three pairs of solemn dark eyes, observing her. It wasn't enough.

She stepped on the sword again and bounced firmly with both feet. Now she could feel the spring in the blade pushing back against her. She bounced harder. It bounced her back. She stepped off, bounced on the other side.

Zoysana stood back looking at the sword, lying there so shiny and smug across its boards. She remembered how she had hated it, how it had taken so much out of her. How could a piece of metal do this to her? It had made her sweat, cry and writhe in agony. That, she could abide. But now it was making her doubt herself. That, she could not tolerate.

She jumped.

From a standing start, she threw her arms back and jumped as high as she could, landing with both feet together, dead in the centre of the blade, straight down. Almost straight down.

Then she was lying in the dust on her back, her feet waving. There was a roar of relieved laughter. She sat up and twisted around to see the three Kyabrans trying to recover their composure. She followed their glance. There, lying half buried in the dust, was her sword. Not so shiny now. Just as dusty as she was. Getting up, she strode over, slid her hand into the guard and picked up the sword, sighting down its length. A pure, straight ribbon of light ran away from her, then returned. She swung her arm. It felt beautiful. She turned to look at her friends, grinning.

"Do you need to try the other side, my Lady?"

"I don't think I dare. It might buck me off again."

"Oh, but you must, my Lady." Janitra was straight-faced. "If you get thrown off, you get right back on again. That is the first of the Rules of Riding. That way you show it who is the master."

Zoe slapped the flat of the sword against an awning post. "Anything that I have battered with a hammer for this many months deserves the chance to dump me on my butt at least once. I don't ever plan to ride on it again. But if you insist."

She placed the sword back on its blocks, straightened up and jumped, just as high as before, but with sure aim. This time she was ready, and when it threw her skywards, she did a flip in the air, landing on her feet. "Is that better, gentlemen?"

She strode to retrieve her sword, brushing the dust from it. She marvelled at the feel of it in her hand. She proceeded through a series of Patterns, each more intricate than the last, increasing her speed until the world became a blur, hidden by the flashing silver of her sword, weaving its protective pattern around her. Finally, she stopped in the 'guard' position, panting, feeling her robe sticking to her back. The sword felt as light as if she had just picked it up. She grinned at them. "I think this Test is passed!"

49. TRAVELLERS OF MANY SORTS

And so, when the summons came, she was ready. Not anxious to leave this quiet haven in the golden-warm months of autumn, but ready with her steel and her newfound knowledge to dive back into the world from which she had come: a world of uncertainty and battle, a world where her friends needed her. She had served her purpose here.

The message came obliquely, sliding into her life like a cold knife through a warm blanket. One day a stranger appeared at the Omanisa Home gate demanding to see her, and her alone. Expecting such a visit, she obeyed. The man was tired and travel-worn, his rangy horse and nondescript riding cloak spattered by mud from a rain which had not reached this far from the mountains. However, he refused to dismount.

"There is no time, my Lady. I am far out of my way on a mission I do not understand. Please allow me to complete it and be about my business."

"Of course, sir. What is your mission?"

"This." He fumbled in a pouch at his waist and produced a small, round packet, bound in parchment. "I am to give you this."

She reached up. "Is there a message?"

"Yes. I am to say, 'It is your turn'." The man looked anxious. "Have I fulfilled my pledge?"

She smiled to reassure him. "Do I understand the message? Yes, you have fulfilled your mission." She hefted the object. "I will thank you further, would you give me leave."

He returned her a relieved smile. "It was a strange mission, my Lady, and one I had no real hope of fulfilling to any degree of satisfaction. I am grateful for your reassurance, as I dearly wished to keep faith with the sender of the message. That is all the thanks I require. It is also an honour to meet you, but now I must go." He saluted in the Petrellan manner, wheeled his horse and was soon a diminishing speck on the road.

Zoe returned to the courtyard musing over the package. She knew what she would find there. A small wheel, intricately carven with tiny human figures. The wrapping would be blank. She had all the information she needed. It was time to go home.

Of course, it was not possible to obey the summons without delay. In fact, it was rather difficult to tear herself away. When word spread that she was leaving, all her new acquaintances insisted on seeing her one last time, and a series of evenings had to be set aside for that purpose. Even those who had argued most strongly against her in the summer's discussions felt a need to pay their respects. There was also a good deal of bustling about in the Priya household, with mysterious preparations that Zoe and Tadeo took care not to notice. It was very difficult to keep any secrets, though, and they had no doubts that the girls were outdoing themselves with going-away presents.

So when Zoe finally departed from the gates of Omanisa Home, she was far better equipped than when she had entered, months before.

Both she and Patu were fitted out with the best of Kyabran harness. Patu's was a gift from Alphard, with the blessing and design assistance of his master, Baridea Rimmon. It was a travel pack, sturdier than most, with enough hardened leather and metal studs built in to act as armour sufficient for anything except a pitched battle. According to the donors, this was the ancient style for armigerents when accompanying their masters on long journeys. They were expected to transport their own food and a good measure of the master's belongings as well. Patu was lightly loaded; there was not that much to carry, as they would be staying at inns, and the weather was still warm enough for light sleeping robes even if they did bivouac.

Tadeo's family presented Zoe with a beautiful scabbard for her sword. Simple and unadorned as suited her, but finely made, strong and light, with a harness adaptable to waist or over-the-shoulder wear. They had also created her a new robe, woven of the fantastic ubrsilk by Falihea, crafted by Merghani, and embroidered by Rhesia. It contained all the usual concealed places, and Zoe felt fully clothed and equipped as she rode out, her grandfather's robe tucked away in the bottom of a saddlebag with her Petrellan clothing.

Tadeo, similarly provided, rode proudly at her shoulder. All knew that he was going off again into foreign lands, to adventure and glory, and many envied him. His awareness of the true difficulties and hindrances of their romanticized dreams did nothing to temper his enjoyment of his reputation.

Their departure differed in many ways from their arrival. Early on a cool fall morning, they were seen off at the gate by a very sober group, with not a few tears hidden by brave smiles. Only Jaddie broke down enough to throw her arms around the neck of each of the three in turn and dampen their new apparel.

Then off at a brisk trot to allow the animals to work off their morning spirits before settling in to their travelling pace. Through the city they moved quietly, but even so, several townsfolk appeared on their doorsteps to wave a friendly farewell. This time, Patu had no restraints. He ranged forward and back, paying last visits to any he met, gracefully accepting grubby remnants of breakfast from small hands, pausing for a pat or scratch, then off again after the horses.

Outside the town they were on the road again, settling down, getting the kinks out, allowing their minds to drift into that half-aware, half-dream state that overtakes the distance traveller as he jogs along, day after day, lulled by the sound of the horses' hooves setting their monotonous cadence.

Beside the shore of the Inner Sea they passed, through the formidable border of Kyabra and into the lands beyond. Then up through the dry passes to the south, away from the moisture of the sea.

It was when they reached the Inner Duchies that they encountered the rumours spreading out to meet them. Petrella was in trouble, but at first no one could give any definite news. War, murder, famine; all were suggested. As they got closer, the news became more specific, but no better. Petrella was in an uproar, and the newly acquired territory of Velikii as well. King Barent was holding his lands in an iron grip from which only a few dribbles of gossip escaped. The Inner Duchies were worried, it was certain. If he were to crush his internal opposition, where would he turn his armies next? It was rumoured that Torey of Arva was arming, perhaps with the aid of Prince Gerth. Would they invade? Merchants were torn whether to rub their hands in glee or run. War was good as long as it happened somewhere else.

They began to meet more traffic on the road, but found few travellers going their way. Those who were able were finding less troublesome places to ply their trades. Pedlars, minstrels, tinkers and itinerant workmen with families: all were leaving.

Those who travelled along in their direction were not the kind one would like to see approaching one's country. Compared to the honest folk fleeing, these were a rough lot. Poorly dressed but well armed, the men often looked capable, but of what was in question. Sometimes a woman or two journeyed as well, better dressed than her male companions, perhaps over-dressed, with too much makeup, too much wine, and too loud a laugh.

Zoe and Tadeo kept apart from the crowds, walling themselves off from their fellow travellers by judicious use of their foreign clothing, Kyabran tongue and prominent weapons. By his mere presence, Patu did his share on the road to discourage over-friendliness, and at night he stabled with the horses, ensuring their safety.

In the privacy of the road, ambling along through an early fall rain, they discussed what was happening. Zoe, though saddened by the woes of her country, could not profess surprise. "We talked about this last spring, the Sivan and I. We knew it would happen. There seemed to be no solution then, and I see none now."

"I do not understand, my Lady. When Janitra first set out for Petrella, he felt it was the most likely kingdom to start trading. There was peace, prosperity, and a strong line of kings. What has happened?"

"A kingdom is as strong as the honour of its king. I'm afraid Barent has allowed his ambition for his kingdom to overwhelm his instinct for what is correct. Once started down that path, it is almost impossible to turn back. Honour once lost is very difficult to regain, except by some great act, usually of sacrifice. Barent has no act of atonement to perform, so he must grimly stay the course and hope circumstances will get better. I hope they will, but I fear they will not. If he can hold out until winter when the roads are poor, perhaps he will get time to straighten his kingdom out before spring. If anything remains." She shook her head in misery. "He was so sure he knew what was best." She kneed her horse ahead so that Tadeo would not see the tears. Patu looked up, his ears flat to his head. She could not stand even his sympathy, and she gave the signal for him to range ahead. Given a mission, he bounded off. As long as he had a task to do, everything would be fine. She envied him his innocence.

50. REFUGEES

It was when they entered Poligny, the last large duchy before the Velikan border, that they met the real refugees. Tadeo misunderstood instructions given in a strong country accent, and they found themselves on the road at twilight on a damp day when their clothing had not dried after a morning shower. Seeing a fire in a copse of evergreens near the road, they pulled aside to investigate.

It was not a reassuring sight. A group of people of all ages ranged around the blaze, huddled near its warmth, holding various articles of tattered clothing out in a vain effort to dry them in the damp air. Children clung to their mothers. There was no screaming or playing, just the high whine of an unhappy baby.

For a moment, the two just sat there on their horses, taking in the scene. There was no livestock, and the only transportation was in the form of dilapidated two-wheeled carts, usually drawn by some beast of burden or other. Over these were stretched rags of canvas to protect against the weather.

A shout, and all eyes turned their way. Zoe had not realized what the effect of their silent appearance, especially with Patu, might be. She cursed herself for not calling out first, but she had assumed that any group this large would post someone on watch. In their misery, these people had not bothered. There was frozen silence as the poor folk cringed away from this new threat, but none moved, none ran or made as if to put up a defence.

Zoe gave Patu the sign to fade, then stepped her horse forward and dismounted to cover his departure. She moved slowly, eyes searching for a leader, someone to address. When no one was forthcoming, she decided on a middle-aged man who seemed less beaten than the rest, sitting on a stump with several older children pressed close to him.

"Excuse me, Sir, but my companion and I were caught on the road by the night, and thought perhaps to share your fire."

A slight relaxation eased through the group at this statement. The man answered in a monotone. "My Lady, if you wish to share our fire, there is none here who could deny you."

"That is not my intention. I am asking your permission, not forcing my way. We could move along if we are not welcome. We thought to share the company and security of a larger group."

The man shook his head. "There is no security here, my Lady, save that of a school of fish that flees in panic and disorder, hoping to confuse the predator that as many as possible might survive due to the sacrifice of a few. That is why we are here. We merely share each other's misfortune."

Zoe looked around. Then she realized what was missing. There was no food being prepared. "I thought perhaps we might also share our meal. We carry a certain amount of supplies for an emergency such as this."

At the mention of food, several of the children swayed forward. The man's voice held them back. "We have precious little to share, my Lady."

She smiled. "I will do the sharing this time, then. Perhaps you can repay me with information."

He looked at her with suspicion. "What kind of information?"

"Nothing you won't freely give. We are travelling into the South, towards Velikii and Petrella. Can you tell us the conditions there?"

The man spat out a curse, then glanced with guilt at the children still gathered around him staring at Zoe. "If you would feed these, I would pay with anything in my power. Conditions in Velikii we know well. Two quarters ago it was our home."

Aware of the group's anticipation, Zoe cut him short with a call to Tadeo, who had remained mounted and holding Jobe's reins, the other hand hovering near his sword. "I think we should stay. Would you tether the horses and bring the food?"

There was silence, then Tadeo's voice floated down out of the darkness. "I...I don't have the food, my Lady."

"Oh, yes, Patu is carrying it, isn't he?"

Tadeo swung down. "Yes. Do you want me to get it?"

"No, that will help." She turned to the child nearest her. "When my friend comes, do not be afraid. Remember, he carries the food." The mute expression on the little boy's face told her that, if he were carrying food, it could be the Fanged One himself and he would be welcome. She whistled. There was a moment of expectant silence, then a gasp from the group as Patu materialized at the edge of the firelight, ears up, alert. Zoe held him there with a hand signal, then looked around, businesslike. "Tadeo, we will camp under that tree, there. Please put the horses on the left side, and the tent to the right." Waving her hands as she gave the instructions, she then turned and spoke to Patu, including his signals in her gestures. "Patu, you come over here so we can see what you have for us. You," she looked down at the boy, "can help me carry things, all right?"

The lad cringed from the huge beast, but the easy way in which it obeyed her commands, plus the emptiness in his stomach, decided him. He nodded and edged forward.

"Good." She strode over to Patu, who stood patiently while she dug in his saddlebags. Reaching out, but not so far that the boy could avoid coming close, she handed him the first parcel. "Now take that over to whoever does the cooking and come back for more. Do you have a sister or brother who could help?" Again without speaking, the boy nodded and pointed to a girl a few years older. "Then send her over, will you?"

The girl couldn't help but hear this exchange and she approached timidly, then stepped forward when her brother nudged her. Zoe walked around to Patu's other side and passed the next package across his back, making the girl almost touch him in order to reach it. Just when she was stretching out her hand, Patu brought his head around to investigate. He gave a small snort, pushing his nose near her outstretched arm. The girl flinched, but did not move.

"Good girl. That is the smartest thing to do when close to a strange animal. He's checking your smell. He likes his ears scratched. That would be a nice way of thanking him for carrying this food for you." Again the magic word, and every barrier fell. Zoe felt guilty, but it was for a good cause. The girl placed her hand gingerly on the muscular neck behind the ears and rubbed. Patu pushed closer for more, and she gained confidence, scratching harder, ruffling his fur.

"Have you ever had a dog?"

"Yes." A shy smile broke out as the armigerent pushed his nose into her hand.

"Well, they aren't too much different. With this one, just make sure he doesn't step on you. Now you take this parcel over to the fire, then you can come back and talk to him all you like." The girl did as she was told, and Zoe grounded Patu, then went to help Tadeo with the tent, leaving the refugees exclaiming over the simple trail fare that was her emergency supply. "Well, Tadeo, we eat light this evening," she murmured as she worked.

"So I gathered. Who are these people?"

"They are not beggars or tramps, that I can tell. I think we will hear a sad but very informative story tonight when the food has loosened their inhibitions against talking with strangers."

369

As she was unharnessing Patu, with the help of his new friend, a sudden thought struck her. "Do you have any livestock with you? Goats, or anything?"

"No, they're all gone."

"That will help." She gave Patu a signal. He brightened and bounded to the edge of the clearing, stopping to look back over his shoulder in invitation. She waved him on. "No, you go by yourself. I'd be no use to you, blundering around in the dark." He made one pleading glance then gave up and disappeared.

"He is hunting. This area is all wild land, and there's no sense in feeding him, with all these extra mouths." She wandered over to the fire and offered to help, but the woman working there refused. She had her pride, it seemed, and if she was receiving a gift of food, she could do her share by preparing it. Zoe's opinion of these people was rising by the moment.

At leisure to look around, she used her observational skills to make her deductions. While their clothing was worn, it had once been of decent quality. Despite their hunger, the children were well mannered and helped each other and their parents willingly. The adults, in their turn, were also polite, and even the most difficult child, a two-year-old with a piercing scream, was treated with firm understanding. Zoe wondered what strange twist of the fates of war had driven these folk so far from their homes. From their easy familiarity with outdoor activities and the assistance two of the men gave Tadeo with the horses, she concluded that these had been farming people. Perhaps not landowners, but well-off peasants, leasing the same land from the lord for generations. It took more than a battle to send such hardy people fleeing.

Her opinion was strengthened by the formality of the meal. It was simple fare: smoked meat and road-bread, a hard crust which travellers called 'road-bed' because of its resistance to the teeth. However, it softened up if warmed over water and was very sustaining.

When the food was handed out, some of the youngsters could not contain themselves, but the others all seemed to be waiting. Curious, Zoe held the morsel she had taken and waited, too. When all had been served, the leader took a small piece and broke it in four bits. Then he dropped each one into the fire, and as he did so the group chanted a word that sounded like 'thanks' in Kyabran. Then he stood back and, raising his hands, spoke with formality.

"For what you give us, Lady, we return all that we have – our gratitude."

All the others repeated the Kyabran word, then fell at once to eating. Tadeo had slipped naturally into the ceremony, pronouncing the Kyabran 'thanks' with the proper intonation, and she did the same, getting a few strange looks. Then she, too, ate sparingly.

There was little sound during the meal, all too intent on their enjoyment to speak, so it was not hard for Zoe to pick out a noise in the forest nearby. Alert, she listened further, then raised her voice to gain their attention. "My friends, I am not sure, but it is possible that the second course is about to arrive." Patu never moved like that unless he was carrying something heavy. Sure enough, he soon appeared, his head held high to accommodate the small buck he was dragging between his front legs. He strode straight up to Zoe and dropped it at her feet, looking very proud of himself. She made the expected fuss over him, then looked up at the astonished faces around her. "I think we might give him a quarter. That's all he needs. We could cook the other and leave the rest for another day. How does that sound?"

The girl who had befriended Patu was the only one to speak. "Will he let us take his kill?"

"Why not? He eats a lot, but he is not greedy. Now. Who will help with the butchering?"

Again, she was politely but firmly set aside. They were the hosts. They would take care of the cooking.

"Then perhaps you would tell me your story as we wait."

There was general agreement. Zoe listened, reclined against Patu's chest as he lay on his side, her arm draped down his foreleg as if on the arm of a chair. The tale was about what she had expected to hear, but worse. They were a small farming community in the less civilized area of Velikii when the war came. First, someone's army marched through foraging and took their livestock. Next, that force was found by their opponents, and a running battle trampled the crops. Then they were left in peace for a few months, but the worst was yet to come. A smaller group of soldiers arrived, taking time to scour the district, cleaning up anything of value that had not been destroyed or stolen. The pickings in their area were small, but these men seemed to take pleasure in leaving a trail of utter destruction in their wake.

Realizing that these bandits planned to stay, the local people gave up. They packed up their few remaining belongings and set out. Having little idea of geography, they headed north for two reasons: it was rumoured to be warmer up there, and it was away from Petrella.

When the man finished talking, Zoe was speechless. Then she gave vent to her rage. "Those are the same scum that always hang around a war when civil order breaks down. Surely you could have stayed for a while longer. When the war was over, King Barent would send his own soldiers around to restore order, and drive those vultures out!"

"My Lady..." the man seemed to find it difficult to go on.

"Yes?"

"My Lady, those were Barent's soldiers."

She jerked upright, Patu's head swinging to attention at the same time. "What?"

"They were Petrellan soldiers, in King Barent's colours. They even had one of his Guides with them. He was the leader, the worst. He always knew where everyone hid their food and valuables. He was the one who... he..." the man was obviously close to breaking down, "...my wife..."

Zoe had noticed the gap in the family that grouped so tight around him, and now it all fitted together.

"The Guide? Who was he? What was his name?"

"Everyone knew it and feared it. His name was Lupent."

"Lupent? I don't know him. Are you sure he was a Guide?"

"The other soldiers seemed to think so. They were afraid of him, too."

Zoe thought this over. She had known all the Guides once. Not personally, but at least their names and faces, and a bit about each one. There had been no one of that name or personality. He must have hired on later, she surmised. To change the subject, she turned her questions to other things, and the moment of grief passed. The other information she got was what she expected or worse. Refugees were fleeing Velikii, and some were even crossing out of Petrella. This group had pushed forward to try to stay ahead of the others, who were beginning to exhaust the ability of the countryside to support them. Only a lack of strength to go on had stopped them here. They had little idea what to do next. The winter rains were setting in. If they stayed here, they would starve.

The smell of roasting meat did much to allay their misery. The children stood at a respectful distance, watching Patu tear his portion and crack the bones. When he was finished, they started to move in. It was rather amusing, and when one of the adults moved to stop them, Zoe intervened.

"He likes children. Let them enjoy themselves."

Encouraged by Zoe's words and the example of the older girl who had first met him, the youngsters were soon gathered around Patu in the familiar huddle, first exclaiming and patting him gingerly, then cuddling in closer, finally mauling him completely. As usual, he suffered it without moving, although the pained expression on his face brought the first sound of laughter she had yet heard from the group.

With their stomachs fuller than they had been for months and the younger children put to bed, the refugees' minds turned to less practical concerns. The leader approached Zoe diffidently.

"My Lady, it is much too long since we held a Remembrance of Our Lady. Would you or your companion care to join us in our devotions?"

Intrigued, Zoe agreed. The ceremony was simple, consisting of a dance in the form of a revolving circle, and a repetitive chant that Zoe, with her knowledge of Kyabran, picked up easily. When it was over, there was peace in the pinched faces around the fire. Gradually, people drifted off to their makeshift housing and soon the flames were dying away alone.

Zoe lay for a long time, thinking. Finally, she reached a foot out of her robe and nudged Tadeo. "Are you awake?"

"I am. These folks go to bed early."

"Hunger requires a lot of rest. I want to be out of here early in the morning."

"Why?"

"For one, I don't want to eat any more of the food. Also, I find I am in more of a hurry to get home than I thought. Another thing, I don't like the look of this weather. It looks as if the fall rains might blend into winter with no abating. The quicker we move, the better."

"Fine. You wake me up if I sleep past daybreak. I'll do the same for you."

51. THE RIGHT DECISION

In the mist of the early morning they harnessed their animals and prepared to depart. When Tadeo began to pack their tent, Zoe shook her head. "Leave it. They will need it before they find somewhere to winter over. I will leave my Petrellan clothes, too."

Just before they mounted up, Zoe approached the leader's tent. There was stirring inside, and his head appeared in response to her low call. She handed him a small bag.

"This is all the money I can spare. I hope it will keep you going until you find a haven for the winter. I suggest you get moving now, while you have strength and food. The weather is closing in."

The man looked at the contents of the bag. "My Lady, it is too much. We cannot take this!"

"It is King Barent's money, and he owes you something. Take it and survive." She turned on her heel and was on her horse and trotting towards the road before he could object again. She glanced back once, to see him standing, perplexed but joyful, looking after her.

Tadeo rode up beside her. "We never even learned their names."

She glanced across at him, then away. "At the beginning, there was no opportunity. When I realized that we had caused all this I was ashamed to say who I was, in case someone knew me." She slashed her folded gloves against the leather of the saddle. "Damn Barent! How could he mess up so badly?"

"From what I can gather, my Lady, he has damned himself sufficiently."

She was contrite. "I'm sorry, Tadeo. I shouldn't. But I get so angry when I see that sort of thing. I know it happens all the time, but it doesn't need to, and I don't want to be a party to it in any way!"

Tadeo made no response, as none seemed required, and they rode on.

They breakfasted at an inn farther down the road where the yard was full of travellers who were not much better off than those they had just left. As they moved on, the road became more crowded, everyone pushing their way, with their belongings, northward. They stopped for their noon break by a small creek, but it was so muddied by feet and hooves that they had to go almost a bowshot upstream to find clear water. There they joined a group with a more prosperous aspect than most; they travelled with oxen pulling their wagons and seemed well fed and clothed.

They treated Zoe's small party with wary courtesy. The leader of the group, a wiry fellow with a sparse, curly beard, invited them to share his fire when it became obvious that he could do no less without seeming churlish.

"You won't get farther upstream than this, my Lady. The forest's too thick, and there's too much undergrowth. You'll just get soaked. Better if you join us."

"Thank you, sir. Zoysana Rochenan at your service. This is my Guard-of-life, Tadeo Priya." She bowed in the Petrellan fashion.

He gave her a sharp glance, then rose from his seat on the wagon tongue to return her courtesy. "Newlin, at yours, my Lady. You speak our language well."

She smiled and nodded thanks. "Tadeo, what have we to eat? I think that skin of wine might help fight the chill."

Tadeo brought out their newly purchased supplies, and they shared their meal and drink with the teamster. The gesture of friendliness thawed him and his curiosity finished the job.

"And where might you be coming from, my Lady? I have never seen robes the like of yours, nor weapons either. Are you foreign fighters going to sign on with King Barent for his great conquests?"

Zoe sidestepped the question with one of her own. "I hadn't heard about any conquests, although word is moving that he will hire fighters. Are there specific plans?"

"Not that anyone has been told, my Lady, but why else would a great general like Barent hire such a large army?"

"Has he hired many mercenaries? I thought he had a fine local army of his own."

The wagon-master snorted in disgust. "Hah! Amateurs. Love a scrap and bita glory, those Warlanders, but the moment it gets down to a siege or working in the mud for a while, they're off home to their own castles. No, your hired man is the best fighter. Does his job, long as he gets his pay. Doesn't argue, doesn't make a whole lot of extra rules. Just does his fighting. Wins most times, too."

"You seem familiar with the mercenary trade."

The slim man drew up with pride. "Spent some time at it myself. Worked in the Duchies, made a good life when I was young. Then I got a good bit of plunder from a city we took. Got lucky, found a stash of jewels. Not much, but enough to get these wagons built. Now I'm in the hauling trade."

"So you aren't a refugee."

The man poked a thumb back over his shoulder at the people around the wagons. "They are. I move 'em where they want to go. They can pay the price, they get there."

"Any trouble on the road?"

He looked her over, then Tadeo and Patu, whose metal-studded harness now looked travel worn and functional. "None that'll bother you, my Lady. Oh, sure, there's a few bandits around, but not strong enough to worry us. My drivers are all

377

handy with a bow or sword, and my passengers aren't helpless." He chuckled. "They'll fight like demons if we're attacked – got their wives, children, and all their fortunes with them. No, we've had no trouble."

He paused. "Can't say the same for Velikii, though. Picked this bunch up at the border. Wouldn't go in there for twice the money. Hear the army's not much better'n the bandits," he leaned closer, "and if you're headin' for Petrella, your body-guard better be gods-bedamned good with his sword, or you won't be no lady when you get there."

He straightened up at the sudden ice in her look, not sure if he had overstepped. He had, but it was not important enough for Zoe to make a point. Here was someone who had spent most of the past months crossing this area, and for his knowledge it was worth putting up with his abrasive personality for a short while. She passed him the wine skin and started asking questions.

She was in a serious mood when they left the wagons and mounted up. Heavy in thought as she rode along, she did not notice the mist thickening into rain until Tadeo rode up beside her. "Hadn't you best put your cloak on, Zoe? You're getting soaked."

She flashed him a grateful smile. "Thanks. You do a good job taking care of me. Too bad I can't continue to take advantage of it."

He was taken aback, not sure he had understood. "Can't continue?"

"I've been thinking. That teamster had a lot of information. Not of the best quality, perhaps, mostly rumour and hearsay, but recent. I think the situation is coming to a head much more rapidly than I had expected.

"I must go to Petrella, but I also need to make contact with Gerth, who, by all reports, is still in Arva. It wouldn't hurt to get to Torey as well. So I want you to take a message there. If you

378

take the pack trail that cuts across the ranges to the west, you'll be there as soon as I could get to Petrella. Faster, since I will be working my way through a very stormy countryside."

She shook her head to forestall his protests. "You can do me better service by acting as my messenger than by trying to look after me now. If I need to, I can always fade into the background and slip through. I couldn't do that with you along, could I? Besides, where will I find a messenger that Gerth can trust, who also knows enough to give useful input to Gerth's plans?"

He muttered for a while, but in the end he could find no argument against her logic. They spent the rest of the day in planning: discussing routes and alternatives, speculating what Gerth and Torey might have in mind and how they could help. In that area, there didn't seem to be much they could plan, being so short on up-to-date information. It all boiled down to one instruction.

"If Gerth decides to bring an army, just make sure he talks to me before he attacks."

"What could you do?"

She shrugged, staring grimly ahead through the rain. "There has been too much killing in the Arlyn family." She turned earnestly to Tadeo. "Gerth must not take the crown from Barent by force. That is what you must get through to him. That was Barent's mistake, and look what it has done to the kingdom. Tell Gerth he must wait."

"For what?"

"Maybe just wait. Barent cannot go on like this. He may solve the problem for us, one way or the other. He may be killed in battle. A hundred things could happen. But Gerth must wait!"

"That message is clear, my Lady. I will tell him."

That was his formal commitment, and Zoe felt relieved. Knowing the Kyabran as she did, she was sure he would do his utmost to convey her warning. Having done all she could for the moment, she rode on through the mist, wondering what it concealed ahead of her.

52. Alone

Zoe pulled her horse to a halt. He stood: patient, or perhaps just glad of a rest. Patu circled back looking up at her for orders. She turned in the saddle, gazing backwards. No one. She regarded the equally empty road ahead. Then she sighed and nudged Jobe with one heel, and he plodded on. It had all seemed so right and simple when she bid Tadeo farewell earlier that morning and set out on her own to solve the problems of her kingdom. Now it was just plain lonely. She was finding out how much she hated to be alone. It had only taken half a day before the silence started to oppress her and she had begun listening for hoof beats, half hoping Tadeo had found it necessary to come with her after all.

Nonsense. I made the correct decision; it's going to be a little harder to carry out than I expected. I'll get used to it. She kneed Jobe into a canter to shake off the depressing silence and warm them all up. The weather was getting colder, and the dampness didn't help one bit. *I am definitely going to find a snug, dry inn for tonight. Some company wouldn't hurt, either.*

The thought cheered her, and the rest of the day's travel went more optimistically. Later on in the afternoon, she passed through a small hamlet with a likely looking hostelry. It was early, but this was probably the only place of its kind in the neighbourhood, so she swung down, anticipating a pleasant evening by a warm fire. Leading Jobe into the inn yard, she became less sure. A group of well-armed ruffians was just leaving the yard, having left their horses with the stable boy, along with a few bullying threats about the care of their mounts. She stood aside to let the men pass, and they ignored her for the moment.

After seeing to Jobe's stabling she went into the inn, allowing Patu to trail beside her. As she entered the long, low room, the other travellers were just sitting down with mugs of ale.

"Hey! Don't let that ugly thing in here!"

She turned. They were all staring at her. "What are you doing, you simpleton? You may live with your horses where you come from, but around here we're more civilized."

She put her back to the roar of laughter that greeted this wit, and approached the landlord, who was hovering behind the bar. "Do you have a private room for tonight?"

He looked uncertain. "Yes, I do, but..."

"Hey, you! Don't let that foreigner bring his stinking animal in here!"

The innkeeper shrugged. "I'm sorry, sir, but you need to take your dog out. The other customers..."

Zoe signalled Patu to wait outside. Turning back, she repeated her request.

The landlord was much happier now. "Oh, yes sir, there is a very nice room at the end, away from the noise."

"Good. I'll take it. I'll put my 'dog' in the stable." She raised her voice. "A better idea. No one will dare touch my horse or gear."

She went out to the stable and put Patu in his usual spot next to Jobe. Placing her saddlebags safely behind him, she returned to the inn. The evening would not be so pleasant, after all. Camping out might be preferable.

When she shouldered the heavy door open again, her fellow guests had been discussing her.

"Hey, you! Yeah, the foreigner. C'mere."

With a sigh, she moved towards their table. Best to get things straight at the beginning. "Yes?"

The loudest of the group looked her up and down. "Where you from, little foreigner?"

"Petrella."

"G'wan! Nobody in Petrella like that. You look like somebody left you in the oven too long!" Another roar of laughter.

"Nonetheless, that's where I am from. How could I convince you?"

"Say, you got a awful high voice. You some kinda fancy boy?"

She decided it was time to take control. "That's none of your concern."

"Ah, but it is. I might want a fancy boy for myself tonight."

So that was how it was going to be. If they wanted to think she was male, she wouldn't do anything to change that idea. She smiled and walked behind the leader, placing her hand on his neck. "If you want to sleep well…"

He grinned up at her, then around at his friends.

She slipped her hand into a different position, "…then perhaps you could start now." Her voice was calm, but her fingers dug in. The bully convulsed with pain, then his eyes rolled up and he slumped forward, his face crashing onto the table. His companions gawked at him, then their eyes turned to Zoe. She stared them down and spoke coldly. "He'll wake up in a while. This time. Another time I might not be in such a good mood."

She held them a moment longer, then walked over and tossed a coin on the bar. "Bring me a meal to my room. See that I'm not disturbed tonight."

The host, realizing that he may have chosen the wrong side of the argument, was quick to lead her down a short corridor to a small room at the back of the inn. The hall ended in a door. "Does that lead to the stable yard?"

"Aye, sir, it does."

"Fine." It would be better to minimize her contact with her recent antagonists, and this way she need not stay inside for the rest of the afternoon. Dropping her pack off in the room, which was fairly clean and big enough for a small person, she used her private exit and went for a stroll. The only article of her Petrellan clothing she had retained was her Guide's cape, and with this shielding her from the rain, she felt inconspicuous.

She followed a rhythmic sound that led her to the local blacksmith, and she strolled into the familiar atmosphere. Her interest in his work and a demonstration of her knowledge afforded her a sure welcome. Perched on a workbench in the warmth of the forge she forgot her troubles for a while, discussing techniques and materials, stories and ballads. He was an able craftsman, and she saw no harm in showing off her sword. He was fascinated but skeptical until she revealed some of its qualities, at which point he became enthusiastic, wanting to know all about the technique. She gave him a rough idea of how to proceed, but when she teased him about forgetting his farming trade and starting out as an armourer, he laughed.

"Wars don't last, the gods be praised. The farmers are the daily bread of the smith, and that's as it should be."

Zoe observed that she wished life were that way more often, her mind returning to the realities outside the smithy door. Soon she bid the smith goodbye and returned to the inn, checking on her animals then going straight by the back entrance to her room.

Early the next morning she was away again, determined to put distance between herself and any possible trouble. It was a vain attempt, however, as the Velikan frontier was just ahead.

Even had she not passed through a border post, she would have known she was in another country. The people were more bent and poorly dressed, the fields straggly, the buildings in worse condition.

She continued to meet refugees in even worse shape than those who had the money or intelligence to leave before.

Grateful that she had already given away all but the necessities, she felt little guilt in leaving them to go on their way. She firmed her resolve to go deeper into the roots of the problem and try to solve it there. Anything she could do here, at this moment, would be like putting a bandage over a sliver. The injury would not be cured, only hidden.

53. RAIN

The weather did not improve. With no tent, sleeping out was not possible, so she started early to look for a room. The day went on and darkness was coming and still she had found nothing. She began to wish she had taken one of the less likely places she had rejected earlier and wondered if she should turn back. Around nightfall she came upon a poor excuse for a village with a broken-down travesty of an inn. This time she made no apologies. Having stabled Jobe in the driest stall and made sure the downtrodden hostler gave him passable fodder, she strode into the common room, slung her bags in a corner near the fire and set Patu to guard them. She did not allow the innkeeper a chance to argue, but laid down her money and demanded a room. Cowed by her commanding attitude, he obeyed at once. She wondered how such a submissive man could ever run an inn and how he dealt with problem patrons.

After seeing her quarters she decided that her luggage would be safer in the common area, so she brought it back with her. She arranged her table so that there was a space behind it for Patu to lie hidden.

The innkeeper himself served her, and although she was sure there must be someone in the kitchen, he was the only person she saw. Two other men slunk in a while later and each slipped into a chair as far from the centre of the room as possible and stared gloomily into his mug.

Soon the reason for all this unhappiness became apparent. She heard the jingle of armour and four rough-looking soldiers bulled their way in. Taking instant command of the tavern, they seemed to fill it with their noise and aggression. She kept her head down but observed them. They were a poor lot, their weapons decent enough, though poorly kept. Clad in what had once been the uniform of the Petrellan infantry, they had embellished their gear with odds and ends of stolen finery and in the process had lost many of the original pieces. The result was that they resembled game birds dragged around by an untrained retriever.

Clothing aside, to the occupants of the room these men were well known, and known to be dangerous. If the innkeeper was flexible before, now he was obsequious. The two other patrons looked as if they wished they were elsewhere.

Three of the soldiers sat down, but the fourth was restless. He strolled around the room as if looking for something to break. He got the response he wanted from the other drinkers, but that did not satisfy him. Then he noticed Zoe sitting in the shadows.

Not a word was spoken. He swaggered over to her table and planted himself in front of it, leaning over her with menace. Glancing back to see that his friends were watching him, he leaned down and was about to pick up Zoe's saddlebags when she decided that was enough. On her signal Patu reared up out of the darkness and put his front paws on the table, glaring down at the dumfounded soldier. The armigerent held his position until he had created the proper effect. Then he yawned. His huge jaws opened, the white fangs standing clear of the black gums. From his angle the soldier's staring eyes could see straight down the dark gullet. Then the teeth rang shut like the closing of a steel trap.

There was complete silence in the room, and then the soldier broke free of his terror. With a treble scream he bolted to the door, hauled it open and disappeared into the night, his companions close behind him.

There was peace after that, broken by Zoe's low chuckle. The innkeeper, at first too astounded to move, began to laugh as well, a high-pitched giggle that went on and on. One of the patrons banged his hand on the table, and the other attempted to take a swig of his ale and choked on it. His fellow strode over to slap him on the back, only stopping when he realized that the coughing had turned into strangled laughter. It was a healthy sound, and it made the room a friendly place.

The patron stepped behind the bar and drew another mug of ale. He set it down on Zoe's table with a respectful glance at Patu, now lying with his head on Zoe's knee while she gave him the attention he deserved. "Would the beast like anything for himself, sir? Whatever I have is his, and for free. That was the best sight I've seen since this damned war started."

"Thank you, innkeeper. He has fed well, but I am sure a bone or scrap from your kitchen would not go amiss."

The man walked over and shouted something through the kitchen door. A querulous answer caused him to go inside, his voice patient as he disappeared. A while later he returned, bearing a large platter of scraps and bones and accompanied by a woman who came under protest, hiding herself as best she could behind him.

"Don't worry, m'dear. The soldiers are gone and won't be back tonight, I can guarantee. Come an' meet the gentleman who turned the tables on them so neat. Sir, I hope you don't mind if my wife joins us this evening? This is the first time in three months that it's been safe. She always used to like sittin' out here, talkin' with the travellers."

"Not at all, sir. Please, goodwife, sit with me. My friend will do you no harm."

"There you go then. I told you he was a gentleman!"

The woman tugged at his sleeve, whispered in his ear.

"What?" He turned and looked at Zoe, then back to his wife. "No!"

She nodded, more firmly this time. Zoe caught her eye and chuckled, and soon the woman was laughing too.

"Your wife has a better eye than you do, innkeeper!"

The poor man stuttered and stumbled. "I am sorry, my Lady. How could I tell? How could a lady be travelling alone through these times?"

Zoe indicated the huge head still occupying her lap, swung her robe away from her sword hilt. "I have not yet found a problem I could not handle."

The locals gathered around after that, asking questions and answering hers in turn. One of the men slipped out to return with two friends. He must have spread the word, for soon more people, men and women, were thronging in, at first astounded at the jollity, then joining in. The innkeeper was required to tell the tale of the rout of the soldiers several times, and in Zoe's opinion it got more interesting each time he told it. Then a lad came in with a whistle, another brought a drum and the tunes started, villagers vying with each other to see who could remember the most songs about armigerents and the ancient wars.

When it was certain that this gala would go on for a while, Zoe excused herself on grounds of her fatigue and, slinging her saddlebags over Patu's convenient back, led him to her room. There he lay inside the doorway, leaving her secure, listening to the happy chatter from the bar. Soon she slept, and late in the night the villagers wore out as well, for when she awakened briefly, all was silent.

The moment she stirred in the morning there was a soft tap at her door and the innkeeper's wife was there, handing a hot mug of tea around the doorjamb. A breakfast of new-baked bread was waiting for her at the table by the fire, with the host himself to wait on her. Nor had Patu been forgotten. More scraps appeared, and he crunched happily through them.

The pleasant aura of the evening still lingered with a small ray of sunlight that spilled through a dirty window, and the owner and his wife became talkative. With no witnesses present, Zoe got a realistic and unpleasant picture of what life had been like in Velikii recently.

"Oh, Lord Rawden was no angel, that's for sure. But at least he was one of ours. His family had a good name once, and his heir had as much chance as any of being a decent man. No, I never thought I would see the day when I wished Rawden back, but here I am, doing it now."

"I understood that Lord Rawden was a hard and grasping ruler."

The landlord nodded. "Oh, to be sure. But he was a smart ruler, if greedy. He knew to the penny what a man could give. He took it every time, but never more. No, we didn't love him, but he let us make our livings. If he took the farmers' seed there would be no crop for next year, for him or for us. So he always left enough. Now it's different."

"How?"

"King Barent's men don't care for the future. They take what they want, of goods and of people, and they leave nothing for us. If they decide to burn this place down one night when they don't like the ale, they will, and with me inside if they can."

"How can they get away with it?"

"What is to stop them? Not King Barent. He has taken his revenge for the beating we gave him last year, and he continues to take it."

"The beating?"

"Of course." The innkeeper's thin chest swelled. "Lord Rawden marched up to the gates of Petrella, and Alarid gave him what he wanted."

Zoe mused. "I suppose you could see it that way."

"Alarid was an honourable man, if a weakling." The man's face turned dark. "But Barent is another matter." He swung his arm in a gesture that included his own situation and that of his countrymen.

Disturbed, Zoe did her best not to show it. Inaccurate as the Velikan's analysis was, it had a thread of truth running through it that was too pointed for her to dismiss. She turned the discussion to other subjects, then ended it by finishing her meal and rising.

"Thank you, landlord, for a fine evening's entertainment, and a good night's rest."

"My Lady, it is us who should be thankin' you for our evening. Times like that come far apart these days."

After these mutual expressions of gratitude Zoe went out, saddled Jobe and took to the road again. The moment's sunlight had been wiped out by high clouds, but they did not look like they bore rain, so she made good time.

But not for long.

* * *

The road now led through a more populated area, and every town had more than its share of armed men with nothing more to do than molest anyone they took a dislike to. Each group she rode past, she had to ignore curses, open insults and even flung clods of earth or dung. She knew that to respond would only bring trouble, but it galled her to be so meek. Finally, one group barred her passage and she had to send Patu out in front to face them down. They gave way grudgingly, and there was a delicate interval after she rode through and exposed her back to them.

That decided her. Mounted and with Patu beside her, she could whip any of these riffraff and send them running, but she also knew that one lucky swing of a sword or a well-aimed arrow could injure or kill herself or one of her animals. It wasn't worth risking her mission for the satisfaction. The next time she met a traveller dressed in Velikan costume, she stopped and asked about a less-frequented road that passed through this area. Receiving information that confirmed her memory of the maps in the War Room at the castle, she soon was off the road and jogging down a trail that wound along the foot of a range of hills.

It was travelled enough to be easy to trace, but no recent tracks marred its covering of fallen leaves. She followed it all day, looping back and forth in slow turns up the mountainside, then over a low pass and into the next valley. There was little hope of an inn for the night, but an empty forester's hut sufficed. She moved on in the morning, refreshed after an exceedingly short bath in a frigid mountain stream. The territory through which she passed grew wilder, and for a while she worried that she had somehow got on the wrong trail, with no sunlight to show her direction. Then she remembered the compass that Janitra had given her. Sighting along it, careful that there was no metal near, she was reassured that at least she was headed the right way.

She dipped down into the valley and the trees changed. While before she had been travelling through a huge, old forest of beech and oak, with their bare trunks exposed to the wintry air, now she was surrounded by a younger stand of evergreens that restricted her vision. It was about this time that Patu started to get nervous.

From their hunting times together last winter, she had developed the habit of glancing at him once in a while, and the moment that he was bothered she sensed it. There were still no prints showing, but he was interested in something his senses told him was happening to the east. Once, he stopped and whirled around in his tracks, nose and ears pointing back up the trail, but nothing showed. Zoe continued warily, one hand on her sword hilt, the other firmly on the reins. She swept Patu out to each side, but he found nothing. She quickened Jobe's pace to make them a more difficult target, and they moved on, every sense alert.

Deeper into the valley they descended, the evergreens now interspersed with willows and the ground mushy with years of dead leaves. The only sound was the sucking of Jobe's feet in the mud, but they strained their ears for anything else.

Patu skidded to a stop, his hackles rising, his teeth bared, staring ahead to the right. The willows were large here, and the evergreens at their feet were impenetrable. Zoe was about to move on when there was a cracking noise behind. Glancing back, she saw a large willow falling across the trail.

Every nerve shouting 'Trap!' she urged Jobe forward, aware that this might be exactly what she was meant to do, but having nothing else in mind. She had a vague hope that she might, by acting quickly, take her attackers off guard. Jobe had not galloped more than a dozen paces before he was pawing for footing as the ground gave way beneath him. Zoe flung herself to the side and managed to worm her way onto level ground. Before she could rise, she looked up at two men standing on the trail, short bows drawn, arrows pointed straight at her. She froze. Then they froze also, as Patu turned and stalked back, his head low, an awful rumble coming from deep in his chest. The bows wavered, swung towards him, then to her. She gauged the dirty faces of the bowmen, and when she saw the uncertainty rise she gave Patu the signal to halt.

"No arrow from one of those little bows is strong enough to stop him, and if you both shoot at him, you'll each have a dagger in your throat before you let fly." She was speaking loudly to carry over the screams of Jobe, who was struggling more wildly than she expected.

"Put down those bows and let me check on my horse." The two glanced at each other and did so, allowing her to approach Jobe.

He was in a pit, deep enough that he could not climb out, but even so, he writhed awkwardly with his front quarters only. Leaning down and grabbing the reins as his tossing head

393

brought them within reach, she soothed him and held him still until he quieted. He continued to breathe with a painful moaning sound. She could see blood on his flank, and when she got closer, a flash of something greyish white. Curtly demanding one of the men to hold the reins, she moved towards the animal's rear.

As she feared, there was a large gash across the belly and the intestines were exposed. Further investigation revealed a sharp stake fixed in the bottom of the pit. It had impaled the animal as he fell, and his struggles only made the damage worse.

In a fury, she swung up to confront the two outlaws. "What in the name of all the gods do you think you are doing? How could you...?" Words failed her, and her clawing hand found the hilt of her sword, sweeping it clear. It was only when they were cowering before her and Patu was snarling at their heels that she gained control.

"What are you doing? Why did you do this to my horse?"

"We are starving, my Lady. We need food. Our families need food. We had thought to trap a deer, but when a rich rider came by... We are desperate, my Lady. Please do not kill us. Our families need us."

Disgusted, she sheathed her sword. With the disturbance, her pony had resumed his struggles, although they were getting weaker. "Patu, guard them!" she snapped. Then, drawing her dagger, she approached Jobe, taking the reins and calming him. Not wishing to draw his pain out any longer, she rubbed his nose and behind his ears, then held his head gently and made a quick incision where the vein stood out on his neck. In the extremity of his agony he did not even notice, and the blood poured down, matting his brown chest in rivulets of red. Soon his head started to droop, but the lowering of his body must have pushed the stake farther in, for he jerked his head up, throwing Zoe aside, and gave a great scream of pain.

Helpless, she watched as he thrashed frantically. Then it was over. His forelegs collapsed and his head slipped down, leaving his hindquarters grotesquely elevated.

Zoe turned away, unable to bear the sight. When she could speak again, she motioned to the two outlaws. With Patu's teeth menacing their backs, they hurried over to her.

"I will see these families of yours. If, in truth, they are starving and if I believe this situation does not exist through your incompetence as providers, then I will not harm you. If I deem otherwise, you will suffer. Can you call your people to you?"

They were eager to please. "Oh, yes, my Lady. I have only to call, and my son will come. He can get the others."

"Then call him, but no other signals."

The man shouted, a high yodel that carried through the bare branches of the willows. A muffled answering yell drifted back, and soon a boy of about ten appeared from down the trail. At Zoe's nod, his father called to him to "Bring everyone."

"While we are waiting, you may figure out how to pull my horse out of your pit. If I decide to bury him there, you can remove the stake and put him back in. Get to it."

With Patu supervising so that Zoe did not have to watch, they removed her equipment from the dead horse and attached ropes with which to slide him from the pit. In a few moments, the rest of their families arrived: a large group to be provided for by two such men. There were two middle-aged women whom she presumed were their wives, a mass of small children and three older folks, one of whom seemed to be blind.

Once the ropes were tied, willing hands heaved the carcass out, and Zoe approached to where her companion lay, covered with mud and blood, a gaping hole in his belly. After a moment, she turned away. There was nothing more to do. She didn't even want to hear these people's story; she already knew what it would be and that she would believe it. The war, the soldiers, the choice of running with a chance of death in the wilds or staying with death all around their homes. Still, she listened carefully and professionally, hoping one small detail might make it worthwhile. The only familiar factor was the name of Lupent, who seemed to have advanced, both in his rank and in the scale of his atrocities.

Breaking off the conversation as soon as she could, she threw Jobe's soiled saddle across Patu's harness and lashed it in place. Strapping her own pack to her back, she turned to the men.

"I will leave you the horse. He is past knowing, and I would not be wasteful. I cannot blame you for your actions, nor can I forgive you for the pain you caused him. One day, when this horror is finished, I charge you with a deed of atonement. You will choose the deed, you will decide if it is enough." She stared steadily at the group, huddled silently together under her icy gaze. "You will survive, if only to do this deed!" She swept them once more with her eyes then turned and strode away, biting back her tears.

Later on that afternoon, when she had taken the time to think, she realized that it was mistake to take the saddle. Patu was strong enough, but it would be foolish to waste that strength when she might depend on it later. So, regretfully, she pulled the saddle off, and, digging a hole in the soft loam with her dagger, buried it. It gave her the opportunity she had missed to say goodbye to her faithful friend. She sat there a while, her arm around Patu's neck for comfort, thinking about their travels together. Then she wiped her eyes, covered the spot with new-fallen leaves and continued down the trail.

54. THE TRUE TEST

The next few days blurred, lacking in event or comfort, as the rain began again. She slogged on, wet through all day, only managing a lesser degree of dampness at her evening fire. Her only solace was the companionship of Patu during the day and his warmth at night. She continued along the trail through the forest, meeting no one, seeing little sign of life. There was a certain pleasure to the quiet and the loneliness, when she considered the countryside of the plains below and what was happening there, but she knew that sooner or later the path would wind back down and spill her out into the main stream again. Although it meant company and possibly a warm meal and bed, she was of two minds about the near future.

On the afternoon of the fourth day the trail began to descend, and soon she could see cultivated fields through the bare branches ahead. She came out in the open at twilight near a small farmhouse nestled into an opening in the forest, the road not far beyond. The weather showed no sign of clearing, and she decided to stop and ask for a bed, if even in the hayloft.

Leaving Patu in the forest and crossing the field, she approached the back yard where an old man was attempting to chop a hard piece of wood with a poor axe. She watched him as he tried for a good swing while the loose head of the axe twisted on its handle, thwarting his attempts. Finally, she spoke.

"How would you like to trade an armload or two of split wood for the use of a bed tonight?"

He jerked up, startled, and held the axe before himself ineffectually.

"Please, sir, I am only a traveller wishing a dry place to sleep. I would be happy to chop wood for you in exchange for the favour."

Her words registered, and he lowered the axe, peering at her. "What's that?"

She reined in her impatience. "You look like you could use a hand, and I need a place to spend the night. May I chop some wood? I might even be able to fix that axe."

He regarded her, then glanced around. "Where did ye come from?"

She tossed her head. "Back there. Down the old trail from the hills."

He nodded is if there were great import to this simple statement. "Ah, then you'll be wantin' a place to stay."

"That's right. May I stay here?"

He considered this. "Of course, you must. Of course. You'll not be the one they're lookin' for."

She glanced around. "Looking for?"

"Oh, yes, the word's out. Lookin' for someone. Don't know who or what, but someone. Soldiers, all up 'n' down the road the past few days. Lookin' for some Warlander: could be a man, could even be a woman. Armed to the teeth. Got a monster with her. Straight from the Fanged One's pits, it sounds like. Oh, they've got theirselves in a fine frenzy, they start lookin' for gods from the old religions. Hah! And what if it was true? Serve 'em right even more!" He looked up at her. "What was that about an axe?"

She smiled down at him and his ramblings. "I was suggesting I might fix your axe. If not, I'll cut your wood with my sword." She flicked her cloak back to reveal the hilt.

His watery eye gained a new sharpness. "Well, I suppose I wouldn't mind to see that. Splittin' firewood with that fancy sword. 'S tough wood, all I could find. Prob'ly snap your blade."

"It's not so fancy and it's certainly strong enough to cut your wood." Swinging the sword clear, she started in. The wood was tough all right, and a sword isn't a good splitting instrument,

398

but she went to it with a will, and soon there were a good number of burnable pieces. She turned to the old man. "See? Not so weak."

"No, not so weak, my Lady."

"And now, if you wish, I'll take a look at that axe."

"Oh, don't you bother with that. I just bin too lazy to fix it. Serves me right. I'll do it up in the morning. Now let's you and me go in and tell Mother that she's got company for supper. Not that she don't already know. Nosey old bag, my wife."

He spoke with the utmost cheerfulness and she couldn't help but grin. But with his next words, the smile dropped off her face.

"You'll be leavin' the beast in the woods, then?"

The old fox! He isn't as senile as I thought.

He grinned in satisfaction. "Better you do. My wife don't mind a bit o' company, but she don't want no Fanged One's beasts in her kitchen."

"He's no beast." Zoe found herself stung into giving out even more information. "He's an armigerent!"

The old man made no comment, but his smile flickered again.

Defeated, Zoe whistled Patu to stay away.

The man trudged over to the farmhouse door, opened it and shouted in. "Hey, woman, there's company for supper. Put another cup o' water in the soup."

A strident voice answered him from inside. "Well, the two of you shuck your boots at the door or you'll be cleaning my floors before you eat!"

The old man gave an apologetic grin and, taking off his boots, motioned her to enter. Removing her own with exaggerated care, she followed.

There was one main room to the cottage. The curtained alcove would contain a bed. Stooped over the fire was a pudgy little woman with wispy dark hair and sparkling eyes.

"Let me present Princess, the light of my life."

"Oh, shut up, you old goat. The day you land a princess the dung-heap will grow its own wings." She gave the pot a quick stir and turned, giving Zoe a formal bow. "We are so pleased you finally got here, my Lady. Please sit down. Will your companion be comfortable where you left him?"

Zoe's puzzled glance caught a meaningful raising of the eyebrows from the old man, and she refrained from comment. But the old lady noticed the look.

"Oh, he didn't believe me, that you were coming. Told me I was goin' senile, he did. But I was right, wasn't I? Hasn't she come, just as I said she would? Hasn't she left in the forest Him that it isn't right for the mortal eye to see?" She smiled at Zoe. "Don't you worry, my Lady. There is those whose eyes are so good, they can't see a thing, and what they see, they don't believe. But we know, don't we?" She made a gesture, familiar to Zoe now, of touching her blouse near the breastbone.

Anxious to get the conversation back in familiar territory, Zoe attempted to introduce herself, but was stopped again by her hostess. "Now don't you bother yourself with that, my Lady. We know who we are and that's all that's needed. Oh! But here I am talkin', and you hungry after walkin' all day." She swung with alacrity to the pot on the fire and ladled out a steaming mass into an earthenware bowl.

"Now sit you right here and eat till you're content." She shot an indignant look at her husband as she placed his bowl in front of him. "And there's no extra water in that, you may be sure!"

They all settled down to eat, and the aroma that enticed her made Zoe realize how hungry she was. The bowl was empty sooner than good manners would allow, and she looked up to

400

see the two old people regarding her with fond humour. Embarrassed, she lowered her spoon and stuttered an apology.

"Never you mind, my dear. You will need your strength, and little time remains. Would you like a touch more?"

Thrown off by the woman's strange speech, Zoe gave way to her hunger and held out her bowl. "If you have enough..."

"Of course. Enough and no more, but enough. After tonight we need nothing here, so eat what you will. As we know, you need it."

To Zoe's puzzled look, the old man answered apologetically. "Mother's got the second sight. Or says she has. Said you'd be comin', she did. I never listen. She never predicted anythin' pleasant for me. Just babies and hailstorms. Dunno which is worse."

"Ah, you don't have to believe me, you old fool. You just wait and see where we are tomorrow morning. Then you say you don't believe me."

"But I don't want to go to your son's place. I told you that, and I'm not going!"

The old lady turned to Zoe. "Independent old coot. Won't leave the home farm, even when my son's place is much better. Not too far away, but back off the road where every tin-pot-hatted soldier can come by and take what he wants. Fact is, he's afraid. He'd rather sit down here and be bothered by scum than come up to my son's place and be bossed around by my daughter-in-law. Got him so twisted around, he asks her if he can sit down, then asks where!" She was off in a high-pitched chuckle.

"She has not! I got proper manners, is all. You don't see me stompin' in and takin' over my in-laws' house. Not me. I got manners."

The old woman became serious. "Now, you mind those manners. The lady don't wanta be hearin' all our troubles.

401

When things get rough, we'll be out the back way and over the hill, don't you worry." She smiled as if satisfied that her plans were in order.

Zoe had finished her second bowl of stew and sat back, contented, when her hostess rose, head cocked to one side. "There! I can hear them coming now!" She bustled about, putting the dishes aside. Sure enough, Zoe also heard something: the sound of harness jingling. Cavalry patrol. She sat still, hoping they would ride by, but the pounding hooves came nearer, then entered the laneway. Soon there were at least four horses in the farmyard, perhaps five. A thundering knock sounded: a sword hilt against the door. Unsure of what was about to happen, Zoe sat still, conscious of her stocking-covered feet.

The old man opened the door and five troopers shoved into the room. The leader, a large man, overweight and sweating, was just sheathing his sword when he saw Zoe.

"What have you got here, old man? Who is this foreigner?" He turned a frown on her host. "This might be the one we're looking for! Do you know what happens to local riffraff who get caught harbouring a fugitive?"

There was no use. Zoe stood, hand on sword hilt. "What do you want, Captain?"

The rider turned. "I might want you. The word's out there's a stranger causing trouble along the road. Where's the rest of your band? Don't tell me we caught you alone."

"My band? I have no followers." Perhaps there was some kind of mix up. Maybe she should go with these men. They were more disciplined than most she had seen so far, and she might get somewhere with them, talk to their commanding officer, find someone who would vouch for her. She was, after all, a friend of the king. What was there to worry about?

A grin split the thin lips that faced her. "No followers, hey? Well, isn't that nice? So it's just you and us." He paused to glance at his men. "And maybe, when we're finished, if you are the one they're looking for we'll pass you along. But first we need to question you. Grab her arms, two of you."

Before the troopers could move, Zoe's sword was out and her back was to the wall. Out of the corner of her eye, she saw the two old people slip out the side door. Too late, she realized that she should have called Patu while the door was open. She doubted she could be heard, even by his ears, through the thick walls and across the field. She whistled anyway.

The leader laughed. "There's nobody around. We checked first. You really are alone, little lady. Now are we taking you whole or in pieces?" When she did not answer, he drew his sword. "Well, in case you do have friends over in the forest, let's do this quick."

His sword whipped towards her in an overhand cut that she parried easily, deflecting the force of his blow. He swung from the side and she deflected it again. She knew not to play around. She must dispatch this man before he discovered that he could not beat her and called for help. Then she had an inspiration. Why had she spent all summer in the blazing heat if not to prepare for a moment such as this? In an eye-blink, she made up her mind.

Her opponent swung a hard slice at her, and instead of deflecting the blow she held her edge up to intersect his sword directly and braced her wrist with her other hand. His weapon came down in a mighty rush, all the strength of his arm behind it, and met hers edge-to-edge. She had the momentary pleasure of seeing the stunned look on his face as his blade shattered, leaving him with a broken stump. Then she realized to her dismay that her own sword had flown from her hand and lay across the room under the table. Her right arm was numb and hung by her side, unmoving. All this registered in a fleeting moment and then the battle went on. The soldier cursed and tried to fling the hilt of his sword at her face. The moment he raised his arm to do so, her left-hand dagger flew straight to his throat and he fell backwards, choking. Darting forward, she slipped the dagger from her sash and drove it between the ribs of the man who had followed his leader too closely and was now too tangled up with his body to avoid her. He fell, wrenching the dagger from her hand. She launched herself upon the next man, trapping his sword in the sleeve of her robe and crushing his throat with the side of her foot.

Regaining her balance, she took stock of the situation. Her rush had taken her to the centre of the room and the two troopers who guarded the door were too far away to attack. Both had their swords drawn and were staring at her. She thought desperately. The weapons left in her robe were all much too subtle to defend against a sword, even if she had two hands that worked. There was nothing in reach to use as a weapon. She remembered her grandfather's house, so full of useful things, and here she was, dying in a similar but completely barren cottage. She considered her arm. The fingers were numb, but she could move the upper muscles. Good. At least she might throw it in the way of a blade.

She thought with fondness of all those who had taught her to fight. *Always keep going. Practice never giving up, even when you're hurt.* She made a silent salute to those men now, living and dead, and hoped that their training would help. If not, she would be joining some of them soon.

Well, there's always the bluff. Don't let them find out you're hurt. Relaxing and calming herself, she let her left hand fall to the same angle as the injured one and slid forward, her eyes focused at a spot between her two opponents, keeping both in her peripheral vision. As she moved, she analyzed them. The one on the left held his sword higher. If she could get under his guard and turn him between herself and his partner...well, it was worth a try. Her supply of options was running low.

She glided forward another step, angling to the left. She was about to move again when it registered that the swords facing her were wavering into defensive positions, the two faces above them open-mouthed in fear. In fact, the soldiers were about to break. Before she had time to consider this new situation they ran, clawing at each other as they collided in the doorway, then out of sight in a jingling of harness and a confused thudding of five sets of hooves, scattering away into silence.

Zoe stood in the centre of the room, astounded. Returning to reality, she darted over and grabbed her sword from the floor, fitting it as best she could into her left hand. At that moment, there was a scrabbling of claws outside and Patu charged in, stopping in comic uncertainty at what he saw. Hackles bristling and growl rumbling, he sniffed at the three fallen enemy. Certain they were harmless, he turned to Zoe for the accustomed praise.

Half laughing and half crying, she threw her arms about his neck and held on. When she was in control again, she straightened and looked around. Now that the action was over, she noted again how bare the room was. Intrigued by its owners, she had not registered it before, but except for the table and its utensils, the cottage was empty. Behind the curtain there would be no bed. She strode over and jerked it open. Sure enough: a bare wooden bedstead built into the wall. Curious. As if the two had meant to move out already and were just waiting for the right moment. Very curious.

Well, there was no time for mysteries. Sooner or later the surviving soldiers would calm down enough to go back to their headquarters and report. She didn't want to be anywhere near this cottage and its contents when they showed up with reinforcements. King's friend or not, they would be too happy to see her dead to listen to anything she had to say. She put on her shoes, shouldered her pack, awkwardly sheathed her sword and faded into the woods, trying to rub the feeling back into her right hand.

Now she was torn as to her route. Wary of soldiers, she wanted to stay off the road, but that would slow her down more than she needed, and she had to investigate what was happening. Barent would want to know. Maybe this was the part she could play, bringing key information from the centre of the uprising.

So she compromised, skirting the backs of the farms, slipping down to listen outside windows at night, and twice she purchased food from farmers who were as eager for conversation as she was.

The border was alive with rumour. A wave of religious fervor was sweeping into Petrella from the north. Its front must be just ahead of her, because all of her informants felt that their facts were the very newest. The Lady Herself had appeared far to the north. Several times, Zoe caught people making furtive signals to each other, the most frequent being the familiar touching of the breast where the medallion of the Lady hung. References to The Lady started appearing, even on the lips of those who seemed unfamiliar with Her creed. Zoe filed this away as well. *How fortunate for me! The insurrection I will be dealing with is one I have personal knowledge of: more perhaps than anyone at Barent's court.*

There was a great groundswell of hatred building among the people of the area, and their resistance to the soldiers was increasing. Zoe wondered if this was a planned campaign by some rebellious military genius, or simply the flowering of popular hysteria. Whichever it was, the effect was the same. An unhappy, repressed population was finding an emotional outlet for their woes. That they would soon boil over into open rebellion was not in doubt. Her history lessons had taught her that. She shuddered at the memory of what often followed such an uprising.

Barent, you always were to ready to leave the beaten path. Now look where you have led us.

She resolved to make better time. *I will soon be needed.*

55. The Final Straw

As she approached the Petrellan border, the rumours and stories increased. There was a swelling of revolt in the countryside and the king's men seemed at their wits' ends because of their inability to get information. Their tactics became more brutal, but this stiffened the people's anger. Zoe moved quickly but with every nerve on end, as there was no telling when a patrol of cavalry or quick-stepping foot soldiers would sweep past her as she lay hidden beside the trail, warned by Patu's nose or ears.

She crossed the border into Petrella by the smugglers' route and even there had to avoid other wayfarers several times. Returning to the lowlands, she decided that now she was in her own country she could afford to be more open.

It was a pleasant feeling to be walking on her home paths again after so many months of strange lands. She swung out, marching at speed. She knew the area, knew how far it would be to a village where she could spend the night, even knew the name of the inn: a pleasant state of affairs.

But she was not so secure as to ignore Patu's warning and the pounding of hooves. Fading into the brush at the side of the road, they waited.

The horsemen were not on the main road, but coming down a small lane that led to a farm. They were Petrellan, and as they swept by, they were laughing and joking. Several had extra bags and boxes slung across their saddles as if recently picked up.

When their noise had faded, Zoe stepped out. She looked up and down the road, then at the lane. On impulse, she started up the driveway.

Soon she reached the farm: small but well-tended fields, a sturdy house and outbuildings on the far side. All seemed normal. Then, as she came closer, she noticed several unusual objects.

The farmer and his family lay strewn about the yard like broken dolls, except that their bodies oozed blood, and their faces, frozen in the eternal moment of their final agony, were far from pretty. She sank down on a stone and sat, transfixed in horror. This was Petrella! These were Petrellan people, slain by Petrellan soldiers, who rode away laughing! Seething anger washed through her, setting every muscle tense, her hands like claws.

A sound made her spin about. Then she relaxed. A young kid stumbled towards her, dragging a leg, a red stain tumbling down one flank. It fell, bleating piteously. She started to get up, but Patu was there first. Taking the little creature in his mouth, he raised it and brought it to her. It lay quiescent in his grasp as he placed it in her lap. She took a rag from the ground nearby and wiped the blood away so she could explore the wound. It was superficial: a light sword slash that had been turned by the animal's growing winter coat. Looking for a piece of clean cloth for a bandage, she avoided the bodies, going into the house for a rag of curtain torn from the wall. As she worked over the animal, the softness of its hair, the warmth of its body against her and its complete trust calmed her. The anger drained out of her, to be replaced by a building determination.

Taking a handful of grain from a spilled bag on the barn floor, she started it soaking in water. The kid's mother was killed or frightened away, and she had nothing else to feed it. By this time of year it should be weaned, though its small size suggested a late spring birth.

While waiting for the grain to soften, she dealt with the bodies. All she could manage was a wide, shallow grave. She wrapped the family in sheets from the house and laid them straight, close to each other. Then, saying a brief passage from the Codes, she covered them over. There was nothing else she could do for them; she had no idea who they were, but still she knelt and cried for them and for her land.

The kid worked the grain around in his mouth and got most of it mashed in his hair, but she thought he swallowed some, and hoped it would help. Picking him up, she placed him in one of Patu's copious saddlebags, taking off her Guide's cloak to pad the bottom and strapping the lid on lightly. Looking around once more in sorrow at the now-bare farmyard, she turned back towards the main road.

As she walked, her mind was working. Without the cloak she felt chilled, so she walked faster. It suited her mood. As she turned towards her destination, the aimless speed developed purpose. She had a job to do. It was time to get started. *Why am I wandering about in the forest when I am needed at home? I must get there as quickly as possible.* What she would do when she arrived was not yet clear, but she had her own confidence and the trust of those who had sent her. *I am important, competent. I will make a difference to my people.*

As she walked on, she noticed that the road was bare. No refugees huddled past, trying to escape everyone's notice. No rich arms merchants with their heavy wagons of destructive creations. No patrols of soldiers. She heard noise ahead of her but her thoughts were on more important things. A small part of her mind catalogued the sounds as they neared: mounted Warlanders led by Light Horse and then foot soldiers, tramping along at their travel pace. She kept walking.

She topped a rise and there they were, stretching off into the distance. Patu bristled and moved ahead, one ear cocked back for her word to attack or hide. Zoe was in no mood to hide. She had been slinking around in the forest for too long. She had somewhere to go. Signalling Patu to follow safely behind her, she kept walking.

The light cavalry, acting as advance guard, came closer. From high up on his horse, the captain sneered at her. "Off the road there, little girl."

Zoe kept walking. When she was close enough for him to hear her voice, she spoke in a conversational tone. "Get out of my way." Then she moved on as if he did not exist. At the last moment, his horse made up his mind for him. Whether through his unconscious signal or of its own accord, it reared up and landed sideways to her, allowing her to pass. His men, observing their captain thrown out of the way, scrambled aside as well.

Approaching the Warlanders, she had a similar effect. When she reached the first horse, its rider had transferred his confusion to the animal. She had only to reach out her hand and it dove away in panic. As she clove through the ranks of mounted Warlanders leaving chaos in her wake, that small thoughtful part of her mind suggested that this was not a normal situation. She ignored it. *I don't care what is normal or not. I have somewhere to go, and I am going there.* She felt no antagonism for those in her way, but they must stand aside, that was all. She kept walking.

The men in front of her took on a misty quality, and they flowed together then parted, leaving her a clear path. She found that she could, at her leisure, focus on any single item she wished. The colour of a soldier's shirt. The feel of the roadway beneath her feet. In spite of the chaos of the surrounding army, the sweet song of a bird in the forest to the left.

Then her attention came back to her path. The easy flow had stopped as if a boulder blocked the course of a stream. Someone barred her way. He was a huge man, dressed as an ordinary soldier. He carried a businesslike sword in his hand and he stared at her. She could see the naked fright on his face, but he stood unyielding. i As she came closer, the sweat glistened on his forehead, but still he held his ground. Then, with a supreme effort, he raised his sword and swung. Gently she reached out and brushed him aside as she would a branch across her path in the forest. There was a snapping sound, and he stumbled back into the arms of his friends, his weapon falling from nerveless fingers to the road. She kept walking.

Then, from the forest on one side of the road and echoing from the other side, came a high, ululating call that reminded her of Kyabran worshippers of the Lady. After a pause it sounded again, starting on the left this time, repeated on the right. Even in her heightened awareness it was difficult to pinpoint the sources. For the soldiers, it was the final push. They broke and ran, up and down the road and into the forest on either side. The whirr of arrows filled the air. Then the sound of their passage, punctuated by terror-stricken yells and cries of pain, died away.

Soon she had the road to herself again, and she came gradually to her normal senses, looking around. Dazed, she found a wayside boulder to sit on, and there she rested.

She was roused from her stupor by the feel of Patu's tongue on her foot, and the muffled bleat of the kid from his bag. Shaking herself, she rose, and after bringing Patu back to his feet and reassuring him, she opened the saddlebag and allowed the kid to stick his head out. His health was improving, his eyes bright with interest as he stared around.

Zoe looked at the sun, peering at her through hazy clouds. Plenty of time to make distance.

She kept walking.

56. HOMECOMING

She moved with even more purpose now, sliding into the Messenger's Pace: a hundred strides running alternated with a hundred walking. At this rate she covered more ground than a horse, and it only took her three days to approach Arlyn Castle.

The final day she walked until late, knowing there was an inn with passable fare in the last village before Escalon Pass. Reaching it after dusk, she stabled Patu this time; she could hardly bring his small passenger inside. Besides, she was in the heart of Petrella now, with only the Pass between her and her destination, and this was a reputable place. Leaving the bemused hostler with instructions as to how to handle both his charges, she entered the main building.

At least, she tried to enter. There was a crowd in the common room, all very excited about something, and the landlord's sales were booming. She squeezed along the wall until she could catch the busy man's attention. There was no difficulty in getting a room. The people were all locals, here to discuss an incredible event of the preceding days. From the sound of it, there was an invading army somewhere close, moving fast. She slid back to her usual vantage point in a corner and listened, but all she heard was hysterical gossip. If the tales were to be believed, there was an army of over a thousand men, led by some sort of fanatic with supernatural powers, all within a day's march north of the village.

She gave up and went to bed. She wasn't going to get any sense out of this and she wasn't in the mood for an evening in a crowd.

In the morning, she breakfasted on a piece of meat stuffed inside a stale roll as she strode out of town, headed south. It was a passable morning, with sunlight now and then and a fresh breeze, but there was an oppressive feeling in the air. If a storm was approaching, she must hurry. Besides, she knew she would be home tonight, so if she showed up tired, she could just sleep in tomorrow. In her own bed. After such a time away, that was a pleasant thought.

As Escalon Pass opened up before her, she scanned the far horizon through the break in the mountains. Sure enough, dark storm clowds billowed. The question was, which route to take? If she took the road and went the long way, she was sure to get wet. If she went over the mountain she might beat the storm, but if she didn't and it caught her, she could end up in snow.

She ruffled Patu's ears and grinned. "What do you think, fellow? Up to a touch of mountain climbing?"

Patu looked up where she had indicated. His ears perked and his tail began to sweep. He probably thought they were going hunting, but it was nice that he agreed with her plan. She addressed the small white head peeking up from the saddlebag.

"You don't get a vote, kid. You're just a passenger."

The little creature bleated at her, unconcerned. The stable hands at the inn had fed him grain, evening and morning, so he was in fine fettle.

Zoe smiled. "All right, troops, left turn and forward march." Going over the mountain appealed to her. It was quicker and had the added advantage of leaving her at the Guides' Postern. She didn't want to parade up the main street of the city and knock at the castle gate. This way she could slip in and find out what was happening before she had to take any action.

So up they went, through the now-leafless forest, under the pines and out on the barren rock, slippery with recent rains. Then over the top, with the wind rising and particles of snow stinging her face, causing Patu's little passenger to duck down into the shelter of his saddlebag. On the southern side, the flakes came down in earnest, but she was soon low enough that they melted to rain and she was forced to steal the cape from under the kid to keep herself dry.

So she was appropriately attired when she knocked at the Guides' door. The Guide on duty let her in, although he wasn't a man she recognized. Once she was inside, he questioned her thoroughly. Having at least heard about her, he allowed her through.

She thought it best to take Patu and the kid to the stable. Ardu was there, so she received a pleasant welcome, tinged with sorrow when she had to explain Jobe's absence. The pony had been a favourite of the stable lad's, too.

The presence of the kid in Patu's saddlebag entranced the boy.

Let loose in the echoing stable, the little fellow ran about to get his legs stretched, then came looking for food, butting his head against Patu's side in the appropriate signal. When nothing was forthcoming, he looked up to Zoe and bleated a command. She and Ardu exploded with laughter.

"Could you find some milk or grain? I'm not sure what to do with him, now that he is here. He can't come to my rooms."

"Can I take care of him? I've looked after all sorts of animals. We had goats back home."

"Would you like to? I'm sure he would be happier here. He can keep Patu company."

With that settled, Zoe hauled her packs over to her quarters. It was strange to open the door and see everything exactly as she had left it. There was the chair she had pushed back from the table when she stood up to leave. There on the bed was the shirt she forgot to pack at the last moment. No one had disturbed anything, although there was no dust, and the floor was cleaner than she remembered.

Just for fun, she decided to wander the castle and surprise any of her friends she ran into. She set out across the courtyard, still in her Kyabran robe, her new sword swinging at her hip.

414

There were few people around. Many were newcomers who regarded her with wary curiosity. It was long past noon, so she strolled over to the kitchens to see what she could scrounge. There she was recognized and rushed over to her favourite corner table to enjoy a bowl of broth and a hunk of heavy bread. However, there was a restraint that she did not remember. She wondered if it was the strangeness of her clothing. She hoped that she, herself, had not changed that much.

So it was with an unsatisfied air that she headed back to the stables with a bag of scraps for Patu. As she entered, she heard Ardu's voice raised in protest.

"You can't do that! He belongs to Zoe!"

Nasty tones boomed in response. "I dunno who this Zoe is, but he leaves a tasty morsel like this running around, he ain't gonna keep it long." There was a harsh laugh and a squeal from the kid.

Zoe hurried her steps, but paused and rounded the corner quietly to see what was happening.

A tall, bearded man in Guide's gear was standing in the middle of the open area by the stalls holding the kid up by its back legs while it screamed in fear. Ardu stepped forward.

"You put him down!"

The man backhanded the boy, knocking him across the cobbled floor. "Don't you tell me what I will or will not do, you little rat, or you'll get more than that!" He pulled his dagger out, his intention toward the kid obvious.

Ardu looked around in panic. No help near. He was sobbing in pain, but he refused to quit. He started towards the man, but the dagger point swung towards him.

Lowering the kid behind him, the man stalked toward Ardu, flicking the dagger at his face, forcing him back against the stall. The boy, in real terror now, screamed out, "Patu!"

Zoe, about to rush forward, had forgotten about the armigerent. At the boy's call the beast cleared his stall door, landing close to the kid's tormentor and crouching there, his lip wrinkling, the beginning of his battle roar a low, building menace.

His target dropped the kid, who bleated and scrambled to Ardu for safety. The man backed away, his face white, his dagger pointed at Patu. The armigerent crouched forward, still snarling. Zoe stood where she was, allowing the man to back towards her. At the correct moment she flashed Patu a signal, and he rushed forward a step, causing his opponent to lurch back. Zoe had only to reach out a foot and the man was flat on the stones, her sword tickling his throat.

She gave him time to realize his situation. "Now you know who Zoe is. Zoe is the owner of both these animals. We come as a package. Still interested?"

The man on the floor crawled backwards, trying to avoid the point.

"No, stay where you are. I have questions to ask. Who are you, and what are you doing here?"

"My name is Lupent, and I'm a Guide, and I've just come in from the north with important information for the king."

"And to whom are you thinking of reporting?"

"I told you. To the king."

"So the Guides report to Barent now, do they?"

Zoe's point had moved aside as a reward for plain answers, so Lupent sat up, sneering. "I do. The others still report to that woman. Loreline."

"I see. Well, you do your reporting to King Barent and then you stay out of my way. I know about you and your style of work and I don't like it. If you are valuable to Barent, you are safe. The moment he doesn't need you any more, you will leave

Petrella. Do you understand?" The sword tip snapped back to its place at his throat.

He glared up at her. "Barent needs me!"

"That's 'His Majesty,' and I don't think you understood." She stepped back. "Patu, do you want him?"

The armigerent started ahead, but Lupent scrambled to his feet, his back against another stall.

"I understand, I understand."

"My Lady."

"I understand, my Lady."

"You may go now. Remember." She indicated Ardu. "The boy, too."

The man snarled an affirmative and slunk out.

Zoe turned to Ardu. "Are you all right?"

She looked at his face, which was bright red on one side but otherwise undamaged.

"Better than I have been for a while. That was beautiful!"

Zoe shrugged. "He has done much worse than that. We are going to get rid of him. I must talk to Barent about it. Thank you for taking such good care of the baby. Can you think of a name for him?"

"Can I name him?"

"I didn't even think to. Why shouldn't you?"

57. A Lethal Division

Those responsibilities taken care of, Zoe went in search of Loreline. She found her, as expected, in the Sivan's office, looking small and forlorn behind the big table.

She rose joyfully and dashed around to give Zoe a long, warm embrace.

"Zoe! You don't know how glad I am to see you! When did you get back?"

"If you're taking the Sivan's job, you're supposed to know that. He always knew where I was before I even got there."

The woman slumped against the table, and Zoe saw the weary lines in her face. "In case you hadn't noticed, I'm not the Sivan."

Zoe laid a hand on her friend's shoulder. "I'm sorry, Loreline. That was a petty thing to say. It's just that, well...I suppose I was hoping, even at the last minute, to walk in and see him still sitting here."

"You think I don't wish for the same, every day I come here? Do you know what this duty is like?"

"I have an idea of what he did. How he did it was another matter."

"Exactly." The sweep of her arm took in the table, covered with papers as usual, and the pigeonholes behind. "I can't make any sense out of most of this. As if it's written in plain language, but it's really a code."

"It is a code. The code is the way the Sivan thinks. If you understand how his mind works, you can figure it out."

"That's one reason I'm so glad to see you. Will you help?"

Zoe grinned. "If you've taken over the Sivan's job, then I am under your command. Say the word."

"Of course that's not true. I have enough trouble with these so-called Guides without trying to give you orders."

"What's wrong with the Guides?"

"What's wrong is the old Guides are gone. At least, most of them. The ones we have now are a new lot, brought in by the king. Most of the old set just disappeared. Some before the Sivan, some after. They were low born, most of them, but they had great pride in their work and they wouldn't do what Barent wanted them to. So, like Guides would, they faded and disappeared. Then His Majesty hired new ones who would do what he said."

"Like Lupent."

"Have you met him?"

"We had words." She rubbed the pommel of her sword.

Loreline waited, then realized that no more was forthcoming. "If I'm supposed to be running this organization, I should know what's going on between its members."

"Yes, Ma'am. If you say so. He was bullying the stable boy, so I put my point to his throat and told him that when he had finished giving his important information to His Majesty he had my permission to leave the kingdom."

"Zoe! You can't send Barent's favourite Guide away!"

"I didn't. I just threatened to. I'll be speaking to Barent about that small matter as well. Do you have any idea how things are going out there?" She tossed her head in a northerly direction.

"Oh, yes. I'm not completely useless, and I get all the reports, such as they are. These new men, Zoe, they're not Guides. They're either bullies or spies, that's all. They have no intelligence, just a low cunning and no honour at all."

"Part of the larger matters I must speak to Barent about."

Loreline raised her head. "If you just came in from the north, you must have an idea what's going on."

419

"I think so, but there's so much hysteria and rumour, it's hard to figure out what. Whenever religion gets mixed up in it, everything becomes more complicated."

Loreline grinned, and motioned Zoe to take her usual chair. "Give me politics any day, plain and simple. Now, Guide, let's have your report."

It was a pleasant respite for both of them: Loreline to hear from a source she trusted, Zoe to find someone knowledgeable to discuss the situation with. Between them they put together a report of what was happening, then made projections of possible future action. When they had finished, they sat back and looked at each other in mutual concern.

"It looks grim, if the common folk are as enraged as you say they are."

"Oh, they're angry, all right. The problem for you and Barent is that your main sources of information are the worst causes of the problem. How could anyone make a reasonable decision based on anything Lupent brought in?"

"I never trusted him, but is he as bad as that?"

"I heard his name specifically mentioned too many times for it to be coincidental. Now that I've met him, I find it even more credible."

"If you are correct, there will be insurrection soon."

"It still depends on this religious fanatic, whoever he is. The whole countryside is like the forest after a drought. One spark and it will explode. He has the potential to be that spark. We must find out more about him. It isn't possible to field the forces your reports say he has without at least a few scraps of evidence showing. I spent the last two quarters passing through that area and I saw no forces. His power is not in men or weapons. I think it is in the minds of the people. If he touches off the spark, every able man, woman and child in these two lands will take up whatever weapon he or she can and attack anything that resembles authority. There will be a conflagration."

"How can he do that?"

"Think of how you start a fire. Flint and steel, right? Barent's men are out there hardening the steel in the people, and this," she reached inside her shirt and pulled out her wheeled pendant, "is the flint."

Loreline gasped. "Where did you get that?"

"You didn't send it?" She stared at the other woman, willing the truth from her.

"Zoe, how could I? You were away for months."

It wasn't a straight answer, but the feeling was there.

"It was sent to me, I don't know by whom. That was a message in itself, that I would find secret help from these people, and I have. But they are the ones who will lead the revolt. How will you deal with that, follower of The Lady?"

Loreline slumped in the chair, her arms spread on the table before her. "I have no idea, Zoe. Are you sure?"

Zoe just waited. That was answer enough.

Loreline pulled herself together. "There is nothing else to do. We must inform King Barent. My responsibility is to him."

Zoe wished things looked that simple to her. "And what about the Sivan?"

"What about him? I decided that long ago. He is not here. He is either dead or gone, in which case it doesn't matter, or else this is part of his plan. I cannot go around wondering what he would expect me to do. I will do what I think is best and hope that it is what he wants."

These words so echoed her own feelings that Zoe felt relieved, but also suspicious. "Damn the man! I still wonder if I'm in the middle of one of his plots."

Loreline smiled. "I'm sure we are, whether he's alive or not. Doesn't it make you feel better to know that someone has this mess figured out?"

Zoe balanced the ideas, one against the other. "No, it doesn't. I don't like to think I'm that predictable. I prefer to look at it this way." She ticked the points off on her fingers. "The Sivan is gone. He has left us to do what he hopes we will do. But he can only guess. We are the ones who will know, when the time comes, what is the right thing to do. We must make the decision. If we do not choose what he wants us to choose, that is his problem, not ours. For myself, I will do what is right for me. I will not consider what his plans might be. If I take his way, fine. If I do not, too bad. Besides which, look at the other possibility. Perhaps he has done all he can." She flicked her fingers, tossing the uncertainty away. "In any case, it is up to us."

"In any case, we must see the king."

"I agree on that. Before he acts on what Lupent tells him."

They were about to leave the Sivan's office when Zoe heard a familiar step behind her. Turning joyfully, she met Kenna with open arms.

"Zoe! How fortunate that you should return now. Did you bring any news from the north? I hear frightening things."

"The news is not good, Kenna. Loreline and I were going over it. Barent is getting unreliable information and we want to talk to him before he acts on more of the same."

Kenna looked grim. "That's why I was coming here. That weasel, Lupent, went in to see him, and I hoped Loreline had some information to check the truth of what he says. Let us go now. You can give me the gist of it as we walk."

The three swept across the deserted main hall, headed for the king's receiving room beyond. "It starts out simple. Barent's soldiers and spies are creating havoc in Velikii and in

Petrella herself. The people, both the nobles and the commons, are primed for rebellion. Now add the rumour of a religious leader with supernatural powers."

Kenna wrinkled her nose. "Some new fanatical religion? From where?"

Zoe could see Loreline grit her teeth. "No new religion, my Lady. These are followers of The Lady, bearers of The Wheel."

Kenna stopped dead. "The Lady? But that is no religion of rebellion! It is the old matriarchal religion of Kyabra, a sect dedicated to the protection and nurture of the land."

Zoe smiled bitterly. "If logic had anything to do with it, a case could be made for the removal of Barent's men as dangerous to the land. From what I witnessed, I must agree."

Kenna walked on slowly. "That religion is Kyabran and very old. What power can it wield here?"

Zoe thought about what she had learned in Kyabra. "You are right about its age, but the Kyabran part is far less simple. The sect is more widespread than that. In more recent times it has taken on the aspect of a secret cult, here and in all the Duchies. It is well entrenched, but with few tangible resources. No, the real power is its position as a rallying point for the feelings of the populace."

"Which are very strong."

"To the level of rebellion."

Kenna regarded Zoe from head to foot and seemed about to say something, but then they arrived at the receiving room door. Ignoring the guards outside, Kenna swept into the room, pulling the other two along in her wake.

Barent glanced up warily from where he was sitting, deep in conversation with Lupent. "Well, Kenna, what brings you here?"

"A report from a source I can trust."

Then he noticed Kenna's companions. "Zoe! You come at an opportune time. What do you bring me from Kyabra?"

"Nothing that will help you in this present crisis, your Majesty. Not from Kyabra, that is."

"Then what do you bring that will help, and from where?"

Zoe indicated that Loreline should give her report, but Barent shook his head. "No, no, I don't want the analysis, Loreline. I want the facts, straight from the source. What do you have for me, Zoe?"

"Information. Recent, and accurate as far as it goes." She proceeded to give him an outline of what she had seen and heard in the past quarter, leaving out the analysis and the solutions she and Loreline had discussed.

When she finished, Barent regarded her, a forefinger rubbing his chin. "Are you sure you are not giving too much credence to this religion? Old religions don't return. Once the old gods weaken, they never recover."

"What about Kyabra herself? Do old peoples never come back? Or do they return with a different type of power? This religion is changed, adapted to modern ways, and very powerful."

Barent regarded Kenna, then shrugged as if giving in. "What can I say? You all seem agreed that this religion is our main problem. So we will deal with it." He became businesslike, almost like the old Barent, joyfully tackling a new problem, about to come up with a stunning and creative solution. Zoe watched him, relieved at this spark. It lightened the shadowed face and put vigour into his slouching shoulders.

"Yes, we must be quick and decisive." He smiled at Kenna. "It is pleasant that we all agree for once. Lupent and I were discussing measures when you came in."

Zoe felt a stab of dismay. What possible good could come of this man's advice? She listened with growing horror as Barent outlined his plans.

"It may seem harsh, but if bloody revolution is coming, we will save more lives in the end. We will outlaw this religion. All members will be imprisoned, their property confiscated." His smile came out as a grimace. "That always brings out the informers – the chance to take over the lands of a rival. We can search everyone for evidence. They make it easy, wearing that medallion all the time."

Zoe glanced over at Loreline, wondering if she, too, felt the weight of her wheel dragging at her neck, a huge lump that couldn't be concealed.

Barent continued with enthusiasm. "We must execute a few of them. Find the leaders, make an example. Then we can figure out where they are hiding their armies and force them into battle, wipe them out for good. Scorch them, cleanse the kingdom of them. Yes, perhaps harsh measures, but quick and effective and the problem is solved."

Kenna had waited long enough. "What has happened to your brain, Barent? That is the stupidest thing I have ever heard you say, and believe me, I have heard a few recently." This was a Kenna Zoe had rarely seen. This was not the quiet and careful woman who manipulated behind the scenes. This was a fully armed Warlander, carrying all before her in her battle rage. "Didn't you hear what Zoe said? There are no armies to engage in honourable warfare! All you have out there is the people. Your people, Barent. You are talking about killing Petrellans, torturing them to find out information that doesn't exist, persuading them to lie to gain revenge on their enemies. I have never heard a more despicable idea, and it little becomes you."

Barent seemed able to weather this, but he picked up one detail. "What do you mean, no armies? Lupent says they routed four hundred seasoned reinforcements I sent out. What kind of army would they need to do that?"

Zoe looked searchingly at Lupent. "I would like to know about that myself. I saw that force, but I'm not so sure what happened to them. Perhaps they weren't routed by an army. All the rumours say that a supernatural power was used on them. My analysis is that they were a bunch of cowards, outwitted and scared off by a clever trickster. But could they come to you and tell you that? No, I think they would invent an army to save their pride. I think that would be a useful tool for another clever trickster, a lever to gain more power. Tell me, your Majesty, who suggested himself as commander of this army you are sending?"

She glanced at Lupent, who snarled but said nothing.

She turned back to the king. "I thought so. Barent, you are getting poor information, slanted to suit the needs of those who bring it to you."

Kenna had not cooled down yet. "Yes, Barent. Listen to her. Get rid of this upstart weasel with his self-serving lies and listen to those of us with the kingdom in our hearts."

Barent's fist slammed down on the table. "I am the kingdom! I am the king, and my welfare is the kingdom's welfare! How dare you lecture me on my duties!" His voice lowered, and again Zoe caught a glimpse of the powerful, controlled man she had known. "You would like to see your son in my place, so you could rule him as you try to rule me. But that will not happen!"

Zoe thought to interpose herself before this got any farther out of hand, but Kenna was beyond the reach of cool sense. "I do not want my son on any throne sullied by your deeds! Better he should never return than endure having his name connected with your actions, past and future. I warn you, brother, that I supported you, yes, supported you even when I disagreed, because I thought you had the kingdom at the centre

426

of your ideals. But now I see that you are corrupted by those you associate with, polluted by the filth they wallow in."

She took a deep breath and calmed herself. "I warn you, Barent, if you do this thing you speak of, I will no longer support you. If I must leave this kingdom, the country my ancestors ruled for so long, I will leave rather than be associated with a deed of such infamy!" She paused, breathing hard again, then shook her head sadly. "Oh, Barent." She turned and strode out.

There was silence in the room after her departure. Zoe looked at the king. All the strength seemed to drain from him. The bend in his back was more pronounced and the drooping of his head in the torchlight accentuated the deep circles under his eyes. Wisps of grey tinged his beard and hair.

She turned away, saddened as well. She was witnessing the end of a great many things, the greatest of which was the man she had known, the man she had loved. It grieved her deeply, but she still could not support him in what he planned. What good could ever come of this situation?

Barent managed to pull himself together. "Leave me." His voice held a husk of its former power.

They waited while Lupent, with a sly grin, slunk out. Then they followed at a distance.

Supper was dismal. Barent made no comment when Zoe positioned herself with Loreline at the Sivan's accustomed spot. He merely sat alone at the high table, staring off into space and eating when he remembered. The two women finished their meal and slipped away. He didn't seem to notice.

58. The Final Choice

Zoe was prepared for another long, thought-tortured night, but the rigours of the trip and the welcoming familiarity of her bed lulled her early, and she slept well. She awoke refreshed but guilty, had a quick breakfast and resolved to see Barent again.

As she approached the Receiving Room door, she found a restless group of men ahead of her: soldiers and officers. There was a notable lack of Warlanders from any of Petrella's leading families. Lukin was pacing back and forth in front of the door, and a few of his Guard milled around, their disheveled clothes and wan faces suggesting a sleepless night. Lukin noticed her and brightened.

"Zoe! I didn't know you were back."

"Hello, Lukin. Where's the Man?" It was a favourite expression of the captain's, and Zoe used it as a casual reminder of their shared experiences.

Lukin jerked his thumb at the brass-studded door. "Been in there all night. Alone. I can't think what to do. We tried to send in some food. The steward just about got his head bit off. I had to tell him about Torey's army, and he listened to that, but he still wouldn't let me through the door." The soldier's heavy head swung back and forth. "I don't know, Zoe."

"What's this about Torey?"

"He crossed the border yesterday. Made no secret of it."

"Has there been any fighting?"

"None. Torey's supposed to be an ally, and Gerth is with him. Barent won't give any orders, so we have no idea whether to fight or let them come. So we let them come. They'll be at the city gates by sundown, but we can't fight Gerth unless Barent orders it. What does he want, Zoe? He always has a plan!"

428

This plaintive plea, combined with the fact that he had forgotten to refer to Barent as king, showed how uncertain the captain was. Zoe would have smiled if it hadn't been so serious a matter. *Such a man as this coming to me for a reassuring pat on the head! Well, I will help if I can. That's why I came home.*

"In the absence of orders, no resistance is the right course. Let them come. They won't do any harm. If we batten the city down tight, we can sit here and wait for His Majesty to make a move. I have no more idea than you do what he has in mind. I just got home yesterday."

"What of Lady Kenna? I heard they had a row."

Zoe grimaced at the memory. "More than that."

The captain raised his eyebrows. In his years of service with Barent, he had weathered many brother-sister disagreements. Those close to the royal family had for years seen them as natural and of little import.

"It looks bad, Lukin. And Gerth headed this way with an army might make it a lot worse. We must be cautious. A small mistake could have serious consequences."

"I agree. But in the meantime, what?" He tossed his head in the direction of the forbidding door of the reception hall.

"As long as Barent is able to make a decision, we wait for that decision. Even choosing not to act is a choice in itself, I suppose."

"But what if he's not able?"

"What do you mean? He was all right when you gave him the message, wasn't he?"

"Depends on what you mean by 'all right.' He looked terrible. Worse than I've ever seen him."

"I can imagine." Zoe's guilt increased. There she was, sleeping happily when Barent needed her the most. She could give him rest, she knew. The old ritual with tea and massage had always pulled him out, got his body relaxed so that formidable mind could work. Hope began to build in her. *I can still try. We were a team once and could be again.*

"I'd better talk to him."

Again the old campaigner shook his head slowly. "He doesn't seem to want company."

"Maybe he doesn't, and maybe he does. He's getting company." With a renewed sense of purpose and competence she strode to the huge, studded door, with Patu at her side and her sword's comforting weight swinging at her hip. There was a general relieved shuffling and several of the watchers fell in behind her. With her hand on the massive latch, she paused. *No, this isn't right. This is a task for me, alone. A duty for Barent's old friend, not some noblewoman from Kyabra with her fancy sword and trappings.* Turning Patu, she signalled him into the 'guard' position and slid out of her harness, laying the sword at his feet. "Look after that, will you, fellow?"

Then she put her weight against the door. It swung until the crack was wide enough for her to enter. She slipped in and pushed it shut behind her.

Despite the bright morning outside, the room remained gloomy. The windows high in the west wall let in no direct rays of the sun, and the dark old stone soaked up what light there was. The ancient banners and tapestries on the rafters and walls hung still in the murky air. There was a dark lump on the throne, unmoving as the walls themselves. As she paced forward she made out the shape of the king, slumped back, staring at an invisible point before him.

She paused, and his eyes flicked to her, then away again. It was natural for her to assume her old position on the floor, her back against one leg of the massive chair.

They had often sat thus for hours in his rooms, looking into the fire, talking of this or that. Long silences were not unusual. She settled down, made herself comfortable and waited.

430

"Zoe, what am I to do?"

She swung round to look up at him, shocked. *His mind is set. Why is he asking me? If he intends to do anything else, why the fight with Kenna? Surely he doesn't mean what to do about the approaching army.*

Divining her confusion, he shook his head. "No, not about this armed threat. I can deal with those two pups. About this." A vague but all-encompassing wave of his hand conveyed everything. His reign, this trouble with his firmest supporter, the whole mess in which he had immersed them.

"I do not know, Barent." She turned away again, staring ahead. "Honour is hard to regain."

"Honour?"

"That's what is missing here. Look around you. There is no honour in this land. There is murder, rape and the underhanded dealings of greedy people. This all comes from the source of power."

"And I am the source of power."

"At this moment, yes. But barely. If you do not regain your honour, your power will be taken from you, or you will retain your power and lose even more honour, through the taking of the lives of your people."

"But they are in rebellion against me!"

She pivoted around to face him. "Of course they are. You misused your power. You must change that somehow. Be seen to act honourably again. Come on, Barent. You are the man with ideas. You can find a way."

She waited, expectant. He slumped there, unmoving. Finally, he dragged up the energy to speak. The words came out slow and heavy.

"Zoe, I have no more ideas. None. Nothing works any more. I try new ways and they are as bad as the old ways. When I saw I was changing for the sake of change and for no other reason, I

431

stopped. It was plain to see that it didn't work. So now I change nothing. I continue down the path I set for myself, knowing full well what lies at the end. But I have no choices left. I must travel that path."

"But you can change! Get rid of these carrion eaters gathering around you. Treat your people with honour again."

Barent smiled, shaking his head. "Too late, my idealistic young friend. Too late. What is the only thing that keeps the people from rebellion? Fear. That is all. If I take away the fear, they will see it as a sign of weakness. Then they will rise against me. No, I must finish the game, Zoe, in spite of what the score will be."

He stared off into space again. "There was a time when I would have cringed at the necessities that face me. I would have been haunted by the faces of the dead men, the bereaved wives, the motherless children. Now they mean nothing to me. I have immersed myself in horror to the point where I am covered over, and even the current of your clear, honest pity cannot wash me clean. It is too late, Zoe."

"Gerth will come and take the crown from you."

"Perhaps, perhaps not. What difference will it make?"

"The difference is that if you had the good of the kingdom in your heart you would not let that happen. The Arlyn family has had too much internal bloodshed. Petrella has had too much of the same. It must not happen again."

"Ah, but I am afraid it must. I am no weakling, to give myself up graciously and grovel at the feet of my nephew and young Torey. I am not what I once was, but I will not give in. If they insist on attacking, what can I do?"

She could see him pondering, trying to regain the old creative skill.

"If I had a unified kingdom behind me I could face these upstarts down, with no warfare needed. Would that suit you?"

A faint hope rose in her. "Isn't it past the time when you could do that, Barent?"

He stood, strode across the room, turned back. "They are not so much against me as you might think. The Warlander lords think of their own personal good. If they felt I had the best chance of coming out on top of this, they would back me." He rubbed one hand through his greying hair. "If only I could think!"

"You never can think when you're pacing about like that. Why don't you sit down where it's comfortable and relax?"

"Relax. That's a thought I haven't had in months. There isn't much relaxing in this work, Zoe. I haven't relaxed since you left for the mountains last year."

"When was the last time you had tea?"

"The Morning Ceremony yesterday."

"And does that no longer comfort you?"

"Not a lot. It calms me somewhat, gives me a chance to think when no one can interrupt, but my thoughts are not of the most comforting."

"Then you will sit over here by the fire, and I will un-knit your muscles and make you tea and you can relax properly. Then perhaps we can come up with a solution." She bustled about, finding the small lamp and other utensils where they were usually stored. The tea smelled dry, but it looked like one of her own creations, so she could cope. As she slipped into the familiar ritual she thought with sadness of the many comforting times they had spent when their problems were so much smaller. Barent seemed to be feeling nostalgic as well, for when they reached the part of the ceremony where she listed the herbs, he smiled sadly. She could see the tension draining from his body and the lines easing from his face. To her relief, the tea was passable and as they sipped their eyes met.

"Ah, Zoe, what changes."

She smiled. "Well Barent, you were always one for change."

"Perhaps not so rapid, though."

"That danger is ever possible. If the changes are ready to happen they will happen at their own pace, not the one you set. We who study our history know that."

"I always thought one studied history to find ideas that had been forgotten."

"And to find mistakes that should not be repeated."

He raised his eyebrow in that old familiar way. "And has this happened before?"

"If one listens to the ballads and tales, it is the most common of tragedies. Good intentions are no shield against poor conduct, if you listen to Sarasha the Lame."

"Ah, homilies. It is so long since anyone has had the nerve to bring them to my attention. So many of them seem to run counter to my own actions."

"The old sayings must ring true or they do not survive long enough to become boring."

"And is that another homily?"

"The homily of homilies, I suppose."

Barent smiled. "I missed this so much, Zoe. I had no idea until now. I feel so much better. Would you finish what you started?"

"Of course." She rose and stood behind him, both looking into the fire.

As she massaged the stiff muscles of his neck, he began to talk. At first about nothing in particular, but as his body relaxed his mind functioned more clearly.

"I should have done this before. I feel like I can think again. Perhaps a solution exists."

"If there is, you have the ability to discover it, and the power to make it work." Zoe also began to feel better. He had never failed before. She could now see how important she was to him. He had often said that it was her perspective that kept him on course, away from the self-serving intentions of his other advisors. Perhaps now she could help him to come up with one of his old, perfect solutions. She bent to her task with more enthusiasm.

"Watch it. That hurts!"

"You always complain. Your back has enough knots in it to keep a sailor busy for a quarter. You do the thinking, let me get on with my share."

"You have me at a disadvantage. I must comply. Let me think, then." He began, as he often did, to muse out loud. She knew that anything she heard she was allowed, and expected, to comment on.

"I was right earlier when I said that, could I show a kingdom united, I would send this invasion packing without a struggle."

"I must agree. Gerth would never begin if he felt he was attacking the whole kingdom, and Torey is no fool."

"So the trick is to get the whole kingdom behind me."

"That is the difficult part." She prodded down his right shoulder, loosening the tension there.

"But simple solutions occur to me."

"I am wary of simple solutions. Try one on me."

"About this religious uprising. I need to squash it, quick and clean. That will remove one source of dissention."

"But that may not be possible. There has been no uprising, and may never be one. I assure you that there is no army to fight. You must deal with that problem by re-creating the people's confidence in you."

"So perhaps I should concentrate on my enemies closer to home."

"I wonder whether you shouldn't be looking even further inwards."

She could tell by the tilt of his head that he was chuckling at her. "Zoe, you place great faith in the concept of honour and the application of the Codes, but those are for normal times. There are always situations the Codes do not cover. We must then improvise to get things back to normal so we can all live happily by the Codes again."

Zoe's calm was disturbed by this reinterpretation of their old discussions. "But don't the Codes help us in times of trouble also, showing us ways to act when we can't find our own paths?"

"Of course, but only for those who cannot make their own way."

Zoe refrained from mentioning that the path Barent had forged for himself lay in shambles around him. *This regained self-confidence is our only hope. If I can get him back to his old, incisive...*

"So, if you don't mind, Zoe, we will look for a more practical solution. As I was saying, we must deal with our enemies closer to home. We must root out the sources of discontent, of disagreement. Close as they may be. Painful as it may be."

Zoe felt a sudden chill of apprehension.

Barent, unaware, continued with his musings. "It would be good for us to be seen as impartial, don't you think? If we were to take no sides, to give no favours? To root out opposition, wherever it is found?"

He could not mean...

"Or perhaps that might be taken amiss as well. Perhaps it would be better if we were subtle. We are removing an obstacle to the peace of our kingdom, not seeking revenge."

He shifted and sat straighter. "Zoe, I may need your abilities. Surely you have ways to kill? Silent, subtle?"

"I suppose."

"Could you kill so that the method would never be discovered?"

"I know nothing of poisons." She could say no more. Her mind was frozen, although her hands kept on working at his back muscles: kneading, pressing, soothing.

"I don't mean poison. That would be real dishonour. I'm surprised that you brought it up. No, I mean physically."

"I have no wish to kill in cold blood, Barent."

"Zoe, Zoe. What is the difference? It is easier to kill in the heat of battle, but the man you kill might be honourable in his own way. He might not deserve to die. When one kills in cold blood as you call it, one can be certain that the victim deserves the sentence. There are no mistakes. The decision can be made rationally, with no rancour or prejudice."

"I suppose that is true, but it does not help how I would feel about it."

"But are we not agreed that we should unify the kingdom?"

"It would be a good idea, yes."

"And we are also agreed that there is no use in attacking the religious sect, and perhaps a great deal of harm. We also agree that it would be an ill thing for the kingdom if Gerth and I were to war over the throne."

Zoe nodded miserably, forgetting that he could not see her. Her hands continued their massaging.

"So the solution is to remove the other most potent force of dissention. A person who defends our religious enemies. A strong supporter of Gerth. With this force removed, all will fall into place, will it not?"

437

A tear rolled down Zoe's cheek, to be absorbed by the multi-coloured fabric of her robe. Inside, a burning pain began to eat at the chill.

"So tell me, Zoe, what is your method of silent killing? I would have no pain, mind you. I wish no revenge. Only the removal of an obstacle."

Finally, her tongue came free. "There is a simple technique, your Majesty. I carry the means with me at all times, concealed in my robe. A long, thin, needle."

"And..."

"It kills."

"And could you use it?"

She had only to think for a moment, although at the single word, the flames stirred within her again, searing. "Yes." She longed for the numbness of the cold again.

"Good. So tell me what you will do." He moved, half turning towards her. "I am not unaware of the deed I am asking you to perform. I would not have you bear the responsibility alone. Tell me!" He straightened again, waiting.

Zoe snuffled. The tears kept getting in her way, blurring her vision, making her fingers slippery where she wiped them from her face, staining her robe where she dried her hand. "It is simple, Your Majesty. There are places on the body, here," she touched him on the left side of his back, close below the shoulder blade, "or here." Once again she touched him, just behind the ear.

"A fine needle, slid in at the right angle, can reach a vital spot, do its job, and be withdrawn leaving no noticeable mark. The victim is dead, apparently by natural causes. Death is sudden, with no pain. Is that what you wish?"

"Yes, that would be perfect. I wish her no pain. After all, she is my sister, and I love her. Are you sure you can do this?"

"I don't know..."

438

"For the good of the kingdom, Zoe. Don't you see it must be done? You have told me you have the good of the kingdom in your heart. Now prove it."

The tears were getting in the way again. Her hands must be dry. She must think rationally. There must be no mistake. This must be a very careful decision. For the good of the kingdom. That was his excuse the first time. Was she acting any differently now? Would this deed condemn her as his had condemned him? *Well, if it does, I alone will suffer. The kingdom will not be harmed.*

That decided her. "For the good of the kingdom."

He leaned back, and she could feel the muscles relaxing again. The needle was there in her hand, the good, impartial steel. The pain in her chest was as hot as a sword from the forge. It rose and flowed along her arm, tempering her muscles to their hardest. As gently as she could, as firmly as she needed, she pressed at the precise angle she had been taught, right behind the ear. How easily it slid in! He gave a start, then slumped, his weight falling against her. She withdrew the needle and hid it in her robe again. The trace of blood disappeared into the lining. She wondered if that was part of the design. It would be.

Gently laying him down, she started the Ritual for the Fallen, as she had done for her grandfather, long ago.

59. REQUIEM

"Zoe?"

Dimness filled the room. The sun must be low. A voice was calling her name. A familiar voice. She was returning, as from a long distance, and the voice was drawing her in. She forced open her eyes.

"Zoe?"

Varli. What was he doing here? Her knees were numb. She looked around. She was kneeling on the floor of the king's receiving room at the foot of the large meeting table. Shadows were gathering in the corners, and a low light from the westering sun suffused the room. Slowly, stiffly, she got to her feet.

"Zoe, can I come in?"

She turned, favouring her legs as the blood rushed back into them, tingling and burning. Varli stood in the crack of the big door, his head hesitating forward.

"Is it all right to come in, Zoe?"

She considered. "I suppose so, Varli. Why not?"

A touch of his usual spirit edged the boy's voice. "Why not? Because Patu has been on guard out here all day refusing to let anyone in, is why not. If I hadn't got here, they would still be standing around dithering."

She made a smile. "But you solved all their problems, did you, Varli?"

He grinned back. "I guess so. I think Tadeo could have done as well, but we thought Patu would be more responsive to me, so I tried first. He was happy to see me. I don't think he was too sure what to do, either." The door pushed open more, and Patu's worried head joined him.

The armigerent's ears were back and his nose was low, as if expecting a reprimand. Her heart went out to him. *Poor animal, left alone all day.* She moved forward holding out her hand, and he joyfully nudged under it. She laid her other hand on the boy's shoulder. "So who else have you brought me, Varli?"

Varli's shoulders straightened. "Nobody. Unless you include Gerth and Torey and their army."

Zoe's face fell as the memory of the afternoon flooded back on her in full force. "That is King Gerth, now, Varli."

He looked less surprised than she had expected. "King."

She shrugged.

"That was one of the possibilities we considered."

"We? We considered?"

"We held a meeting while we waited. All of us: Gerth, Torey, Kenna, Tadeo, Loreline, Lukin. You had to expect that we would be curious. You were in here the full day, and not a sound. The king's private entrance locked, the servants' likewise and Patu on guard at the main door. When we heard how Barent had been lately, we all thought...well, we thought he might..." Varli made a vague gesture towards his own neck to substitute for the word he could not bring himself to say.

"I see."

"So King Barent is dead?"

She nodded numbly, motioning towards the table.

He looked at her, waiting. When she did not move, he came to a decision. "I think we should talk to the others, now, Zoe."

Her head dropped again. Then she straightened up, preparing.

"May we come in?"

She roused her mind. "Of course. I did not mean to keep you out. I just forgot. I was...busy."

441

His glance took in the tearstains on her robe. "Yes." Checking to see if Zoe would object, he moved Patu aside and swung the door open.

Behind him she could see the rest, somberly waiting. Farther down the corridor either way, several members of Barent's Guard stood, silent as well. She moved outside, and Gerth stepped forward.

She had expected him to be dressed in armour, but he was only in his travelling clothes, his great-sword slung in its accustomed position over his shoulder. As he approached, a question on his face, she picked her own sword off the floor, drew it and knelt, presenting the hilt in the appropriate manner for offering loyalty to a new monarch.

He accepted the sword, touched her neck with the edge and motioned her to rise.

She looked up at him. Tears were forming. Forgetting the protocol, she flung her arms around him and was enfolded in turn. They held each other, then separated. Solace must wait for later.

The import of Zoe's action was not lost on the others. They moved into the audience room, Kenna in the lead, and formed a silent crescent at the foot of the table.

She had laid him out in the proper position, with his sword hilt under one arm and the other hand on the royal insignia at his breast. He seemed so peaceful, the lines all gone from his face, but it was neither the Barent she had met here nor the man she had known. The restless spirit had fled. She had finished her mourning for the moment so she left them. Buckling her harness absently, she wandered away down the corridor, Patu anxious behind her.

Quiet footsteps followed, and she turned to find her Guard-of-Life at her shoulder. "It is good to see you again, Tadeo. You don't know how much I missed you. I gather your mission was a success?"

442

"I missed you, too, Zoe, but it was wise that you sent me. They were having trouble deciding what to do. Many wanted an all-out attack, especially those who had suffered. Gerth was hesitant, but did not want to lose the initiative by holding back. Your suggestion gave him a good middle ground; he could bring his army, but had reason for not attacking. As it turned out, it was the right move."

"I suppose it was."

"Of course it was, Zoe. Everything has worked out as you planned it. There will be an orderly succession to a popular king with no bloodshed. A great difference from the situation a quarter ago."

"But Barent is dead! And I…"

He made a subtle motion towards the sleeve of his robe, a question in his eyes. She nodded dumbly.

"Ah. He was very important to you, wasn't he?"

Again, she could only nod.

He laid a hand on her shoulder, turned her to face him. "And you can never talk it over with anyone here, can you? I suppose that leaves me."

He was standing there so close, and she needed it so much that she allowed him to wrap an arm around her and press her head against his chest with his other hand. She put her arms around his waist and they stood for a long while in silence. It felt so good to stop being the one in charge, to let him hold her. It would be so tempting to let it continue, to allow the barriers to fall. He felt so strong, his muscles like cords on his spare frame, so similar in size to hers. She leaned back and looked into his face. Gradually, his arm loosened until only his hand rested on her waist.

"Is that better?"

Once more she nodded, still torn by her desire to let it all go, to let the flood of events carry her for a change, to stop being responsible, to let someone else direct her course.

"I have a question."

She looked at him.

"What is it that bothers you the most about this deed?"

She frowned.

He raised a hand. "No, not that. Think about it. What bothers you?"

Then it came to her. "He asked me to kill Kenna. I cannot believe that. Why would he ask me that? He loves her. He knows I love her. How could he think I would do that? It was the ultimate betrayal. Of both of us."

"Yes, that would be difficult to accept, and it does not sound like the man you have spoken of. Could he have had another objective?"

She thought that over. "Another objective. What else could he...oh. Yes, he might. He might have been pushing me. He knew me so well. He wanted an action that he knew I would not wish to perform. So he found a way to make me. A double blind."

"Perhaps." The corner of Tadeo's lip lifted. "He spent enough time with the Sivan. Perhaps he learned something."

"That would explain it."

"And does that help you deal with the event?"

"Yes. It makes me feel a great deal better."

He smiled. "Good. It is the duty of the Guard-of-Life to minister to his sponsor in the emotions as well as the body. You were in great need of comfort."

How smoothly he places us back on our proper footing. Once again she was in awe of his Kyabran courtliness, which she could never hope to achieve. "Why in the name of all the gods

444

am I sponsoring you? I often think it should be the other way around."

"It is a poor teacher who cannot learn from his pupil."

"Don't quote old ladies to me!" She looked at him. "Where did you learn something from Sarasha the Lame?"

"Don't ignore wisdom, no matter the form of the presentation." His calm was infuriating, but she could not take offence. "And, in answer to your question, no one in all these kingdoms could accomplish what you have done today. Whatever pain it will cause you, always remember the amount of suffering you have eased for so many others. That may be your only reward, but it is substantial. I would continue our relationship if you are willing."

Her response was cut off by Varli, who came skidding around the corner of the corridor then stopped, confused when he saw them standing so close together. "Zoe...!"

She noticed his discomfiture but did not move away. "Yes, Varli?"

As usual, he recovered quickly. "They're having a meeting. Gerth wants..." he paused to straighten his posture, "King Gerth has summoned you."

She started back up the hallway. "Who is meeting? Everyone?"

Varli hurried to keep up. "No, just Gerth and Kenna. Family meeting, they said, and they want you there." He made the pronouncement as if it was the most natural thing in the world that she should be part of an Arlyn family meeting. "The rest are off to arrange everything. Presentation, coronation..."

It seemed the meeting would take place in Kenna's quarters. When Zoe reached the door, Tadeo and Varli turned back with Patu and she went in alone. Mother and son were sitting opposite each other, silent, a chair empty at a third side of Kenna's favourite tea table.

"Come in, Zoe." Kenna had gained no peace, either. The lines in her face were deepened by the light of the fire beside her. "We have things to talk about."

Zoe sank into the chair, hesitant.

"We have a kingdom to run. More than that, we have a kingdom and a duchy to restore. It will take all our resources and all the cooperation we can muster."

The two young people sat, confronted by the enormity of the task.

Kenna continued. "I am taking advantage of the fact that events have been swift and you are both off balance. Gerth, soon you will get your bearings and take charge. I am not the kind of mother to try to rule from behind the throne, but for the moment I will direct you as well as possible until I can return to my preferred style. Do you agree?"

Zoe looked anxiously at Gerth, remembering some of the rows these two had carried out when he was younger.

He only smiled. "Don't worry, Mother. I am not the kind of king to try taking over everything at once. You are the one who knows best what has been going on: who to trust, who to advance, who to punish. We will work well together."

"Zoe?"

"Me? Of course. Whatever you say."

"No, not 'of course,' Zoe. False modesty will do us a disservice. You exert more influence than you think. We need you here, but you have other options. If you choose to return to Kyabra, for example, it will be much more difficult for us. If you should choose to go against us, it would be disastrous."

"Go against you?" She was aghast, hurt. "Why would I do that?"

Kenna laid a hand on her arm. "No, no. I am not suggesting that you would. I merely give an example."

446

Mollified but still puzzled, Zoe nodded. She had no such illusions about her personal power, but she was willing to do all she could to help. *This is my kingdom; these are my friends. My family.*

"So, what is there to do?"

Kenna regarded her, then nodded once as if confirming something. "There are many things to be done soon. We have a coronation to arrange and an injured land to minister to. What I am suggesting at the moment, though, is that we look further ahead. If we make long-range plans, we will find the day-to-day decisions much easier."

Gerth nodded. "We can do no better than that. What do you have in mind?"

"First, the stability of our kingdom. It has just been demonstrated to us, with great force, the lack of wisdom in following a solo course against our neighbours. You took the first step of the solution by confirming our alliance with Torey of Arva. This will prove of use in the future, but he is still only a border lord. The Inner Duchies and those to the north of them consider him more barbaric than we are. Do you agree, Zoe?"

"No question of it. In Kyabra, they think we eat with our fingers and throw the bones over our shoulder to the swine who live in the hall with us."

"There you are. Not charitable, but a factor. So what do we do about this?"

Gerth leaned forward. "Form alliances with lands of a more civilized leaning. Gain credibility through their knowledge of us."

"Good. But we have little to offer that would entice them."

A small stir of enthusiasm warmed Zoe's breast. "We have raw materials: timber, furs, wool. That will attract them."

447

"Economically, we have leverage. But politically? Our army has been discredited because of its behaviour. We must downplay that aspect of our power. What else do we have?"

"Gerth."

"Me?"

"Explain what you mean, Zoe."

"Gerth is a great asset. He will prove to be a powerful, honourable, monarch. He will regain our stature among our neighbours." Fierce pride burned in her now. "He will!"

"I believe you are right, if I say it who shouldn't, being his mother. And that brings us to the other possibility."

Both looked at her, puzzled.

"Marriage."

Zoe felt a chill run through her. Gerth married. She hadn't thought about that too often. She should have, but had pushed it aside. *Now I understand the Sivan's comment about blindness because of emotional involvement. Gerth would some day make a political marriage, she knew.* If she had considered it at all, she had hoped it would not make too much difference to their relationship. Faced with the reality, she understood how naive that hope was. She would lose him, too. A numbness spread out from the core of her being. The fire was gone, but the pain of the cold was similar. She tried to keep her shoulders square, to listen to what the other two were saying.

"Marriage? Now?"

"Yes Gerth, if not now, at least soon. You must stabilize the kingdom and gain allies in the more civilized central areas. You need a wife, preferably from the Inner Duchies."

Gerth laughed. "What dainty princess from the Inner Sea could be persuaded to mate up with a barbarian like me?"

Indignation jarred her from her stupor. "You don't know what you're talking about. You display just as much manners, sensitivity, and civilization as any man in the Inner Duchies! Just...well, more of it."

Kenna chuckled. "It is good to hear you defend him so, you who have the most recent experience with our prospective allies. Tell me Zoe, what kind of girl are we looking for?"

Forcing herself to concentrate on the task at hand, driving the numbness and cold back down inside, Zoe thought as carefully as she could. "Power. She must have a power base. That is what we need the alliance for. Personality as well. Charisma. Our people have been through a rough time. If they could have someone they could love as they love Gerth, it would bind them closer." She thought further, keeping herself from seeing the blush rise across Gerth's face at her words.

"Stamina."

"Stamina? Are we buying a Warlander's horse?"

She reached out and cuffed him, taking refuge in the old teasing. "No, dunderhead. We may be civilized here, but we are not dainty. Our weather is harsher, our distances longer to travel. You need a queen who can handle all that. You do not want a delicate blossom who fades at the first winter frost."

Kenna numbered off three fingers. "Power, charisma, stamina. Is that all?"

Gerth looked helpless. "Isn't that enough? How are we ever going to find anyone who has all that?"

Zoe couldn't help but dig a little. "I suppose it would be nice if she could get along with him. Not necessary, but nice. She doesn't need to be pretty, I suppose, but that would help too?" She made the last a question, in that sweet, reasonable voice all her friends had learned to beware.

Kenna smiled and was about to speak but then she stopped. Zoe had frozen, one hand raised, her head cocked, listening. Alerted, the other two could now hear what had disturbed her. It was a low rumbling sound, felt rather than heard, and it wavered, built and fell like the waves of a distant ocean. Questioning looks darted among them. Then Kenna relaxed and smiled.

"Our time for discussion is past. Gerth, your people want you."

As she rose and made her way to the door it opened and Loreline appeared, hesitating on the threshold.

"Your Majesty, you must come. There are so many people!" The muted roar of the crowd thundered through the open doorway.

Kenna turned with a smile containing many triumphs. "Your Majesty, it is time for your first public appearance."

Uncertainty washed across his face. "What do you mean? How many people?"

Loreline shrugged. "Thousands, Sire. The whole parade ground is full. The Army, the people, everyone."

Zoe was instantly at work. "What is the mood, Loreline? How do they sound to you?"

"Uncertain, I would say. Anxious, half afraid of more bad news, swept now and then by a new rumour, good or bad."

Zoe met Kenna's eyes, and they both nodded. "They are in a mood for good news. They will take what we give them."

"Yes. All they want is the uncertainty to be gone. This is the key moment we spoke of, Zoe, on a grand scale. Time to move with decision." Kenna started out the door, recalled herself and motioned Gerth to precede her. Puzzled and hesitating, he started. Then he paused, rebellion in his voice.

"What are we going to do, Mother? If I am to be a part of some great plan of yours, at least you could tell me what role I am to play."

"This is no plan of mine, Your Majesty. Not now. You must play the role you were born for: the king of Petrella. Your

450

people want to see you, to know that you are real. They hope you will calm all their fears, end their nightmares. They hope you will promise them peace and prosperity. But mostly they want to see you. They want to see the symbol of the strength and security of their kingdom. What you do or say is up to you. But you must meet your subjects."

"Just walk out there and say 'Hello,' to several thousand screaming people? How simple. Why didn't you say so before?"

He looked so worried, Zoe could not help but laugh. She took his arm and shook it. "I doubt if you can say anything over that roar. They only want to see you. What's wrong? You stood in front of hundreds of enemy screaming to kill you, and you didn't seem bothered by that!"

"That was different. I was with an army then. Must I do this alone?"

Zoe looked to Kenna for confirmation. "Of course not. Who do you want holding your hand, your mother or me?"

That got through to him, and the bit of anger helped. "Look, you two, this isn't funny. I've never done this kind of thing before and I need help." A sudden thought brightened his face. "I'm the king, aren't I? If I say you have to come, then you must come, right?"

Zoe grinned. "You're catching on, your Majesty. We'll make a king out of you yet."

"You may be sorry yet. Come on. Let's go. Bring that beast of yours. He can be helpful if the crowd gets too close."

Kenna was smiling, too. "We won't let them eat you, Gerth. You'll be standing above the castle gate where everyone can see."

"Fine. You're all still coming." He assumed a dignified air. "We will proceed."

451

Glancing at each other with amused pride, the two women followed him, Patu and Loreline behind, leading a contingent of the King's Guard.

When they reached the battlements, it was easier than Zoe could have imagined. The others had been doing their work, and the King's Presentation had begun.

60. Long Live the King

The moment Gerth approached, a long blast on the war horns, the "Prepare for the Monarch," drew the crowd's attention. Then a troop of the King's Guard filed out to line up along the top of the wall, their polished armour and weapons glistening in the low rays of the sun. The Banner of the Arlyns was unfurled; carried slowly and somberly by Varli – so proud he could hardly restrain himself – it preceded Gerth to his position.

The traditional Presentation Platform above the main gatehouse seemed constructed for this, although it was originally made for the castle general to use as an observation post during an attack. High above and behind the central gateway, with a low wall in front, it commanded a view of the whole castle and the city below. This meant that a person on the platform could be seen by everyone, inside and outside the walls.

Gerth approached this prominent point, then hesitated. He was pushed forward by another blast on the great war horns, signalling the "Presentation of the King." Glancing back and motioning his mother and Zoe to follow, he turned, squared his shoulders and stepped into public view.

The anxious murmur of the throng rolled under the wave of solid sound that burst from thousands of throats. As those near the castle recognized the man before them, their cries doubled, and the increase swelled back through the crowd as the realization spread. He stood there, his loose hair blowing around his face to make a halo in the golden evening light. He raised his arms in greeting, and the sound rose even higher.

The noise went on and on. He glanced to Kenna, who nodded. There would be no speaking today. Following the ritual, he reached over his shoulder and drew forth his blade, the two-hander he used when fighting on foot. It was longer by a span than any other weapon in the kingdom, yet he twirled it over his head with impressive ease. Then, going to one knee as Zoe had done earlier to him, he presented his sword to his people, the king pledging his own allegiance. The crowd quieted at this solemn moment. The Warlanders and soldiers all knelt, returning his gesture, as did many of the citizens.

Then he stood, the roar of the crowd lifting him. He held the stance, his arms raised. The sound showed no sign of lessening, as the anxieties of the time of terror poured out in a cathartic cry of relief and optimism. After a while, he dropped his arms and turned to Kenna. This time there was no questioning. He motioned her forward, and she moved to his side. He placed his arm around her and raised his other arm to the crowd. Again the roar arose.

Then movement down behind a crenellation near her caught Zoe's eye. Turning, she saw two heads peering out, one dark, one white. It was Ardu the stable boy, his mouth open in awe as he watched. Clutched to his breast was the small white kid, who seemed equally stunned by its surroundings. How the two had made their way up here she couldn't say, but she supposed they could get into no harm.

Then Ardu glanced at Zoe. His gaze froze on her face, a guilty look covering his features. His hands dropped. She was about to smile to reassure him when the kid, realizing he was free, darted ahead. He stopped, confused by the people and the noise. Then, seeing the open space before him, he hopped up onto the wall surrounding the platform and looked down at the crowd.

Zoe started forward in dismay. The little fellow was sure-footed, but this was not his normal ground. With the excitement and the uproar, what if he slipped?

She was too slow. Patu was moving even as her thought began. In one bound he had reached the kid and lifted the small white body gently in his huge jaws. Then the armigerent realized what was in front of him. His ears perked, and he peered with interest at the mass of people below him.

The sudden appearance of the great armigerent beside the new king, the small white animal in its mouth, had a stunning effect on the crowd. There was instant, profound silence. Zoe stood frozen, wondering what to do now. A flicker of motion caught her attention. Gerth was grinning at her, gesturing her to retrieve her friends. Face burning with embarrassment, she moved forward.

As she did so, Patu finished his observation and placed the kid in her arms. She tried to slink back into anonymity, but Gerth stopped her.

"I want them to see you, Zoe."

She was about to protest that this was wrong, that she was supposed to remain hidden, that she had no part in this occasion, but his firm gesture cut her short. She turned, the kid in her left arm, to face the crowd. The comforting warmth of Patu's solid shoulder pressed against her side, and she twined the fingers of her right hand in his ruff for reassurance. So this is glory! She was terrified. She stepped forward.

All this had taken but a heartbeat, and the throng was silent as she faced them. The hush stretched as those who could see her absorbed this new development.

Then, high and wailing on the crisp evening air, came that thin, ululating cry she had heard in the forest. It echoed over the silent throng and died away in the echoes of the mountain behind the castle. Then another cry arose and another, interweaving, rising and falling in strange harmonies. Zoe stood in confusion, wondering what to do. Then many of the crowd went to their knees again, some of the soldiers as well. As the wailing cry spread, louder and louder, and larger numbers of people knelt, she turned to Gerth. He seemed as puzzled as she was. She looked at Kenna.

There was no question on the woman's face, only proud satisfaction. Their eyes met, and then it all came clear. The realization flooded through Zoe, followed by deep chagrin. *How could I be so blind?* The slow approach of The Lady, following Zoe's own path, the rumours spreading ahead of her. The route of the army of reinforcements. The way people treated her. Now Ardu's 'accidental' appearance with the kid.

But this isn't the way...! She turned to Kenna, her mouth open to protest, but her movement was cut short by a shake of the older woman's head and a helpless gesture towards the crowd. The action spoke volumes.

It was too late. Mistake or not, the people had seen her. The impression was made. All she could do was ride out the consequences. With a grimace at Kenna promising dire ramifications, she turned again to the crowd. There was again no need for speech. The crowd's roar had returned, drowning the call of the Followers of the Lady, and Her people surged to their feet, swelling the sound. Gerth stepped over and placed his other arm around Zoe's shoulders and the three of them stood for a long time, the waves of adulation washing over them.

She could see a smile form on Gerth's face. It had begun in wonder, but it was changing to satisfaction. Before her eyes, the youth she had known was turning into a king. She knew him well enough that she could already see the plans forming, even as he received the adoration of his people. Kenna was also smiling, her pride mixed with triumph.

Then the moment was over. The horns sounded again, and the party stepped back from the platform. The sound of the crowd fell away, ending in a low rumble of satisfaction that continued until it was swallowed by the walls of the corridors they passed through.

As they followed Gerth through the halls, Kenna dropped back beside Zoe, counting off on her fingers.

"Well, Zoe, what was it you said? Charisma, stamina, power? Someone he could get along with? Someone the people could love as they love him? Even someone pretty."

Zoe stopped dead in the corridor, forcing Kenna to halt with her. Gerth, noticing something amiss, paused as well. After a glance at Zoe's face, Kenna motioned him to proceed. The royal party continued, leaving the two women facing each other across the hallway.

"What is going on in that devious mind of yours?"

Kenna played innocent. "I thought the facts spoke for themselves."

"How long have you known?"

"Almost from the beginning. As soon as Loreline said you were on the way and the reports started coming in. Even unreliable sources can give information." She smiled wolfishly. "More than they think, sometimes."

Zoe was still trying to put it all together. "What do you know about the cult of the Lady?"

"A lot more than I did before you left. It seemed a good area for study."

Zoe covered her face with her hands. "I have been just...so...stupid."

"I sincerely doubt it."

Zoe tried to get her mind back on the conversation. "Loreline knew I was coming?"

"Sort of. The Sivan told her he would send for you if it became necessary. Then he disappeared, and the rumours started coming in. The descriptions of you were too accurate to be coincidence. That is unless one were to believe that the real Lady was appearing."

Zoe regarded the older woman. "And you wouldn't believe that?"

457

Kenna looked thoughtful as she turned down the corridor. "I'm not so sure. In the minds of the people, she did come. She was real. She was here. Her appearance has stopped a war and started the new king off on a strong footing, with the power to do what the kingdom needs. How can I say the gods do not choose to move in their own ways?"

Zoe grinned as they continued in the wake of the royal party. "I'm not so sure it isn't just the Sivan working in his own way."

Kenna nodded. "Yes, that was strange. Do you have any idea what happened to him?"

"I had hoped you could tell me."

"No, he did not confide in me. Do you think he will return?"

"Watch Loreline."

"Loreline?"

"Surely..." Zoe thought Kenna knew all the castle gossip.

"They spent a lot of time together, but..."

Zoe laughed. "The Sivan would be so pleased! He put something past you!"

Kenna smiled as well. "So if Loreline goes soon?"

"Then he won't be back. If she stays, then perhaps he will. With the Sivan, who knows?"

"Who knows, indeed. Still, it would be good if he were here again."

Zoe nodded. "But if he does not return, I think we can count on his presence being of assistance to us, wherever he is. He has a great allegiance to the Arlyns."

"I don't think so, Zoe."

"You don't?"

"No. His allegiance here stemmed from two factors: personal and professional. He worked here because he had free rein in

458

his work. Then he developed a personal allegiance to Barent. Now Barent is gone. I don't see him returning to his old duties here. He has moved on to something else. If Loreline goes, there will be one tie left. You."

Zoe thought about it before sounding surprised. No false modesty. "Yes. And that adds to my personal power, doesn't it?"

"Which brings us back to the original point."

Zoe grimaced. "Kenna, do you really see me married to Gerth? I don't think it's a good idea. I'm still a nobody and half a foreigner. That's not what Petrella needs right now."

"A nobody?"

They entered the Main Hall and saw that Gerth was busy with a host of court functionaries. They grinned at each other and took two chairs in an alcove to the side, leaving him to get used to it.

"Now. Down to business. What is your status in Kyabra?"

"Sole descendant of a small but ancient name."

"And how much does that matter?"

"The age of the name seems to be more significant than the size of the house, although wealth is important."

"And what about the faction you are allied with?"

Zoe should have expected Kenna's knowledge. "In years to come, they will probably become the strongest force in Kyabran politics."

"And your status with them?"

Zoe smiled, rubbing the pommel of her sword absently as she thought of her summer. "I think I did pretty well. Ask Tadeo."

"His presence alone tells me a great deal. So are you a nobody? An honoured member of the most powerful faction in the politics of a major trading partner. Added to your religious power here, I would say that adds up."

Zoe floundered, stirring in her chair.

"There is another problem isn't there, Zoe? You don't want to marry Gerth, but you can't bring yourself to tell me."

Zoe felt a rush of gratitude and guilt. "Oh, Kenna, I'm sorry. It's not that I can't tell you. I don't know. I haven't had time to get it straight. When we were talking a while ago about him getting married, it felt just awful to think of losing him. But now, when you suggest I marry him, I should be ecstatic. And I'm not. I'm sorry."

"Don't be sorry. I would hate to think you would marry him because I wanted you to. You are lucky. If you were a king's daughter like I am, you would marry where you were told. I did well." A shadow passed over her face. "For a while, anyway. But at least I have Gerth, and that hasn't worked out so badly, has it? He's very like his father was.

"Anyway, we were speaking of you. You are lucky. You can make your own choices."

A sharp, cold pain knifed through Zoe. "I wouldn't say that was lucky." She hesitated, wondering how much she should say.

"Kenna, there is one more reason I couldn't marry Gerth."

"Oh?"

"Do you remember telling me about making difficult decisions?"

"Yes. It was last year, just after the battle."

"You were right. Kenna...I made one of those decisions today."

"I know."

"You do?"

"So does Gerth."

460

"Gerth?"

"Yes, but only Gerth. We knew this afternoon that Barent would never come out of that room. He didn't want to, but he could never bring himself to give up. He needed help. No one but you could do that, Zoe. It is a heavy burden we ask you to bear, but it was necessary. You see that, don't you?"

"Oh, I see, all right. I was there, remember? But I still couldn't marry his successor."

"Do you know what Gerth said? 'I hope she would do the same for me.' You don't need to worry about that."

Zoe tried thinking it through out loud. "I don't want you to think I'm playing difficult, but I still think it's wrong for me. It would be a good life. I love this kingdom, and I could be a good wife to Gerth, and a great help as his queen. But it isn't me. Do you know what I mean? The thought of being a queen is so alien to my way of life. I wouldn't like being a queen, Kenna. Even for Gerth."

"I can see that. All your upbringing, your training. There is also something you haven't mentioned. How do you feel about Gerth himself?"

"Gerth has been my best friend for years. We would make a compatible couple. Oh, I'm not so naive as to think that everybody gets married to someone they adore. Yes, I could marry Gerth."

"But you don't love him?"

"Not like that. But I would come to, in time. No, the problem isn't Gerth."

"Tadeo?"

Zoe smiled wryly. Kenna always considered every alternative. "No, he is careful to keep our relationship on the proper footing. He has too much respect for me, I guess." She shook her head. "And besides, sometimes he is just so damned perfect he makes me want to scream."

461

"But out there somewhere...?"

"Who knows? I suppose I take the ballads to heart. But I'm not looking for someone to marry. There are other things I want to do, other things to learn, other places to see. My visit to Kyabra has opened my eyes to the whole world, and I want to see it all. Being a queen wouldn't let me do that."

"So what do you want to do?"

"At the moment? I want to help put this kingdom back in order. But not from here. I made myself a promise when I was travelling through all that misery. I want to be out there where I can see the results of my efforts. Can't I go back to my old job with the Guides?"

Kenna merely raised an eyebrow, a gesture so like Barent that Zoe felt that cold stab inside her again.

"Right. Barent said it. You can't go back, can you? After that scene on the battlements, I can't go back to obscurity." She tried to laugh. "I think the Sivan would be quite upset about that, in fact."

"The Sivan lost his chance, and I took mine. I don't think he would be too disappointed in the outcome."

"I suppose not. I will stay around here while Gerth needs me. The Guides will have to be rebuilt, perhaps along different lines. I can help Loreline with that." Her face became grim. "I expect there will be a few gaps in the ranks by morning. Especially one particular individual, if he is smart enough to be long gone. Couldn't I keep on as I have been? I could be on the watch for him and those like him. And won't Gerth need a reliable source of information?"

Kenna looked thoughtful. "That might be a good thing. The mere thought of you out there turned the whole countryside upside down. If you were to go out as an observer, making sure that everything went as it should..."

"That would keep everyone honest, wouldn't it? At the same time I could reassure people that the king was doing his best for them." The prospect of travelling again, but with the power to help those who needed it, seemed very important to her. "Could I do that, Kenna?"

The older woman laughed at her enthusiasm. "You're asking the wrong person, Zoe. Let's go and see the king." They rose and strolled over to where Gerth was immersed in castle functionaries. Head and shoulders above them, he saw the two approach and signalled them to wait. They watched with interest, and not a little pride, as he finished off his business, treating each man with individual attention and decision. Servants approached cringing and departed with a lift to their steps, determination on their faces.

When the last one was gone, Gerth looked over to his mother and his friend. "So Zoe is not going to marry me."

Zoe laughed out loud at Kenna's expression. "He is your son, Kenna, and he had all the information you did. He's not dense, like I am." She laughed again. It feels so good to laugh.

Kenna smiled as well, ruefully. "No, Gerth, she has other plans. We'll talk about them if you like." Zoe did not miss the deference she showed her son.

"You're not leaving, are you, Zoe?" He became his old self again, and she had to resist the impulse to tease him. There would be time for that kind of relationship later.

"No, Gerth. Petrella is my home. I'll stay as long as she needs me."

END OF BOOK I

463

BOOK II OF THE PETRELLAN SAGA

"THE INNKEEPER'S HUSBAND"

PROLOGUE

THE CHILD OF WAR

The boy hated uniforms.

He avoided them whenever possible, but could not ignore them, as they were often the only source of food in the ravaged countryside. He stole from them when he dared and hid, snarling, when he had to. But he hated them with all of the pent-up emotion of his undernourished soul.

The boy had been an early casualty of the war. Certain scenes were walled away in his small mind: scenes of fire and blood and flashing steel, and a screaming that seemed to go on and on and never stop until he woke in the cold night with the sound from his own lips.

In the beginning, he vaguely remembered sheltering with others, but then the soldiers had come again and the harsh scenes were repeated. Thrown on his own resources, he relied on himself alone, shunning the poor wretches who huddled together in the protection of their former homes. He scorned and avoided them, stealing from them as well when his hunger drove him.

But for the uniforms, he reserved his own, special hatred.

He had seen them run once. He still cherished that scene, drawing it out before his mind's eye in his moments of peace, reliving it again and again. Like a recurring dream, he could experience it all.

The soldiers were marching, as usual, with their weapons, their horses, and their wagons. He crammed himself in the hollow under an uprooted tree to watch in longing and hatred as they passed.

But then they stopped. *Have they seen me?* No, they were confused, making uncertain noises, moving restlessly in place. He liked that. They almost looked afraid. He felt grim satisfaction, but it was nothing compared to what came next.

A disturbance crept through the line of soldiers, coming from the head of the column and advancing towards him. As the turmoil approached, it looked as if something was rolling down the road through the army. Before the moving object was uncertainty. Men shuffled and strained to see, others pushed ahead, some pushed back.

After the moving thing came pandemonium. The horses of the mounted men reared and plunged, unseating riders and running free. Soldiers fled in terror or froze, some falling to their knees in supplication. Intrigued, he squirmed higher, his face screened by a projecting root stub, his matted hair blending in with the dirt. He had never seen soldiers act like this. Whatever was making the soldiers afraid, he wanted to know about it.

Then, from the forest opposite him, came that scream. It rose and wavered and died, then rose again, repeated and echoed through the trees. The terrible sound startled him, and at first he was afraid, but then he saw its effect on the soldiers. They panicked and ran away in many directions, one almost stumbling into the boy's hiding place in his haste. The boy scuttled down under the broken wood but kept one eye to a crack. He had the satisfaction of seeing the man fall, an arrow through his chest, before he had run more than a few steps.

That bothered the boy, because he had seen no one in the woods behind him with a bow.

Then he noticed the figure on the road. The cause of the disturbance. Two figures, because the one behind was a dog. Or sort of a dog. It terrified him. It was larger than any dog he had ever seen, with a wide head, huge teeth, and great furry feet with strong black claws. It was bigger than its master, who was now revealed before him.

Its master. She must be its master, the small dark Woman in the swirling robe. The dog followed Her with its head and tail low. He knew what that meant. It meant She was the dominant one, and the huge beast was trying, like a scolded puppy, to win Her good will. He watched Her with great interest. Could She be the one who frightened the soldiers away? She must be. Her walk wasn't normal. Her head stayed still, Her eyes focused far ahead, and Her body swayed in a dance-like motion. As he watched, She sat for a moment on a roadside boulder, the huge dog fawning at Her feet. Then She jumped up and continued, walking normally now, around a corner and out of his sight.

For a long while he lay there, savouring the pleasure of the experience. *The uniforms ran! They were afraid, as I am afraid of them! Who is this Woman, with this power? She must be magic.* The word came from somewhere in the storehouse of his mind, a concept from another time, another life. But magic was the right word. *She must be magic.*

Then he saw something more important. A supply wagon lay on its side, horses gone, wheel broken. Spilling out of it was more food than he had seen in months. Meat; loaves of hard, dark, bread; dried fruits! Abandoning his cover, he slunk over to the wagon. He picked up a loaf, unable to believe his luck. It smelled marvellous. He took a bite, tearing the tough crust with anxious teeth. It was real. It tasted heavenly. His saliva flowed, and he gulped it down. He grabbed a handful of nuts from a torn sack. They were real; they went the way of the bread. He was in his own fearful version of heaven. His eyes darting from his feast to the road and the surrounding woods, he gorged himself warily.

Then he heard footsteps returning through the forest. Men's voices. Finding a rag, he hastily wrapped as much as he could carry in its folds and slipped back into the woods just as the men with bows came out. Avoiding them with practised skill, he started off towards his hideout.

Then he remembered the Woman. But She was gone. He thought of Her with longing. *How can I see Her? How can I go to the One who makes the soldiers afraid? Will She kill me with Her magic? The soldiers thought She would kill them. They ran away so fast. Where did She go? How can I follow Her?* His food was too heavy, and he could not leave such riches.

He stopped, torn by his two desires. He opened the makeshift pack and ate more bread, but he was too full. He closed it again. Looking around, he saw a good hiding place, under a rock with thick thorns above it. Sliding his treasure in as far as he could, he backed out and observed it from several angles. *Yes, it is well hidden.* He started away.

After a few steps he stopped and looked back. The food is safe. He turned and went on. Then he stopped again. He looked over his shoulder. *I can't see the food! He rushed back. Yes, it's still there.* So hastily that he got several scratches on his back, he dragged his prize out and opened it. *Yes, it's all there.* He grabbed a handful of fruit and stuffed it in his mouth. His stomach hurt.

He stood for a long time, his arms around the bag of food, staring with longing in the direction his idol had departed. He could not leave the food. He must take it to his den and come back. *By then She will be gone. If She goes into the town, I can't follow her.* They would chase him, in the town. They would throw rocks. *But I must not leave the food.*

Maybe She would come back. *Yes, that's it. I will stay with my food and wait. Then She will come back. When She comes back, I will go to Her. I will put my head down, like her big dog did, and She will know that She is my master. I must practise.*

Placing the bag on the ground he crouched and cringed. *Is this right?* He tried to look at himself. On hands and knees, he arched his back, tucking his buttocks in and holding his head near the ground, neck exposed.

Yes, that's the way. That will work. I will practise, so when She returns, I can tell Her that I want Her to be my master. I will wait. I will eat the food, and She will return and all will be well.

His pinched heart swelled in his narrow breast. All would be well. He would wait for Her.

* * *

About the Author

Brought up in a logging camp with no electricity, Gordon Long learned his storytelling in the traditional way: at his father's knee. He now spends his time editing, publishing, travelling, blogging and writing fantasy and social commentary, although sometimes the boundaries blur.

Gordon lives in Tsawwassen, British Columbia, with his wife, Linda, and their Nova Scotia Duck Tolling Retriever, Josh. When he is not writing and publishing, he works on projects with the Surrey Seniors' Planning Table, and is a staff writer for <indiesunlimited.com>

More from Gordon A Long

Other Titles available at Smashwords, Amazon and
other outlets

"Out of Mischief" World of Change Book 1
"Into Trouble" World of Change Book 2
"Mountains of Mischief" World of Change Book 3
"The Trouble With Tents" World of Change Book 4

"A Sword Called...Kitten?" Romantic Comedy with an Edge
"The Cat with Many Claws" Sword Called Kitten Book 2

"Why Are People So Stupid?" Social Humour with a Point

Look for Gordon's books, selected reviews, poetry and short
stories at <airbornpress.ca>
Gordon's opinions on humanity are at the
"Are People Really That Stupid?" blog
Find his weekly reviews and his ideas on writing at
"Renaissance Writer"